I0564677

Bronco

Bronco

Erick S. Gray

www.urbanbooks.net

Urban Books, LLC
300 Farmingdale Road, N.Y.-Route 109
Farmingdale, NY 11735

Bronco Copyright © 2026 Erick S. Gray

All rights reserved. No part of this book may be repro-
duced in any form or by any means without prior consent
of the Publisher, except brief quotes used in reviews.

To the extent that the image or images on the cover of this
book depict a person or persons, such person or persons
are merely models, and are not intended to portray any
character or characters featured in the book.

ISBN 13: 978-1-64556-759-2
EBOOK ISBN: 978-1-64556-760-8

First Trade Paperback Printing February 2026
Printed in the United States of America

10 9 8 7 6 5 4 3 2 1

*This is a work of fiction. Any references or similarities
to actual events, real people, living or dead, or to real
locales are intended to give the novel a sense of reality.
Any similarity in other names, characters, places, and
incidents is entirely coincidental.*

Distributed by Kensington Publishing Corp.
Submit Orders to:
Customer Service
400 Hahn Road
Westminster, MD 21157-4627
Phone: 1-800-733-3000
Fax: 1-800-659-2436

The authorized representative in the EU for product
safety and compliance
Is eucomply OU, Parnu mnt 139b-14, Apt 123
Tallinn, Berlin 11317, hello@eucompliancepartner.com

Prologue

1944

The thunderous sounds of a massive navy barrage were heard. The power of the guns was astonishing. The heavy gunfire from the navy ships roared through the air and rattled the soldiers' ears. It was a full-blown nightmare coming to realization. Death was everywhere. It seemed inevitable—sooner or later, it would come for each soldier. Cannons from the opposing forces fired back at the nearby landing craft. A roaring boom spewed from the Nazis' artillery, followed by a massive explosion of fuel, fire, metal, and flesh. There was a direct hit on one of the nearby landing crafts. Shells exploded around the soldiers, flaming oil burned on the water, and cannon fire smashed into the bow.

Land and sea were torture and torment. The screams of men brutally dying ricocheted through the air and seemed to echo forever. While the sea became a watery grave for many, the landscape became a hellish mix of craters, billowing smoke, shell-pocked boulders, contorted dead soldiers, and mud. Everything seemed scorched and blackened. It seemed impossible to proceed, but this was what these men signed up for, to fight for their country, to oust the evil that plagued Europe, to overcome and kill the Nazis and Hitler—to have a purpose. But was dying for a country that forever saw and treated them as second-class and marginalized citizens worth it?

A small group of Black soldiers, the segregated 92nd Infantry Division, fought with dogged determination. One of the soldiers was Bronco. He was battle hardened, powerful, and seemed unfazed by the hell around him. His black skin and robust, muscular frame were camouflaged in worn army fatigues, combat boots, a helmet, and a rifle. His face was covered with the faces of his fellow men. A few soldiers began to lose it. They began to shudder and weep. This was hell on earth, but the 92nd Infantry Division did its best to stare straight ahead. But their fear infected them.

Underneath these soldiers' boots were dozens of propaganda leaflets for African American soldiers, trying to persuade colored soldiers to join the Germans because they'd be treated better in their country. The leaflets falsely suggested that African Americans would receive better treatment by the German military and encouraged them to surrender to German troops.

It was nonsense. And the soldiers knew it.

Explosions were happening everywhere, and the Germans were on the edge of a cliff, raining down machine-gun fire and grenades. A river of machine-gun fire poured into the men, and over a dozen soldiers were instantly killed. And although Bronco was among these men hit with intense machine-gun fire from the Germans, somehow he seemed unscathed and survived. With the remaining soldiers, he jumped into a ditch. A fellow soldier stared at Bronco in awe.

"How . . . how did you not get hit?" a soldier asked him. "I saw you get hit."

Bronco remained quiet. The fury of confusion of actual war was playing out in front of him, all of the men, a nightmarish spectacle. They were lying in the mud and dirt under gray, weeping skies. There was an injured soldier next to Bronco, cringing and crying out in pain. Bronco looked down at the man's leg, a mess of blood, muscle, and exposed bone.

"Aaaah. Mama . . . help me, Mama. I'm dying, Mama!" the injured soldier screamed in agony.

"Keep pressure on that wound!" said Bronco mechanically.

The 92nd Infantry Division struggled through the heavy gunfire. They fired up as best they could and continued making for the cliffs' base. Other soldiers tore out bandages from half-burned medic kits and stuffed them against the bleeding. While doing so, a mortar round landed nearby—boom—and showered the men with dirt and debris.

"We's gon' die here," a soldier cried out in his thick Southern accent.

Bronco huffed and replied, "We won't die here."

He gripped the rifle against his chest and stared out from the ditch, ready to react with bravery, prepared to save his fellow soldiers' lives. But before doing so, his eyes widened with confusion. He saw German soldiers encroaching toward the ditch they were hiding in. However, these soldiers were dressed differently, in World War I attire, and armed with Mauser Gewehr 98 instead of the Karabiner 98k. They were dressed in some field gray uniform, not the M36 uniform with a dark green collar and shoulder straps. Surprisingly, his infantry division was not reacting to them. In fact, it was as if no one else saw these soldiers but Bronco.

Bronco fired at these soldiers but to no avail. It seemed like bullets went right through them, and they kept coming. A few men stared at Bronco with bewilderment.

"What do you see, Bronco?" one asked.

"You don't see 'em?" said Bronco.

"See what?"

They didn't see these soldiers. It was an anomaly. *Are they dead? Ghosts?* Bronco was alone. He glanced at the hell in front of him and scowled. Then he decided to charge alone. He pushed toward these apparitions, firing his weapon—the same, nothing. Bullets passed through them. Right away, Bronco was hit multiple times with machine-gun fire from the Germans perched on the bluff. Yet, he didn't go down. He kept charging. It seemed like the bullets were striking steel and reflecting off him. He seemed impervious to the gunfire coming from the Germans, and what remained of the 92nd Infantry Division behind him was shocked.

What is happening? they all thought.

Bronco cut loose with the M2 Hyde he wielded and was able to kill several men. However, the Germans released several mortar rounds and struck his division. Thick smoke and dust wafted through the air, and almost all were killed. Blood and flesh showered the men behind Bronco. It was madness.

Bronco was in shock. He was becoming the last man standing. This ability he had, he felt it was becoming more of a curse than a blessing. The Germans were coming for him with everything they had. Heavy machine-gun fire continued to rip into him, but he stood there unfazed. Bullets bounced off him like he was Superman. The Germans were baffled by this. What was he . . . *a monster?*

Bronco continued with his relentless charge toward the Germans. Still, suddenly, a mortar shell exploded so close to him that his ears shattered with intense ringing, and everything went black.

Chapter One

A Rage in Harlem (1955)

Bronco Jolted awake to the anxious thudding of his heart and cold sweat upon his brow. He felt suffocated and breathless from the vivid nightmare that had just plagued him in his sleep, unsure of where he was or what was real. He was a bit disoriented, and it took him a moment to realize that he was in his own bed, safe from the terrifying sounds of war and bloodshed. He remained on edge for a moment. The one-bedroom apartment he resided in in Harlem was quiet, still, and dark.

Bronco was shirtless and drenched in sweat, with his heart still racing. It was only a nightmare, but they were becoming recurring. He removed himself from the bed, needing a glass of cold water. The sound of Harlem came through his open bedroom window, alive like a Broadway play. He lived above a quaint nightclub and could hear the last of the drunken stragglers exiting into the cool morning air after a night of drinking, dancing, and partying. It was five in the morning, but New York, especially Harlem, never slept. Though the Harlem Renaissance ended nearly two decades ago, Harlem was still buzzing with recognition from fashion, food, music, especially jazz, art, and nightlife. It was the new Negro movement with a new Black identity. Black Mecca at its finest.

But with the new Negro movement came the crime—numbers running, bootlegging, gambling, and prostitution, fueled by postwar prosperity. Men like Bumpy Johnson became godlike figures and controlled Harlem with an iron fist. Politicians such as Adam Clayton Powell Jr. broke the color barrier by being elected to the city council.

But no matter what Harlem was or became, this would always be Bronco's home. It was where he grew up—a few blocks north of 110th Street. Mathew "Bronco" Washington was the only child of Janice and Rosco Washington. His parents had migrated north at the turn of the century to escape segregation and the harsh conditions of the South. Jim Crow and the KKK became the cornerstone for brutal violence, poverty, and injustice for Black people and families, creating the great migration north—the mass movement of about five to six million African Americans from rural areas of the South to urban areas in the North.

In the beginning, life finally seemed fair for Janice and Rosco Washington. Rosco had gotten a job in a furniture factory and become a part-time barber. Janice worked as a seamstress. Together, they made a decent living for themselves and Bronco when he was born in 1923. They lived in a two-bedroom flat and were saving to buy a car. But then the Great Depression hit the country in the 1930s, and it didn't take long for Roscoe to find himself unemployed and depressed. Following his sudden unemployment, Bronco's father became an abusive alcoholic father, turning to the streets for income.

Life became rough for Bronco. His parents had to downgrade their living conditions, and shortly after, his mother lost her job as a seamstress. Roscoe had gradually become an absentee father and husband by the time Bronco turned 10 years old. Unfortunately, his mother took to prostitution to pay the bills and feed her son. Though he was a good student in his youth, when Bronco was 14, school became irrelevant to him. He began to lead a teenage gang in stealing, fighting, and becoming an enforcer for the local crime bosses.

He got the nickname Bronco from a gangster and numbers runner named Pinch. Although Bronco was young, he was a brute on the streets of Harlem, able to knock out grown men and take on multiple enemies simultaneously. His wild and violent actions reminded Pinch of a bronco horse, a wild and untrained animal with unpredictable behavior such as kicking and bucking. A bronco was bred to be fast, strong, and agile. And Bronco was rough and rude.

Shortly after Bronco's sixteenth birthday, his father was killed in a bar fight. This devastated his mother, and she, too, turned to alcohol to escape or cope with the pain of losing her husband and the dramatic downfall of her life. Bronco took out his anger and frustration on the streets, becoming a feared young goon in Harlem. His name began to ring out, and Pinch took him under his wing to school him on numbers running and committing various crimes for Pinch, like robbery, burglary, racketeering, and gambling.

"You're a beast, Bronco. Always have 'em fear you because fear is the only thing men, even white men, respect," Pinch had said to him.

Bronco nodded. He looked up to and respected Pinch. The man ran a profitable business in Harlem, and the ladies loved him.

One day, Bronco went missing for a week. No one could find him. Pinch and his men searched everywhere in Harlem and New York. Pinch began to fear the worst: his protégé may have been kidnapped and killed, most likely by his rivals. It seemed unlikely, but it was Harlem.

The Italians were becoming an opposing force in Harlem, and men like Pinch and Bumpy Johnson were becoming a problem. Then, one day, Bronco turned up suddenly. He was found unconscious in an alleyway on the east side of town, nearly naked and confused with strange markings on his chest. When questioned by Pinch and doctors, Bronco had no memory or recollection of the past week. It felt like his memory had been wiped clean.

"You don't remember nothin', nigga?" Pinch had questioned him.

"No. I don't. Not a damn thing, Pinch," Bronco had replied.

Pinch thought it was odd for a man to suddenly go missing for a week and not remember anything. He began to suspect the worst. Maybe Bronco was cooperating with the police or his enemies. Doubt began to stir within Pinch.

The relationship between Pinch and Bronco began to shift in a different direction and turned sour after Bronco's sudden disappearance. People were in his ear about Bronco's account, questioning his movements, loyalty, and story.

"A nigga don't disappear like that and not remember anything, Pinch. He knows something. He ain't telling it," one of his goons said about Bronco.

Pinch knew he couldn't take any chances, not with the police investigating him and the Mob looking to destroy him. He gave the order to his men. "Do it. Make it quick."

Two men went to retrieve Bronco from his mother's pad one night. He was only 17 at the time. Bronco knew Shortie and Coco really well. He trusted them. He climbed into the back seat of a black 1940 Buick Sedan, and they drove off. Shortie and Coco were quiet during the ride, which Bronco found odd, especially with Shortie. He was always bragging about his rendezvous with beautiful women. He was a playboy.

"Where we going?" Bronco had asked them.

"Pinch wants to have a word with you," Shortie had said. "No need to flip your lid, young'un, you dig?"

Bronco nodded. Still, something didn't feel right with him.

They'd arrived at an old warehouse in the Bronx, and Bronco climbed out of the car. It was late, and Bronco was sandwiched between Shortie and Coco as they entered the warehouse. Surprisingly, it was empty. There was no Pinch. When Bronco spun around to ask what was happening, he saw Shortie and Coco pointing their guns at him.

"Shortie, Coco, what I do wrong?" he'd asked.

"Pinch wanna know who you talked to," Coco had said.

"No one. I didn't talk to anyone."

"Fool, you lyin' to live, beatin' up your gums," Shortie had said. "Don't know how one loses a week's memory after disappearing for a week."

"I don't know what happened to me. I promise you that," Bronco had replied.

"It don't matter to us, fool. Pinch still wants you dead," Shortie had said. "You can't be trusted."

Bronco had scowled. He'd braced himself for the worst. Shortie and Coco were two cold-blooded killers, Pinch's finest. Once someone saw the barrels of their guns, it was lights-out. As expected, Shortie and Coco opened fire on Bronco, striking him in the chest multiple times and not caring that he was only 17 years old. However, the unexpected happened—nothing! Bronco was still alive, breathing heavily. He was sure they didn't miss him. It seemed like every shot had ricocheted off him. Bronco stood there as shocked as the two shooters.

"What the fuck?" Coco had exclaimed.

"We hit the nigga, right?" Shortie had questioned himself.

Bronco remained wide-eyed, knowing they'd hit him. He felt the impact, but his skin didn't break at all. Realization hit Bronco. *Run!* He sharply pivoted and took off running. Shortie and Coco gave chase, shooting at him, and multiple rounds struck Bronco in the back, but nothing brought him down. The two men were taken aback. *How is he still alive after that?*

Bronco had burst through a back door to the warehouse that led into a tight alleyway. He stumbled over some trash cans but kept it moving. Shortie and Coco were right behind him. But Bronco was fast. When he reached a towering, chained fence at the end of the alleyway, the way he scaled it, it was something out of a movie. He was young, and he'd become something different. Shortie and Coco stood behind, dumbfounded by what they had witnessed. It was impossible. But more important, how were they going to explain this shit to Pinch?

Word had gotten back to Pinch about the mishap, or fuckup, and he was livid. He didn't believe a word of what Shortie and Coco had said. No one was bulletproof. But Shortie and Coco were adamant with their story.

"You two fools done flipped your lids," Pinch had exclaimed. "You find him and kill him."

Bronco remained confused and frightened. He had no idea what was happening to him and why or how he'd disappeared for a week with no memory of it. His world had been turned upside down. Pinch went from being his mentor in Harlem to an adversary. He'd decided to hide out in Brooklyn with a girlfriend until he could figure it out. Fortunately for Bronco, the situation worked itself out. Pinch was a dominant force in Harlem, but he bumped heads with Bumpy Johnson, another fearsome crime boss. One day, Bumpy Johnson got the better of Pinch. A few of Bumpy's men had gunned down Pinch outside a popular lounge on Lenox Avenue, and that was the end of Pinch.

The demise of Pinch gave Bronco mixed feelings. It felt like he'd lost an older brother, though Pinch tried to have him killed.

The following three years of Bronco's life were nothing to him, working odd jobs and committing various crimes to earn a buck. World War II was at its peak, and in 1943 came the second Harlem riot. It was a hot August day when a white police officer shot and wounded an African American soldier, and rumors began to circulate that the soldier had been killed. A crowd of about 3,000 people gathered at the police headquarters, and Bronco was among the crowd. A riot had ensued, with the property destruction of white-owned businesses in Harlem. Bronco didn't care why the riot had started. He only wanted to take advantage of it. He'd smashed the windows of an electronics store and grabbed a radio and a small TV. But before he could flee with the items, he was accosted by three white officers.

"Where do you think you are going with those items, boy?" one of the cops had scoffed.

Bronco frowned.

"You think you can steal from a white business and get away with it?" another cop had exclaimed, clutching a billy club.

Bronco recognized the look on the officers' faces. It was familiar to every Black man and woman in Harlem: white superiority and prejudice. And they weren't there to just arrest him but to teach him a lesson.

"You hear me talking to you, boy?"

Bronco had heard the crackers loud and clear. By this time, he knew what he was, what he'd become, and what he was capable of. And three racist cops weren't going to stop or arrest him tonight. Out of nowhere, Bronco threw the TV at one of the cops' faces so fast it seemed like his face exploded, and the cop went down like a hurt boxer.

The remaining two cops had charged at Bronco to beat him with their clubs, but they were no match for Bronco. One was hit with the radio so hard that he flew off his feet and became unconscious, and the latter had struck Bronco against his head with the billy club to no avail. He might as well have hit Bronco with a pillow. The cop stood there in awe, not knowing what to think, and then, like his fellow officers, it was lights-out. Bronco had hit the man so hard that teeth spewed from his mouth, and blood went flying everywhere.

But Bronco knew he'd fucked up. He'd assaulted three cops, and though he knew he was somewhat invincible, he was still outnumbered and living in America, where white men seemed just as invincible because of the unjust laws and status quo. They would come for him with everything they had to destroy or dissect him to study what he'd become.

Fortunately for him, he'd been summoned by the local draft board for military service in World War II. Bronco knew it was time for him to leave Harlem, even though it was to fight in a war.

Bronco splashed cold water onto his face and stared at his rough and beaten image in the bathroom mirror. He exhaled, knowing it was going to be a long day. Being back home was nice, but he had a past in Harlem, one he wanted to forget. His mother was dead. She'd died while he was in Europe, and most of his friends were dead, too, or incarcerated.

Bronco felt alone and trapped in wartime memories.

What he'd done to those cops twelve years ago never came back to haunt him. The only things haunting Bronco were flashbacks of war and the death of his fellow soldiers in his infantry division back in Europe—and something else.

The sun began to rise in the heart of a bustling city. Harlem began to awaken, with the first rays of sunshine reflecting off the windows of buildings. The sunlight added a magic touch to Harlem, becoming a moment of harmony between nature and human innovation. Bronco proceeded to dress for his job at the cemetery. He was a gravedigger. It was an odd and awkward job to have, digging graves for the dead, especially being a veteran. But Bronco found some delight in it. It gave him peace and some time away from a busy city. He spent a significant amount of time beautifying lawns, trees, and the aesthetics of the cemetery.

Bronco moved around in his one-bedroom pad, buttoning his traditional dungarees for work. The place was sparsely furnished, the walls were bland, the fixtures were decades old, and the lighting was dismal. It was an ugly, run-down apartment with cracked floors. But for Bronco, it was home sweet home. It was his, and the rent was cheap, $50 a month.

Bronco snatched a bottle of whisky from the dresser and took a few swigs to ease the tension and sudden visions. The liquor helped—sometimes. But this morning, he would have another incident. Preparing to leave his apartment for the day, when Bronco went to close his bedroom window, he suddenly saw her, a little girl who looked to be about 12 years old. She stood in the center of the street, hauntingly gazing at him. She wore a charred shirtwaist dress, no shoes, and had severe burns to her face and body. It was no mistake. She was the undead, an apparition.

His curse had returned to him.

Chapter Two

Fuck Jim Crow!

Morton, Mississippi, was a small town with a population of 1,600, surrounded by the Bienville National Forest. The town was an unincorporated community near vital rivers that flowed through the forests and was located on a railroad line along that same river. It was a place where the bank was a building smaller than a house and the high school was the size of a midsize church. Doting housewives, hardworking husbands, flourishing agriculture, recreation, segregation, and knowing where home was defined this small-town culture.

It was a beautiful, quiet, and humid night in the country. It was after midnight when three carloads of Klansmen speedily raced through the back dirt roads. They were armed with pistols and shotguns and inebriated from drinking whisky and bootleg moonshine. These men wouldn't wear their traditional white hoods tonight. They wanted their victims to see their faces clear as day. These niggers needed to be dealt with.

"How far this nigger lives?" a Klansman named Joseph asked the driver, Paul.

"Out yonder. Heard this nigger and his family have more acres of land than any white man around," Paul uttered.

"This an uppity nigger, huh?" asked Mark.

"An uppity nigger that needs to be put in his place," said Joseph.

"He and his family are stubborn niggers. Benny gave 'em a good offer for their land, and they turned it down. Benny said he's tired of playing nice with this nigger," said Joseph.

Mark, Paul, and the others knew what Joseph was saying. Each said nothing, but their silence said something.

"What is this nigger's name?" asked Mark.

"Sylvester Baker," said Joseph.

"We'll put this nigger in his place all right. Tonight will be their last night on that land," a man named Keith uttered.

Each man nodded in assurance. Each man in the car was very familiar with implementing cruel and inhumane beatings and punishment, including death, toward Black men and women in Mississippi. They were the decree, and they believed this was their country to protect under the laws of God.

They were in the lead car. Behind them were other blinding headlights, men with wicked intent who navigated through the thick country woods. Without the bright moon in the night sky and the car headlights, they would have lost their way in the dusky forests. And though the entire forest served as a reminder of how beautiful nature could be, tonight it would become the scenery of injustice and viciousness against those who strove for a better future and way of life.

Sylvester Baker and his family were sound asleep in their home. Their four-bedroom log cabin farmhouse sat on 21.5 acres of land in the middle of nowhere. Sylvester was a proud landowner and a farmer. He was a man in his late fifties and a World War I veteran. He was one of the 380,000 Black soldiers who had served in the United States Army during the World War, serving in the 369th Black Infantry Regiment. Sylvester had emerged from the war bloodied and scarred, but he was determined to cut himself a slice of the American dream. Although he was an American soldier who fought with dignity and courage in Europe, back in America, Sylvester continued to face disenfranchisement, segregation, systemic racial discrimination, debt peonage, and racial violence. He also had to endure slander from his fellow white soldiers and officers.

Sylvester was smart and determined, with a dream, a knack for business, and a green thumb. He'd settled in Mississippi with his wife, Martha, in 1922. And as they would say, he'd pulled himself up by his bootstraps by saving and purchasing land for himself and his family. Over the years, he and his family grew tobacco, cotton, tomatoes, carrots, and squash. He owned horses that helped to plow his fields, and his oldest son owned and operated a grocery store in a Black town. While some African American and white farmers struggled with climate, education, financing, and infrastructure, Sylvester was becoming the pinnacle of Black wealth.

But in the past three months, a private land company and a group of investors wanted to drive every Black family off their land and out of the area despite them being there for years. First, the company offered Black families pennies on the dollar for acres of their land. These families lived near a large lake, and this company wanted to acquire most of the land and the lake to drain it for cotton cultivation and other means. Many Black farmers found they could feed themselves and supplement their income by fishing in the lake and farming in the fertile land nearby. This area became their slice of heaven, and they didn't want it converted to exclusively private use. Sylvester was against this and began to rally for the Black families to protect their land and fight for their livelihood and what belonged to them. Boycott. The company retaliated by bringing in the local Klan, and the Klansmen began to hang, beat, and threaten other locals with extreme violence. Sylvester remained steadfast in keeping his land despite the threats and violence against his community.

Sylvester was nestled against his wife in their bed. All was peaceful and quiet. It had been a long day, and everyone needed their rest for tomorrow. Suddenly, a bright light flared through their bedroom window, followed by men shouting and hollering outside. Sylvester sprang awake and leaped from the bed. Looking outside, he became wide-eyed and horrified at what he saw. There was a burning cross in front of his cabin and nearly a dozen armed white men ranting and threatening his family.

"Come outside right now, nigger!" the men shouted.

"Mommy! I'm scared," their 5-year-old daughter, Megan, hollered. She ran into their bedroom and leaped into her mother's arms. The sudden disturbance from outside awakened the entire family consisting of three sons, three daughters, and Martha's mother.

"Oh, my God. God help us," Martha cried in a panic.

"Take the kids in the back room, Martha," Sylvester shouted.

Sylvester went to retrieve his shotgun while his wife gathered their children to hide in the back. He checked to see if it was loaded, and it was. While Martha tried to harbor their children and pray, Sylvester made his way to the front door to confront the Klan.

"We don't want any trouble now," Sylvester shouted. "Get from 'round here."

"Sylvester, you best to bring your black ass out from the cabin right now. Think about your family, boy."

"I am thinking about my family," Sylvester shouted. He cocked back the shotgun, ready to protect his family by any means necessary.

Sylvester was outnumbered and outgunned. He had to think fast. It pained him to hear his family crying and whimpering in the other room. Maybe he could take out one, two, or three white men with his shotgun, but he was trapped inside his own home.

"Sylvester, you come out that got-damn cabin right now. Don't make it worse for yourself, boy."

Sylvester seethed. It wasn't happening. He knew the moment he stepped outside of his home he was a dead man. The Klan was approaching the porch, determined to retrieve Sylvester with violence. When they got close to his door, Sylvester swung it open, pivoted the shotgun in their direction, and fired—boom! He struck Mark in the chest, killing him immediately. The Klan took cover and retaliated with their own pistols and rifles. The cabin came under heavy gunfire, and Sylvester crouched behind the door. His wife and the children began to scream and holler. They were scared.

"Stay down!" Sylvester shouted to his family.

"Got-damn you, nigger!" Paul shouted angrily.

Mark's lifeless body was sprawled across Sylvester's porch. It triggered absolute rage and hatred in every Klan member, and there was no turning back. Sylvester had killed a white man.

Seething, Keith shouted, "Burn them niggers out!"

The lynch mob began to pour coal oil onto the cabin, and they didn't hesitate to set it on fire. The cabin quickly became engulfed with thick, heavy flames. In contrast, Keith and the others stood their distance from the intense heat and waited for their opportunity to come.

"Please, I have my family in here," Sylvester shouted and pleaded.

"Come out now or burn, nigger," Keith countered.

Sylvester continued to plead for his family's safety when he decided to surrender himself to the Klan. He exited the burning cabin, raising the shotgun above his head like waving a white flag in defeat and surrender. The Klan ignored his surrender and opened fire. They shot him so many times that his body was riddled with bullets. But it wasn't going to end there. When all three of Sylvester's sons and a daughter tried to flee the burning cabin, the Klan opened fire on them, too, killing everyone.

Martha exited the burning cabin holding Megan tight to her chest. "Please, I have my child."

Disregarding Martha's pleading, the enraged mob opened fire, and bullets pierced the body of her daughter while she was in her mother's arms. They both fell to the ground, riddled with bullets, with Martha still holding the dead body of her daughter.

Meanwhile, their middle child, Nancy, refused to leave the burning log cabin. Along with her grandmother, she remained hidden in one of the back rooms. They both preferred death by burning rather than placing themselves at the mercy of the mob. The fire grew close and hot.

Nancy cried and screamed, "Mama! Mama!"

"It's gonna be okay, Nancy. Stay with me. Look at me and stay with me, chile," her grandmother uttered with tears trickling down her face.

In horror, Nancy stared at her grandmother wearing a shirtwaist dress with no shoes.

"Pray with me, chile," the grandmother said.

The fire became so intense that the air began to stiffen and boil. The flames roared like an angry beast. The crackling of burning wood echoed, and the walls started to collapse. Their fate was inevitable.

Nancy began to recite the Lord's Prayer with her grandmother. They tightly held hands and recited, "'Our Father who art in heaven . . . hallowed be thy name. Thy kingdom come. Thy will be done on earth . . . as it is in heaven. Give us this day our daily bread . . .'"

The grandmother pulled Nancy closer to her in a tight, secure hug. The flames were upon them, and they began to catch fire with the hot flames dancing and flickering at their flesh. The acrid taste of smoke hung in the air, making each breath sharp and bitter.

The grandmother continued while burning in piercing pain. "'And forgive us our trespasses, as we forgive those who trespass against us . . .'"

Nancy began to char while in her arms.

"'And lead us not into temptation . . . but deliver us from evil.'"

The grandmother began to holler in extreme pain. She could no longer finish her prayer. The fire and heat became unbearable. The cabin started to collapse in flames, with thick, smoldering black smoke stretching toward the night sky beyond the vast, leafy forest for everyone to see.

Hours later, the grandmother's and Nancy's charred bodies would be found among the debris, and the town would become outraged by what happened. But justice would not be implemented, though an entire family of nine people, including children, had been brutally murdered at the hands of the Klan.

Chapter Three

The Native Son

Bronco and several other gravediggers stood off to the side with their shovels and pickaxes. At the same time, the preacher gave the eulogy to the family. This was a family's worst moment, burying a loved one. There was weeping and sadness. Sadness and sorrow were part of bereavement. This was an inevitable part of life—death. Virtually everyone would face losing someone they loved and, of course, one day they themselves would face dying. Death involved some of the most painful experiences everyone would have to endure.

The deceased was the matriarch of the family and had passed away from natural causes at the rightful age of 79.

"As it says in John 14:27, 'Peace I leave with you; my peace I give you. I do not give to you as the world gives. Do not let your hearts be troubled, and do not be afraid.' Brothers and sisters, we do not want you to be uninformed about those who sleep in death so that you do not grieve like the rest of mankind, who have no hope," the preacher proclaimed.

Bronco remembered all of them: the deceased he'd helped bury in the ground. He knew their first and last names like they had been old friends. It was a quirk he had, remembering their names as if he would one day see them again. Maybe he would.

"And the dust returns to the ground it came from, and the spirit returns to God who gave it," the preacher continued.

Bronco had been one of the cemetery's caretakers since he'd returned from the war. Although gravedigging was an activity many would loathe to contemplate, let alone do, Bronco found satisfaction and peace doing it. He would take care of roughly thirty acres of plots and, on more than a few occasions, had to dig five to six different plots in 100-plus-degree heat, then turn around and manage the graveside services. His days started around 7:00 a.m., and from cleaning headstones to digging graves to maintaining the grounds, he would put in considerable work with very little staff.

The job kept him busy and distracted from his own personal demons, most days.

While the preacher continued spewing the eulogy with the family mourning, Bronco stood there aloof. He didn't have any family to worry about dying and burying. He had no children, siblings, cousins, or friends he cared about. He was alone, but he was okay with that. Therefore, his personal work ethic at the cemetery directly impacted the lives of visitors and families.

Bronco stared ahead at a line of trees nearby, becoming lost inside his head and thoughts, waiting for the preacher's eulogy to end. It was a sunny and hot day, and it all seemed normal until it wasn't. Once again, it or she appeared to materialize from out of nowhere. The same little girl he had seen at his bedroom window. Was she an apparition, banshee, duppy, or worse, was this a demon or some kind of poltergeist disguised as a little girl? Whatever it was, it was clear he was the only one seeing this being.

She seemed fragile and powerless. She moved in such a brittle and delicate way that it seemed like any big movement would sweep it away from the physical plane. Her scorched skin seemed painful, and her troubling eyes locked in on Bronco. Her attire was the same in its mangled body, a shirtwaist dress. Instead of wanting to run away, the haunting steps of this little girl made Bronco wonder what had happened to her. Halfway toward him, she unfurled her fingers to reach out to Bronco in an unsettling manner.

Bronco stared at her, knowing she wasn't going to go away. He hated that these visions of the dead were becoming reoccurring. It'd been years since he had an incident. It began in the war. Now he couldn't make any sense of it.

What does she want from me?

"Bronco?" a fellow coworker, Dennis, called out to him, snapping him out of his daydream. "You okay, man?"

"Yeah. I'm fine," he replied.

"You sure picked a strange time to start daydreaming. We got work to do, you dig?" said Dennis.

The preacher's eulogy had ended. It was now time to lower the casket into the grave. He had work to do but couldn't escape that haunting feeling. This wasn't going to be the last time he saw her.

Lenox Lounge was a long-standing and iconic location in Harlem. The legendary Green Book nightclub was nestled among 1880s-era brownstone tenements on Lenox Avenue, and the place had become a major artery in Harlem. Some of the most excellent jazz musicians, including Billie Holiday and John Coltrane, performed at the lounge. It was a Friday night, and the 1,200-square-foot place with beautiful tile floors, Art Deco style, and an interior of mirrors and mahogany was packed. A local jazz band was crooning, wooing the crowd with a combination of saxophone, clarinet, trumpet, bass, and drums, creating that unique twentieth-century sound. A beautiful jazz singer named Elizabeth was blowing her audience away with her vocal skills similar to the timbre of musical instruments.

Elizabeth was breathtakingly gorgeous, wearing a silver sleeveless ruffle V-neck cocktail evening gown. She had high cheekbones, raven black hair, bright, long lashes, and almond-shaped eyes that danced with the light. The men couldn't stop staring at her, and the ladies envied her. Elizabeth snapped her fingers and controlled the room with the microphone close to her lips while moving her curvy hips.

"Go on, girl, sing on," someone hollered elatedly.

Elizabeth smiled and enjoyed every second of the attention she was receiving. She reveled in it. But she didn't have all the men's attention. While she moved across the stage, singing and jiving, she glanced at Bronco sitting at the bar nursing a drink. He was aloof from her performance, and Elizabeth had no idea why it bothered her. But it did.

Bronco downed the last of the whisky and signaled the bartender for another pour. While most of the folks looked jazzy and chrome plated, he remained in his dingy work dungarees. His attention was fixed elsewhere. He was there but not there. Mindy, the bartender, smiled his way and asked, "You doing okay tonight, Bronco?"

"I'm fine," Bronco replied half-heartedly.

"Another pour for you, right?"

He nodded.

Mindy poured him another shot of whisky and continued a warm smile toward him. It was evident that she liked Bronco. He was a handsome, quiet, and mystifying fella. Folks knew about his violent past with Pinch and then going off to war. Bronco came back from the war a different person. He kept to himself and tried to keep out of trouble.

"Hard day at work today?" Mindy questioned.

"It's a hard day every day," Bronco replied tersely.

"I will never understand how you do what you do, Bronco. A veteran like you, digging graves," said Mindy.

"It ain't no easy job, I tell ya," he replied.

"Has anything ever been easy for you?" she asked him.

"The only thing that comes easy is dying."

It wasn't the response she was looking for. "Well, don't you try to do that anytime soon. You a cool cat."

Bronco nodded, taking note.

"I know something that might come easy for you," Mindy chuckled, then nodded toward Elizabeth.

Elizabeth had finished her first set with the band and decided to grab a drink from the bar. Like Cleopatra, she strolled through the lounge with men dueling to catch her attention. But she had her eyes fixed on Bronco.

"Get me a vodka martini, extra dirty," Elizabeth told Mindy. Mindy nodded while Elizabeth shifted her attention to Bronco. "How come you always sit at the end of the bar and don't smile, Bronco? You don't like my singing?"

"You sing just fine," Bronco replied.

"I sing just fine, huh?" Elizabeth moved familiarly close to Bronco, running her fingers up his arm for a reaction.

Bronco remained aloof.

"I don't get you. A handsome man like you, always sitting here alone, no woman. You don't cast an eyeball at my performance. What do you like?"

"I like peace of mind, Elizabeth, something you're not good for," Bronco replied.

Elizabeth was taken aback by his reply. No man had ever talked to her that way. But it was also known throughout Harlem that she was Miles's lady, and Miles was a jealous gangster with a hair-trigger temper. Elizabeth was known to be a temptress, and the men who came into her crosshairs were known to have not-so-pleasurable outcomes.

"What, you don't like pussy, Bronco?" Elizabeth continued.

"You're taken."

"Says who?" she countered.

Mindy placed Elizabeth's vodka martini before her, interrupting their back-and-forth. Elizabeth thanked her, took a sip from her drink, and then continued flirting with Bronco.

"If you think I belong to Miles, you're mistaken, hon. I don't belong to anyone. I'm my own woman," Elizabeth proclaimed wholeheartedly.

Bronco glanced her way. She was undeniably an attractive woman with more curves than the letter S. He was still a man. Still, he knew Elizabeth would be more trouble than she was worth. Miles was underneath a gangster named Barron March, a rival to Bumpy Johnson. He was one of several Harlem kingpins, running numbers, girls, and heroin.

"Like I said, I don't want the trouble," Bronco uttered coolly.

Elizabeth was not giving up. When she wanted something or someone, she got it via temptation, deceit, or force. Elizabeth felt she was entitled to have everything in Harlem, including the man she desired, and she desired Bronco. It intrigued her that he would always ignore her. She didn't like to be ignored.

"Don't tell me the legendary Bronco, a gangster himself, maybe, and a war veteran, is scared of a gangster like Miles."

"Like I said, I don't want the trouble," Bronco repeated.

Elizabeth chuckled at the remark. "There won't be any trouble. I'm worth it, baby."

"Another shot, Bronco?" Mindy asked him with her routine smile.

Bronco nodded, and Mindy began to refill his glass. The two locked eyes for a quick second. Elizabeth scowled at Mindy's timing and her interruption. She noticed how Bronco smiled her way, and she became jealous.

She wondered, *is she his type?*

Not wanting to be bested by Mindy, who Elizabeth thought was average, she took Bronco by his hand and uttered, "Come on, Bronco, let's rattle for a second on the dance floor."

Bronco pulled away from her grip. He wasn't budging from the barstool. Elizabeth was hurt.

While the banter between Bronco and Elizabeth was happening, Miles and his friend, Tommy, had entered the Lenox Lounge. Miles and Tommy were clad in slimmer suits and fedora hats, and their demeanor oozed danger. Immediately, Miles cut his eyes at his woman flirting with Bronco by the bar and frowned. He and Tommy approached the bar, and Bronco noticed them coming.

Elizabeth's demeanor quickly changed like the seasons when she saw Miles. "Miles, hey, baby, we were just talking," Elizabeth uttered nervously.

"Cut the gas, bitch," Miles scolded her. "You know how I feel about you entertaining these fools." Miles glared at Bronco. "You comin' on to my woman, nigga?"

"I'm just sitting here trying to have a drink in peace," Bronco replied.

"Looks to me you cruisin' for a brusin', nigga," Miles exclaimed. "You know who the fuck I am?"

Bronco didn't care at all. He remained quiet and un-daunted by Miles and his street reputation. Although

Miles matched Bronco in height, he didn't match Bronco in physique. The only advantage Miles had over Bronco was the pistol concealed on his person. Still, it was an advantage.

"You hear me talkin' to you, nigga?" Miles exclaimed.

Miles created a scene inside the lounge, but almost everyone was afraid to intervene. Bronco seemed to be on his own. But it didn't bother him.

"Baby, can we just go?" Elizabeth uttered. "It's nothing."

Miles spun toward Elizabeth with a quick backhanded slap, and it damn near sent Elizabeth flying over the bar. The crowd was in shock.

"Bitch, don't fuckin' embarrass me in here," Miles scolded her.

In shock and embarrassment, Elizabeth clutched where he'd struck her. Tears began to trickle from her eyes. Bronco's hands tightened into fists. He was tempted to hit Miles so hard that his mother would cry. But before he could react, the little girl haunting him came to him again. Bronco stared past Miles at her. She was shrouded in the corner, staring at him. No one else saw her. Her attention was more haunting than before.

Bronco stared at her, nearly becoming transfixed by her appearance. This being was trying to tell him something.

"Nigga, do you hear me talking to you?" Miles exclaimed.

Bronco ignored him. He had to deduce why he was being haunted by this little girl. Where did she come from? What did she want from him? Why was her skin burned?

And then it happened. Miles broke a liquor bottle across Bronco's head, snapping him out of whatever daydream or trance he seemed to be in. The little girl was gone. Bronco glared at Miles and was unfazed by the sneak attack. Miles drew a blade and was ready to cut this nigga. *Now things have reached the point of no return.*

"C'mon, muthafucka! I'll gut you like a pig, nigga!" Miles uttered through clenched teeth.

The crowd gasped and became shocked. Things were escalating. Miles was even more bite than bark, a known killer. He clenched his jaw with a hostile glare and lunged toward Bronco with the blade. Although Bronco was like the Man of Steel himself, he was trained for hand-to-hand combat. Bronco wheeled himself away from the strike, then struck Miles under the jaw, banged Miles's nose with his forehead, and pushed him away. Miles stumbled back, blood rushing from his nose.

Bronco cut his eyes at Miles's friend, Tommy. Was he, too, foolish enough to charge at him? He was. Tommy pulled a gun from his jacket, and the crowd panicked and shrieked. Bronco remained undaunted. Before Tommy could squeeze out a bullet, Bronco hit him four times: three lefts and a right in the face.

"Oomph, ugh!" Tommy hollered in pain.

He folded in half and fell to the ground, the pistol spilling from his hand. Everyone was in awe. Afraid, Tommy got up and limped out the door.

Bronco glared at Miles and uttered, "Cut out, fool, 'fore I do worse to you."

Miles was defeated and embarrassed. No one had ever gotten the better of him. He picked himself up from the floor and left behind his friend with his tail between his legs. Elizabeth was wide-eyed and enamored, and so was everyone else. What they'd witnessed was a spectacle.

"You okay?" Bronco asked Elizabeth.

She nodded. Bronco was worked up and agitated. He wanted to sit at the bar and drink in peace. Now it was time for him to go. But he was going to be compensated for his sudden troubles tonight. He placed a few dollar bills on the bar counter for his drinks, looked at Elizabeth with an impious stare, and said, "C'mon, let's go."

He took her by her hand, and she didn't resist leaving with him suddenly. If she wanted to fuck him, then he was going to fuck her tonight.

Miles had pissed him off.

Chapter Four

The Invisible Man

"Ugh! Ugh! Ugh!" Elizabeth panted.

The heat was intense. He wanted to fuck her from the back, position her up against the bed. Elizabeth was fearless. She had no second thoughts or doubts. What she wanted was desire and passion from Bronco but received candid fucking. Bronco's rhythm from behind was mechanical and forceful. Sex with him felt more like a task than a desire. She could feel his large penis filling her up and winding deep into her. She was trying hard to switch things up, straddle him and take control. But he was adamant this was the position he wanted her in, doggie style.

He went awhile until he reached an orgasm. When he did, it didn't take him long to recuperate and go again until he reached a second one. Elizabeth was amazed by his stamina. Bronco was something different, maybe unique. Not too many niggas would have manhandled Miles tonight the way he did. Elizabeth had seen her man belittle and cut down to size the best of them. Miles was an expert with the blade. But Bronco she had never seen anything like before. Bronco was the better fighter.

The scene in the bedroom became intense, wild, and passionate. Bronco squeezed her buttocks while pounding away, and soon Elizabeth reached the point of no return, a deep orgasm that was very loud and wet. When he was done, she collapsed onto her back, breathless.

"That was special," she uttered with a smile. Elizabeth reached nearby to remove and light a cigarette. It was needed. She took a few drags and exhaled.

Bronco refused to lie next to her.

"Are you okay?" she asked, genuinely concerned.

"I'll be fine," he replied.

"Do you wanna smoke?"

"I don't smoke."

"Oh, okay," she replied. "Nice little place you have here. It could use a woman's touch, though."

"I like things the way they are."

She chuckled. "Set in your ways, huh?"

Elizabeth was trying to ignite some kind of conversation with him, spark pillow talk between the sheets, and maybe he would open up to her. She had a knack for that, having men confess their darkest secrets or fears when relaxed, especially after sex. She was the Delilah and Jezebel of Harlem. But Bronco sat at the foot of his bed, aloof and immune from her gossip and honey trap, and stared off somewhere.

"What changed your mind, Bronco? Before you beat my man down, you acted like I was some kind of plague. What was it? Did Miles upset you so much that you felt the urge to fuck his woman tonight? This is some kind of payback?" Elizabeth smirked. "I mean, I'm not complaining. I did have a good time, and I did have my eye on you for a while. But you already knew that."

"You do talk a lot," said Bronco.

"I like conversation, baby. I like to get to know people, and people like to get to know me. I'm a spicy kind of lady," she replied with a cocksure smile.

Bronco continued to stare into some abyss. His attention was elsewhere from Elizabeth's tempestuous chatter.

She came back. This was twice in one day. The visions of her were becoming more substantial, like labor pains. The little girl was closer to him now, and he could see her soulless gaze and the burns on her skin. He could almost stand, reach out, and touch her. It nearly felt as if she was panting with anxiety and fear.

Elizabeth took a drag from the cigarette. Then she asked him, "Where did you learn how to fight like that? Was it in the war?"

Bronco didn't reply.

"What if I became your woman, Bronco? You take care of me, and I can take care of you. I don't care for Miles. I never did. He came with perks, but you, I can love a man like you," she proclaimed wholeheartedly.

By now, it seemed like Elizabeth was talking to herself. Bronco's recurring haunting had his undivided attention.

"What is it that you want from me?" Bronco asked this spirit.

Elizabeth grinned, believing he was talking to her. "Simple. I want love, baby. I want you."

She doused her cigarette against the nightstand, leaving a mark. She smiled and then sneaked closer to him. Elizabeth softened her naked body against him. She wrapped her arms around Bronco, kissing his neck and caressing his chest.

Bronco locked eyes with the restless spirit while Elizabeth began seducing him for a third round in the bedroom. But he sat there impassively. The little girl was sad. He was sad. She wasn't going away.

"What are you looking at?" Elizabeth asked him.

Bronco continued to ignore her.

"You are one strange nigga, Bronco. But I like it," Elizabeth said with a lecherous grin.

She reached for his manhood, but Bronco pulled away, leaving her somewhat confused. He was struggling with something and went for the cheap pint bottle of whisky nearby. It was the kind bootleggers sold in basements and every dry county worldwide. Bronco unscrewed the cap and took a slug. The whisky seared and abraded his throat. Imagine broken glass in a puddle of burning gasoline. He closed his eyes to savor the taste but hoped the thing haunting him would be gone. He'd rather be drunk than be disturbed by a bothersome little girl.

Seeing this, Elizabeth beamed. This was definitely her kind of party. "Now you're talking, baby."

Bronco returned to the foot of his bed and into Elizabeth's grasping arms. She removed the bottle from his hand to secure her taste. It burned her throat. She took another big swig and then handed it back. Bronco continued to pour the whisky down his throat while Elizabeth gently swept her lips against his skin. Finally, she and it were gone, the sadness.

"Relax, sweetie. It's going to be okay. Don't be afraid to let go," said Elizabeth.

Before he could begin to consider the meaning behind her words, Elizabeth settled her mouth upon his, robbing him of any thought. She removed the bottle from his hand and straddled him. There was no fighting it. She was a temptress with curves, and Bronco was a troubled man who could sense supernatural beings. He wanted to drink away his curse and escape the madness with some kind of pleasure, although it would be temporary. As Elizabeth began riding him, Bronco leaned back, closed his eyes, and surrendered.

"Let it go, sweetie," Elizabeth faintly reiterated with her hands pressed against his chest while he was inside her. "Let it go."

They both moaned.

**

The afternoon sun was bursting through the open bedroom window, indicating another hot and sunny day. Bronco awoke to a bright glow on his face and knocking at the front door. He was surprised to see that he was alone in bed. Elizabeth and her things were gone. He was still naked from last night and got out of bed to search for something decent to put on. He grabbed a pair of trousers hanging from the back of a chair, quickly put them on, and reached for the pint of whisky on the dresser. He was disappointed to find it empty. The knocking at his apartment door continued. Bronco wasn't expecting company, but he figured it might have been Elizabeth returning to his place. Maybe she'd forgotten something.

Bare chested and wearing a pair of trousers, he opened the door expecting it to be Elizabeth, but he was taken aback to see it was Mindy. She looked at Bronco, smiled, and uttered, "Is this bad timing?"

"I thought you were someone else," he replied.

"Well, can I come in?" she asked.

Mindy stood before him, wearing a swing skirt with a knit top. She was cute and adorable, having that schoolgirl smile. She coolly took in the apartment and Bronco's living conditions. She'd seen worse, but he could be living better.

"Is she gone?" she asked, referring to Elizabeth.

"Yes."

"I thought nothing came easy for you. Apparently, I was wrong," Mindy teased.

"Why are you here?" he asked her.

"That dustup you had last night with Miles got the attention of Barron March," she explained to him.

"And I should be concerned because . . . ?"

"You, of all people, know the last thing you need is to end up on Barron March's radar. Word got back to me that he's been asking around about you," Mindy said. "He's a dangerous man."

Bronco remained indifferent about the information. He didn't care about the name or the reputation. There was only one thing on Bronco's mind. Mindy followed him around the apartment while he looked for a bottle with whisky left, but they were all empty.

"I have better things to do than worry about some gangster looking for me," Bronco uttered.

"Are you that stupid, Bronco? You beat down Miles, fucked his woman, and now you're looking to get drunk early this afternoon," Mindy scolded him.

Bronco stared at her and uttered, "That was the plan."

"You must have a death wish," she uttered.

Mindy had no idea it would take more than pistols and knives to break or kill a man like Bronco. He was a moving tank. However, he did his best to keep his abilities a secret from everyone, even those he grew close with, which was a small number of people. It was becoming more challenging for him to sleep at night. From the recurring nightmares he was having and being haunted by a little girl, his sanity was crumbling. Surprisingly, a bottle of whisky and having sex with Elizabeth was the remedy he needed for some decent sleep. Whatever that woman had, it put a spell on him.

"Mindy, get with it. You don't need to worry about me. I'll be fine. I can handle myself," he said to her coolly.

"I already know that. But Barron ain't Miles, Bronco."

"And I'm no candy ass."

Mindy, becoming frustrated, sighed heavily and pouted. "I guess you were right. The only thing that's going to come easy to you is dying."

"Why do you care so much about me?"

They locked eyes. The attraction was there, but the last thing Bronco wanted to do was pull a nice and good girl like Mindy into his world. She deserved better.

"I need to run out," said Bronco.

He began grabbing a few things, and Mindy followed him out the door. She continued to try to put some sense into Bronco's head, but he remained unafraid.

Exiting the building, they noticed the 1955 black Cadillac Fleetwood Sedan parked outside. Right away, the doors to the Cadillac opened, and Barron March, along with two thugs, climbed out of the sleek vehicle. Mindy's heart dropped when she set eyes on Barron March. But Bronco remained aloof and unimpressed toward the drug kingpin's sudden presence.

Barron March stood six feet tall and was clad in a tailored black three-piece suit and a fedora hat. He had an oval face and intense black eyes and rarely smiled or laughed. He walked with a long black and chrome walking stick that glistened in the sunlight as he banged it against the ground. His skin was the color of Hershey's milk chocolate, and he had a cigarette-raspy voice.

"Just the man I was looking for," Barron said. "Do you know who I am?"

"I do," Bronco replied calmly.

"Good. I want you to take a walk with me. I want to talk to you," Barron said, not asking but demanding.

Mindy stood there, afraid for Bronco. The two quickly glanced at each other, and Mindy stared at Bronco like she would never see him again.

"There's no need to worry about the lady. My men will look after her," said Barron.

Bronco feared more for Mindy's safety than his. So he relented and decided to walk with Barron through Harlem. Barron March moved with authority and power, and although he moved with a walking stick, it was more for flash and show than stability.

It was a summer afternoon, and Harlem was active and playing like a Broadway show. A store owner swept away the trash on the sidewalk while bare-chested children played skully and a few girls skipped rope nearby. A woman in curlers was buying a cooling fruit-flavored ice drink on a street corner. While they were passing her, she smiled at Barron and thanked him for some previous favor he'd done.

"This will always be home," said Barron.

Barron wasn't in a rush. He was a man who moved like he had nowhere to be anytime soon. You waited for him, not the other way around. He took in the neighborhood, being watchful. He walked comfortably and haughtily among everyone, and they hurriedly and respectfully stepped out of his way.

"You made enemies last night," said Barron, finally acknowledging Bronco.

"How did you find me?" Bronco asked.

"Harlem is a web, my friend, and I'm the arachnid in the center of it. Whenever someone disturbs my web, I know where to find them," Barron uttered. "But I must admit, I'm somewhat impressed with you, Bronco, and I'm not one who is easily impressed. I've seen it all. Not too many niggas would be able to take on Miles the way you did and survive."

"I didn't want no trouble with him," said Bronco.

"Yet, you purposely left with his woman last night," he chuckled.

Bronco remained quiet.

"I remember you. You used to be the little nigga running with Pinch a few years ago, and then he wanted you dead for some reason. Whatever fallout there was with him, that's in the past. He's dead. But I came to breathe some life back into you," Barron proclaimed.

What life? Bronco thought.

They walked by a few boys opening a fire hydrant, and water began spraying onto the road beside the sidewalk.

"Unfortunately for you, Miles is part of my web, under my protection, and you've disturbed that. He wants blood, and I assure you, he'll come to collect in full," said Barron.

Bronco wasn't a fool. He knew what the kingpin hinted. "And you're here to help me, right?" Bronco smirked.

"A man of your talents and skills I can find useful. As you may know, I run a few businesses here in Harlem and I do have competitors. I pay well, and there are perks when you come work for me," Barron charmingly explained.

"And if I say no?"

Barron finally stopped walking, almost surprised. He concentrated on Bronco, trying to read him. No one dared say no to him.

"I believed you to be a wise man, Bronco. You live in squalor, dig graves, you're a drunk, and you're a man haunted by war. Saying no to my offer would be ignorant on your behalf. Why would you be so foolish?" Barron March contested.

Bronco stared back at Barron, not as a man intimidated by his status but as someone who became agitated by wasting his time.

"I know what kind of curses come with them perks," said Bronco. "I've seen horrors that a man like you can't imagine. I've seen cities and people burn down to ashes. I've killed soldiers, not thugs, and I live with my nightmares every day. The day you allow me into your criminal organization is the day I burn it the fuck down. I just want to be left the fuck alone, and that's it," Bronco proclaimed wholeheartedly.

If Barron March was upset with Bronco's response, he didn't show it. He remained deadpan and stared at Bronco in silence for a few seconds. He seldom faced rejection, but he knew Bronco was different. There was no fear in his eyes.

"I can somewhat respect a man with no fear. A man without fear is either dead or happy to die. I'll tell Miles you said hello," Barron March replied with finality.

He pivoted and coolly marched away from Bronco. Bronco knew what was coming next. Although he didn't welcome it, he would be ready for it. The most dangerous creation of any society is the man with nothing to lose.

Chapter Five

Their Eyes Were Watching God

There was sweat on many of the mourners' brows, highlighting the emotions in everyone's eyes. It was one of the hottest days of the year. A massive crowd gathered inside and outside the Pentecostal church in the small Black town outside Morton. The funeral services for the Baker family were charged with mixed emotions. There was confusion. Sadness. Anger. Bitterness. An entire family had been wiped out, brutally slaughtered by the Klan. Yet there weren't any arrests or an investigation. The sheriff was ruling the fire an unfortunate accident. When one local resident made a fuss about shotgun shell casings found at the scene, and some witnesses saw a carload of Klan members heading in the direction of the Bakers' place, all of a sudden that witness recanted his testimony, and it was, "Nigger, what shell casings?"

Sylvester Baker and his family deserved justice. Folks were hollering. Children had perished in that fire. Sylvester was a good man, a God-fearing man, and he didn't deserve to die like that, nor his family.

The vibe in the air was tangible. Hundreds of mourners poured into the church to pay their respects. A few of them gasped at seeing the multiple caskets lined before them. An elderly woman placed her hand on one of the caskets, and she dropped to her knees, still touching the casket.

"Oh God. Why? Why? Why?" she hollered in agony.

Another woman walked out of the church on shaky legs, shocked. Some churchwomen fanned a passed-out woman. A young girl who was friends with Sylvester's daughter rushed out of the church and tilted her head to the sky. The sunlight forced her eyes into an angry squint. Other funeral-goers touched hands and consoled the tearful. It was a sensory overload for everyone.

Elise held her little brother's hand as they slowly approached the caskets up front. The line was long, but Elise was patient. Kenneth looked skeptical in proceeding forward. He was not only a schoolmate of Sylvester's 12-year-old daughter, Nancy, but they were good friends who lived close to each other and played together often. For Kenneth, it was hard to believe that she was gone. Kenneth had a teary eye, grieving for his friend, and Elise was there to console him.

"I can't, Elise. No. I don't want to see her," Kenneth cried out.

Elise sighed. She expected this to be hard for her little brother. He and Nancy were so close that often folks had mistaken them for siblings. Kenneth pulled away from his sister and ran for the door. Elise followed him. Kenneth sprang from the church, pushing through the crowd gathered outside, and retreated toward the woods. Elise tried to chase him, but her little brother was fast. She gave up and huffed. He was upset and emotional. Everyone was. Elise, too, was torn apart by the tragedy. Mr. Baker was an understanding and caring man. He was supportive of Black people needing to be financially independent from white-dominated societies. He believed in unity and uplifting the Negro into better existence from poverty and marginalization. Elise often shopped at his store in town, and whenever she was short, he would tell Elise to pay the remainder when she could.

Elise was a beautiful, petite woman in her late twenties. Clad in a poodle skirt and a white blouse, with her lengthy black hair styled into a simple ponytail, she was a charming, engaging, and articulate woman with smooth ebony skin. She had an infectious smile that radiated charm. Men, white men included, were astonished at her beauty.

"You looking mighty fine today, Elise," she heard someone say out of the blue.

Elise turned to see Sheriff Duke coming her way. She was shocked that he'd shown up to the Bakers' funeral. Word throughout the town was that Sheriff Duke encouraged and was somewhat responsible for the massacre. He was a ruthless racist and would be happy to see Black folks lynched and disappeared for good.

The sheriff's sky blue eyes became fixed on Elise standing before him. He had a lean body with slightly stooped shoulders. There were masses of wrinkles around his eyes, and he had a broad mustache. His wrinkled skin turned into a fake smile when he greeted Elise.

"Good day to you, Sheriff," Elise replied politely.

His voice was deep and croaky. "It's a damn shame what happened to Sylvester and his family. He was one stubborn nigger, though. However, as the sheriff, I came to pay my respects," the sheriff uttered.

Elise couldn't believe the audacity of this man. He was a mean, twisted, aging man with a badge to do whatever he pleased, especially toward Black folks. The uniform he wore was blasphemy to the Negro community. Sheriff Duke's sudden presence created a thunderous tidal wave of anger and bitterness. All eyes were on him as he marched into the church and proceeded toward the caskets, especially Sylvester's.

"I reckon things would have turned out differently if he had listened, sold off his land," Sheriff Duke said.

Relatives of the Baker family were seething. Some wanted to tear the sheriff apart. It was no secret he was responsible for this, and if not directly, then indirectly.

The sheriff had his fair share of confrontations with Sylvester. But many felt there wasn't much they could do. He was the sheriff, and they feared the backlash.

"Sheriff Duke, it's mighty kind of you to attend today," Pastor Melvin Brooke said.

"I came to check on things, maybe have a word with you in private, Pastor. The last thing we want, what anyone wants, is more trouble in these parts. I feel there's still some good Negros 'round here. Just need to shake a few bad ones off the tree," the sheriff said.

"I understand, Sheriff. Let's talk in my office," Pastor Brooke replied.

Folks groaned and mumbled at the sheriff's remarks. But they became more upset with Pastor Brooke's brownnosing and quick submissiveness. A few men cut their eyes at the pastor and sheriff walking away to talk privately. Pastor Melvin Brooke was a portly man with short black hair neatly parted on the side. He wore nice, tailored suits and was known to be a pacifist. Pastor Brooke meant well with his nonviolent beliefs but received criticism and reaction from some folks in his congregation. Brooke's beliefs aligned with Booker T. Washington's, that it was better to remain separate from whites than to attempt desegregation. Black people should accept disenfranchisement and social segregation as long as white people allowed them economic progress, educational opportunity, and justice in the courts.

Sylvester had become one of the pastor's main agitators in the flock. He clearly understood that white men would always feel threatened by Black men whether it was segregation or individuality and liberation. They were always going to attack Black ideology, Black wealth, and Black independence.

While Pastor Brooke entertained the sheriff inside his office, Elise stood outside the church. She watched a group of men standing in a circle fuss and gripe.

"It ain't right for that man to be here," a man named JoJo hollered with contempt. "I don't care if he's the sheriff or not."

"They can't kill us all," Doc uttered.

"Sylvester and his family didn't deserve to die like that. What we need to do is get our shotguns and show these crackers we ain't playing," a man named Jimmy spewed.

"Y'all hush with that kind of talk now," Ms. Mary chided. "You all be foolish enough to go and challenge that sheriff, we'll be burying you all too next week."

"They killed him and his family, Ms. Mary. It ain't right."

"I know what happened to Sylvester and his family is a tragedy, but we can't be out here putting more folks in harm's way with that kind of talk," said Ms. Mary.

"Then what we 'posed to do, Ms. Mary? Huh?" Jimmy asked her. "They want our land, and they tryin' to pay us pennies on the dollar. I can't let them have it. I have a family to support."

Ms. Mary shook her head and sighed. She understood their plight. She didn't have the answers, but she didn't want to see any more of her people brutally lynched and murdered by an angry white mob. Morton, Mississippi, had been her home from birth. She'd lost a father, two husbands, and a son to lynchings and angry white mobs. She was widowed in her early sixties, living alone, over-whelmed by the Jim Crow South, and made ends meet by being a maid in town.

While Ms. Mary tried to soothe the Black mob outside, Elise felt she'd seen enough. The day was hot, the crowd was becoming agitated, she had chores to finish, and she began feeling uncomfortable in the sheriff's presence. Kenneth had run off, and she had an idea where he'd probably run off to.

"Do you mind if I walk you home, Elise? It is a troubling day," Harland Burgess uttered.

Harland was a young, strong, hardworking country boy with thick jet-black hair and piercing brown eyes. He was handsome, tall, and educated, and his voice was sweet and velvety, like chocolate, each syllable mesmerizing. Though he looked intimidating, Harland was a gentle, kind man who loved playing baseball. He believed education was one way out of the Jim Crow South. He had an intense crush on Elise for years and wanted to marry her one day and migrate north. But Elise was adamant that she would never leave Mississippi.

Elise smiled his way. "I'm off to find Kenneth, Harland. He done run off upset," she said.

"I'm sure he's fine. The boy has been through a lot. I know Nancy and him were good friends."

"They were."

"Damn shame what happened to the Bakers. I can't believe they're gone," said Harland. "I'm thinking 'bout leaving town and heading north."

"You're willing to leave behind everything you love so easily? This is where we grew up, Harland," Elise said.

"It's not safe for us here, Elise, never has been. How we 'posed to fight? We do, then we all end up like Mr. Baker and his family," Harland griped.

Elise didn't know how to fight. She didn't want to fight. Jim Crow had always been their way of life, and her only concern was raising and taking care of her little brother. Their parents had been killed in a car accident three years ago, and now she was the only family Kenneth had left. She didn't want to retreat from her home. But she understood that the inevitable was coming for everyone. Corporations saw value in their land, and they were coming for it.

"I need to go find Kenneth before it gets late," Elise uttered, not wanting to discuss the town's dilemma with Harland.

"I'll help you find him." Harland smiled.

The two began walking in the direction of Lake Nur. The large lake lay hidden in the forest like a secret gem. The open landscape around the lake stretched as far as the eye could see. The lake shimmered like a sheet of glass under the afternoon sun. It was an oasis for the Black town where laughter would echo from children during the hot summer days and the summer's heat would turn the lake into a refreshing retreat for the inhabitants. Lake Nur had become a sanctuary, a haven from the chaos of prejudice and bigotry for Black folks.

"There he is," Harland pointed out.

Elise smiled. Kenneth stood at the lake's edge, throwing and skipping rocks against the water. He was good at it. He was alone and brooding. This was where Kenneth and Nancy spent most of their time—at the lake, playing, laughing, and being kids.

"I'll go talk to him," said Elise.

"Do you need me to come with you?" Harland asked.

"No. I need to do this alone," she replied.

Harland nodded.

Elise walked toward her brother with her arms folded across her chest. She sighed heavily, feeling that no adult should have a conversation with a child about the death of another child at the hands of an angry white mob. A 12-year-old boy shouldn't have to deal with that kind of horror. The look on Elise's face was one of sadness and resentment.

"Kenneth?" she called out.

"Leave me alone," he snapped. He continued to skip rocks into the lake without turning back to look at his sister.

"I know it's rough, Kenneth."

"Why did she have to die? She was my friend. Why did they do that to her, to her family? Huh?" he cried out.

Kenneth couldn't stop the tears from falling. His young spirit sank like a stone in water. A wave of sadness struck Elise, too. Seeing her brother so heartbroken, her heart felt like it was being squeezed by a cold, metal fist.

"Come here, Kenneth," she said.

Kenneth stopped skipping rocks and stared at the lake as his eyes glistened with unleashed tears that he quickly blinked away.

"I understand what you're feeling. When I was your age, they took my best friend, too," said Elise.

A heavy sigh escaped her lips as a few tears rolled down her cheeks. Kenneth turned and ran into his sister's arms. He continued to cry.

"I miss her, Elise. I miss my friend so much," Kenneth cried in his sister's arms.

"I know. We all are going to miss her and her family."

A tight gloom overcame them at such a peaceful and serene place.

"All we can do is pray to the Lord to protect us from this evil," Elise said.

Elise held her little brother in her arms tightly, and she didn't want to let him go, was almost afraid to let him go, fearing that if she did, the same tragedy would befall him. The only thing she could do was comfort him.

"We're going to be okay. I promise you," Elise proclaimed wholeheartedly.

Harland watched them from afar. He, too, couldn't help but become saddened. It was a tense and emotional day. He wished he could protect them both from any harm. But he understood that while they lived in the South, white folks were going to keep coming for them, one more vicious and evil than the last.

It wasn't going to end with Sylvester and his family.

Chapter Six

Cry Revenge

Bronco found himself suddenly on fire when he opened his eyes from his sleep. The heat that radiated from the fire was hot and bright. The fire inside his apartment was becoming violent and wild. It seemed like it was angry with him and attacking him. Bronco leaped from his bed as the flames came alive, but it became hard for him to move. The entire area became so dark and thick with smoke that it was hard for him to breathe. Suddenly, he heard the screams and cries of a young girl. He was shocked because he was supposed to be alone. But he could hear the agony of this little girl's voice like he heard the roaring fire.

"Help me! Please. Somebody help me!" she cried out.

"Where are you?" Bronco hollered.

Suddenly, Bronco couldn't move at all. He found himself rooted to the floor like his feet were in cement. No matter how hard he tried to break free, it was becoming impossible. It wasn't about his strength. He couldn't combat this raging and powerful fire. The billowing smoke began to waft into his lungs, crippling him. He felt his skin start to burn, although he was believed to be indestructible.

"Help me. It's hot. Help me!" her voice cried out.

She was close.

But Bronco couldn't get to her. Instead, he fell to his knees and became consumed by the fire and smoke. She was burning from the blistering heat. He could feel it. He could hear her crying out in agony. But he couldn't move. Tears began to trickle from his eyes, but the heat and fire quickly extinguished them. Bronco felt utterly helpless for the first time in a long time. He couldn't break free from the restraints, and a young girl was going to die because of this. Yet he yelled, "I'm coming to help you!"

The girl's cries fell silent. Everything went completely black.

All of a sudden, Bronco woke up coughing and gasping for air. He had another nightmare, but this one felt too real. He was burning with her, dying with that little girl somewhere. It felt like a scream was caught in his throat.

Bronco got out of bed to collect himself. It was morning but a bleak day with a steel gray sky spitting rain. It was one of those days made for books and tea. But Bronco didn't drink tea, and he barely read anything. The nightmare was so disturbing that he kept seeing flashes of it in his head. Besides the sheets of rain outside the bedroom window, his place was quiet. He looked out the window. The streets were empty and wet. The rain had temporarily relieved Harlem of the usually hot and humid conditions.

Bronco stood by his window for a moment, thinking. It had been two weeks since Barron March visited him. He knew men like Barron and Miles didn't forget. Gangsters like them lived for action and fear. The closer to death they were, the more alive they would feel. Bronco knew that feeling all too well. Whatever they had planned, Bronco wished they would get on with it already. It would give him a reason to retaliate. Maybe they feared him because he feared nothing. He didn't want to strike first because, after the war, he'd vowed to put that kind of life behind him. The violence and anger had consumed him at one time. He'd become a killing machine. He was unstoppable. But becoming an unmovable force in war and chaos came with consequences. Bronco felt his mental health was deteriorating. It was becoming harder to deduce what was real and what wasn't. Sometimes he faced trauma and anxiety among the public. Or he would form an increasingly complex symbol for the dark side of everyday life.

The sudden knocking at his door broke Bronco away from his haunting thoughts. He turned and went to see who it was, although he had an idea already. Bronco looked through the peephole to see it was Mindy. He sighed. Mindy's presence was becoming routine. It almost felt like they were in some de facto relationship. She cared about him, and she liked him a lot. Bronco knew this. He cared about her too. Mindy was a sweet, cute girl. She had that "girl next door" demeanor about her.

"I know you're home, Bronco," Mindy uttered.

Bronco opened the door. Mindy smiled at him. She was wearing a raincoat and carrying groceries.

"I know you're hungry. I'm going to cook breakfast for you," she added.

Bronco relented and stepped aside to allow her into the apartment. She had been cleaning and cooking for him lately. No matter how hard he tried to refuse her, he couldn't. She was becoming good company. Maybe she was needed. Perhaps she was becoming the required balance in his life.

Mindy removed her raincoat, revealing the yellow house-dress she wore underneath. She was a simple girl with a bright smile. Her upbeat attitude and ability to demonstrate warmth and tenderness toward others were reminiscent of Bronco's mother before the alcohol and downfall.

"This rain falls like a whisper from the heavens," Mindy said.

For Bronco, it was an odd statement. "What?" Bronco replied.

"The best thing one can do when it rains is let it rain," Mindy added. "I like it. It cleanses the streets and washes away the dirt and grime. Sometimes I wish the rain could cleanse the hearts of man."

"Are you always this positive about life?" he replied.

Mindy smiled. It answered his question.

"What are you making?" he asked her.

"Some good ol'-fashioned hominy grits, fish, and biscuits. I know you can eat. A man always needs to eat," she said.

It sounded great. Mindy continued to smile his way. They looked at each other. The connection and attraction were palpable. But Bronco felt he was no good for her. He was haunted and damaged and figured he shouldn't be invited into her world. But Mindy became consistent and didn't take no for an answer. Although quiet and docile, she knew how to express herself clearly and effectively.

"You go on and wash up and get some rest. Breakfast will be ready soon," she said.

Almost everything uttered from her lips was followed by a warm, genuine smile. Unlike when he was with Elizabeth for vivid pleasure, needs, and revenge, there was something there with Mindy, something unique and unexplainable. Bronco thought, *how could I not see it?* Perhaps he did but wanted to ignore it the entire time. Inviting a woman into your life and falling in love, Bronco felt it was nothing but trouble. He didn't want that attachment. It felt too risky for a man like him. He was used to living alone and being single and thought he would become her rose's thorn. It felt like everything became broken around Bronco.

He wanted to be honest with himself.

Bronco left Mindy alone in the kitchen to cook. He retreated to the bathroom and closed the door behind him. It was small with its space-saving fixtures. Bronco turned on the faucet and began to wet his face. The nightmare he had still played inside his mind. That little girl burning made him scowl, and it made him think, *who is she? Where is she? Why am I seeing her so often?* Bronco wanted to escape it, but it was becoming evident that he wouldn't.

Bronco began smelling Mindy's cooking from the bathroom. She was a good cook, and he was getting used to home-cooked meals. He was becoming used to having her around often, which scared him. The man saw himself as a monster and believed he was cursed. But Mindy began showing him something different, perhaps giving him hope.

Bronco continued to stare at himself in the mirror and sighed heavily.

"Breakfast is almost ready," Mindy hollered from the kitchen.

Bronco closed his eyes and tried to erase the fear and dread he'd carried with him since the war and his days as a young gangster under Pinch's tutelage. He never had a girlfriend but only had sexual relations with the ladies. He barely had any friends. Besides drinking and being a gravedigger, Bronco didn't have any purpose to exist. He looked at himself one final time in the bathroom mirror and exited.

Mindy was dancing around the kitchen, making magic with her cooking skills. Bronco stared at her momentarily, and something stirred inside him. *Desire.* Mindy was standing by the stove frying fish when Bronco came behind her unexpectedly. His arms reached around her waist with the softest caress. Mindy gasped at first, shocked by his sudden embrace, but it was invited. Her arms fell to her side, surrendering to his touch. There was no more waiting. Bronco's hands roamed from her breasts down her stomach and slid beneath her dress. He touched her for a moment while he gently kissed the back of her neck, and Mindy's moan was proof she desired the same thing. She shifted her body to face him, bringing her mouth to his. They passionately kissed. Everything was happening fast.

Bronco lifted Mindy off her feet, into his arms. He began carrying her across the living room toward the bedroom. In his arms, Mindy felt like wings had sprouted from her shoulders and were threatening to carry her off into the sky. He was strong.

Mindy wasn't shy about getting undressed in front of him. When she was nude, Bronco gazed at her for a long time. She became nervous. *Did I do something wrong? Does he not like my nakedness?* "Is everything okay? Are you disappointed?"

"No. No, I'm not. You're beautiful," he expressed.

Mindy blushed. Being naked with him seemed so natural. She reached out to grab his hand. She wanted to do this.

"Are you sure about this?" Bronco asked her.

Mindy nodded. He pressed her down onto her back against the bed. They looked at each other for one single perfect moment before he brought his mouth to hers and was quickly inside of her.

"Ugh. Mmm . . ." she breathed.

Mindy panted from the pleasure of his bare chest pressing against her breasts. Their hands became intertwined as the speed of his thrusts increased. Mindy wasn't Elizabeth. Bronco wanted to make love to her. He wanted this to last. He tried to connect with her physically. Bronco wanted to face her and savored every bit of this moment, the opposite of when he was with Elizabeth mostly doggie style.

Mindy closed her eyes as Bronco suckled her breasts. She felt him shift with his ragged breathing mingling with hers. She straddled him and met him eye to eye. Mindy clung to him as they kissed again. Bronco moaned and grunted, wanting to absorb all her heat into his naked skin. He held Mindy firmly while pushing into her. He was an odd combination of seducer and protector.

"Augh. Ugh. Bronco," she breathed.

Before long, Mindy found her nose pushed into the pillow, on her stomach, with his chest on her back and his mouth at her ear. His sheets smelled just like him—warm and masculine and clean. Bronco continued thrusting, and Mindy closed her eyes and arched her back to take him even deeper into her. Mindy could feel that Bronco's muscles were taut as steel bars. He was careful with her. Pressure began to build in her stomach, her muscles tightened around him, and she soon came with a quiet shudder. Bronco thrust into her one more time before his entire body became tense with his orgasm. He then relaxed beside her with a deep moan.

Mindy became nestled in his arms, their bodies intertwined underneath the sheets, and they both lay in silence for a moment, catching their breath.

"I always loved you, Bronco," Mindy proclaimed out of the blue. "And I don't want to share you with anyone else."

He looked at her. "I'm not meant to be shared."

Mindy smiled. Bronco had become her ship, and she knew they would sail through anything as long as she held on to him.

The rain had stopped, and the sun became a beacon in the sky again. Harlem was bright with sunlight and activity once again. Mindy remained on cloud nine with

Bronco. What had transpired between them earlier was something she would remember. And Bronco was grateful for her company. But it was getting late, and Mindy needed to work tonight at Lenox Lounge.

"I'll walk you home," said Bronco.

Mindy smiled. "I would like that."

She grabbed her raincoat to carry since it had stopped raining, and they exited his apartment to the hallway. Bronco locked his door, and they began to descend the stairway toward the foyer. The three-story walk-up rental building had seen better days. The paint was peeling. There were a few unhinged doors, falling ceilings, and rotten floorboards. The one bright thing about the place was a tidy little herb garden on the front stoop that his neighbor, Ms. Katyln, took care of.

"Are you coming to the lounge tonight?" Mindy asked him.

"I feel I should stay away for a while like I've been doing. Don't want no trouble there with you or anyone else," Bronco replied.

"Well, how about I come by after I finish there?"

He smiled. "I wouldn't mind that at all."

Mindy's eyes were bright with the adoration she had for him. They stared at each other before exiting the building. Mindy didn't want to leave, but she had a job to go to. Besides, she knew she would see him again soon. Bronco was becoming a different man around her.

Twilight had arrived. The sun began to set, draping a velvet blanket over the city and creating a cascade of colors, casting a warm embrace over the world. It temporarily blinded Bronco and Mindy from the west. Mindy smiled at the sunset. She saw beauty in so many things. She was the type of woman who took the time to smell the flowers.

Bronco suddenly noticed the 1950 Chevy Bel Air parked across the street from his place. A tall black man emerged from the passenger's side door of the Chevy, wearing a thin bomber jacket in the summer. He walked with the deliberate, swaggering limp of a thug and glanced cautiously at his surroundings as he approached. Bronco caught a glimpse of a jagged scar across his cheek. At the same time, as Bronco was focused on the man in the bomber jacket, a second stranger bumped into Mindy. Mindy fell against Bronco, briefly throwing him off-balance. The man who bumped into Mindy turned as if he were going to apologize, but his left hand emerged from his jacket pocket as he did.

Mindy saw the gun and screamed, "Bronco!"

The man let off two quick shots before Bronco charged at him, twisting the weapon in his hand until he heard the man's trigger finger break with a sharp crack and pulled the gun out of his hand. Then Bronco brought his right hand up and struck the man in the neck with the butt of the weapon over his jugular. It was a hard enough blow to disrupt a major blood vessel, which killed him instantly. While Bronco was occupied with the first attacker, he found himself staring down the barrel of a .45 from the man in the bomber. The attacker scowled at Bronco with his outstretched gun and fired multiple times.

Boom! Boom! Boom!

Bronco shielded Mindy from the gunfire, and then he grabbed the man's wrist and held the gun against his chest, knowing he had the advantage. The gun went off to no avail. Bronco was still standing, unscathed. The shooter became wide-eyed and shocked. However, Bronco didn't give him much time to react. First, he headbutted the attacker, and his nose began to spew blood. Then Bronco delivered an elbow strike to the side of his face and lifted the man off his feet like he was paper thin. Undoubtedly, they were acting at the behest of Miles or Barron March. Following orders had cost these men their lives.

"Who sent you?" Bronco growled.

The man struggled to breathe.

"I said, who fuckin' sent you? Was it Miles?"

Bronco was ready to break his neck but wanted a name. But it didn't matter. The shooter struggled to breathe in Bronco's tight grip, which felt like a web. As Bronco was ready to kill him, he heard Mindy cry from behind him, "Bronco . . ."

Bronco pivoted, and to his horror, Mindy had been shot twice. Bronco's eyes grew wide in shock and fear. Mindy was lying on her side, immobile, her blood pooling underneath her. Bronco hurried to her aid, scooping Mindy into his arms. His tears were natural. He was invincible, but he felt useless and vulnerable at this moment. Mindy was dying, and there wasn't anything he could do about it.

Each breath was difficult and painful. But a wistful smile graced her lips as she stared up at Bronco. It was as if she was reminiscing about some cherished memory. A regretful expression crossed Bronco's face. Their time together was short-lived. Even in Mindy's final moments, her unwavering gaze conveyed a fierce determination to leave a lasting impact on Bronco.

She was dead.

A gut-wrenching sob tore through Bronco's chest, and he screamed in agony. Finally, he'd felt some purpose with Mindy. Now she was gone. He looked away from her as his face turned demonic. The second shooter was trying to get up, but Bronco knocked him back down. They took something away from him. Now he was going to kill him.

"Fuck you," the shooter cursed.

Bronco's booted foot slammed into the fallen man's jaw with such force that his skull vibrated painfully against the hard ground, and his face nearly exploded. The only sound beyond the crack of his skull on the ground was the soft exhalation that escaped Bronco's lips. Startled pedestrians looked on in horror, but Bronco didn't care. He wanted them to become witnesses to the monster they were creating.

It was closing time at Milly's, a restaurant on Eighth Avenue in Harlem. It was late, and Harlem was winding down for the night. Barron March, Miles, and five bodyguards were the last to leave the soul food place while chairs were being put on tables and the lights were being turned off.

"You tell everyone I want him found and taken care of for what he did to my nephew," Barron griped to Miles.

"We'll find him, Mr. March," Miles assured him.

"This is your got-damn mess, Miles. You better fix it," Barron warned him.

Miles nodded. "I will."

Barron March proceeded toward the car parked farther down the street at the curb, flanked by his five men. The area was nearly empty on a balmy night. When Miles and Barron approached the car, everyone froze in fright. Barron's driver was slumped against the steering wheel. He was dead with his throat cut.

"What the fuck is this?" Barron exclaimed.

Barron's goons quickly drew their weapons while Barron and Miles froze with slight fear in their eyes.

"It's fuckin' him," Barron March exclaimed.

This was payback from Bronco, he'd deduced. He had heard the rumors and superstition about Bronco, that he was a man with nine lives like a cat—hard to kill. Now Barron and Miles went from being the predators to the prey in Harlem.

"A man with no fear," Barron March uttered to himself with a smirk.

Suddenly, from the dark, a burst of gunfire exploded, and one after another, Barron's men began to drop before they could fire off their weapons. They were being picked off with brutal efficiency. The machine-gun fire echoed through the empty streets of Harlem, and then everything fell silent. All of Barron's men were dead. Barron and Miles were surprised to be still alive.

Suddenly, Bronco emerged from the darkness, clutching a Thompson submachine gun. He stopped a short distance from Barron March and Miles. They were now at his mercy, trapped in a corner like rabbits by a snarling wolf.

"The girl wasn't meant to die. You was," said Barron.

Bronco had nothing to say to them. Barron March knew his fate. But Miles began cowering. "Look, nigga, you don't need to do this. We can pay you, make it go away."

There was no reasoning with Bronco. He leveled the Thompson submachine gun at them, and they looked at each other. Barron March stood there, waiting for the inevitable. Bronco opened fire and began cutting them both down with a hail of bullets. They dropped immediately. Their blood and brains were splattered against the Fleetwood Sedan. Their bodies became contorted on the pavement along with the men who were supposed to protect them.

Bronco stared at their bullet-riddled bodies lying in a pool of blood and frowned. He'd killed a drug kingpin in public, but he knew the fight wouldn't be over. He knew it was time to leave Harlem. This couldn't be his home anymore. There was nothing left for him here.

When he turned to leave, there she was again, the little girl staring at him creepily. Bronco matched her eerie gaze and uttered, "Whatever you need me to do or wherever you need me to go, I'll do it. I'm done here."

She began to walk toward him.

Bronco was ready to follow her.

Chapter Seven

The Naked Soul

Elizabeth climbed out of the taxicab on 140th Street clad in an elegant red hostess gown with an opening down the front, revealing slim-fitting cigarette pants underneath. She'd come from another one of her performances. It was a warm summer night. Harlem had fallen into a slumber during the wee hours of the morning. 140th Street was as quiet as a mouse running across cotton. Elizabeth was drained from performing tonight. She only wanted to get inside, undress, and stretch across her bed to get some needed sleep.

When she reached the steps to her brownstone, she stopped suddenly. She sensed an unexpected presence behind her, and when she turned around, she wasn't wrong. Bronco was frowning at her from a slight distance. Elizabeth noticed the pistol he clutched by his side, but she remained calm.

"I heard about Barron and Miles," she uttered. "I figured it was you."

Bronco remained quiet.

"And I'm sorry about what happened to Mindy," she added.

Bronco stepped closer to Elizabeth and raised the pistol to her head. She gasped but remained still. She locked eyes with Bronco and saw his sudden hatred and resentment for her. A heavy sigh escaped her lips as a few tears rolled down her cheek.

"I didn't mean for any of this to happen. I really liked you, Bronco. I wanted you to love me, but I knew you and I would only be a fairy tale. Why would you ever love a woman like me?" she proclaimed.

Bronco remained silent and focused on her. He felt a flicker of irritation when she spoke. All it took was one simple squeeze of the trigger to end her life. Elizabeth's cries were barely clear, like the easygoing whispers of the wind on a cold, lonesome night. She refused to look away or beg for her life. The only thing she could do was confess to him before he ended her.

"I had a wonderful time with you that night, and I think about it every day." She smiled.

Bronco cocked back the hammer of the .357 he gripped. Elizabeth stared at him, teary-eyed, but with recognition of her fate.

"You may have been in love with Mindy, but you and I are the same, Bronco. We're two lost, cursed, and tortured souls. Happiness isn't meant to be for us. Creatures like us are not designed to be happy or content. We are designed primarily to survive like every other creature in the natural world," she proclaimed wholeheartedly.

Her eyes continued to glisten with unleashed tears that she quickly blinked away.

"Just fuckin' do it already," Elizabeth uttered.

He'd never killed a woman before.

Bronco bit back his anger. He felt she was the cause of everything. He wanted to be left alone that night, but Elizabeth decided to flirt. It'd become a domino effect, and unfortunately, Mindy was caught in the crossfire.

Is happiness a real thing? he thought. Bronco's heart felt like it was being squeezed by a cold, metal fist.

"I don't want to ever see your face in Harlem again," Bronco finally spoke.

"You won't," she replied.

He was leaving Harlem but didn't want to let her know it. He glared at Elizabeth with finality, then pivoted and disappeared from her view. An avalanche of relief and sorrow crashed over Elizabeth. She stood there for a long moment, reflecting how close she came to losing her life. Miles was dead, and now she was finally free to live her life on her own.

Bronco sat quietly in his seat, staring out at the sprawling landscape of the South as the steam train roared toward Mississippi. It had passed the Mason-Dixon line hours ago, and Bronco had noticed the extreme changes regarding segregation. He traveled in what the railroad called the "Jim Crow" car. Right away, conductors began to force Black people to move from regular seats to seats in the Jim Crow car, and often with no grace whatsoever. Bronco grimaced when he noticed a prejudiced conductor push a young black woman and her child around as if they were beasts. He rudely addressed them by shouting, "Come on, nigger girl, move on now. You and that boy need to move into the nigger coach area."

When the conductor approached Bronco to tell him that he needed to move into the "nigger coach area," Bronco hesitated for a moment.

"Do you hear me talking to you, boy? You need to get up and move on now. You're no different, nigger."

Bronco scowled. He took his time standing, his towering height and solid physique tremendously opposing the short and skinny conductor. Yet the conductor stared at Bronco as if he were the one twice his size.

"You don't want no trouble on this train, boy. I'll have you thrown off at the next stop," the conductor threatened him.

Reluctantly, Bronco complied.

The rudeness continued inside the Jim Crow car. The racist conductor was appropriating seats for incoming white passengers. He would yell gruffly for everyone's tickets before the train began moving. This was Bronco's first time traveling by train to the rural South. He'd never left Harlem except for his tour overseas during World War II, and he had experienced his fair share of racism there, too. Now he was receiving a rude awakening on how things worked in the South. No luggage racks were in the "colored" section, requiring Black folks to cram their suitcases around their feet. The "colored" bathroom was smaller and lacked the amenities of the white bathroom—a subtle and not-so-subtle reminder that white folks were superior and treated better.

Bronco had been on the train for nearly fifteen hours and hadn't eaten anything since he'd left Harlem. Confined to the Jim Crow car, he had no access to the train's dining car, and the stopovers at stations were not long enough to procure food at the stations, if any were provided for Negros. The experienced Black travelers brought their own food for consumption, knowing about the bigoted environment. They would snack on fruit and peanuts, sandwiches, and water. And when Black passengers could purchase food, their options were limited.

When the steam train came to a twenty-minute stopover in Kentucky to allow white passengers to grab a quick meal at the station's lunch counter, Black travelers weren't permitted such luxuries. Instead, when the train resumed its journey south, the lunch counter's staff sent a basket full of cold leftover food to get rid of it among the colored passengers for sale. For a dollar or more, Black travelers could buy a quarter of an impenetrable dried hen fried the day before yesterday, old bread, and a slice of musty pie. And to add insult to injury, the passengers who bought the overpriced food could not secure cutlery or any beverages with their meals, as railroad employees were not allowed to bring dishes or flatware into the colored car.

Bronco refused to eat anything. He was disgusted by the behavior of it all. White people in the South believed he and African Americans were animals, virtually camels, and could go without food or water for several days.

Bronco had no idea what his next move would be when he arrived in Morton, Mississippi. He was haunted by the little girl, and he wanted to help. But where would he begin? The girl had whispered to him in a dream the town she was from—Morton. Bronco knew nothing about the South, let alone Mississippi. One thing was for sure, he couldn't go back to Harlem, but not because he was afraid to. It was because there were too many memories he wanted to leave behind. He would inevitably begin a new chapter in his life somewhere else.

Morton, Mississippi, seemed like it was in the middle of nowhere. It was the epitome of the country. While Bronco was on the train, he noticed the endless cotton fields and farmland with its fair share of sharecroppers working the land. The town had a population of over 1,500, and it wasn't growing anytime soon. The racial divide was thick, and Bronco immediately noticed it at the train station. The colored waiting rooms were smaller and less convenient. Bronco entered the poorly equipped bathroom, which was ill-ventilated and ill-lit. Bronco sighed. *Welcome to Mississippi,* he said to himself.

Bronco carried a military-issue army duffle bag that was worn and shabby. He didn't need much because he didn't plan on staying long, and everything he owned was in that bag, including a .357 Magnum. Bronco immediately stood out among the colored passengers at the station. He was tall and muscular, wearing a brown fedora hat and baggy trousers. His demeanor was standoffish and daunting. He had no problem eyeing white folks directly in their eyes with a frown. While the colored men and women moved warily with their eyes cast toward the ground, not wanting any trouble from anyone, Bronco carried that Harlem arrogance and boldness. He was tough, aware, and angry. The first thing he wanted to do was hit the bar and get himself a drink. It was needed. It had been a long trip from Harlem to Mississippi by train.

With its blazing heat, the scorching sun was the only thing that wasn't discriminatory in the small town. Everyone was hot and sweating and fanned themselves to try to keep cool. Bronco exited the train station and looked around. He was out of place but remained dead-pan.

"Excuse me, sir," Bronco called out to an older black gentleman wearing overalls.

The man turned and replied, "What can I help you with?"

"How far is the nearest bar?" asked Bronco.

The man chuckled and smiled. "Bar? I say, 'bout two miles that way." He pointed. "You plan on walking? It's a mighty hot day."

Bronco nodded. He had no other choice.

"I have my brothers picking me up soon. You can ride with us if you like."

Bronco nodded. "I welcome it, sir."

"My name is Henry. And you are?"

"Bronco."

"Bronco. Now that's a name you don't hear often."

They shook hands, and Bronco met his very first friend. Shortly after, an old burgundy-hued 1946 Chevrolet pickup truck arrived at the train station. Bronco followed Henry toward the pickup truck. Behind the steering wheel was a man about Bronco's age, and Henry's second brother was sitting in the passenger seat.

"Bronco, this is my youngest brother, Jacob, and my other brother, Moses," Henry introduced them.

"Nice to meet you," said Bronco.

They nodded and greeted Bronco with a smile.

"C'mon, hop on back," said Henry.

Bronco tossed his duffle bag into the back of the pickup and climbed inside. Henry followed him. They sat across from each other while the pickup began to head toward the town. While on their way to town, Bronco took in the acres of lush farmland that separated one home from another. This was the antiquated South, a spark of contrast from the lively Harlem metropolis.

"What brings you to Morton, Mississippi? If ya don't mind my asking. We don't get too many folks here," said Henry.

Bronco didn't know how to answer the question. He obviously couldn't tell him the truth, that he was being haunted by a young girl. So he replied, "I'm only passing through, not staying long."

"No friends or family down here?"

"Nah."

"Where ya from, Bronco?" asked Henry.

"New York," Bronco answered. "Harlem."

Henry was taken aback. "Harlem, New York, now that's nifty," he laughed. "You's a long way from home. A cool and handsome cat like ya here in Mississippi, you must have a gal down here."

"No woman," Bronco said.

Henry was confused.

"No gal, no family, no friends. Well, you have a friend with me and my brothers, Bronco. Welcome to Mississippi. Things are quite different here than up North, I reckon you imagine," Henry uttered.

Bronco nodded, understanding him.

The American flag lined numerous storefronts in the town, with many WHITE ONLY and COLORED ONLY signs. A car filled with white passengers passed the pickup truck Bronco was riding in. Bronco caught their attention, and a few eyes narrowed on the pickup he was in as it rolled past.

"Things have been edgy 'round here since they murdered that family," said Henry.

"Family? What family?" Bronco questioned.

"Good folks I hear, a man named Sylvester. He owned lots of land and a grocery store in the Black part of town. White folks become agitated and angry with him, and . . ."

Henry couldn't continue. The look on Henry's face spoke volumes. He couldn't retell the horrors he'd heard about what happened to the Bakers that night. It was a nightmare they all feared, angry white men and gaping, incensed mobs.

"There is no justice, no laws for us down here," Henry uttered dejectedly. "We on our own. Remember that, Bronco."

Bronco stared at Henry for a moment, taking everything in. Henry was disheartened and made to become a meek Black man because of the Jim Crow South. Undoubtedly, Henry was a hardworking and fair man who only wanted to care for his family and make a decent living. But he'd become marginalized by fear and segregation, and there were limitations on where he could go, what he could do, and the kind of man he could become.

The pickup stopped in town. Henry smiled at Bronco and said, "This is your stop."

Bronco nodded. He was appreciative of the ride. He grabbed his duffle bag and slung it over his shoulder.

"Remember what I said now, ya hear? Keep ya head down and mind ya business 'round here," Henry warned him.

Bronco nodded and climbed out of the back of the pickup. Henry smiled as the pickup began to drive off. Bronco watched it disappear, and then he took in his surroundings. It was a quiet and tired old town. Where in Harlem, during a hot summer day, there would be a flood of people, businesses, and activities, Morton and the people on the outskirts of it moved slowly. They moseyed across the square, shuffled in and out of the stores around it, and took their time about everything. There was no hurry. A day was twenty-four hours long but seemed longer.

Bronco walked around, looking for a place to sit and drink. Henry assured him a bar was nearby, but Bronco believed there wasn't a place for recreation for someone like him. The WHITE ONLY signs were everywhere.

A few white men wearing suspenders and dungarees were sitting outside a meat market. They began to glare at Bronco, a new face—a black man carrying a military-issued duffle bag wandering through their town. One of the men stood up and glared at Bronco with disdain.

"Is this nigger lost?" Bronco overheard him from afar.

"I've never seen him before," another man uttered.

Bronco kept his cool and continued walking, keenly aware of all the white eyes on him. He didn't want any trouble, not at the moment. But he was lost and confused. He had nowhere to go or stay. He didn't know a soul around. He began to regret coming to Mississippi without a plan. But she continued to haunt him for some odd reason, and his instincts brought him to Mississippi.

What do I do now? Bronco asked himself.

He was the odd man out, a stranger in a foreign land, and undoubtedly, trouble would find him soon.

It didn't take long. Bronco noticed the sheriff's car, a black-and-white cruiser with a spotlight and siren, approaching. Bronco stared at the vehicle, knowing what was about to happen. It was a small town but with the same bullshit as in Harlem. He braced himself for the worst. The sheriff's car drew near and came to a stop. The driver's side door opened, and Sheriff Duke climbed out of his patrol car with his full attention fixed on Bronco.

"You lost, boy?" Sheriff Duke asked him.

The sheriff's sky blue eyes were narrowed and intense on Bronco. Bronco stood tall and unflinching before the authority figure, remaining quiet.

"You hear me talking to you, boy? I said, are you lost, nigger?" Sheriff Duke exclaimed.

He moved uncomfortably closer to Bronco and eyed Bronco with a menacing stare. Bronco immediately broke one hidden rule in the South: locking eyes with a white man and not showing him the respect he demanded.

"No, I'm not lost," Bronco replied sternly.

"You sure 'bout that?"

"Yeah, I'm sure," Bronco fired back.

"You cast your eyes on me like I'm your equal, boy, and with that tone . . ." the sheriff rebuked.

Sheriff Duke was ready to reach for his nightstick and heatedly hit Bronco's head with it—it'd been done plenty of times before. The town watched everything unfold, with white eyes ready to see the law at its best and not intervene.

The tension was thick. Bronco continued to scowl at the sheriff. Sheriff Duke fumed. *Who is this nigger?* Everything about him screamed trouble.

While the confrontation was unfolding on the street, Elise and Kenneth exited from a retail store, carrying a few items. Elise noticed the trouble brewing with Sheriff Duke and a stranger. Bronco caught her eye. She'd never seen him around before. He was tall, handsome, and daring. Before the sheriff escalated things with violence and an arrest, Elise hurried toward the two men.

"Good afternoon, Sheriff Duke," Elise uttered politely.

Sheriff Duke fleetingly cut his eyes at Elise and replied, "Elise, do you know this nigger?"

"Yes. I do, Sheriff. He's my cousin," Elise replied quickly.

"Your cousin?" the sheriff replied dubiously.

"Yes. We mean no trouble, Sheriff. He's from out of town, and he's never been to the South," said Elise. "He's just passing through."

"Well, it'd be fitting for you to teach this nigger how things work down here, Elise. If he eyeballs me again, I'll make sure his stay is permanent here," the sheriff uttered with contempt.

"Yes, sir. I'll make sure he'll know," Elise replied passively. "Thank you, Sheriff."

Bronco glanced at Elise deadpan. But he kept quiet. Sheriff Duke glared at Bronco one final time and uttered, "I don't like your cousin's attitude. Don't fuck with me, nigger."

Sheriff Duke pivoted and marched back toward his police cruiser. Bronco stood there with his fists clenched, fuming. He wanted to knock that cop's head off, and he could have done it, too. But he had to remind himself that he was there for a purpose, and it was too soon to stir up trouble.

Once the cruiser drove off, Bronco looked at Elise and said, "I didn't ask for your help."

"Are you stupid and dumb? You could have fooled me," Elise sassed back. "Sheriff Duke was ready to open your head up like a piñata."

"I can stand up for myself," Bronco countered.

Elise frowned at the nerve of him. "Well, a thank-you would suffice just fine, now. Do they have manners and respect where you come from?"

Bronco looked at her. Elise was spirited but attractive. Kenneth remained quiet by her side. He stared up at Bronco, amazed by his height and muscles.

"Are you a soldier?" Kenneth asked him.

"I was," said Bronco.

Kenneth smiled. He'd never met a man with Bronco's brash attitude and stature. "I wanna become a soldier too."

Bronco frowned. The last thing he felt this kid should become was a soldier, but he kept his opinion to himself.

"Well, what is your name?" asked Elise.

"My name is Bronco," he answered.

Elise was caught off guard by his name. *Bronco?* It was different. "Where are you from, Bronco?" asked Elise.

"Harlem."

Elise was taken aback. "Harlem? What brings you to our town?"

Bronco refused to answer. Elise seemed stumped.

"Well, do you at least have someplace to go, Bronco?"

He didn't, and it showed on his face. Elise sighed heavily, and against her better judgment, she said, "If you like, I have a spare room at my home. You can stay there if needed. Mind you, I'm not fond of taking in strangers. But I'm a Christian woman who wants to help."

Bronco stared at her coolly and replied, "I do appreciate the hospitality, ma'am."

Elise smiled. "So we do have manners."

Bronco followed Elise and Kenneth to a rusted, old pickup truck that had seen better days. He climbed into the cab with the two, and Elise started up the truck. The engine cranked to life, and Elise began to drive out of town. Although he didn't express it, he was grateful. Her sudden kindness was a beginning to a nomad like him with a purpose. Bronco sat quietly, and as the pickup was leaving town, there she was again—that little girl with her sad and eerie gaze.

Bronco looked at her in silence.

Nobody noticed her.

However, Bronco knew he was in the right place. He felt it.

Chapter Eight

Another Country

Monroe couldn't hide how scared he was while he rode handcuffed in the back seat of Sheriff Duke's cruiser. It was the middle of the night. Sheriff Duke and his deputy had come to his home and arrested him in front of his wife and daughters. They were terrified. Sheriff Duke threatened his family if he didn't comply. So, Monroe didn't resist when the sheriff and his deputy began to assault and arrest him and tossed him into the back seat of the cruiser.

"We're going for a ride, nigger," Sheriff Duke had told Monroe.

Monroe knew he wasn't on his way to the station because they were deep in the woods, on a narrow dirt road off the main road, traveling farther away from the town. His heart pounded as terror stabbed his heart. Monroe was familiar with Sheriff Duke's violent reputation when it came to dealing with Black men. They wanted his land, but Monroe refused to sign any documents.

"Please, Sheriff. I'll do whatever you want. Just please, sir, let me go," Monroe cried out.

"We warned you, nigger," Sheriff Duke retorted.

Monroe had no idea where they were taking him, but he knew it wouldn't be pleasant. The handcuffs were tight, and he was barely dressed—pants, a torn T-shirt, and no shoes. Sheriff Duke and his deputy began mocking Monroe while driving to a remote location.

"I'll never understand your kind, boy," the sheriff uttered. "We give you an opportunity to move on and make some money, and you reject it."

"I worked hard for everything I have, Sheriff Duke," Monroe said. "I just can't give away my land."

"You think you own something, nigger. This is our country. We give and we take. Now Mr. Lockheart has been more than fair with you to buy your land, Monroe. Why you gon' spit on the man's kind offer?"

"He offering nothin'. I . . . I just want what's fair for me and my family."

"Fair," the sheriff laughed. "You hear that, Calvin? The nigger wants what's fair."

Calvin, his deputy, laughed too.

"It ain't but a hundred years ago you niggers were in chains on plantations," mocked Sheriff Duke. "Now you have these uppity niggers out here preaching equality, justice, and nonsegregation, nothin' but monkeys stirring up trouble in the zoo. If it was up to me, I'd put y'all niggers back in chains where y'all belong."

Sheriff Duke turned to look at Monroe, who was afraid and cowering in the back seat. He continued, "Do you agree with these niggers like Booker T. Washington and W.E.B. Du Bois, Monroe? Do you believe in equality and justice for niggers?"

"No, sir," Monroe uttered meekly.

Calvin laughed. "I do believe he's lying to us, Sheriff."

"And why would you think that, Calvin?"

"Niggers do lie." Calvin smiled.

"You wouldn't be lying to us, Monroe?" Sheriff Duke uttered.

"No, sir," Monroe quickly replied.

"Now you can be honest with me, Monroe. Are you a nigger with dreams? You one of these uppity niggers looking to create trouble here in my good ol' town?"

"No, sir. I just want to take care of my family, Sheriff. That's all. I don't want no trouble."

"Well, you should have signed those papers Mr. Lockheart gave you long ago," Sheriff Duke replied. "You don't do what we ask, then there will be trouble. And I am the law."

"Please, Sheriff. I'm sorry. I don't want nothing to happen to my family. Sheriff, I's begs you—"

"Now you hush on now, Monroe. Mr. Lockheart wants to speak with you about your backlash to his offer. You be smart now and take what he gives you. You understand me, boy? You said you don't want any trouble tonight," Sheriff Duke uttered intimidatingly.

"I don't," Monroe voiced.

"Well, we'll see when we get there," Sheriff Duke said.

Monroe felt helpless. All he could think about were his wife and two daughters. Like Sylvester, he had worked hard and saved up. He'd built something for his family to enjoy and cherish. Now they wanted to snatch everything from him within the blink of an eye. His eyes continued to well with tears. The farther they drove, the more it felt like he was diving into the pit of hell.

The cruiser came to a stop at a large clearing in the woods. Monroe's attention was on a swivel. Sheriff Duke pulled Monroe from the back seat of the car and pushed him toward the cluster of blinding car headlights. Monroe shrank back in fear at the silhouettes of scowling men carrying flashlights awaiting his arrival. One of the men clutched a noose, indicating his fate. Sheriff Duke pushed him closer toward the group and then knocked Monroe down to his knees with a nightstick. Monroe fell to his knees with terror continuing to swell inside of him.

"Look what we have here, boys, another one of them uppity niggers," Paul uttered from the group.

"This nigger like Sylvester?" Mark asked.

"He says he isn't while on the way here, but Calvin and I believe he's lying," Sheriff Duke replied. "What you think, should we find out if this nigger's lying?"

"Look at him, the nigger is ready to shit in his pants," Paul mocked.

A few men laughed. It was thrilling for them to see a Black man in such a humiliating and squirming experience. Monroe whimpered and cowered on his knees, the bright lights from flashlights and high beams blinding him. They stood over him with threatening and menacing postures and continued to taunt him.

"I say we should hang this nigger tonight, get it over with," said Joseph.

"Mr. Lockheart wants to have a word with him. So, we wait, boys," Sheriff Duke told them.

"Where is he anyway?" Paul said.

"He knows the time and place. He'll be here shortly," the sheriff reminded them.

Soon, a blue and white 1955 Ford Fairlane arrived at the scene. The vehicle had everyone's attention. It came to a stop with the headlights remaining on. The driver and passenger door opened, and Benny Lockheart and his associate, Conway, climbed out of the car. Benny Lockheart was a tall man, well over six one, and probably over 220 pounds but neatly put together for his size. He was well-dressed in a tailored blue suit and sporting a white fedora. A pencil-thin mustache and goatee framed his face perfectly. His pale skin exaggerated the depth of his ink black eyes, and a movie star's mole rested just below his left temple.

There was an air of power about him.

All eyes were on Mr. Lockheart. He approached the group with a deadpan gaze toward Monroe, who remained on his knees, frightened. He refused to acknowledge the sheriff and his cronies. Instead, Monroe became his main focus. He towered over the man, slightly shifting his harrowing demeanor.

"I apologize to you, Mr. Monroe. It was wrong for the sheriff to disturb you and your family in the middle of the night. But unfortunately, I'm a busy man with pressing matters that need handling expeditiously," Mr. Lockheart proclaimed politely. "And you, my friend, I'm afraid, have erected a succession of roadblocks to some meaningful businesses and investments on my end. I came to you and your family weeks ago about purchasing your land. I sat in your home, your wife offered me some iced tea, and I believed you and I would come to some kind of agreement."

He sighed heavily.

"Now, unfortunately, it has come to us meeting out here with the creatures and mosquitos. A disquieting place for two men to talk about business," Mr. Lockheart added.

It was shocking to the group of men how polite and well-spoken Benny Lockheart was to a nigger.

"I know you and I both want to get back home to our families. Right, Mr. Monroe?" Mr. Lockheart uttered alarmingly.

Monroe nodded unswervingly. "Yes, Mr. Lockheart."

"It's a damn shame what happened to Sylvester and his family. I hated to hear the news. He was a smart man, but ignorant, too. Sylvester had no foresight of the future. He chose to remain stubborn and defiant, and I know that can be a nigger's way most times. I don't fault him for it. A nigger can be ignorant, but a nigger must also know his place," Mr. Lockheart continued.

Sheriff Duke and the others smiled, agreeing with the statement.

"I admit, you do have a wonderful family, Mr. Monroe . . . a beautiful wife at home and two lovely young daughters. I want you to think about them as we discuss the terms of you selling me your land tonight. Now you can go back to your family in one piece, content on our deal tonight, or I would hate to see something happen to that lovely family of yours, Mr. Monroe," Mr. Lockheart intoned with malice.

The men surrounding Monroe felt like a pack of wolves, ready to tear him apart if he didn't answer correctly or agree to Mr. Lockheart's terms. Benny Lockheart was a charismatic businessman and talkative individual. He was charming and threatening at the same time. He had a way with words and would make polite threats that made folks worry and cringe. He was a walking double entendre.

Sheriff Duke was puzzled why a man of Mr. Lockheart's stature would refer to a nigger as "mister." In his eyes, "mister" should only be reserved for white men.

"So, what will it be, Mr. Monroe? Do you and I come to an agreement tonight? I truly hope so because I do want you to go home to your lovely wife and be able to kiss your children in the morning. It's only land, Mr. Monroe. You and your family enjoyed it long enough. Be content with what I'm offering you for it," Mr. Lockheart proclaimed coolly.

Conway stepped forward, producing the documents that Monroe needed to sign to sell his land. He wore wire-rimmed glasses, remained quiet, and was dressed sharply in a fine suit like his boss and mentor, Mr. Lockheart.

"Go on now, Mr. Monroe. We need you to sign the documents. It will be okay. You and your family will be well taken care of," Mr. Lockheart said.

"It could be worse, nigger," Sheriff Duke exclaimed.

Mr. Lockheart cut his eyes at the sheriff, upset that he had chimed in. It was a silent reprimand—one that Benny Lockheart perfected.

"I apologize for interrupting, Mr. Lockheart," Sheriff Duke expressed fast.

Monroe cried. Signing over his land would become his death. It was all he had, what he worked so hard to maintain and keep up. Besides his wife and daughters, owning land was something he was quite proud of. He planned on passing the property down to his two daughters someday when they became older. Now that was a dream that would be deferred permanently.

Everyone glared at Monroe, waiting for him to put pen to paper and sign his name on the dotted line. Mr. Lockheart was somewhat patient. He knew he was receiving something valuable for practically nothing tonight, and he couldn't comprehend the pain Monroe felt. The man was a capitalist with a giant C. His greed for money, power, and status was palpable, and he reasoned it was for the greater good.

When Monroe finally signed the papers, it felt like he had signed his soul away to the devil. His hands shook, and his tears were endless.

Mr. Lockheart grinned and said, "You've made an astute choice tonight, Mr. Monroe. I'm glad you and I could finally reach an agreement. Now you can finally go back to your family. Sheriff, would you be a kind man and drive Mr. Monroe back home to be with his family?"

Sheriff Duke nodded and frowned. "Sure, not a problem, Mr. Lockheart."

"And you make sure the man makes it home safe. He did a good thing tonight."

Sheriff Duke and his deputy lifted a defeated and sobbing Monroe off his feet.

"C'mon, nigger, let's get you home," the sheriff uttered.

They shoved Monroe into the cruiser's back seat, and everyone departed from the clearing. Mr. Lockheart and Conway climbed back into their vehicle and drove off. There would be no bloodshed or lynching tonight.

The police cruiser arrived at Monroe's home, and Monroe exited slowly from the back seat, gloomed and defeated. His wife, Lorraine, burst from the front door in shock and relief.

"Oh, my God, Monroe, are you okay?" Lorraine hollered.

"It's your lucky night, nigger. We'll see you soon," Sheriff Duke uttered before driving off.

Lorraine threw her arms around Monroe like a blanket and hugged him closely. Monroe's body went completely limp while in her arms, and he dropped to the ground. Lorraine fell with her husband against the dirt and kept her arms around him. Monroe's soul curdled like spoiled milk. He began to sob again while in his wife's arms, with waves of grief and heartbreak washing over him, pulling him under. Lorraine didn't need to ask him anything. She immediately understood what had happened. Their home, property, and land were lost.

"I'm so sorry, Lorraine. I'm so sorry," Monroe cried hysterically.

A haunted, hollow look glazed her eyes. Grief blanketed her, too, like new-fallen snow, and tears began to sting her eyes like shards of glass.

There was relief that her husband wasn't lynched or killed some other way, but the reality of their situation was devastating. They'd been forced out of their home. What were they going to do? Where would they go? This was the only home she and the girls knew.

Chapter Nine

The New Negro

Bronco woke up to the Southern comfort of the sun shining on his face. He'd slept well last night, without nightmares or visits from his ghostly friend. He opened his eyes, and they traveled around the bedroom. He'd slept on a small wooden bed in a small bedroom with the bare minimum of sheets and blankets, hardwood floors, and an oil lamp atop a small dresser. For a moment, he believed he was dreaming. Being on a farm in the middle of nowhere was a strange environment for him. There were no noises outside the bedroom window, no crowds of people gathered underneath the windowpane, no cars honking, no laughter from children, no yelling or argument from adults, no police sirens blaring in the distance. Bronco only heard utter silence besides the birds chirping outside.

Bronco removed himself from the bed and walked to the window. He peered outside. The sun was spreading its light over the vast Mississippi land. Everything was bright and warm. There was nothing but trees, bushes, and land. Bronco donned his pants and a shirt, slid into his old boots, and walked out of the bedroom like a man lost somewhere in a maze. The farmhouse was small, spacious, and the setting for a comfortable way of life. It had three bedrooms, a kitchen and a living area, around 1,500 square feet of exposed wood, and a front porch.

It was one of the many gems of the green fields, and in Bronco's eyes, it was maybe the Garden of Eden.

Bronco stepped out onto the porch and continued with his curiosity. Elise was nowhere to be found inside, so he figured she was out and about somewhere. He stepped off the porch and began walking around the farm. He'd noticed that the place needed a few repairs. The furnace door was almost off its hinges, as were a few doors in the home. There were windows that didn't close as far as possible. The siding of the farmhouse was falling apart, and the place needed painting.

Bronco walked around to the back of the house, where there was an old barn. There, Elise was chopping firewood with an axe. She was clad in old blue jeans and a shirt and seemed skilled at splitting the wood with the downward force of the axe. Elise stopped momentarily, wiped the sweat from her brow with the back of her hand, and exhaled. It was early morning and already a hot day.

"You're quite skilled with that axe, I see," said Bronco, surprising Elise.

She turned around to see Bronco coming her way. "I need to be. Winter can become harsh 'round here," Elise replied.

"Winter is months away," Bronco countered.

"And yet it's only me doing the work here."

"Where's your son?" Bronco asked.

Elise chuckled. "How old do you think I am? He's not my son. He's my little brother."

Bronco was surprised. "What happened to your parents?"

"They were killed in a car accident some years back. I've taken on the responsibilities in raisin' him and keeping this place running," Elise stated.

Bronco was surprised that a beautiful woman like herself didn't have a husband or any children yet. She swung the axe like a man and handled the farm independently, which was impressive.

Elise continued to chop some more firewood, but Bronco intervened.

"I wanna earn my keep around here, so what you need me to do?" he asked her.

"Fair 'nough." She smiled. "You chopped wood before?"

"I'm from Harlem. What do you think?" He was sarcastic.

Elise giggled. "Well, what you need to do is position yo' legs like so, apart . . . Raise the axe up behind yo' head or over the shoulder, and keep your arms extended."

Bronco watched the petite and dainty young girl naturally cut a block of firewood. She was good at it.

"It is easier to split the log if you strike it at the top. It's not much 'bout strength. Speed helps, too. Don't hesitate or second-guess . . . just cut," Elise said.

"Who taught you how to chop firewood?" he asked her.

"My pa, before he died," Elise replied.

Bronco nodded.

"He taught me a lot of things. Always said a woman needs to make her use in this world."

Elise handed him the axe. She picked up another piece of firewood and placed it vertically on the chopping block. She stood by curiously to see how Bronco would do for the first time.

"Every log has natural grains, and it will split along these grains," said Elise.

Following Elise's instructions, Bronco positioned himself with his legs apart, raised the axe over his shoulders with extended arms, and swung the axe with such might and force that the firewood split apart easily like he was tearing a sheet of paper. Now Elise was impressed.

"You sure you never done this before?" she said.

Bronco smiled. "I learn fast."

Elise smiled, and she was relieved. She had help, and it was definitely needed. "You hungry? I can fix you somethin' if you like," she said.

"I would like that."

Bronco continued to chop firewood while Elise turned and marched toward the farmhouse. Bronco glanced at her walking away. Although he was grateful that she'd invited him into her home, he didn't understand why she did it. But what was haunting him was that in the short time he was getting to know her, Elise reminded him of Mindy. She had that same wide, bright smile and a positive and cheerful attitude about life. The last thing he wanted to do was overstay his welcome, so he figured it was best to help out. By the looks of things, she needed it.

Surprisingly, chopping firewood became therapeutic for Bronco. He didn't mind the hard work. It gave him something to do. He swung that axe easily, like putting a hammer to a nail. He had enough firewood stacked within the hour to last Elise through two winters.

The relentless sun and the extravagant summer heat made Bronco sweat profusely. He put down the axe to take a breather and looked around what many considered a quaint homestead. A small, dilapidated whitewashed barn was nearby, with amber stalks of grain obscuring an antique tractor sitting outside. Bronco walked toward the barn and coolly decided to take a look inside. There were abandoned animal stalls, pen gates, hay bales, dust, spiderwebs, old farming tools such as shovels, rakes, and hoes, and above him were rusted exhaust fans. Being from Harlem, this was a new world for him. He'd never been inside a barn before.

Exiting the barn, Bronco took in the endless fields behind it, a colossal landscape of what used to be crops, cotton, or lush green vegetation that took time to harvest. Now it was untapped land. Bronco heard the chickens and the rooster coming from a chicken coop Elise had near the farmhouse. He walked toward the coop and smiled at the chickens and rooster. He'd never seen chickens before. They were fascinating creatures to him.

"They don't bite," Elise joked.

He turned around to see Elise smiling at him. She had changed from blue jeans to a pretty floral sundress. Her smooth ebony skin gleamed in the sunlight, and her infectious smile was just as warm as the sun. Bronco stared at her with admiration. Her Southern comfort was alluring. Her general manner of speaking was gracious and kind. He was attracted to her.

"Breakfast's ready," she said. "You need to wash up."

Bronco nodded. He was filled with sweat and hard work.

Elise noticed the giant woodpile and was taken aback. "You done all this in an hour?"

"I don't mind the work," Bronco said.

She smiled. "I see. Thank you."

"It's the least I could do for you, ma'am. I'm here to help."

Elise smiled and blushed. It had been a while since a man helped her on her land. She was grateful for Bronco but still somewhat wary of him. He was a powerful-looking man who could easily snap her in half with his hands. But there was something unique about him, too. Although he seemed like a brute and standoffish, he was polite and helpful. And when he smiled at her, it was genuine.

"Well, come on inside and get you somethin' to eat 'cause sho 'nuff the sun gon' shine all day. I know you must be hungry."

"I'm famished."

"Famished? Just say you're hungry," she laughed.

Bronco walked with Elise back to the farmhouse, glistening in sweat. His muscles flexed underneath his shirt, and Elise's summer dress blew gently with the summer breeze. When Bronco entered the house, he was hit with the sweet scent of a home-cooked breakfast. It made his stomach rumble and mouth water.

"It smells really good," he said.

"I would hope." Elise smiled. "What you smell is fresh biscuits and gravy, eggs and potatoes, and grits. My pa taught me 'bout farming, and my mama done teached me cookin'," Elise said.

Bronco went into the bathroom to wash up. He pulled off his shirt and turned on the faucet to begin cleaning up for breakfast. As the faucet ran, Bronco took the time to stare at himself in the mirror. His eyes lingered on the strange marking on his right chest—dark particles somewhat creating a tangled ball of lightning. He couldn't explain it. Bronco figured the marking on his chest was the source of his unnatural abilities. It didn't hurt. It was simply odd. But as he stared at the marking and himself, he was hit with déjà vu. The scent of breakfast coming from the kitchen reminded Bronco of the day Mindy was killed. He blamed himself. If he'd stayed out of Mindy's life, she would still be alive today.

Grief and pain had no rules. It didn't discriminate.

"Hey, you okay in there?" Elise asked, knocking on the door.

Bronco broke out of his trance and replied, "Yeah. I'll be right out."

"Breakfast gettin' cold."

Bronco collected himself and splashed some cold water onto his face. He wiped away his morning sweat with a rag hanging nearby and put back on his shirt. He opened the door slowly and exited the bathroom to the continuing scent of breakfast in the kitchen. Elise was drying a glass jar when Bronco entered the kitchen.

She smiled at him and said, "You go on and sit and eat. You gon' need yo' strength."

"Thank you for breakfast. I appreciate this," he said.

"It's nothin'. I love to cook. Never really had anyone to cook for besides Kenneth," she replied.

"Where is he anyway? I haven't seen him around here all morning."

"He likes to go down by the lake to play and fish. Can spend all day there. I s'pose it's his way of escaping things," Elise said.

Bronco took a seat at the table and began to eat right away. Elise frowned, smacked his hand with a wooden spatula, and uttered, "You don't say grace where you come from?"

Bronco was surprised. "Grace?"

"Yes. Grace. You know, a short prayer thanking the good Lord before you eat."

Bronco remained quiet. He'd never said a prayer a day in his life.

"By the look you're givin' me, I see that's a no. Well, in here, we say grace before we eat," Elise said.

Bronco complied. Elise sat across from him at the table. She extended her arms to him and took his hands into hers. She bowed her head. Bronco did the same.

"Lord God, Heavenly Father, bless us and these thy gifts which we receive from thy bountiful goodness. The eyes of all look to you, O Lord, and you give us food at the proper time. You open your hand and satisfy the desires of every living thing. Our Father, Lord God, Heavenly Father, bless us and we thank you for everything. Through Jesus Christ our Lord. Amen," Elise prayed.

They opened their eyes and Elise grinned. "Now was that so hard?"

Bronco sighed.

Just as they were about to eat, Kenneth entered the kitchen wearing high-waisted trousers, shabby Converse sneakers, and a worn ball cap. Evidently, he'd been outdoors playing by the lake all morning.

"'Bout time you come eat breakfast. Go in there and wash up," Elise said.

"I'm not hungry," Kenneth replied.

"Boy, you been gone most of the morning. You need to eat something."

"I said I'm not hungry, Elise," Kenneth fussed.

"Kenneth, don't sass at me, boy."

"I'm not sassing. I'm just not hungry," Kenneth replied. He pivoted and ran back outside.

Elise sighed heavily. "That chile, I just don't know what to do with him. I know he's still angry and upset."

"About what?"

"We had a tragedy here 'bout a month back. His best friend was killed in a fire along with her entire family," Elise said.

"That's terrible."

"It is." Mentioning the tragedy made Elise down. "This isn't Harlem, Bronco. Things operate entirely different down here."

Elise sighed. Her mood changed a bit, and Bronco noticed.

"Well, don't sit there and let your breakfast get cold. Eat up now," said Elise.

Bronco began to dig in, and the moment he tasted her cooking, his eyes lit up, and his mouth exploded with pleasure. He started shoveling food into his mouth like it was a black hole. Everything was good. Elise took in his reaction and grinned. At least someone appreciated her cooking this morning.

"You never did say what brings you here from Harlem," Elise mentioned while they ate.

"I'm simply passing through."

"Oh, and might I ask, where is your final destination?"

"West," he lied.

"West?"

"California," he uttered.

"California? That's a long way from Harlem. Well, I figure you're either escaping trouble or looking for it. Either way, you're welcome here long as you brings no trouble to my farm," she proclaimed.

"I appreciate it, ma'am. And I won't bring any trouble to you," he said clearly.

Elise smiled. "I'll be going into town this afternoon to get a few things if you care to come," she said. "Maybe you can keep me company."

"I wouldn't mind that at all," he replied.

Bronco finished his breakfast and volunteered to help Elise with the dishes. She was grateful, but she insisted he get some rest. He'd been chopping wood all morning but wasn't in the mood to rest. Bronco's stamina could become unmatched, and he usually liked to keep himself busy.

"This lake you mentioned earlier, where is it?" Bronco asked her.

"It's called Lake Nur," she said.

"I think I'll go for a walk there, check it out. Which direction should I head?"

Elise went to the front door and pointed west. "It's 'bout a half mile walk that way. You can't miss it."

Bronco nodded.

"If you see Kenneth, tell him we'll be goin' into town this afternoon," she said.

"I will."

Bronco turned and walked away. Elise watched him from the porch, still curious about who he was and his true intentions. She exhaled and went back to doing the dishes and cleaning the kitchen.

The hot afternoon sun was blazing high in the sky, and the heat became palpable. Temperatures soared to uncomfortable levels, and it was windless. Bronco walked through the woods and toward the lake, sweating like a field slave picking cotton. He soon came upon Lake Nur and took in the beauty of the sprawling lake, the open landscape, and the tranquility it provided. Now he understood why Kenneth and others came to the lake often. Harlem had no such treasures.

Right away, Bronco spotted Kenneth standing at the edge of the lake. He was alone, skipping stones across the water, and he was pretty good at it. Bronco watched him for a moment. Clearly, the boy was troubled by something.

Bronco began heading toward the boy, and when Kenneth spotted him, he frowned and uttered, "What you want? You come to sass me too?"

"No. I came to see this lake. It's beautiful. I see why you love it so much," said Bronco.

Kenneth continued skipping the stones across the lake. There was something magical about the way his stone danced across the water's surface, each skip creating ripples that seemed to echo through time.

"You're good at this," said Bronco.

"It's somethin' to do," Kenneth said.

"You care if I give it a shot?"

Kenneth shrugged. "Plenty of stones to pick up."

Bronco picked up a small rock. He flicked his wrist and sent the rock gliding across the water, but it only went two skips. Kenneth smiled.

"I guess I need some practice," said Bronco.

"You need to flick your wrist more when you throw the rock."

Bronco followed his instructions, and this time was able to skip it three times across the lake. "I'm becoming a natural at this too," said Bronco.

Kenneth grinned.

The two of them stood at the edge, skipping stones in silence, with the sun warming their skin. Bronco bent down, his fingers brushing against the cool, smooth stones. Then he chucked one of the stones. It glided across the water—one skip, two skips, three skips, four skips. It became a fleeting moment of flight, a miniature voyage. And then, with a soft splash, the stone disappeared beneath the surface, leaving concentric circles that expanded outward.

"Look at that, I set a record for myself," said Bronco.

Kenneth laughed. He was connecting with the 12-year-old. The two had become lost in the rhythm of stone and water. Their laughter echoed across the lake, becoming a simple joy.

"If you don't mind me asking, what was your friend's name? The one who died in the fire?" Bronco asked Kenneth out of the blue.

Kenneth sighed deeply. "Nancy," he uttered quietly.

"What was she like?"

"She was sweet, kind, and fun to be with. She never hurt nobody. I hate it that she gone," Kenneth griped. "She was my best friend. We used to stay out, skip rocks, laugh, and tell each other ever'thing."

Kenneth stopped skipping rocks. The loss of Nancy began to anger him. He frowned. He looked at Bronco and asked, "What it like to be a soldier?"

It was a tricky question for Bronco to answer. "It's not fun."

"You killed people?" Kenneth asked blatantly.

Bronco huffed. "I had to."

"I wanna become a soldier when I grow up. I wanna learn how to kill people, and then I wanna come back here and kill ever'one that killed my friend," Kenneth uttered with contempt.

Bronco recognized that anger, and seeing it in someone so young was troubling. He refused to tell Kenneth
the clichés that his friend "was in a better place" or that
"everything happened for a reason." He didn't believe it
himself.

"It's best not to carry that anger around," said Bronco.

"Why not?"

"It can do something to a man . . . change him," Bronco
replied.

Kenneth continued to frown. "Maybe I wanna be
changed. Maybe the only way to forget how she died is to
become angry."

Bronco sighed heavily. He was stuck at the moment,
not knowing the words to say to Kenneth. The boy
was upset, and Bronco understood his feelings wholeheartedly. They were one and the same. And how could
Bronco speak against something when that same anger
was stirring inside of him?

Bronco could only think of saying, "Your sister wanted
me to tell you that she's going to town this afternoon."

"I don't wanna go. Tell her I'm fine," Kenneth said.

He picked up another stone, angrily chucked it across
the lake, and ran off. The stone looked like it was defying
gravity, defying its solid nature. Bronco watched it skip
multiple times across the lake until it sank. And when it
did, that's when he saw her standing at the other end of
the lake. Could it be her, Nancy?

Chapter Ten

How It Feels to Be Colored Me

Bronco stared out the passenger window, taking in the sprawling country landscape. He gaped at the growing crops, including soybeans, wheat, rice, and most importantly to the state, the extensive cotton fields that seemed endless. They were everywhere, shimmering white bolls that stretched to a distant tree line and blanketed acres of fields like a snowy day in New York as Elise's pickup truck traveled down a dirt road.

"You never seen cotton before?" Elise asked him.

"Only in certain books," Bronco replied.

"Well, it's everywhere down here. The king of Mississippi. It's our state's most valuable crop. They call us the cotton belt for a reason," she proclaimed.

"It's hard to believe our ancestors used to pick this from sunup to sundown," said Bronco.

"Some of us still do," said Elise. "Mississippi has become the epicenter of cotton production. The reason they want to take our land from us, to grow more of it, and . . ."

Elise stopped talking. Bronco stared at her, waiting for her to finish her sentence.

"And what?"

"They just don't want us here no more. They want us to pack our things and leave our homes, land, and livelihood like it's easy to do when some of us have been here for generations. Some of us tried to fight, but they kill us. Most of us are afraid now," said Elise, saddened.

Bronco was listening. It was sad to hear about their tragedy. "What about you? How were you able to hold on for so long?" he asked her.

"The sheriff, he take a liking to me, for the wrong reason. He comes to me one day and says to me, 'You'll be the last one standing, Elise, only because I like you.' He's giving me and Kenneth some time to find somewhere new. But I don't wanna leave. My parents worked hard for this place," she sadly proclaimed.

Bronco stared at Elise for a moment. She was pretty and engaging, almost like a modern Southern belle. It was easy to see why different men took a deep liking to her. Elise seemed fragile, reserved, and sexually innocent. Bronco wondered if she was still a virgin. She was beautiful but felt risky to touch, like porcelain. But she had impeccable manners and a core of strength, intelligence, and wit.

"This sheriff, has he ever tried anything with you?" asked Bronco.

"No, but he likes to stare at me. I know what he's thinking, Bronco. I know what they all think 'bout me," Elise responded. "I'm a pretty girl alone on a farm. But I can handle myself."

"I don't doubt that."

Elise smiled. Then she changed the subject. "How long you plan on stayin'?"

"Not sure yet."

"So is there anyone missing you back in Harlem, Bronco?" she asked him. "A handsome and muscular man like yourself finding his way to the South, it still remains odd for me."

"No. I'm pretty much a loner, always kept to myself."

"So you're a nomad?"

"It's beginning to look like that."

"Moses lived a nomadic lifestyle too," said Elise.

"Believe me, I'm no Moses," Bronco reacted quickly.

"I figured that. Although it would be nice for God to send us one." Elise smiled.

Elise steered the pickup opposite the white town, where the cotton fields and farmland seemed to disappear. The pickup truck continued to travel down a dirt road and into a small Negro settlement some fifteen miles from her farm and Lake Nur.

"I thought you said you were going into town," Bronco uttered.

"I need to make a stop first."

The settlement was nestled away in a large clearing in the woods where cabins looked neat and snug, but the majority of the homes in the settlement were dilapidated. It was the kind of town that, when it rained, the dirt roads would turn to mud, and the place would become stiflingly hot and buggy when it wasn't raining. There was a juke joint down the road. And a handful of children were out and about, playing, and some were barefooted. This place was the epitome and the face of economic hardship. But for dozens of Black folks, this had been their home for years.

"What is this place?" Bronco asked her.

"Somewhere long forgotten," Elise replied. "But not by me."

Elise received cheerful waves and smiles from some residents as her truck drove through the place, especially the children. They were happy to see her, and she was welcomed there.

Elise stopped in front of a run-down cabin that stood as a mere shell hidden behind veils of shrubbery and vines. Elise killed the engine and climbed out, followed by Bronco. Elise removed a bag of items from the truck bed. Bronco helped her. They proceeded toward the inviting front porch. Although the cabin stood in a state of melancholic decay, it still represented a picturesque home with some colorful blooms and a garden nearby.

Elise ascended onto the dilapidated porch carrying the items and knocked on an old screen door. Bronco became curious. His attention was on a swivel. He didn't feel endangered but wondered who would live in a neglected place with broken shutters left to the mercy of nature's reclaiming embrace.

"Who stays here?" he asked Elise.

"Miss Shug. She's alone, older, and I try to attend to her every so often. Make sure she's doin' fine," Elise replied.

The front door opened, followed by the screen door, and a short, thin brown-skinned lady with wrinkled skin, a slight limp, and lifeless gray hair appeared in front of them. She immediately smiled.

"Hey there, Miss Shug," Elise greeted her warmly.

"Aft'noon, Elise." Miss Shug smiled.

"I came here to check on you and bring you a few things," said Elise.

Miss Shug opened the screen door wider and stepped aside to allow them inside. "Who is your friend?" Miss Shug asked.

"His name is Bronco. He's from Harlem, and he's staying with me for a few days."

Miss Shug continued to smile and uttered, "Harlem, huh? He is handsome."

Bronco happened to blush and smile back. "Thank you, ma'am."

"I brought you a few things I know you might need, Miss Shug."

"God bless you, Elise. My heart gets so full when you come 'round," Miss Shug proclaimed. Her wrinkled brown skin turned into a bright smile. "You sho' is a blessin'."

"I'm delighted to always see you, Miss Shug."

While the ladies talked, Bronco observed the place, which was in bad shape. Even in its heyday, the old place must have been little more than a glorified shed. A few doors hung on their hinges at a jaunty angle, the roof sagged almost like a giant had sat on it, and some windows had no glass. It was becoming a rotting heap, bowing down, subservient to the elements. Bronco wondered how an elderly woman could stay in such a decrepit location. He began to feel sorry for her.

But despite it all, Miss Shug was cheery and smiled, and there was a delicious smell coming from the kitchen.

"It smells good in here," Bronco uttered.

"That, young man, is some good ol' Southern fried chicken and biscuits," Miss Shug said. "Are y'all two hungry? I have plenty."

Elise grinned. "We would love to join you, Miss Shug."

Miss Shug's smile matched Elise's, and her eyes twinkled brightly. She yearned for some company. "Everything's almost done," said Miss Shug.

Miss Shug entered the pocket-sized kitchen while Elise and Bronco remained in the small, cramped living room. The furnishings were sparse, with a rickety wooden table, some old chairs, and one armchair Miss Shug sat in while she listened to her radio. It was an old wooden radio from 1941, in the cathedral style, with an upright rectangular box with a rounded top. It sat perched on a nearby shelf.

Like Elise's farm, the place needed a ton of repairs. But Miss Shug's shack was worse. The place felt like it could collapse in on itself at any moment. Every time it rained, Miss Shug had to get up and move to one of the dry spots in the house.

Elise picked up on Bronco's concerned look at Miss Shug's living conditions and said, "I know what you're thinking. She's fine here, Bronco. Miss Shug lived here all her life."

"She's not afraid this place will fall in around her?"

"It hasn't in over twenty years," Elise joked. "But we make do here."

Bronco sighed. His tiny apartment in Harlem was a penthouse compared to Miss Shug's shack, but he understood that a home was a home no matter what it looked like.

Miss Shug returned carrying her fried chicken and biscuits. She placed the food onto the small, rickety table and took a seat. Elise and Bronco joined her, although they'd just eaten not too long ago. Miss Shug reached out to Elise and Bronco to say grace.

"Again?" Bronco uttered.

Elise chuckled.

"We'ze thank the Lord for everything we do here," Miss Shug explained to him.

Bronco and Elise bowed their heads, and Miss Shug said grace. Everyone began digging into the fried chicken and biscuits when she was done. It wasn't much, but it was welcome and delicious.

"Mercy to glory, Miss Shug. This chicken is so good it got my eyes watering," Elise praised.

Miss Shug beamed. "Well, I aim to please."

Bronco agreed. He was on his fourth piece of chicken and third biscuit. The cabin wasn't much, but Bronco saw how Miss Shug had made it a home for many years. She immediately welcomed him there, like Elise had done on her farm.

The afternoon continued with Elise and Bronco joining Miss Shug on the front porch. Miss Shug rocked back and forth in a rocking chair while spewing stories about her life in Mississippi. She was 79 years old, rooted in history, experience, and knowledge. She'd seen her fair share of racism, violence, hatred, and discriminatory practices against Black people.

"I's spent my entire life here in Mississippi, workin' on the plantation down the road from here," Miss Shug said. "Yes, I did. My entire family worked on it . . . my daddy, my granddaddy, my mama, my uncles, my brothers, my sisters. Our family must've gone back four generations workin' on that white man's plantation, sharecropping, pickin' cotton, and harvesting crops. It was all we'ze knew. You's see, Mississippi is one of the most fertile areas for cotton production. White men invest heavily in the area, both in money and manpower. But it was families like mine that did the brunt of the hard work here for little to no pay."

Bronco and Elise listened intently. She was a remarkable and strong Black woman. Miss Shug was born ten years after the Civil War ended. Her eyes shared familiarity with hatred, contentment, and pain.

"I's given birth to ten chil'ren. But most my chil'ren done gone to be with the good Lord, taken from me by violence from white men or diseases," Miss Shug proclaimed.

"How many children are left livin', Miss Shug?" Elise asked her.

She thought about it momentarily, smiled, and answered, "Four still breathe today. But they done gone and moved on north from here. The South can be a cruel place most times. So I's understand."

Elise nodded in agreement. She'd seen her fair share of how cruel the South could become.

"They killed my daddy in 1893," Miss Shug uttered.

"Why?" Bronco asked her. He was engrossed in her life like a kid sitting around a campfire hearing horror stories.

"Though slavery ended, it wasn't safe for no pretty girl like me on a white man's plantation," she continued. "Mr. Whitfield, you's see, he took a liking to me, liked having me around 'cause I was good with helpin' my daddy with fixin' things on the plantation. I's became good with my hands for a girl chile. I was the middle chile, and I was useful. Mr. Whitfield liked his niggers being useful. He was an ex-Confederate soldier, fought to keep our kind enslaved. But when the South lost, he nearly lost his home and land. But he managed to keep it with my family's help wit' the promise of things bein' different. He was married, but he began raping me in the barn when I was sixteen, got me pregnant wit' my first chile. My daddy find out and confronted Mr. Whitfield."

Bronco and Elise knew how her story would end. The racial and social mores of slavery remained very much alive in Mississippi right after the Civil War, and it continued in the 1950s. White people grudgingly recognized that Blacks were free. They were unwilling to accept them as social and racial equals.

"A week later, they done found my daddy naked, lynched, and castrated. Mr. Whitfield done lied on my daddy, done say he attacked his youngest daughter. A white mob done gathered to attack my daddy, and he was lynched and burned in front of a crowd. They done cut off his fingers, ears, and genitals, and skinned his face," Miss Shug proclaimed.

Bronco and Elise were shocked. It was a terrifying story.

"Miss Shug, you never told me this before," Elise said.

"Didn't need tellin'. Kept it secret 'cause it's painful to tell so many times. Wit' my daddy gone, Mr. Whitfield continued to climb on top of me and start to rock me away. Mr. Whitfield put a second chile in me, but I done had a miscarriage. God say it wasn't meant to be."

"You was raped, Miss Shug, taken advantage of. Why would God allow that to happen? Why would God allow any of this shit goin' on with colored folks?" Bronco exclaimed.

"God has His reasons, Bronco. Do you believe in Him?"

"Honestly, I don't," Bronco answered. "I can't wrap my thoughts around it. If He created us, then why would He allow such evil in the world?"

"Well, He believes in you, Bronco. And it's not fo' us to question Him, but to trust Him. There's something great in you that I sense. You's different. Don't know how I know this. But God has brought you here to us for a reason," Miss Shug proclaimed wholeheartedly.

"I'm no savior, Miss Shug. I done things, bad things in Harlem," he admitted.

"But you's not a bad man," she replied. "I see it in yo' eyes. And yo' honesty is inspirational. Most bad men won't admit to being bad. But you's here to do something good. I's know it. God made me learn from my daddy and made me good with my hands, which is the reason why I was able to keep this place up for so long. But now I's an old woman and crumbling like my home. We'ze not meant to last here, but to last in heaven."

She smiled.

Bronco slightly smiled. He liked Miss Shug. Something uplifting and comforting about her inspired him. After everything she'd been through, she was still a fighter and firmly believed in faith. It was odd to Bronco to see a woman of her age and stature handy with her hands and her mind still wise and sharp.

"I don't have a problem coming by here and fixin' the place up for you, ma'am," Bronco volunteered out of the blue. "I am good with my hands."

Miss Shug smiled. "I wouldn't be able to pay you anything."

"I wouldn't take no money from you. I just wanna help out."

Miss Shug's smile grew wider. "God bless, you'ze heaven sent."

Elise grinned at Bronco and was impressed with his kindness.

"Miss Shug, I'm afraid we need to head on out now," said Elise.

"I knows you'ze a busy woman, Elise. I do appreciate your visit, so very kind of you." Miss Shug grinned.

"Anytime, Miss Shug."

"And, Bronco." Miss Shug stood up and took Bronco's hands into hers. She stared kindly at him. "Remember what I said. There's something great in you. You'ze different. God knows it. And I's knows it."

Bronco nodded. Whether he believed her or not, he listened. There was something odd and spiritual about Miss Shug. It almost felt like she could see deeply into his soul and sense things about him. Bronco felt stripped completely when she stared at him. Like himself, he wondered if Miss Shug also possessed some supernatural abilities. She was interesting, and he wanted to get to know her better. Also, Bronco thought about what she'd said. Was he a bad man?

"You take care of my Elise for me. She's a good woman. I love her, and I love you too," Miss Shug proclaimed wholeheartedly.

Bronco smiled. "I will, Miss Shug."

Elise and Bronco were soon on their way. Bronco climbed into the pickup truck, and before Elise drove off, he stared at Miss Shug one final time. She stood there on her deteriorating porch, propped up with a cane. She was old but confident. She was small, but her persona was striking, like the Grand Canyon. Her courage was unwavering, and Miss Shug's smile seemed endless. It was the kind of smile that made you feel loved and secure.

She was angelic—an angel.

Chapter Eleven

Known to Evil

"This is God's plan, not mine," Pastor Carmichael hollered at his all-white congregation. "Who am I to question God's way? Who am I to go against the status quo of the Almighty Christ and the heavens? I'm a God-fearing Christian who believes right is right and wrong is wrong. And what God says is concrete. The good Lord has set up the customs and practices of segregation. It empowers us to improve as a race, God's people."

The congregation was on their feet, clapping and cheering him on. They all loved him and believed in him. Donald Carmichael was a grand and charismatic figure with rich blond hair and blue eyes. He stood at five nine and was thin, but his voice and preaching were robust.

"Listen, I have no ill will toward other races. I do believe that we are all God's creation, but there's a hierarchy that must be preserved. And with the passing of this Brown v. the Board of Education, integrating our public school with Blacks, this is blasphemy and a threat to our Christian way of life."

The crowd applauded. Benny Lockheart was among the congregation, standing and applauding proudly. He stood next to his wife of twenty years, Ruth, along with his two young daughters, Susan and Karen. They'd been attending the Southern Baptist church for nearly a decade, and Benny had become good friends with Pastor Carmichael. They shared the same views and felt they were good Christian men with value, legacy, and ambition.

"Ladies and gentlemen, for twelve years I have had the privilege of being the pastor of this lovely Baptist church in Mississippi. And there's nothing better than planting roots, starting families, having morals and belief in our God, and our way of life. But the government's decision to integrate our schools here in the South will annihilate our Christian way of life if we allow it. It won't stop there. Soon, Blacks will be marrying our daughters, living in our neighborhoods, sharing our drinking fountains," Pastor Carmichael exclaimed.

Anger began to stir in the flock.

"Understand this, I have no racial hatred against the Blacks or any other races, but right is right, and wrong is wrong, and integration is wrong. This is sinful. And as Christians, we all must fight to preserve our way of life . . . to preserve God's way. If we stand a hundred years from now, it will still be a white church. I am a believer in a separation of the races, and I am nonetheless a Christian. If they want to give us a fight, then we give them a fight. The difference in color, the difference in our body, our minds, our life, our mission upon the face of this earth, is God-given."

The church was in an uproar, applauding, cheering, and hollering. Benny Lockheart and his wife were profoundly clapping and cheering. Donald Carmichael was their champion. He was their man of the hour, the pastor who'd fight for segregation in Mississippi.

The sunny sky blossomed and radiated from above like heaven's hearth. Church had ended, and the congregation began to pour out of the Southern Baptist church. The children started to run around and play while the adults stood about to talk and congregate in front of the church or parking lot. Pastor Carmichael stood at the door entrance to the church, wishing his flock a safe trip home and holding pockets of small conversation with a few folks.

Benny Lockheart and his wife exited the church into the afternoon sun. Pastor Carmichael smiled Benny's way.

"Hon, you take the kids and go onto to the car. I need to have a few words with the pastor," Benny told his wife.

She smiled and replied, "Don't be too long."

"I won't." Benny grinned.

Ruth and her two daughters trotted down the stairs and made their way to the parking lot. Benny watched them with a proud smile for a moment. His family was his entire world, and he loved them unconditionally.

Benny took his eyes off his family and walked toward Pastor Carmichael dressed in one of his best suits, a gray flannel suit.

"Brother Lockheart, it's always a pleasure to see you and your beautiful family here every Sunday. I know you're a busy man."

"You preached a great sermon this morning, Pastor Carmichael," Benny Lockheart uttered.

"Simply spreading God's Word, brother Lockheart."

"It definitely needs spreading, Pastor. Changes are happening, and not the kind I'm proud of," Benny stated.

"The world is becoming a different place, brother Lockheart. Change is inevitable, unfortunately. I hear they have this movement happening called the Civil Rights Movement. Down in Louisiana, some niggers are boycotting the city's segregated bus system," Pastor Carmichael proclaimed.

"It's a damn shame. It's why men like us need to try to keep things in its place. Righteousness needs stability," Benny said.

"Amen, brother Lockheart. Well said," Pastor Carmichael replied. "Well, it's best you don't keep that lovely woman waiting on you. We'll talk again soon."

"Looking forward to it, Pastor," Benny replied.

The two men shook hands, and Benny began to descend the stairs and walk toward the parking lot to join his family. While doing so, men began to greet Benny Lockheart with respect and admiration and yearned for a minute of his time. He shook their hands like he did the pastor's, and a few wanted his ear for business. But Benny reminded them, "It's Sunday, boys, the good Lord's day. Come by my office tomorrow during business hours."

Benny smiled at his daughters and asked, "Who wants ice cream?"

His daughters suddenly beamed with happiness and excitement. They began to hop up and down and shouted, "Me, Daddy. Me. Me."

"You're going to spoil them," Ruth uttered.

"It's not being spoiled if you totally deserve it," Benny replied.

Ruth smiled at her husband. She was a pretty woman in her early forties with high cheekbones, a slender neck, and a slightly thin nose that gave her a European look. Her lovely face was surrounded by straight, still beautiful, shiny raven black tresses. Ruth Lockheart was once crowned the winner of a Mississippi beauty pageant. Now she'd become the perfect wife for Benny Lockheart. She was pretty, docile, and supportive of her husband no matter what he was into. She'd become his trophy wife.

Benny Lockheart gazed at his wife for a moment, and she began to blush.

"What is it, Benny?" Ruth asked, flushed.

Benny smiled widely and said, "You're beautiful. I love you."

Ruth continued to smile brightly and widely. She loved her husband. Benny was a busy and important man, but she wasn't a fool. Ruth was well aware of her husband's extracurricular activities outside of their home. He was a man who cared for her, their daughters, and their home. He was a good man with a few flaws. He was making the world a better place. However, she wasn't aware of her husband's acquired taste for something undesirable. Benny Lockheart was a God-fearing Christian who wanted better for his community and race.

Benny kissed his wife in front of their daughters like it was his first time, and the girls made funny faces and scoffed. Finally, Benny pulled away from his wife's sweet lips, smiled at his girls, and said, "Now let's go get us some ice cream."

It was the classic colonial four-bedroom Mississippi home spanning more than four acres of sweeping land in the quiet countryside. The beautiful estate featured impeccable styling and spacious rooms with hardwood floors, elegant molding, and garden views. Behind the house was a four-stall barn and a five-green putting green for Benny's convenience.

It was Sunday afternoon, and Benny changed clothes in the master bedroom while his daughters played on the property. He stared at his six-foot-one appearance with his pencil-thin mustache and goatee, always neatly trimmed, and grinned. Benny Lockheart was a handsome man in his mid-forties and believed he should have become a movie star in a different life.

Benny fixed his tie and grabbed his suit jacket from the closet as Ruth walked into their bedroom.

"Are you not staying for dinner?" she asked her husband.

"No time, dear. I have to meet with some folks about business," he replied.

Ruth exhaled. It wasn't anything new to her. In the morning, he would attend church with the family, and after church, he had a minor moment of quality time with his daughters. Then he would change clothes and run off, galloping like a horse to something else that required his time.

"When will you be back?" she asked him.

Benny pivoted in her direction and glared at his wife, quickly showing that he was becoming displeased with her questions. Ruth averted her gaze from his and uttered, "I don't mean to quarrel with you, dear. But the girls and I hardly see you anymore, besides church."

"You know I'm a busy man, Ruth. There's a lot happening. Between niggers trying to vote, our desegregation of public schools, and acquiring the land needed for these investors, I need to micromanage everything. If not, then our way of life as we know it will change indefinitely," he proclaimed wholeheartedly.

Ruth nodded, relenting and understanding. Benny smiled, and then he kissed his wife.

"I'll be back late tonight. Don't wait up," he said.

Benny donned his suit jacket, placed his white fedora on his head, and exited the bedroom.

He stepped out onto the large wraparound porch to see Susan and Karen chasing each other across the sprawling green field. Benny smiled and called out to them. "Susan, Karen, come see your father off now."

The girls immediately ran to him with open arms and huge grins. Benny crouched and wrapped his arms around his daughters.

"I'll be back later tonight. Y'all mind your mother while I'm gone. You hear?"

"We will, Daddy," Susan replied.

"That's my girl." Benny kissed them both on their cheeks and began walking toward his 1955 Ford Fairlane, one of his three vehicles.

Ruth stepped onto the porch as Benny climbed into the car. She stood by her daughters, deadpan, and watched her husband drive off with her arms folded across her chest. Her gaze became pensive. Benny was gone to do whatever while she was becoming the lonely and concerned housewife.

"Girls, go wash up for dinner now," she said.

"Yes, Mother," Karen said.

The girls dashed into the house while Ruth lingered on the porch, her gaze sour and lost.

The estate where Benny arrived exceeded his home by acres. The Greek Revival–style mansion featured twenty rooms and sat on 3,000 acres. It was surrounded by massive oak trees, had several gardens, a pool, a guest home, and a tennis court, and was once a symbol of the "Old South." It was what kings proudly called their home, and women felt like queens there.

Benny parked and climbed out of his car. He ascended the steps toward the pillared porch and opened the front door. Benny was greeted in the large foyer by one of the staff members at the home, Windell. He was an older black servant wearing a black suit and bowtie.

"I'm here to see Mr. Roth," Benny uttered.

"Yes. He's expecting you, Mr. Lockheart," Windell replied. "He's in the back. Follow me."

Benny followed Windell through the mansion. Everything was grand, stylish, and striking. Statues, antiques from different cultures, and rare items from around the world could be found from the great room to a private den. Benny Lockheart was wealthy and successful, but he was provincial. However, Harvey Roth was an extraordinarily wealthy and resourceful man with connections and power beyond that of Benny Lockheart.

Before following Windell outside into the sprawling backyard, Benny stopped to look at a pair of artifacts Mr. Roth had in his possession. They were two statues from West Africa. One was an old African tribal from the Pende people in Congo, and the second was a Benin Bronze African sculpture with peculiar carvings. Benny found them odd and ugly. But he couldn't stop staring at them.

"He's waiting for you, Mr. Lockheart," Windell said, snapping Benny from a trance.

"Oh, thank you, Windell."

Benny Lockheart walked outside onto the sprawling lawn with a large garden, a swimming pool, a patio, and a small pond with a gazebo. It was quiet and isolated—nearly a paradise. Benny walked toward Harvey Roth, where he was about to tee off, although it wasn't a golf course. Harvey Roth clutched the driver with confidence and skill. He flexed his knees slightly for a balanced stance and shifted his hips toward the target. His form was nearly perfect. He looked ahead to only land, grass, and acres he owned.

Benny stood and watched quietly, knowing not to interrupt a man when he was about to tee off. Harvey Roth was focused. His golf swing sequence had become second nature to him. Finally, Harvey rotated his body open through impact, rising with his legs into a follow-through, and he sent that golf ball soaring into the air like a rocket taking off. Harvey and Benny watched it go, and it felt like the ball landed some miles away.

Harvey Roth was pleased. He didn't celebrate excessively, but his mannerism showed cockiness and arrogance.

"Impressive," Benny said.

"Do you partake in the game, Mr. Lockheart?" Harvey asked him.

"I do."

"Then maybe one day we'll hit the green and place a wager on our skills," Harvey said.

"I wouldn't mind that at all." Benny grinned.

Harvey turned to finally stare at Benny. Benny now had his undivided attention. Harvey Roth was a tall Caucasian male with a sharp chin, a lean build, and chiseled features. He almost resembled a comic book character. His body was pretty ripped for a man his age, in his late forties. He was handsome, intelligent, articulate, and extremely wealthy. Harvey Roth had the perfect life. He was an investment banker from Wall Street who made more money than most people could ever dream of making. He had a beautiful wife and three sons in college, and he traveled the world and experienced many different things.

"A proper golf swing involves two main elements: namely, the rotation of the body, and the shift of weight toward the golfer's target," said Harvey.

Benny Lockheart nodded. *Duly noted.*

Harvey removed his golf glove, and Benny followed him toward the patio area, where Windell had placed an expensive bottle of Scotch for the men to enjoy this afternoon. Harvey handed Windell his glove and driver and uttered, "Thank you, Windell."

"My pleasure, sir," Windell replied. He then retreated inside.

Harvey poured Benny a glass of Scotch, and the two began to drink and talk.

"My investors are growing impatient, Mr. Lockheart. You promised us that you would remove the niggers from their land within a short time frame," Harvey said. "Yet, it's been a little over two months, and I'm still not able to move forward with my project."

"I told you, Mr. Roth, these things take time. You're talking about seizing nearly two thousand acres from the niggers. That's almost three and a half square miles of land. That's a lot of area for my men to cover."

"When I came to you, I was under the impression this was your town, your people, and you would move mountains to get whatever I needed done. I'm not paying you for your service. I'm paying you for results," Harvey Roth proclaimed.

"And results you will have," Benny assured him.

Harvey downed the last of his Scotch and poured another half glass.

"Besides, cotton season will end in a few weeks," Benny added.

Harvey chuckled. "You think this is just about cotton, Mr. Lockheart?"

"Why else would you want these niggers' land? It's fertile to grow anything you want on there."

"That area is more valuable to me than growing cotton. This is about the future of America. Specifically, white America. Our population is growing, and our cities are becoming overwhelmed with overcrowded conditions, inadequate housing, and a decline in living standards. Our cities alone can't accommodate the growing population. This is a post-war era, Mr. Lockheart. Our soldiers are coming back from the Korean war to a burgeoning middle class. They want and deserve stability and comfort in private homes, away from the Blacks that are consuming our cities with chants of equal rights and equality," Harvey proclaimed.

Harvey Roth downed the last of his Scotch. He poured another glass and became comfortable on the patio. Benny took a seat across from him, and they continued to talk.

"Mississippi is a beautiful place," Harvey uttered.

"It is. There's roots here, history," Benny concurred.

"I've personally visited Lake Nur and that area myself. Although it's plagued by niggers, it's beautiful and perfect for what I and my investors have planned . . . building several large subdivisions not only for our war heroes, but for the people who want to live the perfect American Dream."

"And while doing so, you're going to make a shitload of money, I bet," Benny said.

"It is America, of course." Harvey smiled. "This is what capitalism is, a system that brings wealth to the many, not just the few."

Benny smiled. "And am I one of the many?"

"Indeed you are, Mr. Lockheart."

The two men raised their glasses and clinked them together. "To a better America," Harvey Roth toasted.

"To a better America," Benny repeated.

Chapter Twelve

The Awkward Black Man

It was another sizzling and sunny afternoon. The blazing sun made it feel like everything was melting or burning. The South was known for its hot and sticky heat, but this felt like hell. The suffocating humidity was swallowing everything up and was making activity outside draining and even deadly. It was becoming an incredibly aggressive summer, and not just with the heat. Tension began growing within the Black and white communities. However aggressive the heat became, work and repairs were still needed on the farm.

Bronco was shirtless and working on repairing the house's roof. He was sweating profusely under the hot sun but didn't mind the work. He liked helping out and being busy. He was approaching a week on the farm, and each day felt refreshing and productive. Bronco and Elise would rise early every morning to attend to chores. She would make breakfast and coffee for him, and Bronco would either get to work on her farm or spend a day with Miss Shug and help with things there. He was beginning to like the routine. Elise was great company. She was easy to talk to and get along with. He also began to grow closer to Kenneth. Some evenings, they would toss and skip stones in the lake and talk. Bronco got to learn a lot more about Nancy and her family. The more he heard about Sylvester, his accomplishments, his bravery, and his way of thinking, the more it angered Bronco what the Klan had done to him and his family.

"Mr. Baker used to take us fishing all the time," Kenneth had said to Bronco. "He done became a father figure to me, was teaching me things. He was smart, and now they both gone. I miss 'em a lot. Now Sheriff Duke and ever'one, they actin' like it never happened. I hear they say it was an accident. I's know it was no accident."

Bronco knew that Kenneth's pain wouldn't go away. The sad thing was that it would grow wilder and stronger, like a raging fire, and become hard to put out.

"In the South, you have the Klan. In the North, we have the police. Different uniform, same fucked-up prejudice," Bronco had said.

"Can you teach me to fight?" Kenneth had asked.

"You're too young."

"But I'm not too young to be killed by white folks," Kenneth had countered.

Unfortunately, Bronco knew the boy was right. White people's hatred and bigotry toward them had no limitations. Growing up as a Black boy in 1950s Mississippi was an incredibly perilous experience. Between lynchings and Klan violence, Kenneth's chances of seeing adulthood could be violently cut short by one wrong action deemed unforgivable by an angry white mob.

"If the time comes, and I'm still around, I'll teach you a few things," Bronco had said.

"You plan on leaving us soon?" Kenneth had asked.

"I don't know," Bronco replied honestly.

Kenneth huffed and puffed. "I's don't blame you if you do leave. Who wants to stay here any's way? This place brings misery and death. I hate it here."

"It's no different where I come from, Kenneth," Bronco had replied.

"But I's hears Black people have their own mecca called Harlem. That's where you come from, right?"

Bronco nodded.

"That's where's I's want go then. Harlem."

"Harlem has its cracks and problems, too."

"But you's don't have to worry 'bout the Klan there, and no lynchings, no white men burning crosses in front of your home," Kenneth had rebutted.

Kenneth had seen far too many horrors at his age. His parents were killed in a car accident, and now his best friend had been murdered. In a way, the two of them were somewhat two kindred spirits. They were becoming familiar with losing loved ones to violence and death.

Kenneth had picked up a stone and thrown it into the lake.

"My sister likes you," Kenneth had blurted.

Bronco was caught off guard by his statement. "Say what?"

"She likes you," he had repeated. "I can tell. I see how she looks at you. She brought you to our farm. She don't do that. But she don't want you to leave. I don't want you to leave, either."

Bronco was taken aback by the statement. Elise was a beautiful young woman, and he knew any man would be lucky to have her in their life. But his history with women wasn't the best. He thought about Mindy. She was something special like Elise, but her death haunted him like Nancy's.

"I'm just here to help out, Kenneth," Bronco had replied.

Bronco thought about his conversation with Kenneth while hammering away on the roof. In his short time there, he'd taken a liking to the boy. Kenneth needed mentoring, but Bronco wrestled with teaching him to fight. He didn't plan on becoming a father figure to him like Sylvester. He had many demons, and one of them was drinking. It'd been over a week since he had a drink, and there were times when it was needed. The good thing about his time on Elise's farm was that Nancy had been coming around less.

It was odd.

The afternoon sun blared down on Bronco while he was on the roof. Suddenly, Bronco looked up to notice a vehicle approaching. A 1945 Ford pickup came to a stop near Elise's farmhouse. Harland climbed out of the pickup and was surprised to see a shirtless man on Elise's roof. The screen door opened, and Elise stepped onto the porch, surprised to see Harland. She wasn't expecting his company.

"Good afternoon to you, Elise." Harland smiled at her. He was wearing jean overalls and a gray flat cap.

"Good afternoon, Harland. What brings you by?"

"I's come to check on you and Kenneth. I haven't seen you around in a bit," Harland said. "Wanted to make sure you and the boy doin' okay." His attention shifted to Bronco, who was coming down from the roof.

"We're fine, Harland," Elise replied.

Bronco was down from the roof and chose to stand near the porch. He was shirtless and sweaty, with dog tags hanging around his neck. Harland couldn't take his eyes off the stranger. Like himself, Bronco was a strapping young man but a veteran. Handsome, too. Jealousy began to stir inside of him.

"I'm done for the day, Elise. I'll be inside, washing up for dinner," Bronco said.

Bronco disappeared into the farmhouse while Harland couldn't hide his jealousy.

"Who he, Elise?" Harland asked her.

"His name is Bronco. He's staying with us for a few days, helping out,"

"Bronco? What kinda name is that?" Harland poked.

"Harland, is there a reason you came by?" Elise uttered, not wanting to quarrel with Harland about her company.

"Yes. There's gon' be a town meeting tonight at Pastor Brooke's church. Wanted to come and tell you myself," said Harland.

"I'll be there, Harland," Elise replied.

Harland nodded and smiled. "Good to know. It's always good seein' you, Elise. Where's Kenneth?" he asked her.

"Where he's always gon' be, by the lake."

"I was thinkin', Elise, maybe I should come by more often, take Kenneth under my wing and take him fishin' like Sylvester used to do."

"He would like that."

"I's figure that. I know I haven't been 'round here often like I want. But I promise you, I'm gon' be here for you."

Elise smiled. "I appreciate it, Harland."

"But I's concern 'bout you, Elise. This Bronco, where he come from?"

"You don't need to worry 'bout me, Harland. I'm in okay hands," she assured him.

"You sure?"

"Go on, Harland. I'll see you tonight," she said.

"Well, it's always good seein' you again, Elise," Harland said. "If you need anything, come see me."

"I will. Goodbye, Harland." Elise smiled.

Harland reluctantly pivoted and began walking back to his pickup truck. Elise watched him climb inside and leave. She sighed heavily. She didn't mean to become dismissive and impolite to him, but his timing was awkward. Harland was a good man. She didn't want to hurt his feelings. He'd always been interested in her more than she was interested in him. They grew up being good friends, and she wanted it to remain that way. But the older folks in their community had always been in her ear about marriage. They hinted how Harland would make a good husband and father. Elise didn't deny it, but there was a passiveness to Harland that Elise disliked. He wanted to run away north and not fight for their home. Elise and her parents had worked too hard to give up so quickly, but Harland was a good man. Still, he wasn't aggressive in their fight for civil liberties and equality.

Once Harland's pickup disappeared from her view, Elise turned and marched back into her farmhouse. Bronco was coming out of the bedroom wearing a shirt this time. He looked at Elise and said, "I hope I didn't bring any trouble to you by being here."

"No, you didn't. Harland is a friend. He's harmless," she replied.

But Bronco had noticed the look in that man's eyes. It was pure jealousy. He'd seen that exact look plenty of times with men in Harlem, including in Miles over Elizabeth. Bronco once had a reputation for sleeping around during his younger years. His appetite for women was ravenous, and he'd been with some beautiful ladies over time. Being unstoppable made him reckless and uncouth. It didn't matter if she was married or had a boyfriend. Bronco always had his way with the ladies. They were attracted to him and flocked to him like he was some Hollywood movie star. He took full advantage of fulfilling his sexual appetite. Bronco even became bold enough to have sex with these ladies in the same home they shared with their husbands or boyfriends. And if the husband or boyfriend came home to find Bronco in bed with their ladies, Bronco would remain cool as a cucumber. They tried fighting, stabbing, shooting, and attacking Bronco with everything but the kitchen sink and would always regret it. Most of the men who became violent after finding their ladies in bed with Bronco would come out of the fight with a broken jaw, a broken arm, a few cracked ribs, badly bruised, and so on. Meanwhile, Bronco would leave unscratched with a smirk.

This reckless attitude continued until one day Bronco began an affair with a reverend's wife named Connie. Connie was exceptional. Bronco had known her since childhood, and they attended grade school together. They'd become close but lost contact over the years when Bronco went off to fight in the war. Then, one day, they'd come across each other in Harlem and reconnected. And although Connie was married to a reverend and became the first lady of his church, there had always been a fire burning inside her for Bronco. She'd begun having sex with him, and their affair went on for weeks until her husband came home early and caught them together. The reverend lost it and did the unthinkable. He pulled out a pistol, shot and killed his wife, and then attempted to shoot and kill Bronco. Bronco, being invincible, where every bullet fired at him seemed to flatten as it struck his skin, lost his cool and nearly beat the reverend to death in his own home. The man survived, but he would no longer be the same. The reverend, who was once a pillar in his community—a good, Christian man who loved his wife and his people—was now a murderer. The reverend became devastated by his actions and killed himself a few months later.

Knowing this, Bronco got to drinking more and fell back from his promiscuous ways because of Connie's death. And Bronco would often see the spirit of the good reverend haunting him. The last thing Bronco wanted was a repeat of his past. Elise was a good woman, like Connie and Mindy, and he didn't want any of his wrongful stench wrecking her life. Bronco saw Miles, the reverend, and other men in Harland earlier. Yes, he wasn't harmful now, but when it came to a woman, men were known to become unnatural and wild beasts.

"You okay?" Elise asked Bronco.

Bronco snapped out of this trance and replied, "I'm fine."

"What was on ya mind?" she asked him.

"Nothing."

"They havin' a town meeting today at the church. I'd like for you to come with me," said Elise.

Bronco looked reluctant at first. He didn't want to get involved with anything about the church or the community. He believed this wasn't his fight. Something else brought him to Mississippi, and he didn't want Nancy to continue to haunt him. Bronco knew he was there for another reason, to avenge a troubled and vengeful spirit. Nancy had returned from the afterlife to seek revenge for her family's cruel and unjust death.

But Elise was persuasive, and Bronco relented.

"An unjust law is no law at all," Forrest Tolson shouted to everyone in the church.

Every person erupted with loud applause, agreeing with him. It was a packed house at the Southern Baptist church with no empty seat. Forrest Tolson was there to speak to everyone on behalf of the NAACP about a growing movement called the Civil Rights Movement. He was an activist, and what was happening in Mississippi made him sick to his stomach.

"These Jim Crow laws allow for our children to be in segregated schools with inadequate resources, overcrowded classrooms, and poorly paid teachers. Our children today face inferior educational opportunities compared to their white counterparts. And now I hear that families here are being forced out of their homes and off their land, land that they've owned for years, generations."

"It's true," someone hollered.

"It is our right to be free from discrimination and this mandated racial segregation in public facilities, schools, transportation, and other aspects of daily life. As a people, we want the right to vote for our elected representatives. We want the protections of due process, and the right to privacy. And we want justice for Sylvester Baker and his family."

The crowd continued to roar and applaud in agreement. There was a fiery rage to Forrest as he stood at the podium, his deep voice spewing mighty rhetoric. Forrest Tolson was a handsome man with smooth black skin and a neat Afro. He wore a dark suit with a narrow tie and browline glasses. He was ready to lead this generation into the promised land. However, Pastor Melvin Brooke sat behind Forrest, looking concerned. He didn't mind Forrest bringing the people in his town together for a speech on justice and reform, especially regarding voting. They needed the morale. However, Forrest wanted everyone to begin protesting in the white towns for voting rights and equality, but what Pastor Brooke feared was the backlash from white folks. Forrest Tolson was an extreme activist, and the last thing Pastor Brooke felt his community needed was more violence and bloodshed. There was always the threat of the Ku Klux Klan looming.

Forrest looked down at Monroe and Lorraine Rice from the pulpit. The couple remained saddened and devastated by the loss of their land from Mr. Lockheart. Mrs. Rice was cushioned in her husband's arms with tears in her eyes.

Forrest said, "Mr. and Mrs. Rice, what happened to you a week ago is a crime, and my heart goes out to you and your family. What was taken from you is a tragedy that should not go unheard or unpunished."

"Amen!" a woman shouted.

The crowd loved how Forrest's voice quickened when he was sparked by adversity against Black people. He was intelligent, articulate, and motivated to implement change, something their community needed.

"Our country's Constitution and federal laws contain critical protections that form the foundation of our inclusive society," Forrest continued.

Elise and Bronco stood in the back of the church, listening to Forrest's fiery rhetoric. Elise clapped and hollered in agreement like everyone else. Meanwhile, Bronco noticed a few eyes on him and a few glares aimed his way. He was a new face in the community. He came with Elise, and a few folks found that odd. One of the people staring oddly at Bronco was Harland. He couldn't stop looking at the man from across the room, standing there with Elise like they were lovers. It was obvious that everyone wanted to know who this man was and where he came from.

Forrest Tolson wanted a few volunteers to join him in the fight for civil rights and voting rights for Black Americans. He wanted a group of people, young and old, to go into City Hall and register to vote. He also wanted to organize a march to protest the murder of the Baker family by the Klan. It would be the beginning of change and a campaign for economic equality no matter what they were facing. Elise was one of the first to volunteer against Bronco's wishes. But he couldn't tell her what she could or couldn't do. He was a guest in her home and in their town.

"I'll be outside, Elise," Bronco said to her.

While Elise began talking to Forrest and Pastor Brooke, Bronco marched out of the church and joined the outside crowd. There were mixed reactions about Forrest's march, vote, and protest plans. Some folks were ambivalent, and others were adamant about following Forrest. They were angry about losing their homes and land, and the brutal murders of the Baker family were still lingering in their minds. However, one thing was sure: although a change was needed, it would be dangerous.

Bronco felt isolated from the community. He didn't know them, and they didn't know him. In their eyes, a place like Harlem was a world away. But he, too, was a world away from home, feeling alienated from his own kind. Their accents were thick with a slow, melodic Southern drawl, while Bronco's accent was distinctive and bold. The South was brand new to him, with its Jim Crow laws and the assumption that Southerners were still in the Middle Ages.

Harland walked out of the church, and he stared at Bronco. Bronco was leaning against an old oak tree, waiting for Elise, trying to mind his business. The two men locked eyes, and Bronco sighed heavily. His intuitions were correct. He deduced that Harland had a thing for Elise, and Bronco's presence would be an issue. He didn't want any trouble, but it seemed that trouble began to follow him around no matter where he went. However, for now, Harland stared at Bronco more out of curiosity than anger.

"You must be Bronco," someone said to him unexpectedly.

Bronco's attention shifted from Harland to an older man wearing classic overalls and a straw hat. Bronco nodded and looked at the man apprehensively. "I am. Why you ask?"

He smiled. "My name's Duncan, Duncan Goff. And this here is my lovely wife, Beulah."

Duncan and his wife extended their hands toward Bronco with a smile. Bronco shook their hands and acquiesced to their kindness. A wizened face peered from under Duncan's straw hat. He looked to be in his mid-sixties with aging skin, but he was a seasoned gentleman of respectable stature with deep smile lines and wise eyes. Duncan was a man who looked after himself and others for his lifetime, a man who had not given in to the frailties of old age.

"Nice to meet you, ma'am," Bronco politely greeted her.

"Miss Shug speaks highly of you. Says you'ze been by most days to help her fix some things. I welcome a man that helps the elders. You'ze must be godsent," Duncan uttered.

People were beginning to tell him that. He hated it.

"I'm just trying to earn my keep while I'm here. That's all," Bronco replied matter-of-factly.

"Well, you'ze doin' a mighty fine job. Keep it up," Duncan added. "How's you know Elise?"

"She's a friend."

"She's a good friend to have around," said Duncan.

Bronco nodded. "She is."

While Bronco chatted with Duncan and his wife, Elise finally exited the church in her blue sack dress and a smile.

"Miss Elise, you'ze the prettiest thing around," a man said, smiling.

Elise grinned and began to look around for Bronco. Meanwhile, Harland began to head her way.

"That's a real pretty dress, Elise," Harland said.

Elise smiled. "Thank you, Harland."

"You really gonna sign up to volunteer with Forrest and get involved with this Civil Rights Movement?"

"They're takin' everything from us, Harland. What choice do we have left?" Elise said.

"We can go north, begin a new life there, Elise. We's both young."

"I'm not running away from my home, not now, not never," Elise replied.

"And when the white man comes to take it, what you gon' do next? Where's you gonna go?"

Elise huffed and slightly frowned. "I don't know. But I know I need to fight right now to try and keep my parents' farm."

"I's just don't want you to get hurt out here," said Harland.

"They already hurting and killing us, Harland," Elise countered.

Harland exhaled, knowing Elisé was stubborn. But he was beginning to look like a coward to Elise. Meanwhile, Elise smiled at Bronco when she saw him chatting with Duncan Goff and his wife. It seemed like they were taking a liking to him.

"Come, Harland, let me introduce you to Bronco."

Harland seemed reluctant to go, but he was curious about the man. He walked with Elise toward Bronco and the Goffs. Duncan grinned at Elise and said, "Elise, Beulah and I been talkin' with your friend here. We want to invite y'all to dinner this Sunday."

"We would be delighted, Mr. Goff," Elise replied.

Harland became disappointed. However, he kept up a smile, and when Elise introduced him to Bronco, the two men shook hands, and he uttered politely, "It's a pleasure to meet you, Bronco. I hear you's from New York."

"Yes, Harlem," Bronco replied.

"That's a good ways from home. What brings you to Mississippi?"

"I'm just passing through."

"Well. It was kind of Elise to take you in. She's a good woman," said Harland.

"Yes, she is." Bronco smiled at her. "I'm grateful for her hospitality."

Elise and Bronco locked eyes, smiling and showing some chemistry. Harland noticed this and spewed, "Well, since you're only passing through, what is your next destination?"

"Wherever the wind takes me," Bronco coolly replied. "But for now, I'm here to stay and help out anyway I can."

Harland's passive-aggressive behavior began to agitate Bronco, but he kept his cool.

Mr. Goff intervened. "Beulah here is a great cook. You and Elise make sure y'all come on by this Sunday."

Elise grinned and replied, "We would like that, Mr. Goff."

"It's settled then. Sunday evenin' after church, you'ze gon' get a mighty fine meal, Bronco. I's hope you bring an appetite."

Bronco smiled back. "I will."

Harland frowned. It bothered him that this sudden stranger had Elise's undivided attention. He stood on the sidelines while Elise stood close to Bronco as if she liked him. He silently fumed and huffed. He was supposed to be her knight in shining armor, not this Northern brute. It was clear to Harland that Bronco would become an issue between him and Elise.

Chapter Thirteen

The Long White Con

"I say this, the niggers has become a menace to our civilization with the passing of Brown v. the Board of Education. And then this nonsense with some Civil Rights Movement stirring up trouble, I wouldn't be surprised if the nigger will soon begin to believe that he is equal to the white man," Cleveland Brown proclaimed in front of his white peers.

"It is idiocy to believe that the Negro is the equal of the Caucasian. God Almighty made the Blacks to serve whites. And we all know God knows best," a man named Jacob McBride proclaimed.

A few men laughed.

"The Negro is the son of Ham, and in the Bible it says God Himself has placed an everlasting curse on the descendants of Ham. Niggers were deceiving, frowned upon, and cursed then, and they will continue to be deceiving, frowned upon, childlike, and in servitude today and in the near future," Cleveland said.

Cleveland Brown was a respected physician and a Harvard graduate. He considered himself a distinguished gentleman and an educated man, and he was a healthy believer in eugenics. His views on race were visibly biased. Cleveland believed that because he was a doctor, a graduate of an Ivy League school, and had spent some time with the coloreds in Haiti and Africa, he could quickly speak on how inferior the Negro race was to the white man.

"Understand this, gentlemen, it has been scientifically proven that the nigger is inherently inferior. And no matter the amount of training you can give a nigger, or the such passing of favorable laws that will improve a nigger's life, it will never make him superior to whites. The nigger is incapable of governing himself. The nigger simply has evolved underneath the white man's government," Cleveland proclaimed.

The men nodded in agreement.

The men were attending a lavish party at the mayor's mansion. Expensive cars were parked on the makeshift parking lot on the sprawling front lawn as wealthy guests arrived by the dozens. Men wore black and white tuxedos, and the ladies wore lovely gowns. The event was in full swing as white guests mingled excitedly under the moon providing natural light, like a bright chandelier in the sky, and lighting into the mansion that held most of the main event. Greetings were offered along the gravel path. Dainty fairy lights added a surplus amount of color to the parade of footsteps. It was a busy atmosphere with champagne-baring waiters and a collection of violinists, harp players, and pianists entertaining the guests.

"If you ask me, I say the nigger is a whiner," a man named Chris Rockaway uttered. "A Negro is always arguing and protesting for their rights when they could spend that time improving their lives."

"Time they could engage in bettering themselves and this country," Rick Holloway chimed. "And am I supposed to believe that civilization began in such a low-quality country like Africa?"

"As you all know, I've traveled abroad and I've witnessed millions of Negros in Africa living little better than a monkey's life," said Cleveland. "They practiced that horrible voodoo nonsense along with cannibalism and will sell their own flesh and blood. They live like savages over there."

"The fact that you have traveled to Africa, Cleveland, is a wonder to me," Benny uttered. "Why the sudden interest?"

"I like to see things firsthand for myself, Benny."

"I'm surprised you didn't come back with any diseases," Chris Rockaway joked.

"I've made sure to receive my shots," Cleveland quipped.

"Well, they can fight for equal rights all they want. But I tell you this, my good men in this room, I will never dine or eat with a nigger. I couldn't stomach it," Rick Holloway proclaimed with pure disgust.

"You might as well be eating with pigs," Jacob McBride exclaimed.

"At least a pig knows its place," Chris expressed.

The men laughed again.

"I say this to you, gentlemen, that each man in this room is indefinably better than the best nigger that ever lived," Benny Lockheart proclaimed.

"I can raise my glass and toast to that," Cleveland followed.

Each man raised their glass of wine or champagne and toasted. "To the future, and God help us if the Negro ever became an equal."

The men continued to talk, laugh, and puff on their cigars. Benny Lockheart was one of the party's wealthiest and most well-connected men. They all gravitated toward Benny like they were in his orbit, including Cleveland Brown.

"Benny, when you have the time, I want to have a word with you about investing with Harvey Roth and the Renolds Corporation. I hear good things about this urban renewal project, that it will become quite a lucrative investment," said Cleveland.

Benny grinned. "We'll talk later, Cleveland. I promise."

Cleveland Brown smiled. He was looking forward to it. Meanwhile, Benny spotted his lovely wife, Ruth, wearing a light blue cocktail dress with a chiffon shawl. Her feet glided effortlessly across the marble flooring, and she held a glass of champagne. She was coming Benny's way with her sunny smile.

"Gentlemen, can I borrow my husband for a moment?" Ruth said to the group. "You can do without him for a twinkling, I'm sure of it."

"He's all yours, Ruth," Cleveland uttered.

"Well, then." Benny smiled. "It seems I'm all yours, hon."

Ruth pulled Benny toward the dance floor, where couples swayed and danced to the soft melody filling the air. Benny held his wife close, too close. His arm fully embraced her back, and she had no choice but to become one with him. She was entirely his. He gave her a quick turn, spinning her away from him. Benny was a marvel on the dance floor. The couple caught the attention of others, folks watching and admiring them.

"I won't be coming home with you tonight. I need to take care of something," Benny said.

Ruth huffed slightly while dancing cheek to cheek for an endless moment, becoming lost in the steady, sensual rhythm. "What kind of business drags you away so late, dear?"

"An important matter," he replied.

"I was hoping to spend some quality time with you while the kids are with my parents."

She stepped back. He spun her beneath his arm, caught her again, and uttered, "I'll make it up to you. I promise."

She frowned in thought. Benny gave her a quick turn, spinning her away from him.

"I'll wait up," she said.

"Don't," he responded.

He drew her close again.

"How will I get home?"

"I'll arrange for a driver to take you," said Benny.

Ruth's eyes searched his face for something revealing, but her husband remained stoic. Her lips grazed his ear and whispered, "I love you."

"I love you, too," Benny replied.

An hour later, Ruth kissed her husband before she climbed into the back seat of a Cadillac Fleetwood limousine. Benny closed the door behind her, and Ruth stared woefully at her husband as the car began to drive away. Benny then marched to his car with a mischievous sparkle in his eyes.

Benny's burgundy 1950s Packard Eight arrived at the alehouse and gambling spot on the outskirts of town. A large group of cars were parked in the grassy area outside a two-story farmhouse with a large porch and a large barn behind it. Apparently, the farm home had been turned into an after-hours spot for a specific unsavory group outside of the Christian community.

Benny marched toward the active farmhouse, still dressed in his suit from the mayor's party. He moved purposefully and walked by Sheriff Duke's patrol car, indicating the man was already inside. Benny Lockheart marched onto the wraparound porch and was politely greeted by two strapping good-ol' boys named Marvin and Daniel. Both men wore straw cowboy hats and were chewing on tobacco.

"Good evenin', Mr. Lockheart," Marvin greeted him.

"Good evening, gentlemen. Where's the sheriff?" Benny asked them.

"He inside, waiting on you, Mr. Lockheart," Daniel said.

Benny nodded and made his way into the place. Inside, the alehouse was thick with cigar smoke and men playing pool, laughing and drinking corn liquor, and listening to Delta Blues. There were women and whores entertaining the men with their scanty fashionable choices and flirtatious behavior. And for the right price, drunken men would disappear with a young, pretty girl upstairs into one of the four bedrooms to continue their good time together in private. There was backroom gambling, mostly poker, where there were the sounds of cards whirring in the hands of the dealers.

But the barn in the back was where the main action took place—gambling. There were slot machines, roulette wheels, and more. There was an impromptu stage for entertainment and a fiesta of debauchery where men could cut loose and be themselves, from dancing to frolicking like animals in a zoo. It was where everyone came to have a good time with no judgment. Folks from across Mississippi and beyond would flock to this backwoods alehouse that left housewives alone most nights.

You would think it was a place where a man like Benny Lockheart wouldn't be caught dead. But he was a frequent flyer at the gambling house. He collected a weekly bribe from the owner, Jimbo, for operating in his town—the cost of doing business. Jimbo was a husky redneck with a big body and slim legs, mousy brown hair, a wild beard, bad skin, stained teeth, and a Southern twang. Despite his appearance, he was a businessman and knew how to run and operate the place. Jimbo carried a spit cup and was as racist as they came. Absolutely no niggers were allowed in his place except for being the entertainment.

"Mr. Lockheart, de Sheriff waitin' fo' you in de back room," said Jimbo.

Benny nodded. "How are we looking tonight?"

"Packed, like most nights," Jimbo replied.

Benny walked by Jimbo, moved through the crowd of men and women having a good time, and traveled down a short, dim hallway toward the last back room, an office. When he opened the door, he received the surprise of his life. Sheriff Duke was leaning against the desk, pants meshed around his ankles, his head slightly reclined, and deep in his bliss of pleasure as a young girl was on her knees giving him oral sex.

"I don't mean to interrupt," Benny uttered civilly.

The sheriff and the girl, shocked at Benny's presence, quickly began to collect themselves. The sheriff hurriedly pulled up his pants while the girl sprang from her knees. She became embarrassed when she saw that it was Mr. Lockheart.

"I'm so sorry, Mr. Lockheart," she uttered.

"I need to have a word with the sheriff, Trudy," Benny said.

She nodded submissively and hurried out of the room to give the two men privacy to talk. Benny Lockheart closed the door behind her and stared at Sheriff Duke.

"I've known that girl since she was eight years old," Benny said.

"I apologize, Mr. Lockheart. I wasn't expecting you so soon. Thought you be still at the mayor's party."

"Well, now I'm here, Sheriff. If I'm not mistaken, you was expecting me."

Sheriff Duke nodded. "Yes."

"And you took it upon yourself to comfort yourself with an eighteen-year-old."

"I'm a single man, Mr. Lockheart. And she is of age," Sheriff Duke countered respectfully.

Benny Lockheart glared at the sheriff with slight disgust. It was no secret that Sheriff Duke had a penchant for young, pretty girls—and his proclivity for young, pretty girls didn't end with white girls.

"I had an interesting meeting with Mr. Roth the other day, Sheriff. He's becoming displeased with the duration of acquiring the niggers' land around Lake Nur," Benny said.

"Me and my men are doin' our best, Mr. Lockheart. It's just there's a lot of land and a lot of niggers to force out. And now since this nigger Sylvester's death, I hear the niggers has brought in some nigger organization called the NAACP into our town to investigate."

"Spare me the particulars, Sheriff. If you need more men, simply ask. The money is not an issue."

"I need more men, Mr. Lockheart, if you want me to carry out this in a timely matter," the sheriff replied. "And I know you want this done quietly, but most these niggers ain't gon' leave they homes without a fight. That nigger Sylvester done gon' and started shooting at us and done killed Mark. Good man like him, I had to go on and tell his wife and kids," Sheriff Duke proclaimed.

"Tell it to someone else, Sheriff."

Benny Lockheart didn't care to hear the story. The only thing that mattered to him was making money and healthy results. The death of a poor white man by a nigger's hands was considered the cost of doing business. He wasn't going to lose any sleep over it.

"Mr. Roth wants it done by any means necessary. He and his company will take care of any backlash from activists, any Black organizations, or the newspapers. The main priority you need to grasp is acquiring the deeds to their homes and lands so Mr. Roth and his investors can begin building," Benny proclaimed. "So consider you and your men untethered until further notice."

The sheriff nodded. "Consider it done, Mr. Lockheart."

Concluding his business with the sheriff, Benny turned and exited the room.

Benny exited the place and marched toward his car. He climbed into his Packard and started the ignition. It was late, but Benny wasn't going home to his wife yet. He planned on making another stop. This stop was just as important.

Benny Lockheart arrived at an abandoned plantation twenty miles away from his hometown. The old plantation belonged in a storybook. It was isolated, in the middle of the woods, overgrown with thick vines, wild shrubbery, and leaves. It had peeling paint, unhinged doors, and shattered windows. Some said the place was haunted. However, the dilapidated plantation was once a thriving place for cotton production, housing dozens of slaves. It was the envy of all plantations over a hundred years ago.

Benny exited his vehicle, holding a flashlight, and walked toward the crumbling big house. He moved toward the hole in a fence and pushed through it. It was 2:00 a.m., and he was the first to arrive at the plantation. So he stood around and waited. Ten minutes later, a pair of headlights beamed from a distance. An old Ford Deluxe moved to the big house up the long dirt road. Benny watched the car with some anxiety. When the vehicle stopped, he exhaled and kept his eyes on the driver's door. It opened, and Virginia climbed out. Benny smiled at her.

"I didn't think you were going to show up," said Benny.

"Has there been a time when I didn't show up?" Virginia replied with a smile.

Benny was excited. He hadn't seen Virginia in over a month, but he was glad she was able to escape her world to come see him tonight, although it would be brief and isolated. Wearing a skirt that came to her knees and a white blouse, Virginia was a beautiful and petite black woman who had captured Benny Lockheart's heart so many years ago. Her dark ebony skin shined as if it was recently oiled, her face was nearly angelic, and her lovely hair was styled into a chic bob. She carried with her a blanket and a bottle of wine.

Virginia fell into Benny's arms, and they began to passionately kiss.

"Oh, how I have missed you, Virginia," he confessed.

"I've missed you too," Virginia said.

To Benny, her voice was harmonious and pleasant. They continued to kiss fervently underneath the canopy of stars and where the grass grew long and unkempt. However, they found the perfect area to lie and enjoy each other's company. It was a warm summer night, and the bugs were chirping, the heat was stifling, and the abandoned big house behind them was haunting. But it didn't stop Benny and Virginia from shedding their clothes and lying with each other on the blanket.

He was quickly inside Virginia in the missionary position while one of her breasts was inside his mouth. The two began making passionate love in the middle of the night, twisting and turning into different positions, moaning and groaning. The way Virginia made him feel was unnatural but perfect. Their chemistry was deep. Sadly, although he loved Ruth, she had never made him feel this way. She never challenged him but remained the doting wife she was bred to become. Their conversation always felt bland and one-off, while Virginia spoke her mind and wasn't afraid to speak truth to power.

Benny and Virginia remained naked, nestled on the blanket, and stared at the stars.

Benny was five years her senior, and the two met twenty years ago when Virginia's mother worked as a maid for Benny's family. He was 21, and she was 16. She came from poverty and segregation, while Benny came from wealth and privilege. But the two had an affinity when it came to politics and books. Virginia was smart, more intelligent than the average Negro, Benny believed, and she was gorgeous for a Negro girl. Their brief and chance encounter grew over time into a secret relationship.

Whenever Virginia accompanied her mother to work, she began looking forward to seeing Benny. However, they had to be careful because it was 1935, and the South was a treacherous place when it came to interracial dating and Blacks mixing with whites. But that didn't stop them. They would sneak in kisses and conversations throughout the house while her mother worked. Benny would give her certain books to read. Virginia would listen to Benny's complaints, ideas, and debates, and would always give him great advice. This went on for years. The two would secretly meet in isolated locations to talk, have sex, and gripe about their worlds. If Virginia were a white woman, she would have long ago become Benny's wife.

Whenever Benny wanted to get word to Virginia to meet, he would depend on a young Negro named Cory to deliver the message. Cory worked for Benny as a gardener on his land. Cory became Benny's messenger for a few extra bucks and kept his secret, knowing Benny's status in town.

"It's ironic that we have to meet in places like this, Benny, at an abandoned plantation with such a brute history," she griped.

"You know my position, Virginia. Who I am and my associates."

"I know you're an important man, Benny."

"And then there's my wife."

"I don't expect you to leave your wife for me . . . a colored woman," Virginia uttered.

"I do love you, Virginia," he wholeheartedly proclaimed.

"And I love you, Benny."

They remained cuddling on their backs, with her head on his chest. He didn't want to let her go. It felt like he could hold her forever—a colored woman.

"I need to ask you something, Benny, and I want you to be honest with me," Virginia uttered.

"Anything."

"What do you know about that family killed in their home by a fire a few weeks back?" asked Virginia. "Did you have anything to do with it?"

Benny sulked. It was a question he didn't want to answer, but he'd always been honest with Virginia. "It was a tragedy that I couldn't prevent. Virginia, you know how this town is."

Virginia rose up from his arms, becoming bothered by his words. "What do you mean you couldn't prevent it? You're a congressman, Benny. You can do or prevent anything you want."

"But it's not that simple. I do have a reputation to uphold."

"And does that reputation mean killing families, babies even? Do you know a toddler and other children also perished in that tragedy? The Klan brutally murdered them children, gunned them down like they were nothing, and then they laugh about it," Virginia griped. "And I know your friends, the higher-ups, are doing their best to bury it."

It was a haunting thought, and Benny didn't want to be reminded of it. It was a tragedy, and he was disgusted, but he felt his hands were tied.

"I've known you for a long time, Benny. I fell in love with you when I was young. I know you wouldn't want this. I always believed you were one of the good ones I came across," Virginia cordially proclaimed.

Benny had to wear two faces: one with Virginia when they were together, and one for his white, prejudiced peers whenever he met with them. He was a congressman looking to get reelected next year because his two-year term was ending. If it ever got out that he was in love and having an affair with a colored woman, he would be ruined. Benny constantly worried about endorsements from his peers, his constituents, and Harvey Roth, a man with absolute wealth, power, and resources to destroy him. But he also couldn't tell her the truth, that he was for pushing the Blacks off their land for profit and property. Benny believed wholeheartedly in social Darwinism.

"If you don't plan to do anything about it, Benny, then I will," Virginia expressed. "I wrote to a friend of mine in the NAACP, informing him of our recent tragedies and the cover-up behind it. I plan on getting justice for what happened here, Benny, with or without your help."

"You're placing me into a quagmire, Virginia, especially with my reelection coming up next year," Benny replied.

"I love you, but I will not allow you, or your sudden ambition to achieve whatever you believe is more important, to impede justice for that family," Virginia said vehemently.

He felt she was being stubborn. But the one thing Virginia didn't understand about Benny was that he was becoming far worse than a racist—he was becoming a capitalist. It became about growth in his town with jobs, real estate, opportunities, and wealth.

Virginia was ready to leave. Her mood had changed. She rose from the blanket and began collecting her things while Benny watched her quietly. As she grabbed her shoes, she shot Benny a concerned look and said, "We see less of each other year after year, and every time I see you, the more you change, Benny . . . and not for the better."

"I'm a state congressman, Virginia."

"But you're a human being first, a Christian, too. So you say," she countered.

"I am a good man, a Christian, but—"

"But what? The only time you care about children dying is if they are white?"

"It's just . . . complicated," he replied faintly.

Virginia continued to huff and puff. It felt like it finally dawned on her that the man she loved for so many years was two-faced—an absolute racist who proclaimed he loved her. But how could he love her and hate Black people? He wanted his cake and to eat it, too. Everything they did together was in secret, and it felt like Benny was getting the best of both worlds: her unconditional love and pleasures from a pretty Black woman, along with his political and wealthy whiteness.

"I need to go," Virginia exclaimed.

"Virginia," Benny called out to her.

She turned to him, ready to hear what he had to say, but he couldn't pour it out to her. Suddenly, the cat had his tongue. The woman he was in love with was about to walk out of his life, upset. But Benny couldn't lie to her. He didn't care. He wanted to be reelected, and he wanted Harvey Roth's investment to happen, even if it was at the expense of completely wiping out Black ownership and farmland. Benny saw the potential financial windfall it would create for him in the future, and it was too lucrative to fuck up. Greed had Benny's heart.

"Goodbye, Benny," Virginia said with finality.

She marched back to her old Ford Deluxe and climbed inside. The vehicle drove off, and Benny began to wonder if he had made a mistake by allowing Virginia to leave upset. He'd fallen in love with a colored woman over twenty years ago, but he never fell in love with her people.

Chapter Fourteen

The Long Dream

Bronco woke up to a visit from Nancy again. This time, he heard her crying. The room was dark, and she stood in the corner, staring abnormally at Bronco. Her eyes were glistening with unleashed tears. Bronco gazed at her, almost trance-like. Something about her was unnerving. She was sad and in pain. All of a sudden, she began convulsing. It seemed like she was having a violent seizure. Nancy's eyes started to roll back, her limbs became rigid, and her body became possessed by something. Every muscle inside of her began to constrict. It was something inhuman and ghastly. It seemed like she was dying again.

Bronco sprang from the bed to quickly aid her. He reached for her, and the moment he touched her, his vision blurred, and everything went dark. He began to panic. What the fuck is happening to me?

When he opened his eyes, he wasn't in the bedroom anymore. He was lying on his back in some modest but eerie cemetery with only flowers and small plaques. Bronco rose to his feet and knew he must be in a weird dream. He had no idea how he'd gotten there or why he was there. He didn't see Nancy around. But he knew he wasn't alone. Something was with him. The sky above was gray and ominous, and the cemetery was surrounded by a sinister-looking forest with dark, spectral trees and branches that looked threatening. It felt like he was in some kind of a leering abyss.

Strangely, Bronco began hearing a school bell ring. He had no idea where it was coming from. But it was echoing from a distance, disturbing the cemetery's silence. Then he began to see some movement at the edge of the forest. Nancy loomed into his view, but she wasn't alone this time. Throughout the trees, a disturbing figure began to appear before Bronco. This nightmarish figure seemed to be of rotting, skeletal flesh. It stood right next to Nancy and took her hand into his. Nancy started to walk Bronco's way, bringing this ethereal and spine-chilling creature with her. But strangely, this unnatural creature began to change as it walked toward Bronco. Its skeletal and decaying state began reconstructing itself with living tissue. Its skin was returning, followed by hair and eyes—life was returning to it. The decaying process was reversed until its final transformation became a fully grown man standing before Bronco.

It was Sylvester—back from the dead.

It was an unsettling feeling for Bronco. What did he want from him?

"I was once a man," said Sylvester chillingly.

"I'm here. What do you want from me?" asked Bronco.

"I was once a man," Sylvester repeated. "I was once a man."

He felt its presence was beckoning him. Sylvester's gaze upon Bronco became intense as he held his daughter's hand. Nancy, too, continued to stare at Bronco hauntingly. Then she outstretched her hand toward Bronco, indicating for him to grab it. Bronco was hesitant to do so. Nancy remained frozen with her arm outstretched, staring at him unblinkingly. It felt like time had become still.

"I am a man," Sylvester uttered, correcting his rant. "I am a man."

His eyes became cloudy while Nancy's eyes continued to well up with tears. Her mouth opened and began moving, but the sound was muffled. She continued to outstretch her hand toward Bronco, thirsting for him to grasp her hand and maybe become connected with her. Reluctant, Bronco held her hand, and cold air immediately filled his lungs. His breathing became labored, and he dropped to his knees, feeling like he was suffering from a severe anxiety attack. He blacked out again.

When Bronco opened his eyes, he stared at the millions of stars glittering overhead. This time, he found himself in a valley of dead trees whose decayed, gnarled limbs appeared to form hands. He was alone. Everything felt still, quiet. Bronco had no idea where he was, but he knew he was still in some kind of dream. Suddenly, he heard movement happening somewhere among the dead trees. Bronco became guarded, with his eyes glued to the edge of the dead trees. He began to listen to a horse neighing. It was distant at first, but the sound grew closer and closer. Bronco's eyes remained fixed on the dead forest from which the neighing came. It was approaching.

Out of nowhere, an eye-catching black bronco appeared from the dead forest. It stood nearly sixteen hands tall, with muscle, and had a lovely, long black mane. The creature approached Bronco as if it was familiar and comfortable with him. It continued to neigh as Bronco began to calm it, running his hand across its midnight coating and gliding his fingers through its beautiful long mane. He knew the word "bronco" came from the Spanish for rough or untamed.

This stallion was him.

Suddenly, the creature began to stir with fright, sensing something evil was afoot. Soon after, a dark figure loomed from the forest, immediately catching Bronco's attention. It was a tall man of no age with pale skin and predatory eyes, wearing a dark, hooded cloak. But it stood there with a devilish glint in his eyes locked on Bronco like magnets. The stallion began to go stir-crazy, rising up and dropping down on its hind legs, becoming scared. Bronco tried to tame him but to no avail. It became terrified and troubled by this tall figure. This tall being began to walk toward Bronco and the stallion, with its cold gaze fixed on Bronco. Bronco's body felt heavy as this tall figure studied him with a predator's unwavering attention.

Bronco felt he had no choice but to mount the horse for his escape. The stallion allowed him to climb on. Spooked, the stallion began to run away from this predator or evil being. It started to squeal while galloping across an open plain with tunnel vision from the adrenalin. Behind Bronco and the stallion was absolute darkness that began to consume everything it touched. The stallion accelerated, almost reaching thirty miles an hour, and it felt like Bronco and the stallion were moving as one. But the fast-moving abyss of darkness couldn't be outrun. Eventually, it began to swallow Bronco and the stallion completely.

Bronco screamed while the horse roared in pain. He was in darkness again. And while he was utterly consumed in the darkness, he began to hear a horrific and bloodcurdling scream that came from Nancy. Suddenly, Bronco found himself inside the cabin, which was on fire. The walls flickered, consumed by violent flames. The place was crumbling. Bronco gritted his teeth in agony. His body became rigid with pain because every inch of him felt like it was on fire. Bronco slammed himself to the floor. The fear of burning took his breath away. He wasn't invincible but now a man able to feel pain and agony.

All of a sudden, a shadowy figure loomed just beyond the doorway. This shadowy figure came into focus, and it was Nancy. However, again, she wasn't alone. The tall, dark being from the dead forest appeared behind Nancy, and she became afraid. She stared at Bronco with apprehension as this being began to shapeshift into something horrifying with a perpetual scowl. This time, its eyes were pure black. They began to shimmer with some inexplicable malice as claws, fangs, and hooves developed. It locked eyes with Bronco with its predatory eyes.

Is the devil real?

Unexpectedly, Bronco began to hear more screams that came from the family who had perished inside the fire. They were everywhere. The screaming became so intense it started to drown out the raging fire.

"She's mine. They are all mine," this terrifying being uttered to Bronco.

The fire continued to rage and grow hot and destructive. Like the nightmare he had a week ago, he couldn't move at all. Bronco felt helpless as this tall being held Nancy in its dark grasp and watched Bronco burn alive. Frustrated and angry, Bronco hollered and tried to escape this torment and agony. Then a sudden bright light danced across Bronco's face, followed by the neighing of a horse—his stallion. It emerged from the fire to aid Bronco. Seeing this, the tall being scowled as it watched Bronco mount the stallion to rescue him from the flames.

The stallion sprinted from the flames, carrying Bronco. He could breathe again, with the stallion running wild, bucking and fighting this entity. The stallion began to move fast, like lightning striking, pursuing this *thing that had kidnapped Nancy. But no matter how fast it moved, it couldn't catch it, and both Bronco and the stallion became lost in the darkness again. He could hear Nancy, but he couldn't find her.*

Becoming lost in the dark abyss again, Bronco could barely breathe. He knew that he was failing her—or losing her. He screamed out in frustration and horror.

Then he sprang awake from his nightmare. At first, he didn't recognize where he was and tried to deduce if it was a false awakening like earlier. For a fleeting moment, he felt the effects of sleep paralysis and labored breathing. He screamed while remaining frozen in the bed.

Elise hurried into the bedroom when she heard him scream. It frightened her. She sat at the side of the bed and reached for Bronco. "Bronco, are you okay?" she asked him. "Look at me. You were having a nightmare."

Bronco regained his composure and stared at Elise and her beautiful features. It was as if an angel were staring at him, and he was able to move again.

"You were having a bad dream," she said.

Bronco huffed and rose up. His dreams and nightmares weren't normal. Elise stared at him with concern. "What happened? What were you dreamin' 'bout?"

"Nothing. It was just a recurring nightmare."

"Recurring . . . of what?" she asked him.

"Just my past, that's all."

Elise exhaled. "One day, you need to tell me 'bout your past, Bronco. Maybe it can help with yo' nightmares."

Bronco looked reluctant to do so. He felt that his demons needed to stay with him. Elise was too beautiful and innocent of a woman to be exposed to such horrors. The last thing he wanted to do was corrupt or infect her with his shit. But then again, she did live in the South. But Bronco's demons were something unworldly.

"I'll make breakfast," said Elise. "Maybe that'll help with yo' bad dreams." She smiled.

"I need to see the scene," Bronco uttered out of the blue.

Elise looked at him, and she was confused. "What scene? What do you mean?"

"I came here for a reason. I need to see where they were murdered."

"Who are you talkin' 'bout?"

"Sylvester and his family. I need to see the scene, Elise."

Elise became utterly bewildered by this request. "Why? Why would you want to go there? You didn't know 'em."

Bronco sighed heavily. He couldn't explain why. She wouldn't believe him. Bronco felt he was a curse and an abomination from God. *Who would want this gift? Why was it bestowed on me?* It angered him that he could communicate with the spirit world—being a telephone or a conduit with the dead. Bronco hated that he wasn't an ordinary man. He wondered if he was still of flesh and blood since he couldn't be harmed. He hated the recurring nightmares of Nancy and seeing the dead like they were everyday people. He loathed the trance state it trapped him in and that he became this vessel for the spirit's voices, pain, agony, and message.

"You don't have to come. I'll walk there. Just tell me which way to go," he said.

He was adamant about seeing where Nancy and her family had lost their lives. Elise was reluctant to take him there but relented and said, "I'll take you there this afternoon after we eat breakfast."

Bronco nodded and was appreciative of her.

"Do I need to be worried 'bout something, Bronco?" she asked him.

"No," he replied.

Elise's pickup truck arrived at what was left of the Bakers' home. It was nothing but burnt rubble in the middle of the woods. There was nothing left. Everything that this family had perished in the fire. It was mid-afternoon and another hot summer day. Bronco exited the vehicle, and Elise followed him with some uneasiness. They slowly crept toward the rubble that once represented a beautiful home that hosted a wonderful, flourishing, and happy family. Now the area was of nothingness and a harsh reminder of how horrible things could become for Black families in the South. Elise prayed for the souls of the family. She hadn't been to the scene since it'd happened. She didn't want to be there, but Bronco insisted.

Bronco said, noticing her uneasiness, "You can wait in the truck or leave, Elise. I'll be okay. I can find my way back."

But she wasn't going to leave him there. "No. We leave together."

Bronco began inspecting the horrifying scene as if he were a police detective. He could sense this family's agony. He could hear their voices and cries from fear of the Klan outside their home. It felt like he'd traveled back to the night of the tragedy, and he saw it play out for himself.

"Come outside right now, nigga!" Bronco heard a man shout. *"Mommy! I'm scared."* It came from a little girl. *"Oh, my God. God help us,"* he heard another woman scream. *"Take the kids in the back room, Martha."* Bronco heard the patriarch of the family like he was standing before him. *"We don't want any trouble now. Get from 'round here."*

Suddenly, there was gunfire and screaming. Bronco stood in the middle of the rubble and took it all in. His eyes were closed, and he could genuinely sense where they all fell and died. He understood why Nancy was so lost, angry, and afraid. She had burned to death while in her grandmother's arms.

Meanwhile, Elise stood away from the place and watched Bronco's weird behavior. She thought, *what is he doing?* It worried her. She never saw anything so odd. He stood there like he was in some kind of trance. His eyes were closed, he remained completely still, and it seemed as if he was meditating.

Unexpectedly, they had company coming their way. Elise turned and saw a brown 1953 Chrysler Town & Country approaching the area. Her gut instinct told her that it was trouble looming. The vehicle stopped behind her pickup truck, and all four doors opened to reveal several white men climbing out.

"Bronco," Elise called out.

Bronco snapped out of his trance to see that they weren't alone. He frowned at seeing four white men on the property: Jacob, Paul, Keith, and Joseph. Two of them were armed with shotguns. They were the same four men present the night Sylvester and his family were killed. The men scowled at Elise and Bronco.

Paul exclaimed, "Do you niggers know this is private property?"

"Says who?" Bronco replied with a stern stare, locking eyes with all four white men, which was a crime in the South.

"You gettin' smart with me, boy?" Paul retorted.

"Last I heard, this here place belonged to a Black man and his family," Bronco replied.

"Well, if you ain't heard the news, nigger, that nigger family is no longer with us," Keith chimed.

"I've heard," Bronco uttered through clenched teeth.

"What you lookin' for anyway, boy?" asked Paul.

"Why is that your concern?" Bronco contested.

Bronco's defiant demeanor began to anger the men. He wasn't about to humble himself or back down from them. They didn't scare him.

"You're new in town, boy. What is your name?" asked Keith.

"My name should be no damn concern to you," Bronco retorted.

He was angry, too. He felt their vibes and knew they had something to do with the tragedy that happened there. Agitated and feeling belittled, Paul leveled the shotgun he carried to Bronco's chest.

"I will blow you away right now, nigger," Paul exclaimed.

Elise had no choice but to intervene. "I'm so sorry for my friend's rude behavior, sir. He's from New York. He's new here to Mississippi."

"I don't care where he's from, Elise. He needs to be taught a got-damn lesson," Paul exclaimed.

"I'll make sure he won't disrespect anyone again," Elise uttered. "I's promise you that."

"Elise, who is this nigger to you? Because he's about to find himself swinging from a damn tree," Joseph asked her.

"He's a friend of mine, and Sylvester's cousin," she lied.

"This here nigger kin to that rabble-rouser? More of a reason why he needs to swing from a tree," said Jacob.

"He's in mourning about his cousin, that's all. He don't mean nothin' by it," Elise explained to them.

Bronco frowned while watching Elise belittle herself in front of these men. The last thing Bronco wanted to do was put Elise in harm's way. But it wasn't easy for him to hold back. He clenched his fists so tightly he was about to break his skin and knuckles. He wanted to snap these racists apart with his bare hands and was capable of doing so.

Knowing that the sheriff was sweet on Elise, they decided to give them a pass.

"We gon' let you be because of the sheriff, Elise. However, this here is now private property. No niggers allowed. If we find you here again, we will shoot you on sight. I promise you that, boy," Paul said while glaring at Bronco. "Do you understand me, boy?"

Bronco fumed and remained quiet. Elise stared at him with complete worry. She didn't want any trouble. She had seen enough death and violence with her people. She frowned at Bronco, nearly begging him to behave himself.

Reluctantly, Bronco nodded.

"Let me hear you say it, boy. You gon' be a good nigger while ya here in good ol' Mississippi? Because if not, you gon' find yourself dead like your nigger cousin," Paul warned him.

"You won't have any problems with me," Bronco replied pointedly.

Bronco stared intently at Paul, causing Paul to react with, "And this nigger better watch how he looks at white folks. This ain't Harlem, nigger. Watch yo' step and watch yo' damn eyes."

Bronco feigned a smile. "Yes, suh. I's gon' be a good nigger, boss. I's promise you that," Bronco mocked.

Paul and the others laughed. He lowered the shotgun, and then Paul warned them again, "Get from 'round here and don't come to this area no more."

Elise and Bronco quickly retreated to the pickup truck—although Bronco looked reluctant to do so, glancing back over his shoulder with contempt. They climbed inside while Paul and his cronies watched them mockingly.

"Go on now, get from here, niggers!" Paul exclaimed.

He then aimed the shotgun into the air and fired twice—*boom! Boom!* It was startling for Elise, but Bronco remained calm and seethed. While Elise hurriedly maneuvered the truck off the property, Bronco glared at Paul with his shotgun and knew his day of reckoning was coming.

When they were back on the road and away from the danger, Elise cut her eyes at Bronco and exclaimed, "What is wrong with you, Bronco? You can't be sassing and talkin' back to white folks like that down here. You could have gotten us killed."

She was afraid, and he understood her fear. But he now had a purpose. What he felt back at that cabin was treacherous and evil. Everyone in the Baker family had suffered tremendously, and Bronco knew that, before he left Mississippi, there would be hell to pay.

Chapter Fifteen

Every Man a King

Elise's laughter was alluring and soft, almost ethereal. To Bronco, her laughter was like a beautiful butterfly drifting in the wind above a field of flowers. Duncan Goff was a funny and affable man. He was familiar with entertaining the room and guests with stories from his past and dealing with white folks. He was a natural at it, like Flip Wilson. Duncan had everyone at the dinner table stirring with laughter as he told a story about dealing with an incompetent white man and a stubborn mule during his sharecropping days.

"That mule done went to kickin' and thrashin' about, like he done seen the devil itself. Gone off and had me hollerin' too," Duncan laughed. "But I sees why it was scared seeing Mr. Samual standing there lookin' pale like powdered sugar. You's see when a donkey senses danger, its reaction is to freeze in place and assess the situation. That damn donkey didn't move a single step at first until it figured out what Mr. Samual was. That kind of action makes the mule appear stubborn. But when Mr. Samual came close with that bullwhip in his hand, shit . . . that mule ain't stupid. He hollered. I hollered too."

The laughter inside the cozy, two-bedroom bungalow was needed. Mr. Duncan and his wife, Beulah, provided comfort, food, and amusement. Sitting before Bronco and Elise on a large wooden dinner table was a spread of food that could rival a king's feast. There were ham hocks, collard greens, fried chicken, biscuits, corn, and beans. Beulah was an exceptional cook, and Duncan was still an admiring eater after forty years of marriage. Their love and admiration for each other was thick and pouring like her gravy for the biscuits. Every time Duncan glanced at his wife, he smiled warmly.

This kind of atmosphere and hospitality was new, but it was growing on Bronco. He'd never been invited into anyone's home for dinner, laughter, and meaningful conversation. He'd never met someone so affable and outgoing, like Duncan Goff. Surprisingly, Duncan made him laugh also. Although Bronco's laughter came as quiet as a whisper, Duncan's laughter boomed like a cannon going off. It echoed off the walls of the bungalow.

Bronco looked at Elise, who sat across the table from him. She looked marvelous, clad in a polka-dot swing evening cocktail dress, while he wore a bland white shirt that barely fit him and some old trousers. Elise's honied laughter continued to echo through the room, matching Duncan's and Beulah's.

"How'd y'all feel 'bout what this Forrest Tolson man said, 'bout volunteering in this Civil Rights Movement?" Duncan uttered, changing the mood from laughter to current events.

"I already signed up for it, Mr. Goff," said Elise.

"You sure it's wise to get involved with somethin' so dangerous, Elise?" Beulah questioned.

"We need to do somethin', Mrs. Goff. I don't want to sit by idly and watch my farm gets taken away from me. That farm, my land, it's all I have and all I know," said Elise.

"White folks won't be happy until they see us stripped of everythin' we worked hard for, or see us back wearing chains," Duncan growled.

"It's why we all need to stick together, and demand change right now," Elise said.

"And you think marchin' down to them white folks' courthouse and forcing somethin' down their throats gon' make them change they way of thinkin'? White man ain't gon' change for no Black man's comfort. They see the world fit as is. It's easier for them to push niggers out their way to get their doin'," Duncan exclaimed.

"I don't want to see you get hurt, Elise. We care 'bout you. That Forrest fellow, he preaches a good sermon, but I sense a lot of good colored folks gon' end up hurt or dead with this movement he's stirring up," Beulah chimed.

Elise huffed. "A lot of Black folks gon' end up hurt or dead if we don't stir something up and make a change."

Duncan downed the last of his rye whiskey and exhaled. "A crowd has no mind, Elise. I've seen what happens when an angry mob comes into town. They tore my granddaddy apart."

"What will you do when they finally come for your land?" Elise asked significantly.

Duncan huffed and grunted. The thought of it was unsettling. He couldn't help but think about Sylvester. He was adamant about making a radical change and fighting for his rights and civil liberties, and look where it got him and his family. Sylvester was intelligent, strong, ambitious, and stubborn. He was a threat to the white man's status quo, and they butchered him. Now Duncan Goff was no punk. He had his fair share of quarrels with white men and survived to tell about it. But he thought about his family first. If anything were to happen to Beulah, he would never be able to forgive himself. She was his everything, and the only thing he wanted to do was protect her. He and Beulah were doting parents to five adult children and grandparents to nine grandchildren.

Duncan Goff felt he was one of the lucky ones to receive a slice of land in Mississippi, which he'd cultivated into earnings to feed his family and build a stable home to raise his children. Duncan was a man of principles and standards. He believed hard work and values made the man. He was also grateful that he and his wife were able to see their children grow up without a mob of white men placing a noose around his neck to lynch him from a tree. Duncan Goff had seen his fair share of lynchings. For a Black man to see old age and prosperity in the South was a blessing. Because in the white man's eyes, one or the latter was a threat to their community, but both were damnation.

His granddaddy on his father's side, his older brother, and three of his cousins all had their lives brutally cut short by the hands of angry and racist white mobs. But it was his granddaddy's lynching that haunted him. Duncan remembered his granddaddy being accused of assaulting and raping a white woman and also assaulting her husband. Subsequently, his granddaddy was chained by his neck and then dragged and paraded through the street, all while being stabbed and beaten. Then, he was held down, castrated, and lynched in front of over 5,000 spectators, including city officials and police, who gathered to watch the attack. Members of the mob cut off his fingers and hung him over a bonfire after saturating him with coal oil. He was repeatedly lowered and raised over the fire for hours. Duncan and his family were devastated and ended up leaving Louisiana when he was 10 years old.

"What 'bout you, Bronco? What's your thoughts on this? You awfully quiet sittin' there," Duncan said.

Bronco didn't want to get pulled into the debate. It wasn't his forte to talk about politics and political movements. He always considered himself a dumb loner. His take on things was if it didn't bother or concern him, then let it be. He wasn't looking for any trouble unless it came his way. But Elise was talking about marching into town with this Forrest Tolson muthafucka to stir trouble and agitate white folks for equality, voting rights, and justice. Bronco knew it was a bad idea. White men were the same no matter if they were up North or in the South. They were a pack of bloodthirsty and carnivorous hyenas ready to rip a Black man apart because they had the power and the numbers to do so.

"It's a risk," said Bronco. "But so is being Black in America."

"If we don't do nothin' to change things, it will become worse. It's a risk to keep still. Like W.E.B. Du Bois say, social change will only happen through agitation and protest," Elise countered.

"I always believed you to be a Booker T. Washington supporter, Elise," Duncan chuckled.

Elise huffed. Yes, she once believed in the teachings of Booker T. Washington, who advocated gradualism. But she was afraid. Black folks and Black communities had developed skills in trade and agriculture to build economic strength and independence. But now everyone she knew and loved was losing their farms and land because of greed and private enterprise. It wasn't fair.

"Well, if you ask me," Beulah began, lifting herself from the chair to start collecting the dishes from the table, "God has the final say on everything, and despite what is happening, we shall not lose faith in Him and His glory."

"Amen to that, Beulah," Duncan agreed.

"But it also says in the Book of James that faith without works is dead," Elise countered. "Our faith should be accompanied by corresponding actions."

Bronco remained quiet and stoic. Elise stared at Bronco silently. Although she was still getting to know him, she wanted him to honestly side with her on this. She didn't want to force his hand. There was still much to learn. And if she were to march with Forrest, Elise knew that if Bronco came, she would feel a lot better.

Laughter and jokes were now substituted by a serious conversation about racism and change. Duncan mentioned his grandfather's brutal demise and his own run-ins with politics and white men.

"My grandfather once preached those same words, Elise. He believed in change while we lived in Louisiana. It was a vile place rooted in hatred, unlawfulness, and prejudice, a dangerous place for a Black man, especially for one with dreams and ambition. But we made do, we pushed on no matter what, and we had something. My granddaddy used to boast that he saw W.E.B. Du Bois speak, and it inspired him," Duncan proclaimed with now a seriousness in his voice.

Bronco and Elise were listening while Beulah continued to collect their dishes.

Duncan poured another glass of rye whisky to soothe his sudden uneasiness about the past. He continued, "My granddaddy was one of the few colored men who was able to read and write in town. So he began a colored newspaper, and my granddaddy was not one to hold his tongue. His paper wrote de truth 'bout white folks. White folks get to reading, they get agitated, and they come lookin' for my granddaddy one night, burned down the store where he published his paper. Then they say he raped a white woman and assaulted her husband. My grandaddy was sixty-two years old when they killed him, almost de age I am now. And that husband they say he assaulted, he half the age of my granddaddy and was built like a bull."

Duncan finished off the whisky and stared intently at Elise and Bronco. Thinking about his granddaddy's lynching was depressing, but there was a point he needed to make. "I's saying this to you both: be careful. White folks and changing they way of life is gon' be like oil and water. There will be challenges and consequences that you will face. And white folks gon' fight tooth and nail before they allow they chickens to come home and roost."

It was a haunting story—one that stuck to Bronco like glue. He liked Duncan and truly enjoyed his company. Duncan could easily be seen as a father figure like they said Sylvester was. He wasn't encouraging or trying to discourage Elise. He wanted her to be careful. The one thing for sure was that every Black person had a tragic story when it came to dealing with white folks, and it was inevitable that Elise would soon have hers to tell.

"I already made up my mind to go and protest with Forrest," said Elise. "I know it's the right thing to do."

Duncan grinned slightly. Elise was like a daughter to him. He respected her courage and morale. Change only came with boldness and courage. When her parents were killed in a car accident a few years ago, the tragedy devastated Duncan and his wife, too. Elise's parents were family. Old man George was like a brother to Duncan. The two men would sit outside on the porch, smoking their cheroots and downing a bottle of rye underneath the canopy of stars. They would talk and laugh for hours, enjoying each other's company. The two men also had an affinity for jazz and played the piano. George Lewis, a war veteran, was a warm, witty, well-read father and a stargazer with an itch for traveling. His wife, Abbey, was a former cleaning woman who dabbled in photography. Together, like Duncan and his wife, they were building something—structure, wealth, longevity, and leaving something behind for the next generation. Owning land was what they always dreamed of, and farming became their passion.

"Bronco, let's you and I go outside for a walk and talk, allow the ladies to finish up in here," Duncan suggested.

Duncan removed himself from the table and reached for his straw hat that hung askew on the wall. Bronco began to follow Duncan outdoors, but before he stepped out of the bungalow, he rotated to see Elise helping Beulah with the dishes. She stared back with a warm, radiant, affectionate smile that made him feel at home.

"I promise you, he won't bite," joked Elise, still beaming.

"My husband is harmless, Bronco. You men go out and talk. I'll take care of the missus in here," Beulah uttered.

Bronco was caught off guard with Beulah calling Elise his missus. It was odd. He was attracted to Elise, but he was a guest and a friend in her home. He didn't want to ruin things when he felt his only purpose was carrying out justice for the Baker family. And getting romantically involved with Elise would most likely complicate things.

It was a warm and cloudless night. Duncan lit a cheroot on his porch and stared up at the sky. The moon was casting a soft, silver glow on fields of land that stretched as far as the eye could see, giving a sense of openness and space. Even at night, the greenery was abundant and thriving, with crops and vegetation flourishing. Duncan was an adept farmer with a green thumb.

Bronco joined Duncan on the porch. Duncan smiled. "Pretty night, ain't it?"

"It is," said Bronco.

"You smoke?"

"Occasionally," Bronco answered.

"The missus don't like me smoking inside, so I's come out here and enjoys a smoke with nature, nothin' like it."

Duncan took a pull from the cheroot and exhaled. It was predictable that this was his favorite pastime. Duncan savored the taste of a good cheroot with both ends open on a warm summer night. The distant hoot of an owl was heard. The farm exuded a peaceful and picturesque atmosphere, with its quaint barn, winding paths, sprawling greenery, and serene landscape.

"I's figure you to be a war veteran, Bronco," Duncan uttered. "I's noticed the dog tags underneath ya collar."

Bronco nodded. "I am, 92nd Infantry Division. We fought in Italy."

Duncan grinned. "I'm a fightin' man myself. The 369th Infantry was the first regiment of the 93rd Division to reach France. I joined the service when I was twenty-four, right when they allowed colored men to register for the draft. Like most colored men, I believed fightin' for this country would win the respect of my white peers. I's wanted the opportunity to prove my loyalty, patriotism, and worthiness for equal treatment for a country that treated me second-class. I's became a good soldier, a got-damn killer for this country. When the Germans were making raids into allied territory, I's fought off an entire raiding party with only a pistol and a knife, killed me six Germans, and wounded others. My actions allowed a few wounded comrades to escape capture and led to the seizure of a stockpile of German arms."

Duncan became absorbed in the tragedies he'd faced in World War I as he continued to smoke and share his stories with Bronco. It was a time in his life that he wanted to forget. Like Bronco, he too suffered from damaging memories and issues such as anxiety and depression from the impact of a war with nearly 85 million fatalities.

The owl continued to hoot nearby while the men felt the dampness of dew-covered grass beneath their feet. Being in the presence of nature and witnessing the cycles of life on a farm was inspiring and uplifting for Duncan.

"For damn near a month, my unit held their position against German assaults. After a brief break from the front, my unit was again placed in the middle of the

German offensive, this time at Méricourt, France. We fought just as hard as them white soldiers with little to no respect or recognition. Yet, a white sergeant decided to hang three colored soldiers for sleeping with foreign white women while my white captain gets promoted for our actions," Duncan proclaimed with tightened teeth.

Bronco understood Duncan's pain and anger. He'd seen his fair share of racism and segregation overseas. Despite promises of equal treatment in the army, African Americans were relegated to separate regiments commanded by white officers. Black soldiers received less pay than white soldiers, inferior benefits, and poorer food and equipment.

Bronco wondered where Duncan was going with his story. He barely knew the man, but he did appreciate his kindness and hospitality.

"I's come back from that war an angry and broken man and stays that way for a while . . . until I met Beulah." Duncan smiled. "She the best thing that ever happened to me. She fixed me. She gave me a purpose to live, along with farming," Duncan said, becoming reminiscent of the past.

The bugs chirped. The moon continued to shine as an orb in the sky, and the balmy night made their skin sweat quietly. Even at night, the Southern heat was a beast, and their sweat was a badge of courage.

"It's hotter'n blue blazes tonight," Duncan uttered. He removed a hankie from his back pocket and wiped the trickling sweat from his brow.

The men walked farther from the house, trotting on the dew-covered grass toward an open and extensive field where, surprisingly, Duncan was growing cotton across 400 acres. The shimmering white balls seemed to stretch forever toward the horizon, looking like a whiteout.

"Ironic, huh? My grandaddy and daddy, once slaves, used to pick this from sunup to sundown. Now here we are two generations later, where their grandson and son is profiting off the same thing they slaved doing," Duncan said reflectively.

"We came a long way," Bronco said.

"Have we?"

"We ain't in chains no more," said Bronco.

"Yet, they still keep us in bondage." Duncan chuckled, which was reserved. "The sacrifices and hard labor that comes with life on a small farm. The unending hours of sweat, the many days of the blistering sun and so many nights of achin' muscles, the weeks of dullness and years of hopeless toll, all to reap the vague harvest of the dark, brooding earth . . . all for some man representin' a company to try and take it all away for nothin'."

"Who's trying to take your farm?" Bronco asked him.

"I was approached by a man named Mr. Lockheart a few weeks ago. He wanted to know 'bout my debt, then gave me a price to purchase my land and said it was fair. He gave me two weeks to make a decision, although I knows already he done made it for me."

Duncan exhaled, brooding, knowing this was a fight he couldn't win by himself. He was a midsized farmer barely making do. Every year, it was becoming more challenging for him to maintain, from equipment failure, farm production expenses increasing, the price of his crop going down, and facing discrimination and disenfranchisement as a Black farmer. He'd been denied loans he was entitled to and told he wasn't eligible for specific federally funded farm programs that were put out to give farmers support.

The boards were dominated by segregationists. If a Black farmer needed money to grow his crops next year, the board would ensure that the farmer would never side with the NAACP or go out to vote or march against segregation. In other words, toe the company line. If you went against the board, you were most likely denied loans and funding and eventually lost your farm.

"I never thought after fightin' for this country that forty years later I would have to fight to keep my land, fight for my livelihood," Duncan proclaimed vehemently. "The worst of it is I haven't told Beulah yet . . . that they might come for our land. I don't know how to tell that woman in there that this might be all taken from us. It will break her."

"They haven't come for anything yet. There's still a chance to do something," Bronco said.

"We'ze bein' pushed out, Bronco. Every Black farmer in the region," Duncan said sadly.

That affable and jolly man he met the other day unexpectedly transitioned into a man with a million and one worries. The look in his eyes showed exhaustion. But Duncan remained tough and steadfast with this agility to keep fighting for what he loved and believed in no matter what.

"They will come for Elise soon," Duncan uttered. "You and I, I's knows we the same. I felt somethin' different 'bout you the day we met."

"What you think is different about me?"

"It's you against the world, like I was once," said Duncan. "I's see that fight in you, and I know Elise is gonna need it. Damn it. We all gonna need it."

Chapter Sixteen

Fight for Freedom

It was a beautiful Tuesday afternoon in the small Mississippi town of Monroe. The town had a Southern charm, where Main Street was lined with mom-and-pop cafes and bars located in wooden buildings and anchored by a gazebo in the town square. There was a whistle-stop saloon, a drugstore, the local theater showing the latest sci-fi movie, a post office, and a sweet shop selling lemon phosphates and cherry Cokes and all the candy one could buy. The soda fountain shop was the hangout spot for adults and children, and the local barbershop was the town's social network hub. Old and young men were the translation and new sources of local interest that took place while they were waiting their turn for a haircut or a shave. The shop had three chairs for barbers, and the talk of sports, unions, work, politics, and segregation was habit. Milly's Diner and Restaurant was one of the oldest establishments in town. It had a limited menu and seating for fewer than twenty folks. For seventy-five cents, patrons could enjoy some of the best hot roast beef with potatoes and gravy served open-faced with sauce on the bread and potatoes. It was everyone's favorite.

In the small town, Sundays were for church, family dinners, and social gatherings and activities. The locals would play sports, card games, or board games at these family gatherings while enjoying homemade ice cream and a cool glass of lemonade and receiving news updates. Monroe was a slice of Southern comfort and happiness. Still, segregation was blatant and flagrant, like a tackle on a football field. News of marches and protests from the "coloreds" began to spread throughout the town, and everyone was growing concerned. Folks didn't want their way of life interrupted by some meaningless boycott or incident.

"Are the coloreds plotting something, Sheriff?" a resident named Agnes had asked him out of the blue.

"No need to worry about a thing, Agnes. I protect this town. I know what's happening," the sheriff had replied.

The sheriff and local authorities were trying to soothe everyone's concerns by letting them know that he and his deputies had everything under control. They were well aware of something brewing from the colored side of town. Sheriff Duke had a network of spies and Black loyalists on his payroll. The name Forrest Tolson started to become a frequent name from his moles.

"He a colored man from up North, Sheriff Duke. I don't know from where exactly. But he tryin' to stir up trouble in the church. He wanna organize things, he steadily shoutin' and hollering 'bout wantin' justice for Sylvester and his family, and marching for voting rights here in town," his mole had spewed willingly.

"And this nigger, what he look like?" the sheriff had asked.

"I say he a handsome man, Sheriff . . . he kinda tall, dresses nice, and talks with big and fancy words."

"Do you know where this nigger stay at?"

His mole shook his head. "No, sir. I don't. But I can find out for you."

"You make sure you do so, ya hear, boy? But you did good," the sheriff had complimented his mole. "Keep me updated, and I promise you, you and ya family will be fine."

Sheriff Duke had huffed and frowned. He hated when agitators and activists, Black or white, came into his town to stir trouble and disrupt their way of life. He, too, had heard about the Civil Rights Movement. The men at the barbershop began talking about it. Recently, members of the Regional Council of Negro Leadership (RCNL) coordinated an effective boycott against Mississippi gas stations that denied restroom access to Black patrons. This form of protest unsettled figures like Sheriff Benny and Harvey Roth, who recognized the growing influence of organizations such as the RCNL throughout the South.

The group played a key role in exposing misconduct by the Mississippi State Highway Patrol and encouraged Black residents to deposit their funds in the Black-owned Tri-State Bank of Nashville. The bank subsequently offered crucial financial assistance to civil rights activists who were impacted by the "credit squeeze" enforced by the White Citizens' Councils.

Meanwhile, in Montgomery, Alabama, law enforcement officers and their allies became aware of the arrest of Claudette Colvin, a young Black woman who, in March, had refused to give up her seat on a bus to a white passenger. In Montgomery, Alabama, the sheriff and his cronies also got wind of an arrest made of a colored woman named Claudette Colvin back in March for not giving up her seat on the bus for a white passenger.

One of Sheriff Duke's main goals was to find this Tolson nigger and make an example out of him for coming into his hometown and poisoning the minds of the niggers here. Unbeknownst to the sheriff, he would run into Forrest Tolson real soon.

A blue Packard, a black Chevrolet Deluxe Club Coupe, and an old pickup truck with passengers in the back

arrived in the town square surrounded by historic buildings from the early nineteenth and twentieth centuries.
The buildings displayed civic pride. The vehicles came
to a complete stop outside the small-town courthouse.
The doors opened, and several colored men and women
climbed out of the cars and stared apprehensively at
the courthouse, knowing the task would be challenging.
Among the group of activists was Forrest Tolson, who
led the charge like a general on the battlefield. He was
dressed neatly in a black suit, a black fedora, and black
patent leather shoes on his spirited feet. They had the
element of surprise during the early afternoon when
most townsfolk were at work, home, or busy doing
chores during the day.

"Remember, we came to register to vote. We stay calm,
polite, and answer their questions the best we can," said
Tolson calmly. "This isn't going to be easy or kind, but it's
our beginning. This is how we shape our future."

The group nodded.

Forrest Tolson was the first to ascend the stairs toward
the courthouse, and they all followed his lead with ner-
vousness and vigor. Each step closer to the courthouse
lobby felt like traveling a mile on a field full of landmines
for the activists. They moved together, in sync, focused
on their objective like ants marching, sweat dripping
from their brows courtesy of the hot summer sun. A
small group of local whites noticed the group of colored
folks ascending the courthouse stairs and frowned.

A dozen colored men and women entered the courthouse lobby on a mission to register to vote and dressed
in their Sunday best. Thanks to Forrest, they arrived with
their registration documents completed with meticulous
handwriting. Everyone smiled with satisfaction as if
completing the document were a mountain conquered.
They moved toward the register as a coalition and im-

mediately caught the attention of the registrar, a thin, balding 40-year-old male reading the newspaper at a window marked ADMINISTRATION OFFICE. Seeing several colored folks enter the lobby made the registrar stand up and scowl.

"You niggers can't be in here," he exclaimed.

"And why not?" Forrest Tolson interjected. "We came here to register to vote. This is the administration office, right?"

"This is not the time and place," the registrar fired back.

"You are open, aren't you? We came here to register to vote," Forrest Tolson protested.

"You stirrin' trouble, nigger?"

"No, sir. We don't want no trouble. We all came here politely to vote. The Fifteenth Amendment states that the right of citizens of the United States to vote shall not be denied or abridged by the United States or by any State on account of race, color, or previous condition of servitude," Forrest proclaimed wholeheartedly.

"You some uppity, smart nigger, boy?"

Forrest gritted his teeth and held his head high. He stared at the registrar intently, still keeping his composure, and replied, "No, sir."

The registrar stared at the ascetic black faces standing politely but firmly behind Forrest Tolson, each orchestrated with a purpose. They'd all seen their fair share of mistreatment, marginalization, and dehumanization because of the color of their skin. Enough was enough. Change was needed. The only thing between them and voting was a form and the registrar. But something so simple and easy for white folks, like it was Sunday morning, was challenging and hazardous to their health, like a battlefield.

The registrar was familiar with one of the ladies standing behind Forrest. He smirked and uttered, "Ain't you

Mrs. Garrett's maid? Wonder what ol' Mrs. Garrett would think seein' her nigger maid stirrin' trouble at the courthouse. Or how 'bout I ring up the sheriff, have him deal with you niggers?"

"Like I said, sir, we ain't stirrin' no trouble. We here to vote," Forrest repeated coolly.

Forrest walked toward the window and placed his form on the counter. Soon, others followed his lead and began placing their completed registration forms on the counter. Seeing this, the registrar's brows narrowed tightly. He began to burn with anger and brim with hostility.

"You niggers are making a huge mistake," the registrar exclaimed.

"The mistake is not allowing us to vote, sir. We came here for a reason, and we're here to stand on that reason," Forrest Tolson contested.

The problem wasn't going away, and the man needed backup. The registrar marched toward the phone behind the counter and snatched it up with a sense of urgency. While he began to dial for help, he glared at Forrest Tolson with such disdain it was as if he saw the trouble-maker as a cockroach he wanted to crush with his shoe.

Sheriff Duke's patrol car arrived at the small court-house. He and his deputy, Calvin, climbed out of the patrol car to a growing mob of white onlookers perched outside of the courthouse. Word had quickly gotten around town about coloreds entering the small court-house, and they'd swiftly gathered around the court. White folks stood around in groups. Some stood on car roofs or the backs of pickups. A few brandished clubs, and some were waving Confederate flags. They were angry. They heard rumors that the registrar, Billie, may have been assaulted. But it wasn't true. They also began to shout, "Niggers, go home!"

Sheriff Duke casually placed the Bullock shantung straw Western hat with the star symbol onto his head and looked around. He kept his professional composure, but what he saw made him proud to be the sheriff of this town—good ol' white folks coming together to keep the niggers out and away.

"Sheriff, get them niggers outta there right now! How dare they walk into that place like they own it?" a portly man in his forties exclaimed.

"I will, Roger. Me and my deputy will handle things," Sheriff Duke replied with a smile.

"You do that, Sheriff!"

The crowd's rage was manifested through bigotry and anger. The sheriff glanced at his deputy and nodded. They began to walk up the stairs toward the courthouse with authority. There was a mean arrogance about them. They were all too ready to eradicate niggers from the courthouse with extreme prejudice and violence. The badge and their pale skin color gave them the authority to do so. Their mission was to protect their people's way of life and safety, and they did so with aggressive behavior, even if it caused injury, discomfort, or death to their victims.

Sheriff Duke and Calvin entered the lobby of the building to see over a dozen colored men and women standing firm and silent by the window of the administration office. The presence of the sheriff and his deputy now altered things. This was it. This was what they'd prepared for, an altercation with law enforcement. But however it went, they were trained and taught to remain calm and firm.

Sheriff Duke glared at every black face inside his courthouse and fumed. "Who the nigger in charge of this buffoonery?" he shouted.

At first, no one responded. Each man and woman stood there in silence, blocking the registrar, who was seething behind the window. He was finally relieved to see the sheriff's presence. He wasn't alone with the coloreds. He had help.

"I'm not gonna ask politely again. I said, who's the nigger in charge here?"

The sheriff began to grow impatient. His hand slightly rested against his holstered revolver, and his eyes were like icy daggers against the troublemakers.

Forrest Tolson stepped forward with bravery and calmness. "I am," he uttered with nerve.

Sheriff Duke shot Forrest a threatening glance that didn't make the man flinch or quiver. The sheriff approached Forrest, removing his nightstick from its perch. It was a tool the sheriff recently used to break bones in faces and hands, crack ribs, and shatter colored men's kneecaps.

"You that nigger named Forrest Tolson, aren't you? The nigger that's causing trouble in my town?" Sheriff Duke exclaimed.

Forrest wasn't surprised that the sheriff knew his name. It was expected. *When a Black man begins preaching for civil rights, justice, and liberties against tyranny, segregation, and depression, they immediately become targets.* Forrest felt the Sheriff's stifling breath down his collar. But he refused to become a timid mouse in his presence.

"I'm not here to cause anyone no trouble. I'm here to help my people."

"You helping niggers is causing me trouble," the sheriff growled.

"I'm here to correct the plight of and prejudice against my people. And that begins with our right to vote."

"Your people," the sheriff scoffed, tightening his grip around the nightstick. "Your people have no rights here. This is a public facility for whites only."

The activists behind Forrest stood there with fear fluttering in their stomachs and dread twisting in their guts when seven local white men from outside decided to aid the sheriff and the deputy in confronting and dispersing the activists from the courthouse. A large growl of aggression and excitement rose from these white men as they were ready to implement violence against the coloreds. They began shouting and cursing, "You niggers looking for fuckin' trouble?"

One of the activists, Emily, kept shifting from one foot to another, her hands trembling and feet fidgeting. She began to shrink back in fear. The mob inside was growing and festering with rage. She was 19 and began believing this was a mistake. Others wanted to cower too and retreat from their agenda. However, they all were in awe at how Forrest Tolson stood tall with bravery, not folding under fear or intimidation. He was remarkable, unequivocally steadfast with his demands, and they couldn't let him down. He was there fighting for them. Besides, there was no easy way out.

"Nigger, I said leave this place now before I arrest your black ass for trespassing," Sheriff Duke exclaimed heatedly.

Forrest Tolson refused and repeated, "We came here to register, Sheriff."

The remark angered the sheriff. He scowled and heatedly began poking Forrest in the chest with the nightstick. The other white men behind the sheriff were hoping for resistance with their clubs raised, glaring at the activists. Forrest frowned and clenched his fists. The sheriff wanted a reaction from him.

"Come on, boy. Hit me. I'm worth it," the sheriff taunted.

Forrest Tolson wanted to knock his head off, but he knew the repercussions that came with striking a white man, a sworn-in sheriff at that. He knew he couldn't win this way. The law wasn't on his side.

Sheriff Duke sneered and gave another sharp poke into Forrest's chest. Then he shoved Forrest into the others with force and spewed, "Hit me, nigger." The sheriff dared him.

Forrest seethed but remained unruffled. His stomach clenched. Things were getting out of control. The sheriff and the small mob wanted violence and bloodshed instead of their immediate arrests and retreat from the courthouse. Everyone was agitated. Calvin had his nightstick clenched between his fists, eager for harm. He glared at one particular colored boy named James. James was tall and muscular for his age. He was 19, wearing a striped polo shirt. Calvin shot his ice-cold blue eyes at James and shouted, "You got a problem with me, nigger?"

"No, sir," James replied politely.

"You eyeballing me, nigger?" Calvin chided.

"No, sir. I wasn't."

Calvin had already decided that he was getting his hands dirty today. The coloreds' audacity to charge into a civic place and make demands was ill-mannered, disrespectful, and reckless. He and Sheriff Duke believed they needed to be taught a lesson to discourage other niggers from doing the same thing.

"You niggers think you can do whatever you want?" Calvin continued.

Calvin stepped closer to James, dripping with bigotry and hatred. He didn't give it a second thought when he raised the nightstick and furiously brought it down on James's face. Blood spewed and James reacted. He charged and punched the deputy in the face so hard the man damn near lifted off his feet and stumbled backward.

The activists began to holler and scream. The incident gave the mob a reason to charge and implement their brand of justice.

Sheriff Duke began attacking Forrest, hurling insults at him. "You're under arrest, nigger!"

The two men began grappling with each other, and it's what the mob was waiting for. They launched into the activists, clubbing, punching, and stomping, finding joy or pleasure in hurting Black people. A young female protester took a particularly devastating blow to the head, and she went down. One of her cohorts tried to cover her with his body, but he was brutally kicked and attacked. A black man in his early twenties balled his fists and struck the sheriff from behind as he was trying to arrest Forrest. But two white men grabbed him and slammed him into the wall, and then they began beating him with their clubs and knuckle-dusters. He fell to his knees, surrendering, but they didn't care. They continued to beat him until he was unconscious.

Chaos continued to ensue inside the small courthouse. Activists who hadn't been tackled, beaten, or subdued escaped into the street and were immediately met with yelling, screaming insults, spitting, and cursing from dozens of white onlookers who surrounded the courthouse.

Meanwhile, Forrest Tolson was shocked and concerned for his cohorts. Things had grown uglier than he predicted. While the sheriff was beating him and placing him under arrest, his allies for civil rights were being brutally beaten right before him. James continued to wrestle with the deputy. He was a powerful boy with young, brute strength, and it was apparent the deputy had bitten off more than he could chew when he decided to attack James. Although James was injured and bleeding, he was still a wrecking ball of might mixed with resentment.

Therefore, the cavalry came with full force as several white men were on James like white on rice.

Calvin continued battering James with his nightstick when he decided to remove his revolver and calmly shoot James twice in the chest and stomach. The gunshots resonated throughout the area like a firecracker going off, followed by a moment of stillness. It finally registered what had happened, and the ladies began screaming. James slumped to the floor.

He was dead.

Chapter Seventeen

White Butterfly

"What in the hell happened at that courthouse, Sheriff? This is a fuckin' disaster," Benny Lockheart griped. "A colored man shot dead by one of your deputies?"

"Niggers happened, Mr. Lockheart," Sheriff Duke replied. "We tried to get them to disperse, but they were stubborn and began attacking us. You know how niggers can get, rude and violent."

Benny fumed. The last thing he needed was bad press. It was one thing for colored folks to be harmed or killed on their own grounds and in their neighborhoods, but it was a different story when a tragedy of this magnitude happened on state property—and inside a civic place.

"How many were there?"

"Oh, I says over a dozen or so, but we got things under control," the sheriff replied. "And we finally arrested the nigger that's been stirrin' trouble 'round these parts, Mr. Lockheart. He's the ringleader of this disaster that's been putting foolishness and nonsense inside these niggers' heads. His name is Forrest Tolson."

Benny huffed. "Where is he?"

"Where the nigger belongs, in a cage."

"Take me to him."

***

Forrest Tolson was in bad shape. He and the other activists had been badly beaten, arrested, and thrown into holding cells at the police station. A few men needed to go to the hospital. They were clustered shoulder to shoulder and in pain. However, the sheriff was adamant that they would suffer in a stark, cramped cell where a single bulb cast a harsh, unforgiving light across the cell, creating long shadows that danced along the walls. It was an oppressive move. The women were in an adjacent holding cell, scared and weeping. Forrest suffered from broken bones in his left hand, a black eye, and cracked ribs. He and his advocates could feel the constant gaze of the deputy and his cronies. It felt like they were an unblinking eye that watched his every move.

James was dead, and everyone was devastated. Forrest was so heartbroken that the physical pain he felt was nothing compared to a young man dying under his watch. He knew there would be no justice for James. He knew they would make James out to have been the aggressor, utterly lie, and say he was the one that'd attacked the deputy first. Forrest's once proud stance against the oppressive regime and voter suppression was now tilted under the weight of the unintended consequences. His teary eyes were wide with a mix of internal conflict and guilt, and for a moment, they held a depth of regret that spoke volumes.

Benny Lockheart arrived in the depths of the police station accompanied by the sheriff and his deputy. The site of Deputy Calvin made everyone inside the cell cringe with anger, upset, and worry. The sheriff and his deputy stared at the occupants inside the jail cell with no remorse for what had happened. In fact, Calvin smirked and uttered, "If you ask me, we should put every last one of these niggers outta their misery."

"Have they been seen by a doctor yet?" Benny asked the men.

"No, sir. I don't know no nigger doctors," the sheriff replied.

"Get them a fucking doctor, or take them to the hospital, Sheriff. With one man shot dead at the courthouse, the last thing we need is all of the got-damn NAACP coming into this town raising hell. I don't want this thing turning into more of a damn disaster than it already is," Benny Lockheart replied with finality.

"I'll see what we can do, Mr. Lockheart," the sheriff said indignantly.

Benny Lockheart pivoted and marched out of the holding area, fuming. He was upset, but not about James's death. He was worried about the unwanted attention to the death of a colored man being killed by a deputy during his attempt to register to vote. Although James was considered a second-class citizen among his peers, it was still a bad look on the town. The death of the Bakers was a nightmare. Still, Harvey Roth's political and media connections somehow buried the tragedy from the people and the public. If word had gotten out about a family being wiped out for their land, Benny knew that his Mississippi town would have become ground zero for this Civil Rights Movement that was growing.

Benny slammed the Panama hat onto his head as he stormed out of the police station and into the sun-drenched, busy town. There was nothing timid about the July heat. The radiating temperature had him sweating in the haze of the afternoon, and he could already feel his shirt begin to cling to his back. He had a lot on his mind.

"Good afternoon to you, Mr. Lockheart," a passerby politely said.

Benny replied with a simple nod as he briskly walked toward a 1949 Chevrolet Business Coupe. He was in no mood for chitchat with the locals. He climbed into his vehicle, started the engine, and then hesitated behind the wheel for a moment to collect himself. He then drove off toward home. Despite the terrible incident at the courthouse, Benny still had other duties to execute, one being a husband and a father. The afternoon was hot, sunny, and enchanting. Mr. Roth had invited him and his family to attend an exceptional gathering at his home. Mr. Roth insisted that Benny bring his family.

Benny's Chevrolet Fleetline arrived at the vast estate, where numerous vehicles were parked and spread across the far-reaching front lawn to the massive estate, indicating things had already begun. The doors flew open, and Benny's two daughters, Karen and Susan, immediately flew out from the back seat excitedly, clad in what they would consider their Sunday's best: matching blue dresses with white shoes, and blue bows tied in their long blond hair. Ruth climbed out of the passenger seat wearing a straight-neck sleeveless polka-dot and striped flare tank dress and carrying a cute handbag. Benny had changed into a casual knit polo sweater golf shirt with a collar and short sleeves, and nice khakis.

Mr. Roth and his wife, Catherine, were hosting a garden party on their estate. It came with the best that money could buy on their lush, floral-filled property with blooming flowers, lush greenery, and natural beauty. It was a social gathering held outdoors near his wife's attractive and sprawling garden. It included a gazebo, a large pool, and more land than the eye could see, where numerous guests enjoyed food, drinks, and socializing in a picturesque setting. These gatherings allowed people to unite, socialize, and strengthen relationships in a relaxed setting.

The girls' eyes grew wide with interest and excitement as they saw how big this house was compared to theirs.

"This house is so pretty, Daddy," Karen said.

"You girls stay close and behave," Ruth uttered to them.

The girls giggled and ran off while Catherine Roth marched toward Ruth and Benny, wearing a sleeveless floral dress that hit at a midi length and a pair of pretty sandals. She was a beautiful woman in her late thirties with long golden hair, porcelain skin, hollow cheeks, and emerald eyes that seemed she had stolen from a cat. She clutched a martini and had a smile on her that seemed forever.

"You must be the lovely Mrs. Lockheart," Catherine said.

Ruth matched her smile and replied in her thick Southern accent, "Guilty as charged."

The ladies giggled and greeted each other with polite kisses to each other's cheeks. "I'm so proud the two of you could come, and you've brought such lovely young girls."

"Thank you for inviting us," Ruth returned. "This is so beautiful."

"Thank you for coming. My husband and I are delighted to have you both. Me casa, your casa. Feel free to grab a drink, mingle, and meet everyone. You know exposure to nature can reduce stress and improve overall well-being."

Ruth smiled. This was her element, what she had worked so hard to achieve: becoming a socialite. She knew she and Catherine would become best friends because they were the same. Ruth and Catherine began to chat like old best friends.

"Pardon the interruption, but is your husband around?" Benny asked her.

"He is. He's entertaining the men with his shotguns and skeet shooting farther down the lawn, near the lake," Catherine replied.

Benny nodded. "Thank you."

"Have fun, dear."

"She'll be fine, Benny. I'm going to take good care of the missus," Catherine said.

There was no doubt that she would. Benny turned and began the trip through the scene of blooming flowers, lush greenery, and some folks playing croquet. This classic lawn game added a touch of elegance to the garden party. Farther down, a game of bocce ball was being played. It was a game that encouraged friendly competition and teamwork. A gentle breeze created a serene ambiance that enchanted the overall experience.

Eventually, Benny arrived at the spot where Harvey Roth was hosting several men for a round of skeet shooting. The event involved using shotguns to try to shatter clay targets that were launched rapidly into the air from different directions.

Harvey was positioned with the double-barreled shotgun in his hands.

"Pull," Harvey exclaimed, and three clay targets immediately flew into the air. Harvey expertly took aim and fired. Subsequently, the clay targets exploded in midair, being met with gunfire from the shotgun.

Everyone clapped.

Harvey nodded, impressed by his skills. Harvey was accompanied by seven other men entertaining the sport with him. While Harvey chose the double-barreled shotgun, others gripped either the pump-action or the semiautomatic. When he spotted Benny's arrival, he nodded his way with a slight smile.

"Mr. Lockheart, I'm glad you could make it," said Harvey.

"It's always a pleasure," Benny replied.

"I want to introduce you to a few close friends and my investors," said Harvey.

One by one, Harvey began introducing Benny to his associates. "This is Gabriel Spector, one of the best got-damn closers in the city, and a good friend of mines for nearly twenty years."

Gabriel was a tall, handsome man with bright blue eyes like the sky and a muted smile.

"This is Rick Macht, a Harvard law graduate and a senior partner at one of the top law firms in New York City."

Rick Macht was the opposite of Gabriel: he was a short, balding man with thick stubble across his lip. Harvey went on to introduce Benny to Adam Nesbitt, an expert on all financial matters; Edward Eton, an investment banker with a net worth that nearly rivaled Rockefeller's; and Ryan Gray, one of the cofounders of a hedge fund that moved more money than the combined GDPs of several countries. Benny Lockheart was astounded to socialize with men of such wealth and caliber. He knew these men were the future for him and his town.

"Do you partake in the activity?" Harvey asked Benny.

"I'm afraid not," Benny replied.

"Too bad. It's a relaxing pursuit. It helps with focus and quick judgment, knowing when to execute. You don't shoot at the target directly. You predict where the target will be and then take action," Harvey said. "It's like any investment. Projection is the key to success."

Benny nodded. *Duly noted.*

"Come take a stroll with me, Mr. Lockheart. Let's have a talk," Harvey said politely.

The two men started to walk away from the skeet shooting range and headed toward a small lake that sparkled like a surface of crystals in the bright afternoon sun. Harvey walked alongside the lake, holding the shot-gun and pointing it away from Benny. He seemed lost in thought, staring ahead with something on his mind.

"I find it interesting that you liked to be called Mr. Lockheart rather than Congressman," said Harvey.

"It helps me to remain connected with the people, reminds everyone that I'm still one of them," Benny explained.

Harvey chuckled softly. "Deceptive, because you're not one of the people. You're a man in a position to help form and build this country where it needs to be. If you were one of the people, then you and I wouldn't be in business."

Benny was somewhat taken aback by the remark.

"The people, they're nothing but sheep that need a shepherd. And sometimes that shepherd needs to carry a shotgun or sword rather than an old stick. You think a stick will keep the wolves away? We keep the wolves away by becoming wolves ourselves. But we must also remind the sheep that they're sheep, even if we need to punish and discipline a few of them to keep everyone in line," Harvey proclaimed.

Benny was listening.

"I heard what happened down at the courthouse the other day," Harvey mentioned.

"It was an unfortunate incident, Mr. Roth. I'm handling things as we speak."

"One nigger is dead because a few other niggers believed they no longer wanted to be sheep anymore, because they decided to become equal like a shepherd. Shepherds are meant to lead the flock to greener pastures and water and areas of good forage. The day niggers walk on two legs like a shepherd and think they can lead the herd to greater pastures is the day I go broke and poor. And as you know, I have more money than God Himself," Harvey proclaimed with gravity.

Benny took in the lake as they walked. It seemed fresh, simple, and timeless. However, it was nothing compared to Lake Nur, where that lake would shimmer like a sheet of glass under the morning sun.

"I'm ready to bring a lot of money into this town, Mr. Lockheart. The lake, the land, the people—it's all worth the investment. The investors you've met are growing impatient. Therefore, I need those nigger deeds to their farms and lands so I and my investors can proceed with enhancing this town with the best we have to offer," Harvey said.

"It will get done, Mr. Roth."

"You're a fuckin' congressman, Mr. Lockheart. You hold one of the highest positions a man can have in this state. The people elected you. They trust and respect you to guide them toward greener pastures. I see it. So imagine the level of admiration and reverence you'll receive when we create more jobs, bring to this town better homes and a suburbia that will make folks feel safe, secure, and a part of something special. Along with increasing economic growth," Harvey proclaimed.

"It's what we all want," Benny replied.

"It's what everyone wants."

Harvey Roth paused to observe a hawk soaring above his land. The bird circled high in the sky, homing in on something below. Suddenly, it veered into a steep dive. The hawk had spotted its prey and wasted no time. It swooped toward the ground with its sharp talons, ready to snatch something. Swiftly and accurately, it struck its target, then ascended with powerful wing movements, gripping a squirming rodent in its talons.

"Sometimes, in order to create, something must be destroyed," Harvey uttered while watching the hawk disappear into the sky, its prey helpless in the bird's strong grasp.

Benny had also observed the hawk. It happened quickly and was something special to see—birds of prey circling above, soaring predators, or guardians of the sky taking what they needed to survive. The hawk resembled

Harvey Roth, a predator with many talons looking to hunt the weakest and easiest prey below.

The men kept talking and walking. Three thousand acres was quite a lot of land. The man owned so much land that it seemed to have its own zip code and could even have a landing strip for planes to arrive.

"Are you and your wife having a good time?" Harvey asked him.

"Yes. We were happy to be invited," Benny replied. "And the kids love your home."

Harvey smiled. "I'm happy to hear that. The most important things in the world are family and love."

"I agree. Family is not an important thing. It's everything," Benny stated.

"I feel we are two kindred spirits, Mr. Lockheart."

"It seems we are."

The two men began heading back to the others, where the men were still occupied with skeet shooting. It seemed like it was something that the group could do forever. Each man was highly skilled with the shotgun and their aim.

"Come, let's familiarize you with the activity," Harvey told Benny.

Eventually, Benny gave in, and Harvey handed him a pump-action shotgun to start. Benny wrapped his hand around the forearm, which was linked to one of two bars operating the action—both chambering the first round and cycling the gun after each shot to load the next shell. To fire smoothly, the shooter had to pull the forearm back and then push it forward, a motion that often-caused slip-ups on the skeet range because it required quickness, consistency, and accuracy.

"Pull," Benny hollered.

Two clay targets flew into the blue sky. Benny quickly took aim. He missed the first target by a mile but hit the second before it was too late.

"You see that? You're a natural at this. We're going to do great things, Mr. Lockheart," Harvey said.

The hot summer day transitioned into a beautiful, balmy night with fireworks for the guests. Benny, along with his family and other guests, took comfort on cozy cushions and rustic benches, the proper seating arrangements to view the impressive fireworks display that made the children's jaws drop. It was an unforgettable sight as they exploded in the sky and filled it with colors and light. The colors were so bright it almost felt like daylight.

While Harvey stood beside his wife, they observed the spectacular fireworks display. He turned to Benny, accompanied by his family, and smiled as he raised his glass of wine slightly, indicating that the best was yet to come.

The girls were asleep in the back seat of the Fleetline while Benny drove his family home. It was late, and it had been a long day. Ruth leaned into Benny's shoulder while he focused on the road. She felt content about the day. Catherine Roth had become her new best friend. They were like two schoolgirls on a playground. The wives sipped wine, gossiped, and shared stories about marriage and were two peas in a pod. Their husbands were usually two businessmen who forgot they had wives at home.

"Catherine is great," said Ruth.

"I'm glad the two of you hit it off," Benny said.

"We did. I wish they had invited us over sooner. There's so much to do with her and to talk about. We have a lot of catching up to do."

Benny smiled. It was good to see her happy. He wanted his wife to remain close to Catherine. Harvey Roth was an important man. If their wives got along, it was great for business.

They arrived home right before midnight. Benny parked close to the wraparound porch, which made it easier to carry their girls inside. However, Ruth became baffled when he left the car idling while escorting the girls into their home.

"Do you plan on going back out at this hour?" Ruth asked him.

"I won't be long, dear. It's—"

"Business, right?" she interjected gruffly.

Benny was temporarily stunned and caught off guard by her response. He picked up on the slight bitterness in her tone. She stared coldly at him with her dark eyes and tightened brow, a sign of concern or confusion. It was a subtle yet expressive gesture that conveyed a lot. Ruth stared at her husband, yearning to ask that daunting question. It was on the edge of her tongue, and she was ready to blurt it out faster than lightning could strike. Instead, she sighed sharply and muted her concern. As an alternative, she surrendered to remaining the doting and naive housewife and said, "Just don't be out too late. I'll put the girls to bed."

Benny softly smiled. "I love you."

"I love you too."

He pivoted, marched back to the idling Fleetline, and climbed back into the driver's seat. From the porch, Ruth watched her husband leave and felt a flick of irritation. However, she swallowed her frustration and went into the house to put the girls to bed.

Benny arrived at the abandoned plantation an hour after midnight. The previous day, he'd sent Virginia a message via Cory asking to meet tonight. Benny followed his routine toward the old plantation home, passing through a hole in the fence, and proceeded toward the grounds while clutching his flashlight. He was carrying a bottle of wine and a blanket. He wanted to make up for

their last encounter, when they'd argued over the Bakers'
tragedy.

An hour passed, and Virginia had yet to show up.
Benny began to worry. Was she still upset about his
earlier actions? Eventually, he concluded that she wasn't
going to show up. He released a heavy sigh, his lips
pressing together tightly, and retreated to his vehicle.
Collapsing into the driver's seat, a profound emptiness
opened inside him, threatening to swallow him whole as
he returned home to his wife.

Chapter Eighteen

Don't You Want to Be Free?

News of James's death spread like wildfire throughout the community. Folks were devastated and angry. The boy done got himself killed protesting for his civil rights. It wasn't anything new—a lynching by gunfire, but James was only 19. He was supposed to have an entire wholesome life ahead of him. Instead, the boy was going to be buried next to his daddy today. His father was killed ten years ago, lynched by a white mob for something as terrible as looking too long at a passing white woman. Forrest Tolson and the others who were with him had been beaten, jailed, and then treated for their injuries at a colored hospital. The sheriff wanted to bring up charges against everyone, from disorderly conduct to aggravated assault on a police officer.

Meanwhile, the men responsible for James's murder and the severe beating of several Negros wouldn't be charged with a crime. Why would they? Black folks in Mississippi were treated as second-class citizens.

The Pentecostal church was packed like sardines with mourners. His mother, Gloria, was beside herself with absolute grief. She was clad in all black, along with wearing a black funeral hat with a thin veil to try to cover the forever tears for her son. She became weak in the arms of the boy's stepfather, Ulysses. Her tears splashed against his suit fabric, but he didn't mind. He was grieving the loss of his stepson too. Since James's daddy died, Ulysses stepped up, married his mama, and became the boy's daddy. They liked and respected each other. James was well-liked—a good, Christian boy who wanted better for himself, his mama, and his stepdaddy. He'd wanted to become an influential person growing up, a lawyer to fight for his family and community.

The mood at James's funeral matched that of the Bakers' a few weeks ago. Folks were charged with anger, sadness, resentment, and loss, and some yearned for vengeance. They fussed about having equality, but some believed the only way to achieve that was by creating Black armed mobs to retaliate against the white mobs— an eye for an eye.

Guests fanned themselves with church hand fans to combat the afternoon heat as they sat in the pews, gazing at James's Lancaster pine casket. The mortician had done an excellent job with the body, and the young boy looked sharp in a brown tweed suit. There were many flower arrangements on and around the casket. A soloist named Lucy Jane, a portly black woman with a stellar voice and a small choir of eight, stood to the left of the church, ready to sing "When We All Get to Heaven."

Melvin Brooke, wearing a black tweed jacket and black leather shoes, sat in a high-back wooden chair with arms on the slightly raised platform. He remained expressionless as he stared out at his congregation in mourning before him, with James's casket just below his feet. He leaned back into the chair in an angle, shifting his weight to the right, and absentmindedly stroked his goatee, brooding about something. Suddenly, the pastor spotted Elise among the mourners before him. She was sitting with her male friend, Bronco. Something about the stranger bothered the pastor. He'd been in town for a few weeks, and there was this unnatural presence to him that the pastor couldn't place his finger on.

The drummers began with a rhythmic beat, followed by the bass guitar and organ. Lucy Jane took her place in front of the podium and passionately sang the song.

As Lucy Jane sang more and more, Gloria cried harder while grasped in her husband's arms. Her tears could flood the Grand Canyon. Though he was no longer a boy, her little boy was gone forever. James was her only child, and now she was childless. The hopes of any grandchildren had expired like a quick summer breeze. Gloria felt the cruel impact of hatred in the Jim Crow South, with her son becoming another victim of Sheriff Duke.

Everyone sang with Lucy Jane.

Unfortunately, today wasn't a day of rejoicing but grieving. After the selection, Pastor Melvin Brooke slowly stood from the chair. He marched toward the podium with a deep sadness to him. His blood felt like concrete because it was hard for him to move. He'd known James from when he was 7 years old, and he watched the boy grow up. He helped shape James from boy to manhood with the Good Book, encouraging words, and absolute faith.

A heavy sigh escaped from his lips, and he felt his spirit sinking like a stone in water. His eyes glistened with unleashed tears, and he quickly blinked away. But a wave of sadness washed over the congregation, pulling them under with sadness, rage, and fatigue of the status quo. They all needed to hear something from the pastor—motivation, guidance, or strength. They were a flock in need of their shepherd.

"This here, it hurts. It cuts deep," the pastor began, exhaling sharply. "I mean, they all hurt, every last one of them. Every last child of God cut down by hatred, bigotry, and racism. And I know we are to never question God and His ways, for He always has His reasons. But Lord Almighty, we need you. We need you right now. I stand here before a fallen child of God, killed because of the color of his skin, gunned down because he wanted things to be fair and righteous and had the courage to fight for what he believed in, then was killed because of it."

The congregation nodded, agreeing with his preaching. Some were bothered by it, too. However, nearly no eye was dry in the building.

"Preach, Pastor. Preach it," a woman hollered out of the blue.

Pastor Brooke gazed at the closed casket in front of him and let out a heavy sigh. He needed a moment to compose himself, gather his thoughts, and find the right words to carry on. He was angry but knew he couldn't deliver a sermon while consumed by resentment and fury. He couldn't risk losing control of his emotions and expressing the same hatred and rage that had resulted in James's death. As a man of the cloth, he understood the importance of maintaining his composure, particularly in the presence of his congregation. However, he also felt the need to be sincere.

"I'm not going to stand up here and lie to you all. I am angry. I am upset, but as a man of God, I will not allow my emotions to control me. Because I'm not the one in control. God is. And the men who did this to him are weak individuals with no self-control of their actions and hatred. The Bible warns us that if we do not have self-control, we will be slaves to what controls us. It is not our right. As it says in Ephesians 4:31–32, 'Let all bitterness and wrath and anger and clamor and slander be put away from you, along with all malice. Be kind to one another, tenderhearted, forgiving one another, as God in Christ forgave you.' Why? Because as in Proverbs 20:22, 'Do not say, "I'll pay you back for this wrong!" Wait for the Lord, and He will avenge you.' He'll pay us back for this wrong. God never lies, and this will be corrected," Pastor Brooke hollered with vigor and passion.

However, the pastor was beginning to lose some of the flock with his message of forgiveness and patience. They were tired of sitting and not doing anything. They were starting to feel like fish in a barrel, completely helpless and being shot down individually. A few folks stood and marched out of the church, upset and furious. But Pastor Brooke continued to preach about forgiveness and the future.

A few tears rolled down Elise's cheek. James was only a few years older than Kenneth. Elise couldn't help but imagine it was her little brother lying in that casket. She was dressed in black, nestled against Bronco while squeezed in the pew with others and looking for comfort from the man she'd taken in. Elise felt guilty. She was supposed to be there that day when her peers stormed into the courthouse looking to register to vote. But Kenneth had fallen ill the night before, and she had to be by his side to tend to his sickness.

After delivering the eulogy, an attendant opened the casket to allow everyone one last opportunity to see the boy, James, before he was laid to rest. Attendees approached the casket to have their final moments with him. Pastor Brooke moved closer to the casket and closed it after the last person had viewed James. He then signaled to the pallbearers, who approached and prepared to move the casket toward the exit.

The procession included a walk to the nearby cemetery, with a succession of folks following right behind the casket being pulled by a horse-drawn hearse. The crowd sang the hymn "Victory Is Mine," a favorite song among them.

I told Satan to get thee behind.

Got up singing and shouting victory.

The rusted gate of the cemetery creaked open, and silence blanketed the still grounds. The gravestones loomed in their view, casting eerie shadows from the afternoon sun. Superstition seemed to grip everyone like a mysterious ambiance had settled over them. The gravediggers were already at work, armed with shovels, picks, and other tools for digging graves.

Bronco was well acquainted with the process. He had dug many graves and laid many souls to rest beneath the earth. He remained nonchalant, as he was only there to support Elise, who didn't want to attend the funeral alone.

The gravediggers began slowly lowering the casket to the ground. They were surrounded by people watching. Seeing her son being lowered into the earth, Gloria dropped to her knees, wailing like a banshee. Her husband dropped with her with his arms blanketed around his wife for comfort and support. It was heartbreaking to see.

Pastor Brooke recited "O God, Our Help in Ages Past," clutching his Bible while the casket lowered.

Bronco soon saw what the others couldn't see: a ghostly James standing adrift, attending his funeral. James had milky white eyes, and there were gunshot wounds to his chest and stomach, with his shirt covered in blood. James stared hauntingly at Bronco, but Bronco remained composed, locking eyes with the apparition. James was sad and lost. His senseless murder became one of many Black men's in the South. Bronco closed his eyes and sighed. When he opened them again, James was gone.

As the mourners grieved and the pastor delivered the final prayer, Harland's gaze shifted toward Elise standing close to Bronco. He frowned, feeling consumed by jealousy. It was difficult for him to accept the possibility that Elise might be developing feelings for this stranger. Bronco was in the position Harland desired—to be the one to comfort Elise in times like these and to be by her side. He longed for Elise to love him, but no matter what he did, he always felt rejected and unappreciated. It hurt him deeply to witness the woman he had known almost forever falling for an outsider.

"Your soul is finally at peace and at rest with God and His eternal Kingdom, James. And one day, we will see each other again," Pastor Brooke concluded.

James was finally buried.

It was a warm, nice night with the moon half full. It was blazing hot, too. But despite the heat and the funeral that had taken place earlier in the day, folks tonight wanted to take their minds off their troubles and drift into a different world of drinking, dancing, gambling, and jive talk. What the whites called nigger town was just beyond the trees, lining a descending, deeply rutted dirt road, where there was a pocket-sized commercial strip consisting of a feed store, a cobbler shop, a general store, a cooperage, and a seamstress. And burrowed deeper into the woodlands at the road's junction, the paved lane was a mixture of shacks and tiny houses. The smell of cooking fires and hot food was strong. Black folks were sitting on their porches husking peas and corn and cleaning collard greens for tomorrow's supper. The women gossiped, and the men smoked their corncob pipes. But for some folks, the fun was at an old choke house turned into a juke joint. It was near a small clearing in the woods, a secret spot offering food, drinks, dancing, and gambling for tired workers and oppressed individuals to unwind after a hard day's work.

The high-pitched music of the blues carried into the warm night air. The Red Rooster was a small, funky, and intimate venue that featured live music almost every night of the week. Some of the best musicians in the area came to the Red Rooster to perform. It was owned by a talented blues singer named Bayou. His name came from the locals because he was from New Orleans and traveled the country to sing the blues. Now, as a 60-year-old legend, he had settled down in the backwoods of Mississippi and opened the Red Rooster.

A few men who had come from the funeral were sitting at an old pub table, drinking moonshine and whisky, while a game of pool was happening behind them.

"I's hear it was that coward deputy who shot that boy cold-blooded. They done got to beatin' on him, and he fought back," JoJo alleged among friends. "What a man s'posed to do when they beatin' on you?"

"Marchin' into that courthouse was a mistake in the first place. What you's expect gon' happened when you invade them white places?" Doc uttered.

"Then the pastor gon' preach forgiveness and turnin' the other cheek at the boy's funeral. When white folks gon' turn the other cheeks our way? Huh? We'ze tired of this. James never hurt nobody. He was a smart Negro. College bound one day. I's has it in my right mind to grab my rifle and march into the town square myself."

"And then we's be buryin' you too, JoJo," said Jimmy.

JoJo huffed and puffed and downed the rest of his corn liquor. He was deeply perturbed. He slumped forward with his elbows on the table grudgingly. "I's don't care no more. I's says an eye for an eye."

"Hush that damn babbling, JoJo. God gave you good sense, use it," Washer exclaimed to him. "You's got one rifle, white men got plenty of rifles, more guns, and the law on their side."

Washer stood six feet tall, with a deep black complexion like mining coal and a shaved head. He embodied the essence of an old-fashioned country boy.

"So we's s'posed to continue to sit 'round here while they take our land and our lives? How much more we gon' take?" JoJo griped, having a frosted temperament.

"White folks gon' keep on comin, JoJo . . . one more vicious and evil than the last," said Washer.

"That's why I say we need to leave here, go north, New York, Chicago, start life up there," Harland interjected. He sat at a nearby table, nursing a cup of whisky, overhearing the fellows talk. "I hear it's easier there, with better jobs, better pay, and a better way of life."

"Head north?" Doc was baffled. "I don't know nothin' 'bout up there, Harland. Far as I know, white folks just as evil up there like they down here."

"But we would have a better chance of surviving, building something, and raising a family," Harland countered.

JoJo snickered when Harland mentioned family. "Raising a family? It seems to me good ol' sweet Elise done took a liking to that Harlem fellow lately. I thought she would become yo' woman, Harland. You's been sweet on that girl since knee-high."

Harland frowned.

"Quiet, JoJo, don't mock the man," Doc said.

"It ain't no mockin' being done, just the truth bein' told, that's all," JoJo quipped. "That Bronco nigger came to town and done did in a short spell what was taking Harland forever to do, ain't that a bite."

Harland stood up suddenly, enraged from being teased. He grabbed his cap and angrily slammed it on the table. "Do you have a problem with me, JoJo?" Harland shouted.

"Yo' problem isn't with me, nigger. It's with that other nigger Elise is sweet on," JoJo countered. "All that handsomeness and strength wasted on a fool."

Washer and Doc stood between the two men. JoJo was known for being a fierce fighter, and Harland was a big man with hands like mitts. If the two started fighting, it would have been quite a spectacle. However, they didn't dare to disrespect Bayou's establishment. He was tough and very strict about rules, one of which was not to fight on his premises.

"You two been friends fo' how long now?" Washer shouted. "Both of y'all sit. Ain't no need for Bayou to come out here and throw y'all both out."

Both men cooled their anger and sat back down. Washer uttered that the next round of drinks was on him, which made everyone settle back into drinking and laughing. The night continued with a talented singer named Leanne hypnotically singing the blues.

An hour later, it seemed like it was destined for Harland to have an unlucky and irksome night when Elise entered the place with Bronco. All eyes shifted in their direction. JoJo cut his eyes at Harland and chuckled quietly. Things were about to get interesting, he felt.

At Elise's request, Bronco accompanied her to the Red Rooster for a night of drinking and dancing. She needed it. She wasn't a frequent flyer of the juke joint, but from time to time, Elise was human and yearned to unwind and dance like the rest.

Seeing Elise in a colorful cocktail dress made men stare awkwardly, and their hearts fluttered. She was beautiful. Harland felt a lump hug in his throat, and jealousy continued to stir inside of him. *Why did she bring him here? Is she trying to make a fool out of me?* Elise saw Harland and smiled his way. He uneasily smiled and downed the rest of his whisky.

Bronco and Elise found a table and sat down to enjoy a night out together. However, Bronco felt like he was being watched and gossiped about. He didn't want any trouble, but he could tell that trouble might find him, especially with Elise drawing attention to herself. Still, it was precisely what Elise needed after everything that had happened. Despite that, Bronco wasn't a fan of the Red Rooster. It was a crowded, rowdy place filled with stragglers, only one way out, with a menacing presence in the form of Harland.

"Come, let's dance," Elise suggested.

Elise stood up happily, grabbed Bronco with both hands, and pulled him from his seat. Bronco looked reluctant, but how she smiled at him made him have no choice but to relent. Leanne's sweet voice over the mic created a soft melody that filled the air and made her feet want to hit the dance floor. The two figures began to sway gracefully on the dance floor. Their movements were synchronized and unhurried. Surprisingly, despite being masculine, aloof at times, and muscular, Bronco was light on his feet when it came to Elise. Their bodies moved harmoniously, gliding with gentle precision as they embraced the tender rhythm. Each gaze from them locked in a silent conversation, creating an intimate moment of connection amid the surrounding tension. Elise's eyes danced with amusement.

They danced for a while, turning and looping over the hardwood floor, while other dancers drifted around them, lost in their own worlds. Elise twirled free of his arms, her dress flaring for a moment from her hips, then spun back to him, her hand finding his once more.

"Looks to me she 'bout to be real gone over that nigger, the way they cuttin' up on the dance floor," JoJo uttered.

Harland could feel the glass breaking between his fingers. He couldn't help but notice how smitten Elise became. He tried to be the better man, but it felt like the two of them were throwing shit into his face when they'd arrived together at a place Elise knew Harland liked to frequent. *Why is she doing this to me?*

While Harland fumed quietly from the sidelines, Elise leaned forward and delicately exhaled in Bronco's ear.

She was so close that Bronco could feel the warmth of her body on his skin. Her hand crept up the back of his neck, and his breath caught at her nearness. The music wrapped around them, gentle as a summer's rain.

"Thank you for everything," Elise told him out of the blue. She pressed herself lightly to him. Her hand remained light on the back of his neck.

"Ain't no need to thank me," said Bronco. "I like the company, and I don't mind the work."

He drew her close and spun her around slowly, savoring the simple pleasure of dancing. Elise's eyes searched his face, wondering if his feelings for her were as strong as hers were for him. Even though they were close, he still seemed somewhat distant. Elise hadn't meant to develop such strong feelings for this man, but everything about him made her walls melt away.

Everything was going well. Elise was all smiles and having a good time. Until Harland couldn't take the scene of them dancing anymore. He lifted from the table with a purpose, clutching an empty beer bottle in a manner not for drinking. Before anyone could deduce his following actions, Harland marched behind Bronco. Anger rose in him like a tide. There was no time to think about it. His jealousy pushed him to react.

Elise closed her eyes as she danced, lost in a special moment with Bronco. When she finally opened them, she saw Harland approaching from behind him. It didn't take long for her to realize what he was up to. His jealousy had taken over. Harland raised the beer bottle, ready to attack. Before Elise could cry out or warn Bronco about the impending danger, Harland angrily brought the bottle across the back of Bronco's head. The beer bottle shattered, and Bronco turned around to scowl at Harland.

"I want you to stay away from her," Harland shouted.

The crowd inside became stunned by Harland's action. He wasn't that kind of guy, but tonight, he'd been transformed into this green-eyed monster over Elise. His friends knew it had to be the whisky giving him liquid courage. Surprisingly, Bronco wasn't fazed by the attack, not one bit. In fact, he clenched his fists and frowned at Harland but decided to give the man a chance at redemption. He could smell the whisky on Harland's breath.

"You hit me again, you gonna regret it," Bronco uttered coolly.

"Fuck you, muthafucka! Who you think you are? You come into my town, woo my woman, and mock me. Fuck you!" Harland shouted with contempt dripping from his tone.

Elise tried to get between the two feuding men. She looked like a butterfly caught between two snarling dogs. "Harland, you's drunk. Go home," she bitterly said to him.

"No. I's goin' nowhere, not without you, Elise," Harland replied gruffly. "I love you. I always loved you."

Elise was uncertain about what to do. Tonight was the night Harland decided to express his emotions for her. The alcohol gave him the courage. Unfortunately, it was terrible timing. She was caught in a difficult situation because she cared for Harland and didn't want to see him get hurt or become upset. Harland took a step forward, crowding her.

"You fuckin' this nigger?" Harland shouted for everyone to hear.

Without thinking about it, Elise slapped him with an open left hand across his face. It shocked Harland, and he took a step back.

"How dare you?" Elise hollered, seething from the remark. "Don't have me hate you tonight, Harland. Please don't."

Harland was feeling embarrassed and devastated. Everyone, including his friends, watched his nightmare unfold. He clenched his fists, but his anger wasn't toward Elise for striking him. It was aimed toward Bronco for putting the woman he loved in a difficult position and turning her against him. Bronco read his look and tried to warn him subtly, *don't do this*. But Harland had been embarrassed enough. He felt it was time to redeem his manhood, especially in front of everyone.

Harland attempted to tackle Bronco but failed. Bronco effortlessly dodged his charge and pushed him to the ground. Harland fell heavily on his side as if he were a drunken sailor. Laughter ensued. Despite some strong words between JoJo and Harland earlier, JoJo remained his friend. JoJo calmly flicked open his pocketknife, ready to help his buddy if needed.

Harland got back up, fuming like a bull seeing red. He was livid and wasn't going to be embarrassed again. Elise tried to yell some sense into him, but it was too late. The floodgates had opened, and Harland was content to flood the place with rage and anger. He clumsily went after Bronco. He swung at Bronco with all his might and missed. It was a mistake. Bronco countered with a quick right to his jawbone, followed by a sharp uppercut underneath his chin that struck Harland like a cannon blast. Harland went falling backward, arms splayed, and collided against the floor with finality, his eyes rolling upward.

JoJo had seen enough. While Bronco was distracted with Harland, he'd crept behind the muscular man and thrust his blade into his back without a second thought. It was a move indeed to bring about harm or death to an individual. However, the blade broke apart like a pencil snapping. JoJo was baffled. It seemed like he'd thrust his knife against a brick wall. Bronco pivoted toward JoJo and smacked the knife away. It clattered from JoJo's hand and skittered across the floor. JoJo became wide-eyed with fear. His only defense against this man was gone. Bronco had had enough. He grabbed JoJo tightly by the collar and lifted him off his feet, subsequently headbutted him, breaking his nose, and tossed him across the room like a toy. JoJo hit the floor with his body feeble and shrunken.

The evening began with fun but quickly escalated into a chaotic brawl. Several men jumped out of their seats to confront Bronco or each other. Bottles and chairs were thrown across the room as intoxicated men punched, kicked, and wrestled with each other. Bayou emerged from his back office with a shotgun, appearing angry and concerned that his establishment was on the verge of being destroyed.

"Got-damn it!" he hollered. "I warned all of you niggers!"

Bronco and Elise became surrounded by chaos. It was time for their retreat. Bronco pulled Elise closer to him. He covered her from flying bottles and chairs like he was a human tank, and anyone who got in their way between the floor and the exit would soon regret it. Bayou aimed the shotgun toward the ceiling and fired. Boom! Then he screamed, "I told you niggers, don't ever disrespect my place."

Bronco hurried with Elise out the front exit, and they moved toward her pickup truck. He escorted Elise into the passenger seat and got behind the wheel. Before any more trouble followed them, they were gone.

A mile away from the place, Bronco said, "I'm sorry 'bout that."

"You don't have to apologize, Bronco. It wasn't your fault," Elise assured him.

But Bronco wasn't so sure about that. Although he considered them friends, simply being with Elise was creating problems he wanted to avoid. Men like Harland steadily came after him because they were jealous or fearful of him. It didn't matter if he was in Harlem or Mississippi. There would always be a Harland or a Miles ready to challenge him because of a woman.

Chapter Nineteen

The Right Mistake

The sunset was drinking what was left of a hot day. It had been another beautiful summer day, and it was coming to an end as the sun gradually dipped below the horizon, with the fleeting colors of dusk beginning to fade away. The sunset across the wildflower field was bold, brilliant, and rich in color. These flowers grew without any help from people, and they belonged there naturally in their environment.

"My mother used to say to me, 'Every sunset is an opportunity to reset,'" Elise said to Bronco, her voice carrying the weight of her mother's wisdom and the significance of the moment.

Bronco and Elise strolled leisurely side by side across the lush wildflower field that sprawled throughout the countryside, its vibrant vegetation a testament to nature's artistry. The area exuded a serene charm, a hallmark of the countryside. The stillness was punctuated by the gentle hum of bees and insects, a soothing symphony. A soft breeze caressed their skin, a welcome respite from the day's heat. Elise, in her elegant atomic-print sundress, let her long hair cascade around her shoulders, while Bronco, in his trusty Levi jeans and rolled-up sleeves and old Moc toe boots, exuded a rugged charm.

For a moment, they ambled through the delightful field, their thoughts consumed by nothing but the beauty of the scene.

"Sometimes, life doesn't offer a chance to pause," Bronco mused. "The world's moving too fast for some of us."

"The world is changing fast, but you don't have to follow suit."

"You don't follow suit you get left behind," said Bronco. "Besides, the world's a cold place. You keep still, you freeze."

"My father believed in planting roots, keeping still, and growing best where you believe you belong," said Elise.

Their views were somewhat opposite.

"I never felt I belonged anywhere."

"Not even in Harlem? Isn't that your home?"

"It is. But there wasn't anything much for me there . . . besides trouble, maybe. I worked odd jobs, lived alone, and took to the bottle most nights. I'm a man of simple means. I don't ask for much."

Bronco didn't want to spill out his demons. He didn't want to scare her with his truth. He had seen and implemented so many horrific things against men and society that the devil himself could give him a medal—and seeing the dead made him feel like he was a walking nightmare. Bronco felt cursed. He felt no matter where he went, there would be no pure happiness for him—no escape from his demons and torment. He wanted a drink, but helping Elise with the chores on the farm, connecting with Kenneth, and grudgingly involving himself with community activities was somewhat keeping his attention away from the bottle.

"You ever loved someone before?" Elise asked him shyly.

Can I call it love? Bronco wondered. He'd grown close with Mindy and had experienced something that could bear a resemblance to love, but it was short-lived. It still ate at him inside that she was killed because of him.

"It didn't work out," he replied tersely.

Elise didn't want to pry. The slight grimace on his face told her that it was something he didn't want to talk about or, maybe, be reminded of. She didn't bring him to such a beautiful place to stir up old and bad memories. The two continued to walk side by side, but Elise drew closer to him, yearning to touch him, wanting him to take her hand into his and grasp it. She wanted to continue to connect with him and have him open up to her more. She wanted to open up to him with her world, dreams, and hopes.

"I come here all the time," said Elise.

"I can see why," said Bronco. "The place can take your mind off the troubles of the world."

They reached a gentle slope on the hill, where a patch of tall, airy bright blue wildflowers spread out before them. The wildflowers displayed a wide variety of colors, including white, pale blue, pink, and purple.

"Why did you sign up for the war?" Elise asked him out of the blue.

"Honestly, I got into a bit of trouble in Harlem, needed to leave," he replied.

"Oh." She was beginning to know him better.

"It was a mistake, came back different, like most men. They say we fightin' for freedom, to stop the spread of evil, to stop Hitler. But Hitler ain't do me no harm. White men I fought for and fought with did more harm to me and my kind than Hitler," Bronco griped.

"But you still killed for them," Elise said.

"It just came natural," he admitted.

His comment didn't cause Elise to hesitate in her judgment. Instead, it sparked even more interest in him.

"Like Lincoln said, 'There's no honorable way to kill, no gentle way to destroy. There is nothing good in war. Except its ending.'"

It felt like they'd walked a few miles, becoming lost in the tranquility of a bright orange and red sunset and the lushness of abundantly green and healthy flowers that reached to their waists. They were in a state of calm and attention.

"You ever think 'bout leaving Mississippi?" he asked her.

"Where would I go? Not much opportunities for a colored woman, especially a farmer's daughter," she countered. "This farm is all I know, all I believe in."

"And what happens the day when they come for your farm?" asked Bronco.

It was something she didn't want to think about. This place belonged to her daddy, and he put his blood, sweat, and tears into it. Losing the place, her home, and what she'd helped build, they might as well snatch her life, too.

"I don't want to go that far into thinkin' 'bout it," said Elise. "My daddy would want me to fight until I's can't fight no more to keep his land. That's the kinda man he was. And that's what I's plan to do. I's know he would want me to one day pass this land down to my children. But I can't lie to you, Bronco. I'm scared. Do you get scared?"

"It's been a long time since I've been truly scared 'bout something," said Bronco.

"You's not scared of dyin', especially when you fought in the war?"

"No, because I did my best to get myself killed in that war, but it didn't happen," he replied.

Elise was shocked. "Why's would you want to die?" she questioned with a raised brow. "Don't you's have anything you want to live for?"

It felt like she'd asked him the true meaning of life or his existence. It may have been a complicated answer for him.

"Death is the easiest thing one can do . . . something we all can expect," said Bronco. "Unlike the days and nights, we all get one sunrise and one sunset."

"Hopefully, not anytime soon."

Bronco was truly afraid of falling in love and losing someone he cared about. But he didn't want to admit that to Elise. He had developed feelings for her over the time he'd gotten to know Elise. He tried to remain aloof and indifferent and focused on his purpose there—executing justice for the Bakers. But most of the folks there liked Bronco, while some gave him the side-eye and stink stares, expressing doubts about his sudden presence in their town. A few folks, including Harland, were beginning to express scorn and criticism about Elise moving a stranger from Harlem into her home. They knew nothing about Bronco. Where did he come from, and why was he there? And although Bronco was a Black man, he wasn't considered one of them, a Southerner who'd been fighting Jim Crow all their lives and had a lot to lose. But some didn't like Bronco because they were jealous of him. He was handsome, rough, nonchalant, and he carried an appealing rugged charm about him.

"I wake up most times and feel . . . nothin'," Bronco uttered.

"Not even love?"

"Especially that. My pa died in a bar fight when I was sixteen, and my ma became no good to me after that, so I learned how to take care of myself. And every day it felt like I had the weight of the world on my shoulders, and any hope for a better future, I didn't see," Bronco proclaimed.

Finally, he opened up to her, and Elise liked it. She wanted to know his past, pain, hurts, and dreams, if there were any, and if he could ever love again.

"I got into a life of crime. Did it all: numbers running, robbery, burglary, racketeering, and gambling. Even murder," he confessed.

Still, there was no judgment from Elise, but an ocean of curiosity and phenomenon. She grew more intrigued to hear more about his life. He was an open book to her, filled with endless chapters, each completely different from the next.

"After a while, everything became dull and meaningless for me," Bronco continued. "My life, it became this odd chore that I didn't want to participate in."

Elise wanted to hold him and comfort him. But she also wanted to be wrapped in his arms and held lovingly by a man as strong and masculine as him. Elise wanted to be consumed by his masculinity and strength. It had been a while since she'd fallen in love with a man. Harland wanted to be in the running for her unconditional love, but she always saw him more as a friend than a boyfriend. But Bronco was different. He was a mystery she wanted to solve.

"Do you ever want to find love?" she asked him.

Again, it felt like another complex question because he often felt emptiness, dead inside, and apathetic toward his surroundings.

"Not if it's gon' be taken from me so suddenly," he replied.

"My great grandmother, Cherry, she settled here in Mississippi from South Carolina after the Civil War. She made a life here for herself after slavery, a good life, too," Elise began. "She would pass down stories 'bout monsters and demons she encountered on the plantation durin' an uprising in 1850. Said demons and monsters do exist, seen it wit' her own eyes. She talked 'bout a runaway named Solomon. They sold off his wife and he ran off to find her, became somethin' demonic, and killed his masser an' others. But no matter what he became, he didn't give up on love. He didn't give up on findin' his wife. Everything wants to be loved. 'Specially God."

"Been wonderin' if God ever loved me," Bronco uttered. "But I didn't know you believed in monsters."

"If you believe in God, then you got to believe in the devil, and the devil has his demons. But the only monsters I've come across were white men."

Bronco was considering telling Elise a story about himself, about what he was—becoming something different, odd, uncanny, and scary, like a monster. It was easy to believe that he was a monster because there was a heaviness that ached inside him, a curse he'd carried since they found him in that alleyway without any memory. It felt like all the surfaces inside of him had been rubbed raw, and there was this voice in his head and visions of the dead. His nightmares were becoming surreal. Sometimes, it felt like he was breathing with a plastic bag over his head and trying to understand what was happening and feeling.

They continued to talk and walk. It was a surreal experience for Bronco, an intimate and intriguing conversation with a pretty woman. He began to open up about his past in a country field with a beautiful sunset that would rival the movies. Bronco also confessed many times when he felt empty in the middle of a fantastic moment. But this wasn't one of those moments. Something about Elise brought character, honesty, and light out of him. He was becoming different around her.

They began to head home. Surprisingly, as they began to walk the way they came, Bronco coolly took Elise's hand into his, and they started to hold hands.

"I . . . I just wanted to touch you," he uttered almost nervously.

"I'm fine by it." She chuckled quietly.

Finally, it's what she wanted from him, touching, passion, and closeness. Elise smiled at him. It was a deliberately sensual smile that she had longed for and wished to possess at this moment. She felt safe and protected with him, and there wasn't any doubt he would never cause her or Kenneth any harm. In fact, the relationship that Bronco began developing with Kenneth made Elise like him a lot more. He would go to the lake to talk and skip rocks with her little brother. Elise admired that about him. He knew how to speak to her little brother and treated him kindly and respectfully. One day, Kenneth had expressed to his sister how he wanted Bronco to stay with them permanently. Surprisingly, Bronco had a way with kids.

The two walked a quarter of a mile toward the farm, but Bronco suddenly stopped in his tracks. Elise followed, baffled. He then began to stare at her surprisingly and oddly.

"Is everything okay?" she asked him.

"It's fine . . . never been better," he replied.

Although Bronco kept telling himself that he was there for something else and didn't want to develop any feelings for her, the inevitable was happening. His feelings for Elise were already there, growing stronger each day like hardening concrete.

Bronco stared at her quietly with her hand still gently in his. They locked eyes with his giant walls of indifference and aloofness gradually collapsing, and brightly behind it, a second chance maybe with a beautiful woman who wouldn't die because of him. Maybe there was still hope for him, and life in the South and a life with her was possible. Bronco wanted to forget Harlem. He tried to forget the war. Before meeting Elise, he tried to forget about this unnatural monster he'd become. He'd been with so many women over time that sex naturally became a blurred emotion for him, but none besides Mindy made him feel this way.

Bronco leaned closer to kiss her without asking, and Elise didn't resist or shy away. Their chemistry was compelling and natural. He slowly pressed his lips against hers, and things took off. Bronco's mouth clung to Elise's lips like magnets, pouring all the words he couldn't say into that kiss. It was passionate, lingering, and meaningful. Elise found herself fully enveloped in his arms like a blanket wrapped around her with their tongues tangling.

When they finally dragged their lips from each other, they were caught in the moment, panting heavily, and their eyes were glazed with passion. *But am I wrong to kiss her?*

"I'm sorry. I don't know what came over me," said Bronco humbly.

Elise grinned. "I wanted you to."

Bronco huffed. He didn't want this to become a mistake. He didn't want his curse or actions to disrupt or harm Elise and Kenneth. He honestly did care for them.

"Let's go home," said Elise.

Elise was now the one who took charge. With Bronco's hand in hers, she began to drag him home playfully. They'd started something—and it was something that needed to be consummated in the privacy of the bedroom.

Bronco kissed Elise tenderly in the bedroom. He took his time, kissing her mouth and neck as he slowly peeled off her sundress down from her arms and between her shoulders and allowed it to drop to the floor, leaving her naked for him to admire. She stood before him in her perfect curves and soft, smooth ebony flesh, almost possessing a divine appearance. There was no doubt to Bronco that Elise was breathtaking.

"You're beautiful," he uttered warmly, but then he froze or paused as if something had suddenly seized his thoughts.

Bronco remembered uttering those exact words to Mindy right before they made love and only hours before she was killed. The thought of Mindy held his thoughts on that dreadful day, which was one of the happiest and worst days of his life. It wasn't too long ago when he held Mindy in his arms while she was dying.

"Bronco, is everything okay?" Elise asked him, snapping him from his painful thoughts. "Where did you just go?"

He didn't want to explain it to her. It was peculiar, and he wasn't about to bring up another woman's death while they were almost in the throes of making love.

"Nowhere," he stated nonchalantly.

Elise cupped his face into her hands and stared at him fondly. Her beauty and magnetism held his attention, and she said, "Just focus on me. I do want this."

She leaned forward and kissed him. She breathed in his smell, something profoundly masculine, the very opposite of her. He began to kiss the swell of her breasts, gently cupping them. She moaned when he took her nipple between his lips, and she began to shudder as the pleasure of it shot through her. Bronco pulled off his shirt, evenly undid, then removed his pants, and the two soon eased onto the bed and quickly became entwined. He began to thrust slowly inside of her. They moved together deliberately, quicker, and better. Her nails dug into his back while he was on top of her, and a deep pulsation began inside her.

"Ugh! Ugh! Bronco," Elise moaned as Bronco took her hand in his, their fingers knotted, their breath intermingling, and their expressions sated as their lovemaking intensified, with Elise soon about to find her climax.

The aftermath was peaceful and cordial. Bronco and Elise remained naked and nestled together tighter than a python's squeeze, flesh on flesh and skin on skin. Elise smiled inanely and was at peace momentarily, enjoying their quaint pillow talk. Everything felt absolutely perfect.

"My mother used to say to me, 'The world is a book, and those who do not travel read only one page.' She always wanted to find adventure and excitement. It's one of the reasons my parents came to Harlem. Unfortunately, life didn't turn out how my mother expected it," Bronco stated.

"Sound like she was a beautiful and interesting woman," Elise said.

"She was, but then, an unlucky woman, too. Everything she dreamed of never came true."

"What happened to her?" she asked him.

Bronco sighed heavily. The only thing he could say was, "The Great Depression happened, and my parents were never the same."

Elise leaned to kiss him again, but something abruptly trapped Bronco's attention. It was Nancy's charred body appearing on the threshold of the bedroom. If Elise could see what he was seeing, she would be terrified. Fortunately for her, she couldn't see this ghostly charred presence pregnant with the weight of purgatory, forgotten justice, and unspoken sorrows. She was becoming a spectral choir echoing through the passageways of time. Bronco knew how to keep his cool. His visions were becoming repetitive.

"What is it now? You's keep going in and out for a spell," said Elise.

Before Bronco could respond, their special moment was interrupted by loud and disruptive banging at the front door. It startled them both. Bronco sprang from her arms and leaped from the bed to hurry and put back on his pants. Elise became wide-eyed with horror and concern. *Is it the Klan? The sheriff?* She would soon find out.

"Elise! Elise, help us. Help us!" they heard Beulah cry out.

"Oh, my God, it's Mrs. Goff," Elise exclaimed.

She leaped from the bed and followed Bronco's lead in getting dressed. By the time she was putting on her sundress, Bronco was charging toward the front door. Kenneth exited his room confused, awakened by the disturbance, and Elise hollered, "Kenneth, go back into your bedroom now!"

Kenneth was taken aback. He had no idea what was happening. But he was scared, too.

"They took him! They took him!" Beulah shouted in anguish.

Bronco hurriedly opened the front door, and Beulah collapsed into his arms in absolute grief. She continued to rant, "They took Duncan. They took him into the woods to lynch him!"

"Who took him?" Bronco quickly asked.

"The Klan," she hollered.

Chapter Twenty

Blood Grove

Beulah was utterly beside herself with worry and anguish. She cried in Bronco's arms as if knowing her husband was already dead. She was barefoot and in a tattered and stained nightgown. Her feet were caked with dirt, and her eyes were transfixed with horror. The ache in the bottom of her gut was telling her that they were going to lynch her husband.

"They gon' kill him," Beulah hollered.

Elise hurried from the bedroom, her eyes widened with alarm, and shouted, "Mrs. Goff, what happened? Where's your husband?"

"They took him, Elise. They took him! Men came to our home and attacked my husband and dragged him into the woods," Beulah screamed.

Elise gasped, covering her mouth in shock. Stifling a scream, her mind raced through worst-case scenarios, and she realized a nightmare was unfolding after her sweet moment with Bronco.

"I . . . I need to go find him." Beulah's voice trembled with fear, and her legs were like jelly as dread and panic coursed through her veins.

"No, you two stay here. I'll find him," Bronco exclaimed.

Bronco sprang from the floor, and Elise went to be by Beulah's side and console her. She pulled her friend into her arms to hold and comfort her. Beulah's breath became ragged in her throat as she let out a strangled cry. Her heart began stumbling over its own rhythm.

"It's gon' be all right, Mrs. Goff. It's gon' be all right. Bronco will find them. He will. I know he will," Elise babbled with Beulah recoiling in horror in her arms.

The time felt like it was going slow as the gravity of the situation weighed it down. Thinking about her husband, Beulah's chest grew tighter. Breathing was becoming difficult. Until she knew her husband was safe, it felt like she was about to die.

Bronco hurried into the bedroom, snatched his shoes, shirt, and his sheathed M3 trench knife, and was out the front door in a flash. He began a frenzied run toward the Goffs' home, about a mile from them. He sprinted through the dense woods like a galloping mare with his heart pounding. He wasn't about to let anything happen to Duncan, someone he considered a friend. Bronco dashed through the thick woods, weaving expertly between the trees and shrubberies. He became a blur in the darkness. The muscles in his jaw were tensed. He was angry, and tonight, there would be hell to pay.

Bronco approached the bungalow and saw the door wide open. He hurried inside to see the place in disarray, with chairs and tables turned over, broken glass on the floor, and nobody there.

Shit! He had to find them. Bronco leaped from the bungalow into a shroud of darkness. He knew he had to search the area quickly. The forest was thick and vast, with trees towering above and their branches twisting and gnarling like grasping fingers. The air was thick with the scent of trouble. Bronco had to think, *where is he?* He listened sharply, trying to pick up a scent. But surprisingly, he had help. Nancy had reappeared at the edge of the tree line, and she took off running like a bat from hell. Bronco ran after her. He began to think that she was leading him somewhere. He ran deeper where the forest seemed to close in around him. The trees were growing thicker, and the underbrush was more tangled. Sticks broke, and leaves crushed under his feet.

Bronco began to hear the faint sound of something happening in the distance, movement, and voices. He quickened his pace, desperate to reach Duncan before it was too late. Finally, Bronco arrived where the commotion was happening, and absolute rage seared through him. Four men—Paul, Jacob, Keith, and Joseph—had Duncan surrounded. They were taunting and beating him with their rifles and fists while hurling insults at him, calling him "nigger," "boy," "a dead man," et cetera. Duncan was helpless against the ground, bloodied, and badly beaten. But his eyes were harsh with anger instead of fear.

"We warned you, nigger, to pack your things and leave with that bitch of yours," Paul shouted. "Mr. Lockheart done told you already."

"This is my land. I's own it, and I's go nowhere," Duncan retorted.

Paul struck Duncan with the butt of the rifle so hard that blood spewed from his face like a water balloon bursting open, and his face became twisted with pain. Duncan became rigid with agony. They were going to kill him.

"Why are all of you got-damn niggers so fuckin' stubborn? You bring this on ya damn self!" Paul exclaimed, his tone dripping with antagonism. "String the nigger up, and let his feet tap dance on air."

Jacob tossed a knotted noose across a thick tree branch, and it came dangling back down, ready to implement a man's death. The noose was a dark representation of Jim Crow. Duncan frowned and cursed, "Fuck all of y'all."

Paul continued to become agitated by Duncan's defiance. He felt his kind, his men, they deserved to be feared and respected, especially by niggers. But lately, niggers' defiance started to become a problem—like it was some kind of plague that was spreading throughout Mississippi, and Paul was willing to put the fear of hell back into niggers.

"All of you niggers will learn that we are the superior. You don't get to sass and curse at me, boy, and think you'll walk away. No. I'm sick and tired of all of you. You don't own a got-damn thing, nigger," Paul exclaimed through his clenched teeth with disgust.

This time he slammed the butt of the rifle into Duncan's stomach with such force Duncan folded over in pain and then collapsed on his side against the dirt. Paul towered over him, grimacing. The gaping barrel of the rifle was thrust into Duncan's face, and at any moment, he knew that flash could come. But they didn't want to shoot him. They wanted to lynch him. They wanted to see Duncan suffer from asphyxiation. They wanted to witness his body squirm and twist violently in the air and observe the life gradually fade from his eyes.

Paul gave them the go-ahead. Keith and Jacob forcefully grabbed Duncan to fix him upright so they could place the noose around his neck. But Duncan fought and squirmed in their grasp, fidgeting and hollering to be heard. "Get off me. Get off me! Help me!"

"Shut up, nigger. No one is coming to save you," Keith shouted.

It became a struggle, but finally, they placed the noose around Duncan's neck, and he was forced to his feet. Duncan's anger transitioned into fear, with sweat trickling from his forehead. His stomach began to contract into a tight ball, and a hard knot constricted in his throat, making it hard to breathe. His breath grew thin and ragged.

"You's all will burn in hell fo' this!" Duncan screamed at them.

"Nigger, you first," Paul fired back coldly.

The four men were about to string him up, but something immediately caught their attention. Bronco loomed into their view, scowling at all four white devils like they were the Antichrist. Duncan's eyes gleamed with some hope when he saw Bronco appearing to help him.

Paul smirked, recognizing Bronco, and uttered, "Look at what we got here, boys, that nigger from the Baker farm. I guess God is kind, 'cause we is 'bout to have a two-for-one special tonight."

Bronco approached the men with rage surging through him like molten lava. "Remove that noose from around his neck," Bronco growled.

"You a feisty nigger, I see. It's time to know your place here in the South, nigger, and this time, there is no walking away," Paul said with a cocksure smile. "I warned you not to come 'round here no more."

Paul and his cronies believed they had the upper hand on Bronco, although he was an imposing and muscular man. There were four of them, and they were all armed with a rifle or pistol.

"I'm gon' gut you like a fuckin' pig, boy," Paul exclaimed vehemently.

With a crazed roar, Bronco charged at the men like a bull. Paul hurriedly raised his rifle to fire, but Bronco got to him before he could do so and knocked him down with such force that it felt like his soul had evaporated from his body. The nigger was quick, and Paul didn't know what'd hit him. Jacob and Keith reacted. Keith pulled his pistol and shot erratically at Bronco but missed. The shot went wild and over Bronco's head, but it wouldn't have made a difference if it did strike him. Before Keith could fire again, Bronco whacked the pistol from his hand and grabbed him tightly, then slammed him into the dirt, the back of his head hitting so hard he could see a burst of light in the dark.

Joseph aimed his shotgun at Bronco's back while he was busy with Keith on the ground. Seeing that Bronco's life was being threatened and unaware that his skin was tougher than steel, Duncan sprang into action. He forcibly nudged Joseph with his shoulder, throwing him and his aim off balance. The shotgun exploded in Joseph's hand, completely missing his target. Joseph cursed, pivoted, cocked back the shotgun—chk-chk—and now Duncan was in his sight.

"You stupid nigger!" Joseph hollered, leveling the shotgun to fire it again.

Duncan became like a deer caught in blinding head-lights. The gaping double barrels of the shotgun were wide, like two wide tunnels to him. Bronco leaped from Keith and hightailed it toward Joseph before he could fire the weapon again.

"Hey!" Bronco screamed out to get his attention.

It worked. Seeing that Bronco was charging from behind, Joseph wheeled in his direction with the shotgun to stop his charge. Bronco remained undaunted. He moved fast with light speed, and then it seemed like his feet lifted high off the ground like he had wings. Joseph became dumbfounded by how fast he moved. And before he could react, Bronco headbutted Joseph hard across the bridge of his nose. When Joseph stumbled backward with blood spewing from his nose, Bronco surprised him by grabbing him from behind with a deadly chokehold. Then he quickly snapped his neck like it was a twig. Joseph dropped dead like a doornail at Bronco's feet. Paul had come to from being knocked down like he'd gotten hit by a truck just in time to see Bronco take Joseph's life. He and Jacob were utterly taken aback.

"He killed Joseph," Jacob hollered, upset.

Paul fumed with a crazed stare at Bronco. "I swear to God Almighty, I'ma fucking kill you, nigger!"

Bronco was ready for all three of them. He was just getting started. Paul rushed him, but Bronco met him with an unforgiving shoulder and knocked him back onto the ground. Once again, the man had no idea what'd hit him. It felt like he'd been struck by lightning. Quickly, Keith lunged next with his drawn blade. He began to madly swipe and thrust toward Bronco with it. Bronco kicked him to the dirt and pounced on him, driving what felt like an iron fist into his chest that knocked the wind out of him. Keith sucked in his breath like he was drowning.

Jacob sprang his way, gripping a pistol this time. Bronco stood promptly, then veered in Jacob's charging direction while unsheathing his knife. He'd become an expert with the blade and gripped the weapon with his dominant hand with the handle pointed away from him. Bronco cuttingly propelled the knife at his target as he grasped the blade's tip with a well-timed release. He skillfully hit Jacob with the steel right between the eyes. Jacob's body went rigid. His eyes grew wide with shock, and then he collapsed backward to the dirt with the knife protruding from his skull.

Paul came up from the ground, gripping his huge knife, ready to cut open Bronco like he was deer meat. Seeing Jacob dead, his icy stare charred into Bronco. He was itching to kill this nigger, then made a sudden lunge at Bronco, the blade first. However, Bronco easily dodged Paul's knife thrust and grabbed his arm, which he twisted and then broke with a loud snap. The knife fell from his grasp. Paul staggered back, growling in pain and gripping his paralyzed and broken right arm.

"You muthafucka!" he screamed.

This was payback. Now it was Bronco's turn to show him who was boss. Paul was helpless and now at Bronco's mercy.

"You'll pay for this, nigger. You kill me, I swear to God, they will come for you and everyone you love," Paul threatened with a withering stare.

Bronco planted his right foot on Jacob's chest, and then he crouched to pull the knife from his skull. He stood and watched Paul cower away from him with a limp and broken arm. Bronco came face-to-face with this oppressor and pushed him to the ground. Paul landed on his arm and side with a thud and howled from the pain.

"Fuck you! You muthafucka!"

Bronco had nothing else to say to the man. Paul scrambled beneath him, kicking and cursing in the dirt, blood dripping from his ruined face. Bronco knew what they'd done to Nancy and her family. Men like him had been getting away with killing Black people for generations. Now, it was time for retribution. Nancy's restless spirit had led him there for this moment, to make men like him pay for their sins and suffer greatly.

Bronco was on top of him, straddling him. There was nowhere for Paul to go. His fate was sealed. Before Bronco would take his life, he began to cut off his ear. Next, he gouged one of Paul's eyes out with the tip of the blade. The torture Paul felt was a blaze of pain.

Meanwhile, Duncan witnessed Bronco's brutality on the Klansman and didn't cringe. In fact, he, too, was used to seeing this kind of violence when he was active in World War I. The rage in Bronco's eyes was a familiar feeling.

Finally, with one hand around Paul's neck, Bronco began squeezing his throat. For Paul, it felt like his neck had been placed into a clamp and started tightening. Paul desperately grasped at Bronco's arms with his hands twitching spastically and his arms wailing about, trying his best to fight death, but it was inevitable. His breathing shallowed, and his mouth twisted wryly. Then he fell limp.

Bronco stood up from the body only to be hit in the chest with a shotgun blast. It propelled him backward a few feet, but it didn't knock him off his feet. Keith was the last man standing, gripping the double-barrel smoking shotgun. He was flabbergasted. He did shoot the nigger in his chest, yet he was still standing. *How is that possible?* Keith cocked the gun again and fired at Bronco, striking his target again, then again. The two continuous blasts pushed Bronco back and off his feet onto his back. Although Keith and Duncan were surprised it took that many rounds to take him down, they believed he was dead.

Keith stood frozen and traumatized with the smoking shotgun now loosely at his side. He felt somewhat relieved. However, Paul, Jacob, and Joseph were all dead. It wasn't supposed to end like this. Lynching one nigger turned out to become a disaster, and now Keith was ready to finish what they'd started. He spun to Duncan, glaring at the nigger with such contempt that he wanted to beat him to death with the shotgun. It was emptied. Duncan matched his hateful scowl and uttered, "This is your chance to leave. They're dead."

But no, Keith wasn't going anywhere until he killed the nigger first. He angled and clutched the shotgun like he was holding a baseball bat and was prepared to strike Duncan with it. Although Duncan was older, and Keith had him by size, weight, and age, he wasn't about to go out without a fight. However, suddenly, something garnered their attention. Bronco was still alive. The man lifted himself from the dirt and onto his feet and dusted himself off like he didn't get shot multiple times in the chest from a shotgun. Keith became wide-eyed with fear, and his skin lost all color, becoming chalk white.

He stammered, "I . . . I fucking killed you, nigger. I shot you."

"Try again," Bronco mocked.

Duncan didn't know what to believe. He saw it with his own two eyes. His friend was supposed to be dead. It wasn't possible to survive that kind of shotgun blast from such a close range. Yet, the man stood before him on two feet, breathing like a healthy young bull. There was nothing else to do for Keith but to run. He was scared. This nigger was the devil himself, he believed. He sharply pivoted and fled into the woods. Bronco knew he couldn't allow him to escape, so he ran after Keith. A foot chase ensued through the woods. Keith ran recklessly in the dark, trying to miss slamming into trees with his heart pumping fast. Sweat poured from him profusely. The predator had now become the prey.

Of course, Bronco was faster. He moved swiftly, like greased lightning, weaving through the trees fluently, focused on his catch a short distance away, and was ready to pounce on the last Klansman alive. Keith leaped over a wild dwarf shrub but quickly lost his footing. He stumbled and fell face-first into some brushwood. He tried to get up again but toppled over something else because he panicked. Before he could fully stand and run again, Bronco pounced on him from behind, like a lion leaping from a secured crouched position in tall grass onto the back of unsuspecting prey. Keith went down and screamed. His fate had caught up to him.

Bronco rolled him over and glared at him. Keith began to beg for his life. "I'll leave and won't never come back. Please. I won't harm another nigger again."

It was too late for his begging and pleading. Bronco had become his judge, jury, and executioner. Keith was so scared that his breathing came in ragged huffs. He thrashed before Bronco like a squealing pig. "Please. Please! I don't want to die!"

Unfortunately, his begging for mercy fell on deaf ears. Bronco produced his M3 trench knife, now stained with white men's blood, and he pressed it against Keith's throat. Keith's eyes became transfixed with horror. His heart hammered against his ribcage. a thunderous beat reverberated through his body. Bronco showed no hesitation when he began cutting his throat from ear to ear. Keith's body went rigid with agony as his blood spilled from him and pooled onto the ground.

Bronco stood feeling no contrition for his cold-blooded actions. He exhaled. It needed to be done. If Keith had gotten away, then time would have become of the essence. What needed to happen next was that the bodies had to disappear. However, four white men going missing suddenly would stir up questions, anger, and resentment toward him and the Black community among the whites. Just the mention of their deaths would be like Tulsa and Rosewood all over again in Mississippi. So, to give everyone some time to plan and readjust before the inevitable happened, Bronco planned on burying their bodies.

Bronco arrived back to the area where they were going to lynch Duncan. When Duncan saw Bronco looming from the trees clutching the blood-stained knife, he knew Keith had been dealt with accordingly. Duncan didn't know what to think or believe. That was one of the coldest and most unbelievable things he'd ever seen. Both men locked eyes in silence. Who was going to speak first?

"That was cold-blooded murder," uttered Duncan, but with no judgment, just a declaration.

"Would you rather have had them go through with lynching you?"

Of course not. But Duncan also knew even though he'd survived tonight, the wrath of a white mob would come for all of them. Then there was the elephant in the room. "What is you? An angel or somethin'? I's seen you get shot three times in the chest, and yet, you still be alive. How?"

Bronco stood silent momentarily, reflecting on his situation. Duncan wanted an answer. He wasn't frightened of Bronco but curious.

"I don't know what I am or what I became. I'm just this way somehow. No one ever explained it to me," Bronco replied.

"You's don't know what you are?" Duncan replied incredulously.

"I told you, no."

"Wells, whatever you are, I's promise I's keep your secret. You saved my life and I's owe you that," Duncan said.

Bronco nodded respectfully, thanking him.

"You need to go," Bronco said. "Take your wife and leave here for a spell."

"And goes where? This my home, Bronco," Duncan refuted.

"It's no longer safe for you and Beulah. They'll come back, especially after the disappearance of four white men."

"But you's can protect us. I knows it. You'ze godsent, Bronco," said Duncan enthusiastically.

Bronco frowned slightly and replied, "I'm no angel, and I'm not godsent."

"Then why did you just help me?"

Bronco sighed heavily. He wanted to put some sense into Duncan's head. He was helping a friend. But Duncan was an older man who believed in miracles, angels, and prophecies. He was stubborn, too. He was a fighter and planned on fighting until the day he died.

He had a noose around his neck and was knocking on death's door, yet he continued to curse the Klan until his dying breath. Bronco was impressed by that.

"This my land, and they gon' have to carry me off it dead before I's let it go," Duncan protested.

"I'll look after it while you're gone," Bronco said.

"Look after it?" Duncan replied, confused. "I's can look after my own land, Bronco. This all I have, what me and my family worked hard for. You's just want me to up and leave. I's can't do that. I do that, and they win."

"Think about Beulah, Duncan. She's more important right now. If you don't leave now, they'll keep coming for you and her, eventually. What if next time she can't run for help? What if next time they kill her to hurt you?"

Duncan knew he was right. Bronco was invincible, but he and Beulah were not. And if anything were to happen to her, Duncan knew he would never be able to forgive or live with himself. She was his world. Without her, he didn't exist.

Duncan sighed heavily with realization and replied, "I's s'pose I can stay with my brother for a spell in Georgia. That's a good nuff ways from here."

"Go there. Until it's safe for you to return."

"And when will that be?"

Bronco huffed. He had no idea. But he wanted Duncan and his wife to be safe in the meantime.

"Do you have a shovel, and gasoline?" Bronco asked him.

Duncan nodded. "Yes. In my barn."

"Go to Elise's. Beulah's waiting for you there. I'll take care of everything here."

Duncan didn't want to leave the man alone to clean up the bodies, but Bronco insisted. This was his forte, burying dead things into the ground to never be seen again. Paul, Jacob, Joseph, and Keith had to disappear forever. Undoubtedly, these men had families of their own who'd come looking for them soon. The first place they were going to march to was Duncan's place, subsequently interrogating the Black communities for their whereabouts—and by interrogation, he knew it would be with guns, violence, and death. It was bad. Because Bronco knew it was going to get worse before shit got better. Although he planned on discarding the bodies for everyone's safety, white folks weren't about to listen to colored people's reasoning. Still, their bodies needed to go—no bodies, no crime.

While Duncan hurried toward Elise's to reunite with his wife, Bronco began digging a deep hole to dump their souls into. It was a lengthy process, but Bronco's stamina was unique. He dug and dug and dug with resentment and necessity. When all four bodies were placed into the ground, slumped against each other in a heap, Bronco began pouring gasoline onto them. Then he lit a match and tossed it onto the bodies. Immediately, the hole became ablaze with flames and heat. Bronco stood at the edge of the hole and watched the bodies burn. When their remains were charred and unrecognizable, he began refilling the hole with dirt.

Good riddance, he felt.

Chapter Twenty-one

Trouble Is What I Do

When Duncan, disheveled and worn, stepped through the threshold of Elise's cottage, Beulah's heart leaped with relief and joy. She rushed to her husband, enveloping him in a hug so tight it threatened to squeeze out the breath he had fought so hard to keep. Tears of relief and happiness streamed down Beulah's and Elise's faces. Their love and concern for their loved one were palpable.

"I's thought I lost you," Beulah cried out.

"You's know I'm never leavin' you that easily," Duncan joked.

Ironically, he found humor in the situation. All Beulah could do was hug and kiss her husband repeatedly, knowing he meant to keep his promises to her.

"You's a mess, though," said Beulah, scrutinizing her husband's torn clothing and the ugly bruises on his face.

Duncan was a tough old man. This incident with the Klan would only become another collection of war stories to tell their grandchildren when they would be gathered around him. Duncan knew he was a lucky or a blessed man. He wanted to take a seat, thank God for Bronco, and never leave his wife's side again. But he would have to tell Beulah the unfortunate news, that they would have to leave Mississippi for a few, until things cooled down for them.

Elise smiled at their reunion. Then she thought, *where's Bronco?* He should have marched through their door the same as Duncan. She'd gotten so caught up in seeing their reunion and happiness that she had temporarily forgotten about the man she'd fallen in love with.

"Where's Bronco, Mr. Goff?" Elise asked apprehensively, fearing the worst.

Duncan turned his gaze toward her, his eyes shining with hope. "Don't worry, Elise. Bronco's okay. He risked everything to save me." His words, filled with gratitude and admiration, painted a vivid picture of Bronco's bravery and sacrifice, leaving Elise in awe.

Elise was happy to hear that. Still, she wanted Bronco to hurry through that door in one piece so she could hug and kiss him too. The way Bronco hurried to rescue Duncan was extraordinary. He didn't hesitate, and she found that exciting and remarkable. But then she thought, Duncan came back alive after being taken by several Klansmen. So, what happened to the Klansmen?

"Come now, let's get you cleaned up," said Beulah to her husband.

Beulah helped her husband into the kitchen to attend to his wounds. At the same time, Elise remained in the living area, pacing the floor with her arms folded across her chest. Every minute and every second were on Bronco and his return. She would occasionally step out onto the porch and look out for him, but it was quiet and dark. Nothing was heard or seen for miles. Where was he?

Several hours had passed. Elise had fallen asleep in an old chair on the porch with a rifle by her side. Beulah and Duncan had fallen asleep in her bedroom. It was the least she could do after Duncan had to relay the grim news that they had to leave Mississippi. Beulah's joy of her husband's return was somewhat short-lived.

Although Duncan specified that it would be temporary, Beulah couldn't fathom leaving their farm for Georgia. She had so many questions, but Duncan remained vague. He didn't want to tell his wife what he'd witnessed. How would she and Elise cope with that thought or vision? But lastly, Duncan had broken the disastrous news to his wife, Bronco had to kill those men to save his life. Beulah and Elise knew what that meant for them and everyone else. Beulah was happy that Bronco did so, but Elise remained ambivalent toward the grim news.

The sound of a breaking branch snapped her awake. Her eyes became wide open and alert. She spotted someone's silhouette looming from the tree lines and immediately reached for the rifle by her side. But she relaxed when she saw that it was Bronco returning. Bronco looked a mess, too. His clothing was tattered and dirty and stained with blood. His hands were caked with grime, and he reeked of gasoline and death. Elise stood to smile and greet him, yearning to hug him. But seeing the condition he was in, she was taken aback. She already knew what he'd done because of Duncan spilling the beans. Bronco stopped at the foot of the porch, his attention fixed on Elise, who had the rifle by her side. It had been a long night, and he wanted to wash up. He was weary and wanted to get some rest.

"Duncan done already told us what happened," Elise said quietly.

"I had no choice."

Elise sighed heavily. She looked at him in a way that made him wonder if she had finally seen the monster inside him. He always kept this wild side hidden, making him question his own humanity. But there were times when he had to let that side out. Living in a world where it was challenging to keep concealed, Bronco had done what he thought was best to save a man's life. But at what cost?

"How many are dead?" she asked him.

Bronco exhaled and awkwardly replied, "Four."

Hearing that four white men were dead terrified Elise. Tears began to well up in her eyes with the realization of the particular horror that would follow. They had to tell everyone in the community and warn folks about the pending dangers that would come.

"Are we safe? Do I need to wake Kenneth and leave?" Elise asked.

"I'm goin' to protect you and him, at any cost," Bronco replied wholeheartedly.

"That's not what I asked you," she griped.

"When they come, they won't find their bodies."

"And you think that will stop them from terrorizing this community?"

"Would you have wanted me to let them kill Duncan?"

"No. Of course not," she quickly replied, becoming overwhelmed with uncertainty.

Damned if you do, damned if you don't. She understood that he didn't have much of a choice. But that choice now brought about an inevitable fate.

Bronco knew that once word got out about the attacks, they would point to him and blame him no matter the reason he did it. He was the new face in their town. He would become their scapegoat to save their town from the deadly onslaught of a white mob coming for their revenge. He knew human behavior. He knew Black people's fears and insecurities. He had a few of his own.

"You need to wash up and get some rest. Tomorrow's another day," Elise said.

Bronco nodded. "Will do, but I'm gonna stay out here for the night, keep watch over everything."

"Is that necessary?"

"It isn't right now. But I'll feel better doing it, just for tonight," said Bronco.

Bronco moved up the steps toward the porch. The moment he set foot near Elise, she dropped the rifle and threw her arms around him so tightly that it caught him off guard. She exhaled against him, her tears falling against his clothes. She was scared, and it showed. Bronco embraced her and held her tightly for a lingering moment. They didn't want to let go of each other.

They were in love.

Bronco followed Elise into the farmhouse, where he went into the bathroom and began to undress. He wanted to wash away the filth and the blood from his skin. He'd shown no remorse for the men he killed. In fact, Bronco was delighted that the maggots and bugs would gorge on their burnt and rotten flesh. He drew himself a hot bath and then completely submerged into the tub water, inherently feeling liberated. He closed his eyes and exhaled. The bliss of a hot bath. It was like wrapping himself in a cozy cocoon of warmth and leisure. As Bronco lingered in the water's warm embrace, it quieted his mind and reduced his tension and anger. However, moments later, the bathroom door creaked open, causing Bronco to open his eyes and see Elise entering the small space. She was clad in a blue house robe, obviously naked underneath it. She said nothing to Bronco as she untied her house robe and let it fall from her shoulders to the floor. Her nakedness was a gift to see.

Bronco stared quietly at her as she slowly sank into the tub to join him. She came closer to kiss him. It was sweet and enduring. Bronco enfolded his arms around her. Her breasts were pressed against his strapping chest. She wanted this again. She wanted him before the inevitable chaos ensued in their community or if they were to part ways forever. Elise straddled Bronco while they were submerged, and he was soon inside her.

She shuddered and gasped, "Ugh! Oh, Bronco." Her tone was soft and sweet to his ear. There was something about water sex that felt inherently liberating. Elise bit her lip as he thrust slowly into her. Her arms stayed around him. Her eyes were closed. Then they opened with mixed tears of bliss and unease. It took a moment for Bronco to release sweetly inside of her. But when he did, they both clamped on to each other while submerged in the tub, savoring their lovemaking, and exhaled. Elise smiled inanely. She was at peace for those few moments of lovemaking, and it felt absolutely perfect.

Bronco got dressed, retrieved the rifle Elise had with her earlier, and stepped out onto the porch. The moon was nearly gone, but the stars overhead glistened as if they had been nearly polished. As planned, he sat in the old porch chair with the rifle in his lap and stared at the stars and the trees.

The sun shone through the tree branches as Bronco, Duncan, Beulah, and Elise packed some of the Goffs' belongings into a Ford station wagon with wood paneling. The sky was a perfect blue, and the only sounds were birds chirping. The events of last night still haunted everyone. No one knew when the Klan would come looking for their friends. Duncan and his wife needed to be long gone when they did, as they would be the first in mortal danger.

Duncan and Beulah carried the last of their things from their home. They squeezed them into the back of the station wagon, fully packed with their clothing, many boxes, a few pictures, and some personal items. Elise hated to see them go. She'd known them all her life. Now, they wouldn't be right down the road from her anymore. Georgia wasn't too far away, but it could have been. Elise had always been in Mississippi.

Bronco could have protected the Goffs, but he couldn't be in two places at once, so it was best that the Goffs left town for a while.

"I's don't know what I'm gon' do with y'all gone," Elise sadly uttered.

Beulah sighed heavily. Elise was like another daughter to her. When her mother died, Beulah stepped into the position. She'd become so close with her and Kenneth that it felt like she'd birthed them both herself.

"This is where we be stayin' at," said Beulah. She handed Elise an address. "It's Duncan's brother in Georgia."

"I's promise I'll write to you both or call when the time comes," Elise replied.

"I'll be lookin' forward to hearing from you, Elise."

The ladies looked at each other sadly. It was heart-wrenching for them to depart. Tears began to well in Elise eyes. She quickly wiped them away with the back of her hand and huffed. It felt like she was losing her parents again.

In the meantime, Duncan and Bronco chatted by the car, which was packed and ready for the long drive east to Georgia.

"I's still can't explain what I saw the other night, somethin' short of a miracle. But I want to thank you again for saving my life, Bronco. You's an angel sent from above, remember that," Duncan proclaimed unequivocally.

"I'm no angel, Mr. Duncan. I'm just a man trying to find his way in this crazy world," Bronco replied.

Duncan glanced over at Elise talking to Beulah, then looked back at Bronco and replied, "I believe you already have, Bronco. She's something special. Take care of her for us."

Bronco nodded. "I will."

"And don't worry, yo's secret is safe with me. I won't tell a soul 'bout what I saw."

"I appreciate it, Mr. Duncan."

"But you's be safe, too," Duncan blurted sincerely. "Despite what you's capable of, white folks are sneaky, and they will try to find a way to bring you down. We's behind enemy lines, Bronco. And they always have a way to destroy and take away somethin' you love."

Bronco nodded. *Duly noted.*

"I'll look after your farm while you're gone," said Bronco.

Duncan smiled. "I know you will. You's a good man with a good soul. Don't let anyone else tell you different."

The two shook hands and slightly nodded. It was respect and admiration for each other. Duncan then turned and hollered, "Beulah, we's need to get goin' now. We have a long drive ahead of us."

"Well, this is it," Beulah said to Elise with a quiet smile. "Give my goodbyes to Kenneth. I wish I could see him one last time."

"Hush that talk. You's not gone forever. I know y'all coming back," said Elise.

"God knows when though," Beulah replied reflectively. "This madness with the farm, the Klan, and my husband. I can't lose him now."

"I know."

"I'm gon' keep you and Kenneth in my prayers. But I know you's in safe hands with him." Beulah gestured toward Bronco.

Elise glanced in Bronco's direction and beamed brighter than the sun on a hot summer day, indicating she was head over heels for him. Beulah recognized the smile and blush that betrayed Elise's feelings, which mirrored those she harbored for her own husband.

"I's know you in love with him," said Beulah with her knowing smile.

"I didn't mean to fall in love with him."

"No one never means to fall in love. We just do it naturally. The beauty of love is that you can fall into it with the most unexpected person at the most unexpected time."

Elise exhaled. The ladies hugged each other goodbye. Then Beulah climbed into the passenger seat of the station wagon. Duncan gave Elise a paternal and lasting hug and said, "You's take care of ya'self, Elise. Ya hear? And you's take care of ya man, too. Y'all gon be all right together."

Elise nodded and faintly smiled.

Duncan finally climbed into the driver's seat, and Elise and Bronco watched them drive away from their land. She stood close to Bronco. He reached for her hand, and hers warmly became gripped into his.

"They'll be back. I'll make sure of it," said Bronco heartily.

Bronco hated to admit it, but Duncan had become somewhat of a father figure to him too.

The two arrived at Elise's farm to find Kenneth pouting on the porch. Kenneth glanced at them with a sad and bothered expression, then lowered his gaze to the floor. Elise and Bronco nervously exited the pickup truck.

"Is everything okay with you, Kenneth?" asked Elise.

"No. Are they comin' to kill us too?" Kenneth asked them.

Elise was shocked by the question. "No. No one is coming to hurt you, Kenneth."

"How's you know that, Elise? You's sees the future?"

"No, but . . ."

"Mr. and Mrs. Duncan are gone now because they tried to hurt him last night," Kenneth griped. "What 'bout us?

They done already killed my best friend. They won't stop until we all dead."

Elise gasped, then exhaled sharply. Kenneth was scared and still hurting. She didn't know what to do. The men he had grown close to—his father, Sylvester, and Duncan—were now gone. Although Duncan was still alive, he was in a different state, and it was uncertain when Kenneth would see him again.

"Kenneth . . ." Elise started but was at a loss for words. What could she say to comfort him, to give him security? She was scared too.

"Go inside. I'll talk to him," Bronco told her.

Elise looked surprised. "You will?"

Bronco nodded, and Elise smiled gratefully. She went up the stairs, passed Kenneth, opened the screen door, and entered the house. Bronco rose and casually sat next to Kenneth on the porch. The boy remained seated, with his head bowed, and in a sullen, quiet state.

"Do you wanna talk about it?" Bronco asked him kindly.

Kenneth simply shrugged his shoulders, not bothering to answer the question.

"Mr. Duncan, he'll be back," Bronco stated.

"Are you gon' leave us too?" Kenneth asked him out of the blue.

"I'm not going anywhere, Kenneth. I promise to protect you and your sister," Bronco replied.

"But before, you's says you wasn't sure. Says you's was simply passin' through."

"I know what I said, but I know now I have a purpose here," Bronco said.

"And what's that?"

"To make sure no one bothers you and your sister ever again," he answered.

"How you gon' make that happen? You gon' kill every white man around?"

Bronco smirked. It was possible, but he knew that would only bring them much more trouble elsewhere—an act like that would provoke a nuclear backlash.

"I have my ways, Kenneth. But I know you're scared. I get scared too," Bronco admitted.

Kenneth stared at Bronco as if he didn't believe him. He felt it was impossible for a man like Bronco, with his muscles and experience, to become scared.

"You's get scared?"

Bronco nodded. "I do. It's okay to be scared. Being scared means you're about to do something really, really brave," Bronco proclaimed.

"Do you really believe that? I'm just a boy, and if somethin' was to happen, I can't fight."

"How about this, tomorrow morning, we'll both come out here, and I'll teach you a few things that I learned in the army," said Bronco.

That made Kenneth perk up and smile. "You will?"

Bronco nodded. *Of course.* "And here's something to help give you some courage," Bronco added.

He began to unclasp his dog tags. Next, Bronco placed his dog tags around Kenneth's neck and said, "They belong to you now, a reminder that being scared is part of being alive. But having courage is doing what's right. Accept it and walk through it."

Kenneth no longer hung his head down toward the steps. He wasn't sulking anymore. He sat up straight with Bronco's dog tags around his neck, feeling different. He smiled with newfound confidence and excitedly exclaimed, "Thank you. I'm never gon' take them off."

"I know they're in good hands," Bronco said.

Kenneth leaned closer to Bronco, and Bronco placed his arm around the young boy. It was an unexpected moment for him. They'd grown close. Kenneth became the little brother he never had.

Elise had remained by the screen door, eavesdropping. She'd heard their discussion, which made her fall more in love with Bronco. How he'd comforted and talked to her little brother sincerely melted her heart. The man had an unexplainable way with Kenneth and her—it was nearly enchanted or hypnotic. If Bronco would ask her to marry her right now, she wouldn't hesitate. Her answer would have been a screaming and an excited *yes*. She'd never looked at a man the way she did Bronco. She did not want him to leave. She loved him.

Bronco opened the screen door and entered the house. Elise's eyes lit up brightly with a smile. Elise was a woman who always wore her heart on her sleeve. He was the one she wanted to spend the rest of her life with. She threw her arms around him and hugged him. What came next out of her mouth caught Bronco off guard.

"I think I love you."

Chapter Twenty-two

Jim Crow's Last Stand

The heat of the sun was causing steam to rise from the earth. The weather was balmy, and it would be another scorching day. While the blazing sun was good news for playing children, it became hell on earth for others. The hot noon sun filtered in through the slats of the window blinds, laying out parallel strips of sunlight on the hardwood floor. A loud, whirring fan stood upon the sheriff's desk, doing little but pushing warm air around. Sheriff Duke sat behind his desk, trying to keep cool with the remains of his homemade lunch littered before him. The sheriff sat pondering the niggers who had been released. It'd rubbed him the wrong way how Mr. Lockheart chastised him in front of the niggers. He didn't care about their health or well-being, so why should a state congressman care? The niggers had become unruly in a civic place, and consequences needed to happen. Sheriff Duke didn't care if that nigger Forrest Tolson lived or died. He'd brought trouble into his town. And he also didn't give a fuck about the NAACP. Suppose they had the stupidity to invade his city with their nonsense about equality and civil rights. In that case, he'd be ready for them with his deputies and the good ol' boys spreading that good Southern nigger hospitality.

There was a sudden knock on the sheriff's office door. Sheriff Duke sat upright and said, "Yeah?"

Deputy Calvin stormed into the office with apprehension. He locked eyes with Sheriff Duke and quickly blurted out, "Boss, we might have a problem."

"What is it, Deputy?"

The sheriff could hear the voices outside of his office. They were incoherent but loud, full of griping, grumbling, and concerns. Behind the deputy, Sheriff Duke saw the silhouettes of people rustling about outside his office. They looked like scared cattle to him.

"What's going on out there?"

"Well, that's the problem I wanted to bring to you, boss," the deputy uttered. "It seems four men went missing last night."

"Four men, who?"

"Paul, Keith, Joseph, and Jacob," the deputy answered.

"What? They went missing where?"

"In the nigger community, I believe."

Sheriff Duke sprang from the wooden chair, baffled by the sudden news. He marched from behind his desk, moved by his deputy, and hurried into the main room, where he was met with the wives and family of the missing men. Immediately, they rushed toward him like a tidal wave and cried out about their concerns.

"Sheriff Duke, Paul didn't come home last night. He always come home," Paul's wife, Marry, spewed worriedly. She was a rail-thin woman with short black hair.

"Sheriff, where is my damn husband?" Keith's wife, Cindy-Lou, uttered. She was the prettiest of the ladies with blue eyes, long blond hair, and slender curves—a former winner of the Miss America Pageant.

"My kids and I are worried sick, Sheriff. Joseph told us he was doing something for you and Mr. Lockheart, but now he hasn't come back home to his family. Find my got-damn husband, Sheriff!" Abigal cried out, tears welling in her eyes.

Sheriff Duke was overwhelmed with wives, brothers, sons, cousins, and daughters. Four white men going missing suddenly was uncanny. The news began to spread throughout the town like wildfire, and the natives were becoming restless with rumors and gossip.

"Folks, I apologize for any inconvenience this is causing for everyone. But I promise you all that I will get to the bottom of this," Sheriff Duke proclaimed wholeheartedly. "I know these men personally, and they are good men, and we will find them."

The crowd continued to grumble and swell with frustration, making it clear that they wouldn't leave until the matter was resolved.

"Calvin, get on the horn and get me Mr. Lockheart. We gon' get to the bottom of this nonsense," Sheriff Duke instructed.

Calvin nodded and began to make the phone call. The sheriff continued to try to tame the chaos. He knew something terrible must have happened to these men for them not to have made it home last night. Paul was a survivor, and the sheriff believed he would never let any nigger get the best of him. But was it possible that a nigger, or a few niggers, did the unthinkable? It was something he kept to himself. There was no need to trouble the family with his thoughts.

"He's not picking up, boss," Calvin said.

Sheriff Duke frowned. Now wasn't the time to not answer his damn phone. This was a crisis that he needed to deduce.

The sheriff had his deputies handle the scene at the police station while he went back into his office. He reached for his gun belt, fastened it around his waist, put on his wide-brim cowboy hat, exited his office, and waded through the crackling family members. Before he went, he stared at the wives and uttered with certainty, "We gon' find your husbands, ladies. I assure you, they probably got drunk last night and most likely passed out in a heap. They have likely woken up by now with some blinding headaches and some explaining to do."

Deputy Calvin took charge while Sheriff Duke hurried from the police station and briskly headed toward his patrol car. After climbing into the driver's seat, he lingered behind the wheel momentarily. Did he believe what he had said to the wives back there? Yes, all four men did drink, and sometimes excessively. However, they would usually be found staggering at the local saloon or supper club, where they'd be slightly chastised for their drunkenness but eventually make it home to their families. Once there, they'd face another round of reprimands from their wives.

Sheriff Duke activated the police sirens and drove off speedily.

The sheriff arrived at the classic colonial four-bedroom home in Mississippi within the hour, parking his patrol car outside. Mr. Lockheart's invitations to Sheriff Duke's place were rare, and he could count the times he'd been there on one hand. He exited his vehicle, marched toward the house, and ascended onto the porch. Then, he began to knock on the front door. The door opened, and Mrs. Lockheart loomed into the sheriff's view. She was surprised to see the sheriff but politely said, "Good morning, Sheriff."

"Good day to you to, ma'am. Is your husband in?" he asked her.

"Yes. He's in the back, tending to his horses. Is everything okay, Sheriff?"

"No need to trouble yourself, ma'am. I just need a few words with him."

The sheriff followed Ruth through the house, toward the rear, and exited into the lush backyard where he spotted the thirty-by-thirty-six four-stall barn.

"He's in there," said Ruth.

"I'll see myself to him, ma'am. Thank you," the sheriff politely told Ruth.

Ruth smiled and disappeared into her home. Sheriff Duke made his way toward the barn, walking briskly in his yearning to get to the bottom of the men going missing. As he entered the barn, he noted its A-frame profile, fairly square footprint, tack room, washroom, and a crucial secondary space. The sheriff coolly stepped foot into the place where he witnessed the best money could buy. This was his town, but Benny Lockheart and his investors pulled the strings.

Sheriff Duke stood at the edge of the barn, not seeing Mr. Lockheart, but he heard a horse neighing.

"Mr. Lockheart, it's Sheriff Duke. Can I have a word with you, sir?" he called out.

Benny Lockheart was in one of the stalls attending to one of the two horses he owned. "Sheriff, I'm in the stall. Come join me."

The sheriff strolled toward one of the four stalls and spotted Mr. Lockheart running his hand along a sleek black horse, admiring how the sun reflected off its coat.

"I got a new stallion last week. I hope to birth some racing colts with this one," Benny said. "She's a beauty, isn't she?"

The sheriff stared at the animal. It was a beautiful animal, a high-class stallion able to move with simplicity and grace. "She is, Mr. Lockheart," the sheriff replied.

"My wife prefers to ride the mare because the stallion is too big and difficult to control. Myself, I love the stallion. They come with lots of energy and aren't suitable for most riders. The stallion's reputation is that he has a lot of character, is difficult to manage or control and is sometimes even considered a dangerous horse. Not all horses are fit for all riders, whether it be geldings, mares, or stallions."

Sheriff Duke nodded. He knew nothing about horses.

"What can I help you with, Sheriff?"

"Four men went missing last night, Mr. Lockheart," the sheriff informed him.

Benny became bemused. "Who are the men?"

"Paul, Jacob, Joseph, and Keith."

Benny Lockheart sighed heavily and muttered quietly, "Damn," indicating he knew something about what happened.

"Do you know anything about this, Mr. Lockheart?" the sheriff asked.

"I sent them boys to Mr. Goff's farm for an eviction because Mr. Duncan Goff's time had expired."

"You sent them into the nigger community without informing me about it first?" Sheriff Duke griped.

"I don't need your permission to do anything in this town, Sheriff. It was a matter that needed to be expedited. And they were compensated."

"It would have been nice to know this. Some common courtesy would have been polite, Mr. Lockheart. Now I have four men missing and their families are hounding me like a dog in heat about their whereabouts," Sheriff Duke protested.

"It's an unfortunate incident, Sheriff. A matter you and your deputies can resolve. Time is of the essence, and these investors are becoming impatient. They need to acquire every deed in that community by month's end, or else, everything I've worked so hard to build will come crashing down on me," Benny proclaimed.

"I understand your dilemma, Mr. Lockheart. But now we have a crisis on our hands. We need to begin looking for these men."

"Then begin searching for them. I suggest you start with Mr. Goff's land. It's where they were sent last night," Benny nonchalantly replied. "And please do it quietly, Sheriff. The last thing I need is for Mr. Roth and his investors to become spooked about this and pull out last minute."

The sheriff sighed heavily. He was growing tired of being Mr. Lockheart's underling. He was a man with a badge but was being kept in the dark about specific activities and events in the town he was policing. Sheriff Duke hated surprises. Mr. Lockheart was an important man, but he didn't have to deal with the day-to-day events and the niggers encroaching and unlawfulness. They were becoming a handful to deal with. Mr. Lockheart lived in a lovely big house. He had a beautiful wife and sweet, pretty kids, and his reputation proceeded him. But the sheriff, his deputies, and their cronies were in the trenches. They were out there in no-man's-land doing the higher-ups' bidding, ensuring business for them went smoothly without any hiccups. The only thing he wanted from them was communication and respect.

Benny Lockheart continued to run his hand along the sleek horse while the sheriff frowned. It was apparent to him that four missing white men meant little to him. What was more important to Mr. Lockheart was his business and his appeasing of investors. But what was important to the sheriff was the fundamentals of loyalty, law and order, the protection of good white folks in his town, and keeping the status quo of Jim Crow and the niggers oppressed. There would be no such thing as equality and desegregation among the niggers—not while he wore the badge and was in charge.

"Will there be anything else, Sheriff?" Mr. Lockheart uttered dismissively.

"No, Mr. Lockheart. I'll keep you updated, sir."

"Good. I'll take it that you'll see yourself out," Benny said.

The sheriff nodded. "I will."

Sheriff Duke pivoted and walked away, annoyed. He marched toward his vehicle, climbed inside, and grimaced. His gut feeling continued to twist and turn like butter was churning inside his stomach, telling him that all four men were dead and niggers were behind their demise. And if so, he was ready to bestow hell and brim fire on every nigger in that community.

The hot summer day seemed to melt into an even more humid summer night. The air was so moist that it pressed upon everyone's skin like sweat. The polished stars twinkled across the dark blue blanket of the night with their ethereal glow, and the silver orb of the moon illuminated all the land below like a spotlight. Hundreds of fireflies were all aglow and lifted off the dewy grasses from the previous rain, the bullfrogs were chorusing, and the crickets were chirping in the night. Also active in the woods was the Red Rooster. It was up and running again from the previous incident. Bayou had added extra security to make sure things didn't repeat itself. Davis and Rodney were there to prevent any trouble from happening. Davis was a dark-skinned solid chunk of a man with thick eyebrows, and Rodney was a broad-shouldered light-skinned man with a pronounced jaw and a face only a mother could love.

At the Red Rooster, the air was filled with romance and desire. Every man looked impeccable for the evening's event. The creases in their suits were sharp enough to cut, and their shoes shone like mirrors. All attention was on Stephanie James, a remarkable jazz singer with a voice reminiscent of Josephine Baker and Mamie Smith combined. Stephanie stood on a small stage with her band, including Swan, her guitarist, ready to give a stellar performance.

Stephanie James, an attractive woman in her early thirties with soft, curly black hair, red lips, and gentle eyes, wore platform heels and a red sequined long-sleeve evening dress that accentuated her hourglass figure.

A crowd of mostly men surrounded Stephanie while she was on the stage. You could barely see her from a slight distance inside the place, but everyone could hear her sweet laughter and sugary voice. She was loud and vibrant—a joy to be around. Her jazz singing was even louder and more vibrant, and it was what everyone came to see: her phenomenal beauty and magnificent voice.

"How you boys doing tonight?" Stephanie addressed the crowd.

"Better now that you're here, Stephanie," someone shouted from the crowd excitedly.

Stephanie laughed. "Well, I'm glad that I was able to bring a little piece of heaven with me tonight."

"Yes, Lord. Amen."

"You're beautiful, Stephanie," a voice shouted.

"Thank you." Stephanie beamed.

As Swan began to tune his guitar, a sudden silence fell over the crowd. Stephanie continued to smile and giggle in her glowing red dress that complemented her bright black skin and shiny black curls. She stood with one hand on her hip. Just as she was about to start singing, a loud train passed by, and the flashing lights of the train were visible on the walls of the Red Rooster. After the train had passed, Stephanie did what she did best—she started to sing!

As Stephanie sang, her eyes drifted over the crowd, and her words to the tune she'd been humming began to take her audience to heaven. She noticed lovers kiss each other while leaning against the wall, and another couple began dancing together. Her attention subtly rested on Doc, JoJo, Washer, and Jimmy in the crowd. Each man became mesmerized by her beauty and voice. They were rooted to every note and syllable spewed from her lips.

"Fellas, I's believe I'm in love," Doc joked.

Meanwhile, unbeknownst to the patrons inside the Red Rooster, Sheriff Duke and a few of his deputies had arrived in three patrol cars. The sheriff and his deputies climbed out of the vehicles with their hands on their holstered revolvers, their attention itching to create chaos and mayhem tonight. The men saw that the Red Rooster was packed, and their timing was perfect. Each deputy circled around the sheriff, who had the floor.

"Listen here. While the niggers are in there having a grand good time, four good men done went missing the other night, and we intend to find their whereabouts right now. Not a nigger come outta that place without the proper interrogation. If you catch my drift. Do you men hear me?" Sheriff Duke exclaimed.

They nodded and replied, "We hear you, Sheriff."

They could hear Stephanie's voice spilling from the place, along with the guitar and drums banging. The sheriff frowned at the noise and exclaimed, "And someone please shut up that nigger bitch's wretched noise."

Deputy Calvin smiled as if to say to his boss, *I'm on it.*

"Also, if Doc is in there, leave him for me. I want him placed in my car for further questioning tonight," the sheriff said. "We gonna get to the bottom of these missing men."

They all marched in sync toward the Red Rooster like a band of Hitler's Nazi SS moving through a German street. They smirked and looked forward to ruining the niggers' night with their sudden rowdiness. They were ready to leave behind a trail of broken bones, concussions, and unconsciousness—and maybe death if a nigger didn't give the correct response.

The Red Rooster was alive with singing and dancing as Stephanie James commanded the crowd with her powerful voice. She swayed from side to side, happily snapping her fingers while her voice echoed through the establishment. At the same time, Swan worked magic with his guitar. Bayou stood off to the side, observing everything with a slight smile. Davis and Rodney stood out like two pillars in the crowd, ready to impede any incident that would erupt. However, Stephanie James brought out the best in everyone.

Suddenly, the tranquil atmosphere was disrupted as the sheriff and his deputies stormed into the establishment, ready to enforce their will with brute force.

"Listen here, if any one of you niggers try to leave out this place without speaking to me or one of my deputies, you'll be shot down like a dog in the street!" Sheriff Duke shouted.

The revelers were caught off guard and shocked. The women shrieked. The men scowled and became overwhelmed. Panic began to ensue throughout the establishment because the deputies began assaulting the revelers with their batons and billy clubs, walloping Black men across their heads and bodies, and assaulting the ladies. They tossed chairs, broke bottles, and turned over tables. One patron panicked and tried to bolt for the exit. He was quickly met with the butt of a shotgun viciously slammed into his face, immediately breaking his nose.

"I said, no one fuckin' leaves this place," the sheriff shouted.

Bayou seethed at seeing his place destroyed again. He stepped toward the sheriff, scowled, and exclaimed, "What is the meaning of this, Sheriff? I paid my dues to you already."

"This ain't 'bout your nigger money, Bayou. This is something different," Sheriff Duke replied vehemently.

"Like what?" Bayou demanded to know.

Sheriff Duke glared at Bayou, his nostrils flaring as he tightly clutched a baton between his fists. The blood of a few individuals he'd struck with it dripped from the tip.

"Four white men had gone missing from here the other night, and not a nigger around here is safe until we find them. Or we find out what y'all niggers done to them," Sheriff Duke said gruffly with a steely glare.

Bayou was utterly shocked. "I don't know nothing about no white men gone missing."

"Well, you better find out, Bayou, cuz things only gonna get worst for you and everyone else until they're found," the sheriff retorted.

By the stage, Stephanie squatted down around the chaos and attempted to stanch the flow of blood that was pouring out of the gash in the side of Swan's head. He'd been struck hard by the deputy, and he was dazed with his eyes wandering without ever fixing upon a stationary object.

"You just keep this to your head, Swan," Stephanie told him.

She put Swan's hand on the rag she used to hinder blood flow. Her performance had been ruined. Her eyes were filled with tears as she witnessed multiple attacks and beating of Black men and women by nearly a handful of armed white goons. Stephanie stood up in horror and cursed, "Fuck all of you white devils! Go to hell!"

Sheriff Duke spotted the man he wanted to talk to the most: his golden boy, nigger snitch, Doc. The sheriff and Calvin roughly grabbed Doc and took him back to the car to interrogate him in the back seat while, at the same time, the chaos continued inside the Red Rooster. Sheriff

Duke angrily prompted Doc with hard, crunching blows with the baton on his arms and legs. Doc doubled over in pain and hollered.

The sheriff waited, taking joy in seeing his suffering.

"Listen here, nigger, what you know about four missing white men?" Sheriff Duke growled at him.

"I's don't know nothin' 'bout no missing white men, Sheriff. I's swear to you," Doc cried out.

"Wrong answer, nigger," Sheriff Duke replied pointedly.

The sheriff struck Doc's forearm with a quick, hard stroke, causing Doc to cry out and moan in pain. Sheriff Duke looked at him contemptuously and asked again, "What happened to the men, Doc? You'd better tell me something, or you're not leaving this back seat alive."

"All I's can tell you is it might have somethin' to do with this new nigger in town. He looks like trouble. He started a fight in Bayou's place the other night."

"What's his name?"

"I think they call him Bronco."

"Bronco?" Deputy Calvin chuckled.

"You can't miss him. He a powerful and mean-lookin' nigger," said Doc. "I think they say he's from Harlem."

"Now, was that so hard, Doc? It was all I wanted from you," the sheriff muttered. "Why you niggers always so got-damn stubborn and stupid?"

"Can I go now, Sheriff?"

For good measure, the sheriff plunged his baton into Doc's gut, causing him to fold over once again from the pain, and he coughed violently. His deputy added to the abuse and struck Doc's arm repeatedly with his billy club, and Doc cried out, "Aaaah, you done broke my arm. I's gave you all I got!"

"Now you can get the fuck out my car, nigger," Sheriff Duke exclaimed.

Doc struggled to climb out from the back seat of the sheriff's car, managing to do so despite the severe pain. He rolled into a clumsy heap on the ground. He heard the sheriff say, "Tell our men to finish up in there and come on. Burn it all down."

Calvin nodded and grinned. "Yes, sir."

Chapter Twenty-three

White Man's Justice, Black Man's Grief

"I heard they killed three people last night at the Red Rooster," a short, wiry man named Bell uttered, upset.

A few people gasped at the statement.

"And they done burned it down, too. I heard with Bayou still inside it," a woman hollered from the thick crowd inside the Baptist church.

"Bayou ain't dead. That man too stubborn to die," someone countered.

"They almost killed Stephanie James and her guitarist!"

The church was filled with people. The leaders of the community had called an emergency town meeting. News of what had happened at the Red Rooster had spread throughout the Black community. People were scared, angry, and confused. However, what terrified folks even more was hearing that four white men had suddenly gone missing. No one had any idea what had happened to these men, and if it weren't for the sudden white backlash coming toward them like a tornado, they wouldn't have lost any sleep over it.

Pastor Brooke stood behind the podium, shaken by the tragedy. Seated behind him were other respected individuals from the Black community—men and women who owned stores and businesses, had received education from some of the best schools, and had become the de facto leaders of the town. Everyone was eager to resolve the brewing situation. Sheriff Duke was on a rampage of destruction and death. He had made it clear that there would be severe consequences if he didn't receive any information about the missing men. Their families were worried.

"I say good riddance to them crackers if they are found dead," Haywood shouted in resentment. He was a tall, lean man with wire-frame glasses.

"And what you believe gon' happen to us if they are found dead?" Ms. Mary replied.

"They come for us when we keep to ourselves and mind our business anyway, Ms. Mary. We dammed if we do, and we dammed if we don't," Haywood countered. "An eye for an eye."

"You got that right," someone hollered.

The chatter among the group became louder as emotions ran high. Some were defiant about the absence of the white men. In contrast, others believed they needed to reach a resolution before history repeated itself—Tulsa, Rosewood, Springfield. Fear was paralyzing them.

"If anyone knows about them white men suddenly goin' missing, I bet you it's that nigger Elise been sweet on lately," JoJo shouted.

A few folks began to agree with him.

"He is a strange one," a woman uttered.

"Much trouble has been comin' 'round here lately since he came to town," a plump, dark-skinned man named Darryl concurred.

"I's tell you we need to be questioning that nigger. He got that look of a killer. I's know it. What he did at Bayou's club the other night, the nigger looked possessed to me," JoJo added.

Murmuring and gossip started among the crowd.

"Do you really think that man took on and killed four men with his bare hands?" Washer replied.

"You's seen the nigger in action, Washer . . . what he capable of doin', how he tossed me to the side like I was some toy. And I swears to you, I got the nigger right in his back and he didn't flinch," JoJo uttered.

"Thou shall not kill, JoJo," a woman recited.

"Do onto them as they do onto me," JoJo retorted.

The same woman puckered her brow and sneered back at JoJo.

Some people were surprised by the news. It was possible that JoJo was fabricating stories, as he was known to exaggerate sometimes. They found Bronco mysterious, knowing only that he was from Harlem. They wondered why he was in Mississippi, why Elise felt at ease giving him shelter on her farm, and where he came from. There were numerous questions and too few answers.

"What about that fifteen-year-old boy that done went missing in Money, Mississippi?" a woman bellowed out of the blue.

"I heard the Klan done got to that boy, too."

"What 'bout Duncan and his wife? You think he got somethin' do with this? I heard they done cut out and left for Georgia suddenly," said JoJo. "Why's that, Pastor?"

No one knew why.

The conversation in the church became increasingly heated. It resembled a seesaw, with emotions fluctuating as people shouted their opinions and feelings back and forth. The pastor struggled to maintain control of the meeting and had to bang the gavel to gather their attention.

"Listen, everyone, we need to stick together on this," Pastor Brooke shouted.

"And how you s'pose we do that when the sheriff out for blood?" Jimmy replied. "Look at what they did to Doc."

Doc was seated in the crowd, his left arm in a sling. He had cracked ribs, a black eye, and bruises.

"Tell 'em, Doc, tell 'em what the sheriff done told you," JoJo bellowed.

Doc slowly stood up to address the crowd. He was still recovering from the attack, feeling a throbbing ache in his side. It was a fresh pain. He opened his mouth to begin to speak, his voice tight with agony. "He told me there's going to be a warrant out for Bronco's arrest because he gathered sufficient evidence against him."

The crowd erupted with emotions.

"We should turn that nigger in ourselves to save our community," JoJo cried out.

"They taking it away from us regardless with all this land stealing," Washer retorted.

They were fighting a losing battle but didn't want to sit around and not do anything. They had all come too far to give up now. But the situation grew uglier and uglier every day.

During the ongoing town meeting, Forrest Tolson's sudden appearance shocked everyone. The room fell silent as all eyes turned to him. Forrest walked through the angry and bitter crowd, with some believing he was partially responsible for James's death. His expression was blank, in stark contrast to the anger and resentment of a few people. He was accompanied by a beautiful woman named Virginia Brown, and no one knew who she was.

"What is he doing here?" Ms. Mary wondered.

"I thought he done gone on and left town," a woman murmured.

"Who is that woman he's with?" a man asked.

Forrest Tolson marched toward the platform with indifference. He had somewhat healed from his wounds a few weeks ago, and despite what had happened at the courthouse, Tolson still had that determined look in his eyes. He was ready to continue fighting for civil liberties and voting rights for Black people in Mississippi and the South. He had been hurt, beaten, and jailed, but he wasn't broken. Instead, he had become more determined to fight for what was right every day and continued to demand equality. This was only the beginning.

As Forrest walked toward the platform, he encountered James's mother, Gloria, beside her husband. On seeing Forrest, a few tears fell down her cheeks. Forrest felt at a loss for words and locked eyes with the grieving mother. He wondered what he could possibly say to comfort her, knowing that she had lost her son because he believed in change. A dark cloud seemed to hang over Forrest as he struggled with the guilt of the young boy's death. The church fell silent, waiting to see how Gloria would react to Forrest's sudden presence, anticipating an outburst of anger. To everyone's surprise, she stood up and approached Forrest, filling him with sadness.

"Ma'am, I am completely sorry for what happened to James that day, and I take full responsibility—"

"You hush now," Gloria interjected. Her attention went from sadness to heroism. "Don't let my son's death be in vain, Mr. Tolson. He believed in something with you. So you continue that fight in his name, and fight for what he was killed for."

Forrest's eyes glistened with tears, and he quickly blinked them away. "I will, ma'am. I promise," he said.

Gloria faintly smiled and surprisingly gave him a hug. The church was utterly taken aback. A woman hollered, "Hallelujah! Thank you, Jesus!"

It was a touching moment as Gloria sat next to her husband, and Forrest turned to Pastor Brooke to say, "I'd like to speak, Pastor Brooke, and I've brought someone with me."

Pastor Brooke looked reluctant to address Forrest. He didn't want this Negro talking that "by any means necessary" madness to these people. They were already upset, scared, and riled up. They were already about to burst as it was.

"I'll let you address the crowd, Mr. Tolson," said Pastor Brooke kindly. "But keep it respectful. We don't need to keep poking the hornets' nest. Me and the leaders with me, we have a plan going for real progress. The last thing we need is for these people to pick up their guns and start shooting white folks. Before you know it, the National Guard will be here firing on us so quick we won't realize it 'til they lower us into the ground."

Forrest sighed heavily at the pastor's remark. How could he remain respectful when white people were ready to kill Black folks as if it were an apocalypse? He and Pastor Brooke had different approaches. Forrest considered the man a coward, as Pastor Brooke always leaned towards pacifism in the face of white terrorism.

"I simply just want to introduce someone, Pastor," Forrest replied.

Pastor Brooke's attention was drawn to Virginia. She was beautiful, educated, and elegant. However, there was something about her that was unsettling. As Forrest and Virginia walked onto the platform, the expressions of the movement leaders changed. It was evident that they were all apprehensive about what was happening. The church looked in their direction with a mix of awe and curiosity. Forrest stepped behind the podium to speak briefly. He gazed at the congregation, something he had done many times before, but this time, his speech wouldn't be as forceful as in the past. His conscience was weighing heavily on him.

"I came here to this town because there's an iniquity upon Black men and women called segregation, an iniquity that has plagued us for generations too long. You all know me, and my efforts to fight discrimination is to lift the Negro from this brutal era of injustice and inequality. And unfortunately, it's a fight that will come with a cost," said Forrest. He fleetingly glanced at Gloria and her husband, thinking about James.

He continued. "We must all bear the cross like Christ if we expect change to happen . . . a burden or trial one must put up with. But our fight against systemic racism must come in every direction, not just with protests and marches but also with education, documentation, awareness, exposure, and removing those from political office who don't have our self-interest in their hearts. When Jesus said we must deny ourselves and take up our cross daily, He spoke about 'dying to self,' not dying physically on a cross, but dying to our own selfish desires, to do God's will of God . . . . daily. The Christian life is a life of surrender and sometimes sacrifice."

The congregation began to holler. "Yes, Lord. Hallelujah!"

"This woman with me tonight, her name is Virginia Brown, and she has something to say, something important. She wants to reveal her truth to everyone in this room," Forrest introduced her politely.

The church instantly grew silent. Forrest stepped away from the podium, and Virginia immediately took her place before the microphone. She appeared confident and significant in her full-length skirt and blue blouse. She exhaled briefly, ready to reveal something to the folks: her truth.

"Good night, everyone, my name is Virginia Brown. Many of y'all don't know me, but I'm a civil rights activist and newspaper publisher. I'm also the cofounder of a Negro organization called the Color for Change. I began my career as an educator right here in Mississippi where my work caught the attention of Anna J. Julia. But I didn't come this way to talk to y'all about my credentials. When I heard about the tragedy that happened to Sylvester Baker and his family, I knew this was a crime that couldn't be ignored or go unpunished. I'd reached out to multiple people from the NAACP for their help and support and acknowledged in my weekly newsprint this inexcusable and horrendous crime where children were killed. Unfortunately, there's an entity among us that's doing its best to suppress this information," Virginia proclaimed.

She exhaled and glanced at Forrest, who stood nearby quietly, gathering the confidence needed to proceed with something else.

"I myself am guilty of something. I came to speak about a man I've been in love with for over twenty years, a man I've known since I was sixteen years old who is married with children. This is a man who has done his best to hinder and impede changes to this community. He's a man who is after your land right now as we speak and chose to remain silent toward the tragedy of the Baker family. And although I love him, and still do, and I'm carrying his child inside of me right now, I can no longer remain selfish with my own selfish desires and decided to bear my cross to everyone of y'all in this church," Virginia bemoaned.

The room filled with mumbling and grumbling, and the congregation exchanged questioning looks. Who was the man she was talking about?

"Life shrinks or expands in proportion to one's courage," Virginia continued. "And my courage is to expose him for the fraud he is, and to confess my sins among the people. To surrender and sacrifice my selfish needs for the truth tonight. And the truth is, I'm pregnant with his baby, and I've been having a twenty-year affair with Congressman Benny Lockheart."

The crowd gasped with bewilderment as a whirlwind of shock and disbelief swept through the group like a tornado. Pastor Brooke sat in his seat, dumbfounded, while Forrest Tolson knew about her secret. He nodded and smiled slightly as if telling her, "You're free now."

Meanwhile, Harland had heard enough. He stood in the back of the church, keeping his opinions to himself. His fight with Bronco the other night was a humbling experience. He knew it was his fault that Bayou's place had erupted into a full-blown brawl, and he felt terrible about it. It was hard to accept that someone he loved was in love with someone else. However, he wanted the best for Elise, and if Bronco could make her happy, then so be it. It was time for him to let go.

After leaving the church, Harland got into his Ford pickup and drove off. He had decided to leave Mississippi for Chicago for better work opportunities. He had read positive things about Chicago in the *Chicago Defender,* an African American newspaper that he received once a month. For Harland, Chicago appeared to be the promised land for Black Southerners, with plentiful job opportunities in the steel and meatpacking industries.

He arrived at Elise's farm home sometime after 9:00 p.m. It was dark and quiet with a rhythmic cadence of crickets chirping, orchestrating the passage of time with their unseen serenade. It seemed like the world had been hushed away into a stillness reserved exclusively for the nocturnal. A slight glow of light came from the main bedroom, perhaps indicating someone was still awake. Bronco spotted Elise's pickup truck nearby. He climbed out of his truck and approached the porch with a bit of uneasiness. He opened the screen door, knocked a few times, then stepped back and allowed the screen to close back into position. He waited.

Shortly after, the main door opened, and Elise appeared, fastening her housecoat.

"Harland, what brings you by here?" Elise asked him.

Harland managed to smile as Bronco came behind her and glared. He wasn't keen on seeing Harland tonight, but they didn't want any trouble.

"I came by with some urgent news for Bronco," Harland said.

Elise was taken aback. But Bronco remained deadpan.

"What's goin' on, Harland?" asked Elise.

"They's comin' for him, Elise. I's just got back from the town meeting at the church. Doc made it known that the sheriff has a warrant for his arrest."

"What?"

"The sheriff is raising hell 'bout them four missing white men. Bronco's name came up, and some folks ready to turn him in to save they own skin," said Harland.

Elise was surprised by this, but Bronco wasn't at all.

"Why are you telling me this?" Bronco finally spoke with suspicion.

Harland exhaled sharply. There was plenty to say, beginning with an apology. "I know since you arrived here, I've been unkind and unfair to you. I's want to apologize for my actions toward you. I don't believe you's a bad man. I's just really care 'bout Elise, and I only want what's best fo' her."

Elise grinned. Bronco remained deadpan.

"But I wanted to warn you, Bronco, and also to tell Elise, I's plan to leave here soon."

"Leave and go where, Harland?" she asked him.

"Chicago. There's nothin' here for me anymore," he answered matter-of-factly.

"Chicago?" Elise repeated, baffled. "That's a mighty long ways from here."

"I know. I need a fresh start, a new beginning," Harland said longingly.

The sudden expression on Elise's face revealed her sadness at seeing Harland leave. He had been a great friend to her, but she knew she couldn't change his mind.

Before he left, Harland stared at Elise wistfully, slightly smiled, and said, "You take care of yo'self, Elise. And you take good care of her, Bronco. That woman right there is something special."

Bronco nodded. She was.

Harland turned to leave and began descending from the porch toward his pickup. Bronco, however, decided to have a final word with him.

"Wait one minute, Harland," Bronco called out.

Harland turned to find Bronco approaching him, not with hostility but concern. The two men locked eyes, and Elise watched them worryingly from the front door.

"Did you mean what you said back there?" Bronco asked him.

"'Bout what?"

"You going to Chicago."

He nodded. "Yes. Why you ask?"

"I want you to be careful there. The big city moves fast, a lot always going on. There's many swindlers everywhere ready to pick you dry," Bronco advised him.

Harland nodded. *Duly noted.*

"And thank you for warning me," Bronco added.

"You's worried 'bout them comin'?"

"I can handle the sheriff," said Bronco.

"He won't be coming alone."

"I know."

"Just make sure Elise and Kenneth don't get caught up in this," Harland said.

"I'm ready to protect them both with my life," Bronco replied.

After exchanging a final stare, they felt some growing respect for each other. They shook hands, and then Harland turned to leave. Bronco had gained some respect for Harland now that he had admitted his jealousy and insecurities. Their relationship wouldn't be brotherly, but it was the starting point of their mutual appreciation.

Bronco watched as Harland left in his pickup, then turned and returned to the house, where Elise stood behind the screen door.

"Is everything okay?" she asked Bronco.

"Everything's fine, Elise. Just men talking. Go get the rifle. I'm gonna stay up tonight and keep watch," said Bronco.

Chapter Twenty-four

Death Wish

The air was thick with tension. The town grew restless and fidgety like a 2-year-old sitting in church and hyped off sugar. Word of Paul, Jacob, Joseph, and Keith suddenly going missing spread throughout the town, and everyone was worried and fired up. It'd been forty-eight hours since their disappearance since they went into the nigger community, and by now, the gossip roused that they were dead. It was the only logical solution to why they hadn't returned home to their families yet.

A large crowd of people began to gather outside of the sheriff's station, and they were becoming disorderly and intent on creating trouble for the niggers tonight. A truck filled with armed thugs stopped outside of the station. Several men hopped out of the truck armed with shotguns and weapons. Each man was scowling for revenge and seeking to implement retribution for their fallen brothers. They were hooting and hollering with anticipation into riding into the nigger community to bring about desired chaos. There was a particular joy and amusement these men felt tonight—a few were simply looking for a good time and a reason to kill a nigger tonight. The families of the men were also present: brothers who were vexed, sons and cousins who grew angrier by the hour, and wives saddened and apprehensive about their husbands' sudden disappearance. Emotions were running high and all over the place.

"What's the sheriff saying, Jerry?" a man named Conway asked.

"He sayin' we need to wait," Jerry replied.

Conway huffed and puffed. "Wait? Wait for what? These men have gone missing for too long while the niggers plot."

"He didn't say, but he seems as much displeased 'bout this as we," said Jerry.

"I'll be damned if we sit 'round here for another hour on our asses why good men may lie dead."

Conway was a big fair-skinned man with reddish hair and thick eyebrows. Although he had only a basic education, he was an expert in the woods, particularly in hunting and marksmanship. His friends often mentioned that he had incredibly precise shooting skills, being able to shoot the whiskers off a cat and the eyes out of a quarter.

"This Bronco nigger may try and leave town before we gets there," Conway continued to gripe. "I want this nigger's balls twisted upside down."

Jerry guffawed at the statement. Jerry was a wiry, not overly tall, and scratchy-looking man with big blue eyes. He wasn't conventionally handsome and had an odd presence about him. Jerry and Conway were the best of friends, and together, they were the epitome of bigoted rednecks—crass, unsophisticated, and closely associated with the Klan.

"I say we don't need to wait for permission from the sheriff. We just ride out and handle this nigger right now. We go on and burn that nigger town to the ground, the way my granddaddy and daddy woulda done in they day," Conway heatedly proclaimed.

The crowd continued to grow restless outside of the sheriff's station. There was a caravan of pickup trucks and cars idling and waiting to ride out into nigger town. This was personal and social hate. The type of anger and hate that grew strong and became tough to control as the crowd's fury was ready to spring to life. Conway became the de facto leader of the crowd. Paul and Jacob were good friends of his, and to know that they'd possibly been killed by a nigger, anger thrummed through his veins, and rage quickened his blood.

The pitch forks were out.

As the crowd grew restless, Benny Lockheart arrived in his Chevy Business Coupe and parked. He climbed out to the crowd's anger and frustration. They were blocking the entrance to the sheriff's station. He stood tall and handsome, wearing a stylish gray suit and a Tremont hat, having come from a previous business engagement. The unexpected happenings outside the sheriff's station prompted him to leave and deal with the predicament impulsively. Once everyone spotted Mr. Lockheart, their attention immediately shifted to him, as if he were the savior of their crisis.

"It's good to see you here, Mr. Lockheart," Conway greeted him civilly. "We gon' get justice for our boys, Mr. Lockheart. If you care to ride along with us, we'd be mighty appreciative of that. You being here shows support."

Mr. Lockheart shoved Conway and the others to the side dismissively with little interest in their pursuit for justice in nigger town. Yes, he was upset about the four men missing or presumably dead, but having a caravan of drunken, violent shotgun-wielding white men riding into what they dubbed "nigger town" would be a political disaster for him and a hinder in his investment in the area.

Benny Lockheart was pondering Conway's intelligence
and his associates' intelligence. It was a familiar scenario
in the South: a group of angry white men entering thriving Black communities over minor incidents. However,
this situation was unusual. A white group had a valid
reason to be upset, as some of their own people had gone
missing.

He continued to hear the name Bronco from folks.
Benny never heard of the man before, but it was clear to
him that this Negro was becoming the core of this backlash happening. From his information, the man was from
New York City, and Benny believed the Negro was some
kind of city slicker with immoral ways creating trouble in
his town and being unsuited for life here in Mississippi.
Benny believed Negros like him, these damn Yankees,
had this sense of superiority over rural folks—even if they
were Black.

Benny Lockheart walked into the sheriff's station
and found the deputies in a frenzy, grabbing shotguns and swearing in some locals for a raid that night.
It was chaotic as everyone was busy preparing to storm
through the streets of a nearby town and make the residents feel like it was 1921 Tulsa, Oklahoma.

"Where's the sheriff?" Benny demanded to know from
Calvin.

"He's in his office, Mr. Lockheart."

Benny hurried past the deputy and burst into the
sheriff's office. Sheriff Duke was standing away from
his desk with a case of shotgun ammunition and a pistol
on the desk. The sheriff had his back turned to the door,
chewing on a lit cigar and deep in thought about tonight's
events.

"I want you to bring that man in alive tonight, Sheriff,"
Benny demanded out of the blue.

Sheriff Duke turned to the voice and was immediately taken aback by his request. "Alive? Are you serious?"

"Yes. I am."

"This got-damn nigger murdered four white men the other night, and God knows what he done did to their bodies, and you want my men to spare his life?" Sheriff Duke retorted. "I thought the plan was to run these niggers off their land, Mr. Lockheart. Tonight would be the perfect opportunity to do so, along with getting justice for our boys."

"I want justice for these men, Sheriff. But I also want to know where their bodies are buried if they are dead," Benny countered. "Don't you believe they families deserve that? These men and their grieving families deserve to be buried by their loved ones here in our town and not remain rotting in the ground on niggers' soil. If you go on and kill this man, then their whereabouts will be unknown to us."

Sheriff Duke exhaled sharply, knowing Mr. Lockheart was right. But the thought of sparing Bronco's life was agonizing. He wanted to strip this nigger naked, skin him alive, and subsequently have him swinging from a tree with his balls unattached.

"I'll bring this nigger in alive," the sheriff replied reluctantly. "But my boys want justice, Mr. Lockheart. They out there right now itching for it. What I'm s'posed to tell 'em?"

"Tell 'em there needs to be an interrogation done first. When he gives the location of these men, then feel free to do with him as you please."

"It won't be that easy. My men already smell blood and want a taste of it."

Mr. Lockhart sighed heavily as he looked at the door. Over a dozen armed men were waiting outside, and they had to find a way to appease them.

"If they want action, I'll give them permission to destroy and burn down Duncan Goff's home. He and his wife done left town suspiciously, and it was there where I sent them boys. Where they were seen last," Benny said.

The sheriff huffed. He was utterly baffled by this proposal and felt defeated. He and Mr. Lockheart were in a deadlock. These men weren't going to accept burning down some nigger's home and farm for compensation, especially when that same nigger may have been responsible for the death of four white men. The sheriff had a lot of respect for the congressman. Still, he felt Mr. Lockheart was beginning to lose his way and forget what truly mattered—the people, white people. They wanted justice, and they wanted blood. Tonight, they needed to set an example to the niggers that if you kill one white man, there will be trouble. But if you kill four white men, then that would create an apocalypse in their town. Also, the sheriff didn't forget about how he'd chastised him in front of that civil rights nigger, Forrest Tolson.

"What happened to you, Mr. Lockheart?" the sheriff contested. "If this was twenty or thirty years ago, we wouldn't be having this foolish conversation about bringing a nigger in alive and preserving an entire nigger town. My men have their ways in makin' a nigger confess. What that nigger Bronco did was an abomination. Now, I can give my deputies the order to bring that nigger in alive, but them other men out there, now that's a barn door I can't close."

The sheriff was wholly flustered and couldn't hide his anger and resentment. Benny Lockheart stared at the sheriff and began to smolder with umbrage. He felt like he was losing his grip on the town. The authority figures began to rebel and break free from his reins of control. The sheriff was right: an angry mob had no sense of direction. The only thing that could appease a mob of violent white men was bloodshed.

The only thing Mr. Lockheart could counter with was, "And what if the niggers are armed, Sheriff?"

"Then it'll be a reason for us to kill 'em all," the sheriff replied foolishly.

Mr. Lockheart huffed. This wasn't happening. He had an election to win next year, a lucrative investment coming his way, and this wouldn't be his end. Some nigger named Bronco wasn't going to bring him down and destroy everything he'd built. He wanted the Negros removed from their land, but it had to be done as unobtrusively and smoothly as possible. The Bakers' massacre was the only hiccup so far. However, the continued chaos and the bloodshed and four dead white men would scare away potential investors and create gaping problems that could possibly cost him reelection next year.

"Now if you can excuse me, Mr. Lockheart, I have a warrant to serve to this nigger, and I would like to do my job. My men are waiting," Sheriff Duke uttered with finality.

He took a final pull from the cigar he smoked. He brusquely extinguished it against his desk, leaving the cigar disintegrated against its ashes. The sheriff grabbed his shotgun and pistol and went for the door. Benny Lockheart could only watch and pray they brought Bronco in alive without an incident. That tonight wouldn't make headlines like Money, Mississippi. Emmett Till's body had been pulled from the Tallahatchie River near Graball Landing in Tallahatchie County. It was confirmed that the boy had been badly beaten, and the incident was receiving national attention. It was the last thing he wanted for his town—that kind of negative attention would scare Harvey Roth and his business away. With Harvey's influence, they were fortunate to have kept the Bakers' massacre away from the public. The killings became gossip and were quietly brushed underneath the rug. But this was different.

Benny Lockheart was seething inwardly and nervously shuffled around the sheriff's office after the embarrassing encounter. He was clearly uncomfortable and helpless in the situation. The people in town felt like they were about to make history, but not in a good way, and there wasn't anything he could do about it.

Sheriff Duke and his deputies marched out of the sheriff's office, and all eyes were on them. Sheriff Duke stared at everyone with pride and enthusiasm, then hollered, "C'mon, boys, we got a warrant to execute. So, let's go arrest this fuckin' nigger and take nigger town by surprise."

The crowd cheered and celebrated. They began firing their shotguns and pistols into the air. The gunshots triggered an almost immediate response from the crowd, yelling expletives and calling for Bronco to be tortured, burned alive, and lynched. Sheriff Duke continued to deputize some of the men in the mob and instructed them to, "Get a gun and get a nigger if he resists."

It was a magical hour just before midnight. The stars shone brightly, like diamonds scattered across a velvety sky, creating a breathtaking display. All was calm, with a gentle hush enveloping the surroundings. It was a night that invited one to behold the magnificent dance of God's celestial stars on the grand stage of the heavens. The farmland transformed into a captivating nocturnal spectacle as creatures emerged under the dazzling canopy of stars. A possum swiftly darted across an open field, utilizing its remarkable skills to forage for food and navigate its surroundings. However, the possum's movements did not go unnoticed, as an owl perched high in a tree was drawn to it, poised for an opportunity to hunt. Seizing the chance, the owl swooped down on the unsuspecting possum, capturing it with its talons and swiftly ending its life. With its prey secured, the owl carried the possum into the starry night for its meal. Meanwhile, other nocturnal predators, such as coyotes, bats, foxes, and raccoons, roamed the farm, adding to the captivating scene.

The night appeared calm, but there was a sense of intense activity lurking in the shadows. It felt like a nocturnal stage, where time seemed stretched and compressed. Unbeknownst to the predators with pale skin, their target, Bronco, was actually the alpha predator, a creature they were unprepared for. They were about to make a grave mistake by underestimating him.

The sheriff's car and two pickup trucks filled with armed thugs came to a stop on Elise's property. The thugs hopped out of the trucks with their shotguns and pistols and began stalking the area with their weapons. Sheriff Duke and Calvin proudly marched toward the front door, ready to execute the warrant for Bronco's arrest with zeal. If the nigger resisted, this was going to be fun. If he didn't resist, it would still be fun for them. Mr. Lockheart wanted him to bring the nigger in alive, but not before he and his boys had their way with Bronco. Either way, Bronco was going to pay for his sins.

"Conway, Jerry, Luther, you three go 'round back and make sure that nigger don't slip out from our grasp," Sheriff Duke instructed them.

The men nodded and did as the sheriff asked. Sheriff Duke was sad to know that Elise was harboring a fugitive. He was sweet on her, but she, too, needed to experience the brunt of the law tonight. Sheriff Duke gave a particular look of disgust to his deputy and the men standing behind him. He sneered and said, "Mr. Lockheart want us to bring this nigger in alive."

The men began to groan and fuss. There was no way they were going to bring him in alive. "We can skin him first, right?" someone hollered.

Sheriff Duke chortled. "We can hurt him, boys. And I must say I disagree. But Mr. Lockheart has his reasons. We need this nigger to tell us where he buried our brothers. We need to bring 'em home and give our men the proper burial. One that they deserve for their bravery. They don't deserve to stay buried on niggers' soil."

Unfortunately, the mob agreed with the sheriff. They all felt that it was blasphemy to allow Paul, Jacob, Joseph, and Keith to remain buried and rotten in some unmarked graves in nigger town. The thought of it made them want to torch and burn down the entire community, and it was projected, but first, they had to find the bodies.

"We'll get that nigger to talk, Sheriff. I can guarantee you that," Markest shouted. He was a young and muscular white boy wearing a sleeveless shirt and jeans.

Meanwhile, Elise was snuggled between Bronco's masculine arms in the bedroom. They were lying naked and sleeping soundly after they'd finished making love a few hours ago. The house was still and quiet except for a few faint snores from Bronco. Suddenly, Bronco heard a few vehicles skidding to a stop outside with tires crunching gravel. It didn't take him long to deduce what was happening. He immediately pushed Elise off his chest and leaped from the bed. He ran to the bedroom window and gazed out to see his prediction coming true. He saw the sheriff's car and the pickup trucks stopped on Elise's farm. Armed men began to get out. *Shit!*

Elise woke up, baffled by his sudden actions. "What is going on?" she questioned.

"Get up and get dressed. They're here," Bronco said promptly.

Fear and horror immediately crossed her face, though she had anticipated this day. Despite being a black woman, Elise's complexion turned pale as her expression contorted into a mask of terror.

"Go wake up Kenneth, get him dressed, and be quiet about it," Bronco instructed with bated breath.

Elise was overwhelmed by dread as she hurried to get dressed and run to Kenneth's room to wake him up. She snatched the covers off her little brother and whispered quietly, "Kenneth, wake up and get dressed." Raw panic was in her voice.

Kenneth had awoken to see panic flaring in Elise's eyes. "Elise, what's happening?" Kenneth uttered with concern.

"Put some clothes on. The Klan is outside," she said.

Kenneth's eyes widened with alarm at the mention of the Klan being right outside. His chest grew so tight that it became hard for him to breathe. All he could think about was Nancy and how she was killed. Did she and her family feel this way too—this evil dread of death looming? Suddenly, a bright light from a flashlight shined into the bedroom, and they could hear men walking and talking outside the house. Kenneth clung to his sister's arms, hoping their closeness would protect them both. Then, the pounding on the front door began, and they both heard the sheriff's voice.

"Elise, I want you to open this got-damn door right now and give up that nigger you got in there with you. Open this door, Elise!"

Bronco retrieved the rifle and moved into the hallway. Elise and Kenneth hid around the bedroom doorframe, peeking out only long enough to see what was happening.

"Y'all stay closed inside that bedroom," Bronco told them. "Everything gonna be okay. I promise."

Kenneth wasn't so sure about that. His look said it all. He was scared to death. Bronco noticed and said,

"Remember what I told you, Kenneth. Being scared means you're about to do something really, really brave. We're gonna walk through this."

Kenneth nodded nervously and clutched the dog tags around his neck.

The loud pounding at the front continued. "Open this door, Elise!"

Bronco approached the front door with the Mauser short rifle and positioned himself for battle. The Klan had the place surrounded, and although he was indestructible, he knew he had to think about the well-being of Elise and Kenneth. They were not, and this farm was Elise's livelihood.

"We know you harboring that nigger Bronco in there!" the sheriff explained. "We know what he did to our boys. He come out, then we let you be."

"You lookin' for me, Sheriff?" Bronco bellowed calmly.

The sheriff was quickly taken aback by the fact that Bronco was responding to him. "You that nigger Bronco?"

"I am," Bronco answered.

"You best come out right now. We got a warrant for your arrest."

"You tell your goons to back away from this house and there won't be any trouble," Bronco replied boldly.

"Look here, nigger. We ain't playing no games with you," Sheriff Duke roared with frustration. "Either you open this door willingly, or we'll make our way inside there. And I promise you, nigger, I'm gonna take my time with you when we do for what you did to those good men."

"First cracker through this door will get a fuckin' bullet," Bronco warned them.

"You do that, and you'll be a dead man walking," the sheriff countered.

Bronco heard the white men's crackling voices outside. Each voice was itching to grab a piece of this nigger and beat him seriously. Somehow, Bronco distinguished over a dozen men's voices spread out. He could have easily pinpointed several from the windows and snatched their lives before they saw it coming.

Bronco glanced back at Elise and Kenneth, who were peeking out from the second bedroom and looked scared. He knew he had two choices. He could resist and fight the men with his abilities and strength, possibly killing a few of them but risking harm to Elise and Kenneth in the process. Alternatively, he could surrender to the men and go peacefully, hoping they would spare them and the farm. It was a difficult decision to make. If he had been alone, he would have already taken action.

"Listen here, Sheriff. I'll surrender myself to you under one condition," Bronco shouted.

"Nigger, you don't have any conditions," Sheriff Duke retorted.

"You want this to be peaceful or not? Because I promise you, it won't go the way you expect it. You or your men. I'll will kill you all where you stand," Bronco exclaimed through clenched teeth.

There was a moment of silence from the sheriff. Most likely, he was debating or mulling it over with his deputies. Bronco could hear the white boys fussing outside the door. They were anxious to storm into the house, and if they did, it would be the biggest mistake of their lives. Bronco had the rifle aimed at the door, poised to kill as many men as possible with it first. Then, he would rely on his strength and bare hands. He didn't need the weapon to protect himself but killing a few intruders from a distance would be helpful, saving him the energy.

"Listen here, Bronco," the sheriff called out, annoyed. "Whatever weapon you's carrying behind that door, you drop it now and, I give you my word, my men will not harm you. We'll bring you in peacefully."

Bronco didn't trust him. It was bullshit. He'd killed four white men, and there was no way these men weren't going to try to severely beat him before placing him into custody. It was who they were. The animosity to belittle and rough up Negros was in their blood. And Bronco knew the sheriff was a racist and violent cracker who hated Black people. But it wasn't he who he was worried about. Bronco was able to handle himself. It was Elise and Kenneth's safety that troubled him. He didn't want to repeat what'd happened in Harlem with Mindy. Bronco didn't want to see someone else he was fond of, or perhaps loved, be killed in the line of fire. Kenneth and Elise were the only things he cared about.

Bronco sighed heavily and knew what he had to do. He looked back at Elise and Kenneth, who remained terrified by the bedroom door. Their thoughts spiraled as Kenneth clung to Elise's arm. Both were paralyzed in fear. Their eyes widened in sheer horror.

"I'm gonna go with them to keep y'all safe," he said.

"They'll kill you," Elise cried out.

Surprisingly, Bronco grinned, and Elise became confused by the reaction. Why was he grinning at a time like this?

"I have something they want," he said.

She knew what he meant. But it was risky to believe they were willing to bargain with him. Elise knew that the first thing these monsters were going to do was bash his head in with their weapons and violently beat him until there was nothing left of him.

"I'll be okay. Just trust me," said Bronco confidently.

Elise steadied her breath and tried to calm her panic as she observed Bronco place the rifle on the ground and coolly walk to the door.

"I'm comin' out, Sheriff. My rifle is on the ground," Bronco hollered.

"You need to hurry up and open this door, nigger," the sheriff exclaimed impatiently.

They both knew that his fate was uncertain once he opened that door. Bronco was prepared to become Clark Kent instead of Superman. The ache in the pit of Elise's stomach told her that this wouldn't end well for them. Bronco coolly reached for the locks, undoing them bit by bit, and turned the door handle to allow this vile evil into her home. The moment the sheriff and his goons had the opportunity, they pushed their way inside with flashlights brightly shining in his face, and they came barreling into the home like a pack of wolves ready to kill.

"You dirty fuckin' nigger," the sheriff scolded.

Sheriff Duke grabbed a handful of Bronco's shirt, ready to rough him up. At the same time, his deputy took it upon himself to slam the butt of the shotgun he carried into the side of Bronco's head. Shockingly, they didn't get the reaction they expected. The shotgun violently wobbled in the deputy's hand because it felt like he tried to hit a steel wall. Meanwhile, Bronco stood there unfazed with a smirk. More deputies came to attack Bronco, yearning for a piece of the nigger and spewing out insults and racial slurs. They heatedly struck Bronco with their weapons, batons, and fists. But suddenly, they became dumbfounded when they could barely put a mark or scratch on the man. He was unmovable—and it was like they were striking a statue.

The sheriff, the deputies, and the deputized goons continued to try to beat Bronco until each man became breathless. Batons broke quickly against his skin. A deputy broke his hand when he tried to punch Bronco in the face. Another man injured his foot when he tried to kick him in the side. A baseball bat splintered when an assailant swung it at the back of Bronco's head. Fed up and flustered, several gunshots went off, echoing loudly through the home. Elise shrieked with fear. But Bronco remained standing while the men continued to become dumbfounded.

"What kinda nigger are you?" someone shouted.

"Your worst nightmare," Bronco replied.

Elise and Kenneth watched in horror and awe as Bronco seemed invincible. What were they seeing? What was happening? Kenneth was shocked and thrilled to see that the man he looked up to was fighting back—if he could call it that. Because Bronco hadn't lifted a finger to fight back yet, he remained undaunted and unharmed. White men were falling over themselves to try to bring the nigger down with their weapons but to no avail. But it was when the sheriff went after Elise and Kenneth and pointed his revolver at the two that Bronco knew the fun was over.

"Nigger, if you don't surrender yourself right now and put on these handcuffs, I'll shoot this bitch and this nigger dead," the sheriff said in a gruff tone.

Bronco scowled. He didn't want to risk it. He was strong, invincible, and a skilled soldier, but he wasn't faster than a bullet. He fretted and uttered, "Don't hurt them. I'll surrender to the warrant, Sheriff."

Bronco fell to his knees so they could handcuff him. Calvin hurried to subdue him with the handcuffs. While doing so, he threw a barrage of insults at Bronco and prodded his back with his knee, hoping to inflict some discomfort. Bronco remained indifferent to it. However, Sheriff Duke kept his revolver trained on Elise and Kenneth, seething. This man's hatred and anger from being humiliated and defeated seeped through his pores like sweat and blood.

"You touch a hair on their heads, Sheriff, and I'll kill you and your buddies like I did your friends," Bronco warned him wholeheartedly.

The sheriff's and his deputy Calvin's eyes widened at Bronco's audacity. Sheriff Duke couldn't control his anger. He pivoted toward Bronco and snatched the shotgun from one of the deputies' grasp. He vivaciously raised the weapon and slammed the butt of it into Bronco's face, hoping this time it would break his nose and face. But shockingly, it was the sheriff who was taken aback. He damn near stumbled and tripped over himself when he tried to harm Bronco. There was no blood, no bruises, and no bones broken after the hurting these boys tried to put on him. The nigger was becoming a force to be reckoned with. The sneer Bronco gave the sheriff afterward indicated this wasn't going to play out the way he'd expected. An impetuous look in Bronco's eyes captured the sheriff's fear. It stated that he was a cold-blooded killer, some kind of monster they'd never seen before, and that this nigger meant every word he spewed.

"Get that nigger outta here, and take him to my car," the sheriff demanded with frustration.

The deputies began escorting Bronco out of the home. Elise and Kenneth could only watch, feeling relieved that Bronco was still alive—and they, too. But they felt helpless. Sheriff Duke holstered his revolver, and before he exited their home, he glared at Elise with disgust.

"I thought you were one of the good niggers, Elise. I liked you. It's why I planned on sparing yo' land for last. But you harbored a fugitive in yo' home. We'll be back for you and this land," he vehemently proclaimed.

The sheriff left.

Elise's eyes began to water. She felt this gaping sorrow inside of her. She pulled Kenneth closer to her and exhaled sharply. What was happening? And she thought the same thing the sheriff thought: what kind of nigger was Bronco?

As Bronco was roughly escorted to the back of the
sheriff's car, he noticed thick, billowing smoke coming
from Duncan Goff's farm in the distance. He realized that
they had burned the man's place to the ground. He had
promised Mr. Duncan that he would watch over his land.
Sadly, if Mr. Duncan were to return from Georgia, there
would be nothing for him to come home to but ashes.
Bronco was tempted to break free from his handcuffs and
end this nightmare, but he spotted Elise and Kenneth
standing inside the front door. Seeing Elise heartbroken,
dropping to her knees, and surrendering herself to her
grief, he subsided his thirst for revenge. Her eyes were
flooded with tears.

Bronco stared at her before he was placed into the back
seat and quickly uttered, "I'll be back. I love you."

Chapter Twenty-five

Fear Itself

A growl of aggression and excitement rose from the growing white mob outside the sheriff's station. Word had quickly spread throughout their community about Bronco's arrest and his confession that he'd brutally killed those white men. There was a call for immediate action from the mob. They wanted justice, the brutal kind where they would be able to get their hands on him when he arrived at the station and do with the nigger as they please—to tear him apart like a pack of snarling wild dogs would do to a hare. Whites were parked in cars and standing around in groups. Some were standing on car roofs and on the backs of pickups. A few waved the Confederate flag and anticipated the nigger's arrival.

When the sheriff's vehicle arrived at the scene, they were surprised to see the entire community gathered to confront Bronco. Both the sheriff and Deputy Calvin wore arrogant smiles on their faces.

"They are ready to tear you apart, nigger," Deputy Calvin scoffed. "They are all pitchin' a hissy fit with a tail on it."

"Gettin' this nigger inside is gonna be a problem," said the sheriff.

"I say we just leave him be, handcuffed, and push him into the crowd. We all know this nigger's lower than a snake's belly in a wagon rut," said the deputy.

"Did you forget, Calvin? Mr. Lockheart wants him alive. He needs to tell us where he buried them bodies."

Calvin groaned. He hated to see Bronco still breathing, and they had to protect him in police custody.

The sheriff's car slowly maneuvered through the thick, growing crowd of folks with Bronco handcuffed in the back seat. He remained nonchalant as the white crowd attacked the sheriff's car, slamming their fists against the glass and nearly rocking it back and forth. Seeing Bronco sit smugly in the back angered them and drove them insane.

"Let that nigger out, Sheriff. Give him to us," someone hollered.

"He killed good men!"

"Kill that fuckin' nigger!"

"Where is Paul? Where is my fuckin' brother, you stupid nigger?"

The sheriff's car finally stopped outside the station. A crowd of angry, determined people was ready to take action against Bronco. Due to the force of the crowd against the door, getting Bronco out of the car was challenging. Sheriff Duke was the first to get out of the vehicle, standing among the angry crowd with his hand on his holstered revolver.

"Sheriff, give that nigger to us," a stout man with a receding hairline shouted.

"I can't do that, Charlie. Mr. Lockheart wants a word with him first. He needs to tell us where he buried those men."

"I'll get that nigger to talk. We all will," Charlie countered.

A surge of deputies reluctantly had to form a barricade against the crowd from the sheriff's car to the station entrance to hurry up and escort Bronco inside so the crowd wouldn't get to him. Bronco remained undaunted

by the white mob demanding his hide. Their faces were
demonic, like they were possessed and contorted with
hatred and rage. Unbeknownst to them, he was a man
who, if he had to, would kill them all for his benefit,
and most likely, they wouldn't be able to stop him. But
he remembered Mr. Duncan's words before he'd left
for Georgia—despite what he could do, he was still
vulnerable and behind enemy lines. Because they would
immediately go after what he'd fallen in love with—Elise
and her little brother.

The back door swung open with Sheriff Duke hollering,
"Hurry up and get yo' ass out that car, nigger!"

Bronco shimmied toward the door, and Sheriff Duke
gripped his arm to pull him out of the back seat. He
needed to hurry Bronco from the public and into the station. It was going to be easier said than done. The crowd
sprinted toward Bronco and the sheriff, not wasting any
time, breaking into hysterics. They spewed racial slurs
and tried to throw wild blows to his face. A beer bottle
was thrown at his head, and a woman ripped at his shirt
as the energy of the lynch mob intensified. The mob was
beginning to attack his deputies, too. So, the sheriff had
to pull out his revolver and aim it into the air.

He fired two shots.

Pow! Pow!

The crowd froze. They stared at the sheriff holding the
smoking gun flanked by his deputies.

"Listen here!" he hollered. "I know you're angry, trust
me. I understand. I want this nigger to pay for what he
did to those men too. But Mr. Lockheart wants a word
with him, and we need him to tell us where he buried
them. But this nigger will pay for what he's done. I promise you all that."

The mob scowled and fussed, but they reluctantly
backed off. The sheriff and his deputy continued to usher

Bronco into the station. He'd kept this smug and composed demeanor during the ordeal, and his arrogance continued to anger the sheriff and his men.

Moments later, they shoved Bronco into the jail cell and closed the bars behind him. He was alone. Bronco took a seat on the bench and sat there with his eyes fixed forward. Sheriff Duke stood at the bars. He scowled at his prisoner and exclaimed, "I don't know what you are, nigger. But you will tell us where those men are buried. If not, I promise, I'll go pay yo' girlfriend and that pickaninny of hers a visit tonight, finish what we started."

Hearing this, Bronco stood at full height and matched the sheriff's intense gaze. "You do that, and I'm gonna kill you real slow," he threatened the sheriff in a guttural and low tone.

The sheriff was undisturbed by the threats. He pivoted and walked away. Bronco returned to his seat and suddenly smiled when he saw her—Nancy. She had accompanied him in the jail cell, sitting right next to him, and she appeared different. It was as if her spirit was healing and finally being set free. Her usually gloomy expression now seemed more at peace. She could only stare at him with slight content. Her ghostly presence wasn't disturbing like before. Bronco knew then that he was fulfilling his purpose.

When Benny Lockheart arrived, he was surprised by the size of the mob gathered outside the sheriff's station. He had heard that they had captured the fugitive named Bronco alive. Benny hurried to the station to speak with the man who had been daring enough to kill four men and think he would escape punishment.

When Benny climbed out of his vehicle, he was immediately met with the lingering crowd outside the station.

They'd swept him into their turmoil of anger, frustration, and a series of questions he had no time to answer.

"Mr. Lockheart, what's going to happen to that nigger?"

"He needs to be lynched for what he did to those men."

"Me and my men are ready to tan that nigger's hide faster than a hot knife through butter."

It was the middle of the night, and Benny was tired, frustrated, and becoming impatient with what was happening suddenly. The mob was becoming another threat to him. There was ranting about attacking nigger town for vengeance. The beehive had been poked, and the bigoted swarm was ready to soar, sting, and attack anything black that moved.

"He's alive like you asked, Mr. Lockheart," Sheriff Duke uttered with detest.

"You need to get control of that mob outside, Sheriff," Mr. Lockheart replied.

"Not much I can do 'bout that, Mr. Lockheart. Like I said before, they want blood. And knowing we have the nigger in our custody without a scratch on him, they madder than hot grease. Now I can talk to them, but they got a mind of their own. They angry. I'm angry."

Mr. Lockheart sighed with frustration. "Take me to see him."

He followed the sheriff through a narrow corridor, going from room to room, descending short stairs toward the holding cells, and stepping into an area filled with bitter and confused men, all of whom had long, dissatisfied faces.

"That's him there," said the sheriff curtly.

Benny Lockheart appeared at the bars and stared at Bronco. He was surprised to see that the sheriff was right. There wasn't a mark on Bronco. *How is that possible?* He was confident that, despite what he'd told the sheriff and his deputies, the prisoner would have been beaten to a bloody pulp by now. Sheriff Duke was known to bring in niggers so severely beaten that each breath they took afterward would be a miracle. And they'd been beaten for lesser offenses. Mr. Lockheart expected the prisoner to look like ten miles of bad road. Instead, Bronco sat there calmly with his eyes fixed forward. He had confessed to killing four white men and then disappearing their bodies. Yet, he remained undaunted by the chaos happening around him.

"I'm shocked to see the man in one piece, Sheriff," said Mr. Lockheart.

Sheriff Duke frowned at the remark. It wasn't like they hadn't tried to beat the nigger senseless. They gave it everything they had and remained unproductive. "There's just something wrong with this nigger, Mr. Lockheart. He's tough, and he's slicker than owl shit."

Benny Lockheart was baffled by his words. Either they did or didn't. "Why the equivocal statement? I'm confused."

"Ain't no confusion to be had, Mr. Lockheart," Deputy Calvin interjected. "Markest done struck the nigger in the back of the head with a baseball bat, and the damn thing done splintered apart with him still standing. And if you know how powerful Markest can swing a bat, he shoulda done took that nigger's head clear off."

Mr. Lockheart remained more confused.

"Excuse my deputy's ignorance. He's only got one oar in the water," said the sheriff.

Deputy Calvin pouted at the remark. They all knew it was true. They'd done everything they could to beat the nigger badly, and it was frustrating to see him unharmed.

"You the nigger I keep hearing about, right? The fool that had the audacity to kill four white men in my town?" Mr. Lockheart exclaimed. "Why did you do it?"

Bronco remained silent.

"Do you know how much trouble you're in? You need to help yourself and tell us where you buried those men."

Bronco continued to sit there like he was on someone's front porch in the country. It was disturbing to see that the man was so calm and collected inside a jail cell surrounded by dozens of angry white folks who would love to see him suffer. Mr. Lockheart glanced back at the sheriff and his deputy. They shrugged and smirked as if to say, "I told you the nigger was stubborn and slick."

"Do you hear me talking to you, boy?" Mr. Lockheart shouted, losing his patience.

"I do. But you don't mean shit to me. Neither one of you crackers do," Bronco countered arrogantly.

Benny's face turned bright red with anger at the comment. Sheriff Duke marched toward the jail cell, clutching his baton. He angrily clattered the baton across the bars and growled, "Who do you think you are, nigger? I'll come in there and tear yo' hide, boy."

Bronco simpered at the sheriff, mentally saying to the man, *come on in and try*. He'd called the sheriff's bluff. They didn't want to admit it, but they feared him. Sheriff Duke became redder than a chili pepper.

"What do you want from us?" Mr. Lockheart asked.

"I want justice."

The sheriff and his men snickered at the remark.

Bronco stood from the bench and approached Mr. Lockheart from behind the bars. They were both equally tall and intimidating men, but something about Bronco was incredibly challenging. He was built like a tank, with powerful arms, a strapping chest, and an undaunted manner. The fiery intensity in his eyes indicated to Mr. Lockheart that he wasn't afraid of him or anyone else. His demeanor also revealed that he had killed people before, regardless of their race. It didn't matter to him. He was dangerous. Mr. Lockheart had never seen anything like it. Bronco's presence was mesmerizing and formidable.

"You're going to stay behind these bars until you tell us something. And there's no telling how long we can control that mob right outside this station," said Mr. Lockheart chillingly.

"Let 'em come," Bronco uttered daringly.

Unbeknownst to the people holding him captive, Bronco had surrendered himself because of love. He didn't want any harm to come to Elise and Kenneth, so he scaled back his abilities and had to think before he acted. However, he knew that the cage wouldn't hold him for long. He had smashed through a brick wall before and wondered about the extent of his strength and limitations. He was bulletproof and had the strength of multiple men. Still, he didn't understand the origin of his abilities or whether they were permanent. The uncertainty bothered Bronco, and he wondered if he could die.

"Her name was Nancy," Bronco quietly said out of the blue.

The men were baffled by the name. They had no idea who she was, and they didn't care.

"Who is she to you?" Mr. Lockheart questioned

Bronco stared past Mr. Lockheart angrily at Sheriff Duke and his deputy, Calvin. He felt nothing but contempt for these men. He said, "She visits me. Men came and slaughtered them on their property during the night. Her father, Sylvester, her mother, Martha, her grandmother, and her siblings including her infant sister perished that night. She burned to death while being held in her grandmother's arms. You wanted his land and killed his entire family for it. The same men that did this, I brutally killed them with my bare hands then burned and buried their bodies to rot in an unmarked grave. And I hope they burn in hell for what they did. And I'm gonna kill you and the sheriff, too."

Deputy Calvin had heard enough. He unholstered his weapon and charged toward the bars. Enough was enough. He outstretched his arm with the revolver at the end of it, and he was ready to shoot Bronco between the eyes. He screamed, "I'm gonna kill you, nigger!"

Bronco remained standing and unconcerned by the deputy's threats with his revolver. He chillingly replied, "You can try. But y'all have tried already, and now we're here."

"Put that damn gun away, Deputy," Mr. Lockheart shouted at Calvin.

Calvin fumed. "This nigger thinks he can threaten my life and get away with it."

"I said put it away. Now!"

Calvin grudgingly did what he was told. He holstered the revolver and seethed. The hatred that manifested in his eyes for Bronco made the deputy want to spit in the nigger's face and skin him alive.

"Maybe we can come to some kind of compromise, Bronco," Mr. Lockheart said rationally.

"The only compromise is justice—death."

"Listen here, nigger," Sheriff Duke interjected impatiently. "There are over two dozen armed white men outside this station, itching to charge in here and do us the favor. You don't control anything in my house. You hear me, nigger? You either tell us what we want, or I'll make you regret the day you were born."

Sheriff Duke's anger spiked. He became bright red like a fire truck and clutched the baton in his fist so tightly that he began to trickle blood from his fingernails. He glared at Bronco with the urge to open the cell door and try again beating the nigger senseless with the baton. Bronco's lingering smug look was taking its toll on the sheriff. Never in his life had a nigger gotten the best of him and made him look weak and foolish. Tonight wasn't going to be that night.

"Maybe I should let my deputy shoot you in the got-damn head," Sheriff Duke exclaimed.

"No one's shooting anybody," Mr. Lockheart inter-rupted. Surprisingly to everyone else, he continued to remain the cooler head. "What happened to Sylvester and his family was a tragedy. It was implied that he was a good man with a loving family. I give my word to you: I'll implement an investigation into their deaths and get to the bottom of such an egregious crime."

Sheriff Duke and Calvin shared a fretful glance. The man couldn't be serious. It had to be smoke and mirrors. Mr. Lockheart and the people he was in bed with were the catalysts for such a tragedy. They wanted Sylvester removed from his land, and when he failed to comply, they sent the sheriff and the Klan to intervene.

"All we want from you, Bronco, is to tell us where you buried those men," Mr. Lockheart added politely.

"He ain't talking, Mr. Lockheart. This is one ignorant nigger you're dealing with," the sheriff uttered with repugnance. "We be better at giving this nigger to the crowd outside before he talks."

"That be fine by me," the deputy concurred.

Bronco stared at them, deadpan. He knew he was get-ting under their skin, toying with them. It was satisfying to see them falling apart. But sooner or later, he would have to make his move and get back to Elise. He didn't want to bring any trouble to her front door. But the taller man in the superficial suit, with his kind and engaging words, was trying to toy with him. Bronco knew he wasn't anything but a liar. His words were like the hissing of a snake. He was the devil in a clean, proper fabric. Bronco deduced that he had to be some kind of politician by the way he phrased his words carefully.

"Now, we're trying to be nice here, like the men we are," Mr. Lockheart uttered calmly. "But like the sheriff said before, there are men out there waiting to kill you. And it won't just end with you, but they're ready to go after everything you love and hold dear. You see, they are angry. Those four men you killed, they were beloved in this town. Now, those men outside this station, they're going to grab their shotguns, and pistols, and other weapons, then ride out to the nigger community with the sole attempt to kill and destroy everything they see. But I can prevent that. I can talk to them because they listen to me, and they respect me. But for me to do that, you need to give me something."

"Who are you, a senator, the mayor, a congressman or something?" Bronco questioned.

"My status is none of your business," Mr. Lockheart countered.

"The way you speak, opposite of those two clowns, you care about your reputation. And I guess me telling you where I buried those men helps solidify your status a lot more as the muthafucka that can get shit done with your kinfolk. You can't let a nigger outsmart you because you're the smartest man in the room. But there's something about you I sense that's different . . . a secret maybe," Bronco proclaimed smugly.

Benny Lockheart gasped, becoming uncomfortable. *What does he know?* Benny wondered.

Bronco was immediately drawn to something else only he could see inside the room. Out of nowhere, a ghostly black male figure, seemingly from the early 1900s, appeared in the room. It moved closer and closer behind Mr. Lockheart, almost as if it wanted to attach itself to the man. It remained so close behind the congressman that it was surprising that Mr. Lockheart didn't feel its haunting presence. This being didn't care about Bronco. It cared about Mr. Lockheart with a simmering and lingering intensity. It remained standing closely behind him, and suddenly, rage filled his face as it became emotionally devastated. The floor underneath their feet seemed to turn into a puddle of blood. Bronco stared at this ghostly being, unable to comprehend its purpose behind the politician.

"What the fuck is he looking at?" the deputy exclaimed.

Bronco's sudden blank stare into the abyss confused everyone in the room. He had grown quiet and was focused on something. It felt like this thing wanted to tell him something. It was angry and nonplussed, and then it mouthed something to Bronco. "Benjamin. Benjamin. Benjamin." Bronco deduced that this angry spirit was somehow related to Mr. Lockheart.

"What is your secret?" Bronco asked Benny evenly. "What is it that you're not telling everyone? Who is Benjamin?"

Mr. Lockheart was utterly taken aback when he heard the name. "Where did you hear that name from?" he exclaimed. "Who fucking told you that name?"

Bronco smirked. Little did everyone know that the ghostly figure Bronco saw was Benny Lockheart's father, Benjamin John Boone. Benny Lockheart was passing. His mother, Lana Lockheart, was once a fair-skinned lovely Southern belle. However, his biological father was a black man who had traveled to Mississippi from Philadelphia and never returned home.

Lana, who was beloved by her father, a known racist and Klan member, had fallen in love with Benjamin Boone, the son of slaves. Benjamin was an educated Black man. He was a well-known poet, painter, and scholar from the north. They'd fallen in love, and Lana soon became pregnant by him. Soon after, Lana's father had found out about the affair and pregnancy, and he'd sent a lynch mob after Benjamin. A month before Benny was born, the lynch mob had castrated, lynched, and burned Benny's father. A week after his birth, Benny was taken from his mother and sent to be raised by his aunt and uncle, who couldn't have any children. He was white enough to pass in the South and received the proper upbringing. Benny knew the story because his aunt had confessed to him while on her deathbed when he was 17 years old.

A hellish look washed over Benny Lockheart's face. He'd kept this secret for so many years that he planned to take it to his grave. If it'd ever gotten out that a part of his ancestral was African American it would ruin him, his family, and his children. How did some Black stranger know of it? Or who did he know and tell? Suddenly, the location of those white men became irrelevant. Benny knew he had to get rid of Bronco to keep his secret. He also knew there was a possibility that others close to him might know, too. Benny couldn't take that chance. He turned to the sheriff and coldly uttered, "He's not talking. Just get rid of him. We'll find their bodies ourselves even if we have to burn everything, starting with the bitch's farm."

Benny turned and marched away from the jail cell, looking flushed and nervous. Sheriff Duke and his deputy were proud to do so. Both men grinned like the Cheshire cat.

"You heard the man. The nigger needs to go," Sheriff Duke said.

They were waiting for this moment. Bronco, too.

Chapter Twenty-six

America's Soul

The mob outside the sheriff's station had swollen out of control. There was no longer containing it. They wanted Bronco's head perched on a pitchfork and were ready to parade it around town. The nigger had to die tonight. What he'd done was unwarranted, and the gravity of the situation was dire. The crowd was fed up and wanted justice, followed by butchery. The lynching mob had splintered off, and a caravan of angry whites began to head for the Black community to implement their own brand of justice and a search for the bodies buried in nigger town. The second group decided to heatedly surge into the sheriff's station and deal with Bronco. The deputies by the door couldn't control the mob that began pouring into the building with their hostile glares, bared teeth, curled lips, and faces contorted with rage. Men of authority were pushed to the side like furniture and were forced to watch fate take its course. The deputies willingly acquiesced with the mob's decision to carry out their own justice.

"We want that nigger now, damn it!" a man screamed frantically.

In a staggering surge of violence ignited by Bronco's confession of killing four white men, the mob cordoned off the area, snatched keys from the deputies who stood idly by, and charged forward toward the holding cell below, screaming and yelling. There would be no stopping them. They all couldn't wait to seize this nigger and expressed their discontent with his brutal and painful death.

Sheriff Duke, his deputies, and Bronco heard the swarming mob coming for Bronco. There was rumbling of charging footsteps and loud voices looming toward the holding cell. Sheriff Duke hollered, "Damn it, how they get past my deputies? They gon' tear this place apart."

Calvin smirked at Bronco and uttered, "They coming for you now, nigger. You're in a heap of trouble. I'm gonna be glad to see them tear you apart."

Bronco remained standing, maintaining his calm composure. It sounded like he would have his hands full but would be ready for whatever was coming. His only fear was not getting back to Elise in time. He didn't want anything to happen to her and Kenneth. He had to return to them before it was too late. The events were unfolding rapidly and spreading like an oil spill.

"Where is that fuckin' nigger!" the de facto leader of the mob, Charlie, shouted with his face hardened with anger.

Sheriff Duke tried to take charge by intervening with the palm of his hand slightly against his holstered revolver. He didn't care about the well-being of his prisoner. The only things he was concerned about were the destruction of his station and the safety of his deputies. This mob was seeing red, charging everywhere like a bull in a china shop, and they didn't care who they had to hurt just to get to the nigger they wanted to sink their teeth into.

"Charlie, you and these men need to stand down, now!" Sheriff Duke screamed with authority. "I told you, I have everything under control. This is my house."

"We can't do that, Sheriff. We all tired of waiting. That nigger needs to die tonight," Charlie angrily countered.

The sight of Bronco standing unharmed and casually behind the bars infuriated the crowd much more.

"Where are the fuckin' keys, Sheriff? Give us the keys to open that damn cell," Charlie screamed madly.

The holding cell became flooded with a hateful crowd of angry white men. Bronco suddenly became surrounded by the hostile group. Men in a frenzy pushed against the bars, reaching inside, trying to grasp and pull the nigger toward them, yearning to break his arm, punch him, and get things started right away. It became a madhouse of emotions and rage.

"Everyone, you need to leave this place now," Sheriff Duke hollered.

"Give us the fuckin' keys!" Charlie shouted.

Men wrestled with the sheriff to grab the keys to open the jail cell. Sheriff Duke, although he wanted Bronco to suffer in pain and agony for what he'd done, suddenly found himself on the receiving end of the brutal mob. They didn't care who they had to attack to get to the nigger. Someone had punched the sheriff in the face, and then he'd lost his footing and crashed on his back. He felt the brunt of their hatred for his prisoner as they desperately removed his holstered revolver and ripped the keys to the cage from his gun belt.

Bronco witnessed the ordeal and scowled. He clenched his fists and became primed to implement a ghastly death for the nearly two dozen men looking to bring about his sudden demise. They believed the odds were in their favor, assuming Bronco was a caged animal. He thought if he had been an ordinary man in this predicament, how horrifying and horrific this nightmare would have been for him. But he wasn't normal. Whatever supernatural force God had given him, these abilities, which he once believed was a curse, were now in his favor. And the fact that he was a trained soldier able to kill at will, this mob had no idea what they were getting themselves into. They were being controlled by their hatred and rage, emotion, and sensation that left hundreds or thousands of Black men lynched and killed since the birth of this country.

Charlie gripped the keys and hurried to the jail cell, not to release the prisoner but to storm their way into the cage and beat him severely at first. They planned on dragging him out of the cell into the street and punishing him in public. The town needed to see how they dealt with the killing of white people accordingly. But unbeknownst to them, they were about to open Pandora's box.

Charlie maneuvered through a crowd of men, determined to reach the jail cell with the keys. They pressed against the bars, allowing Charlie to unlock and open the cell. The loud roar of their angry voices echoed, almost shaking the room.

"You do this, and you will all die," Bronco gave them fair warning.

His statement ignited a deep fuel of rage that felt more powerful than dynamite going off. The audacity of this nigger giving them a warning.

"Open it!" someone screamed from the top of their lungs.

"Get that nigger outta there!"

Finally, the cell door opened, breaking the barrier between life and death. There would be no turning back. The crowd was too far gone to reason. They were coming for Bronco with everything they had, bats, batons, knives, and guns. The only thing they saw was an opportunity to get justice and kill themselves a nigger.

"Your ass is mine, nigger," the first man to attack Bronco shouted excitedly.

He lunged for Bronco with a baseball bat. Bronco expected it, anticipated it. His eyes were deep and dark. He didn't talk. When the man tried to swing the bat at Bronco, he gripped it mid-swing, stunning the attacker. The man's face turned white with shock. Bronco forcefully pushed him into the others, and they began to topple over themselves like bowling pins going down. The next wave of attackers came for Bronco. One received a swift kick in the groins so fast and hard that he crumbled to the floor with a resounding tormented howl. Then, another invader got tossed to the side like a leaf in the wind.

Charlie indignantly charged for Bronco with the sheriff's gun, screaming, "I'm gonna kill you, nigger!" But before he could raise the weapon and fire, Bronco smashed an elbow into the side of his skull, the soft spot high on the temple. Then he thrust him forward and flung his body to the ground. Blood filled his mouth, and the pain was blinding. That move was followed by when Bronco hit another attacker right in the V under his ribs where the sternum ends. It paralyzed him as he gasped and doubled over and then pitched forward onto the ground. They continued to aggressively throttle into the cell. Bronco's fist collided with someone's cheek, shattering teeth and breaking his jaw. Bronco grabbed another man into a chokehold, quickly snapping the man's neck like a tree branch. Then he banged someone's nose with his forehead, subsequently plunging the heel of his palm into another man's face as a satisfying snap filled the air, telling everyone it was a broken nose. All his victim's blood leaked onto the stone floor. Bronco gave one man a sharp round punch to the chin with a sharp blade, then stared at the river of blood that appeared and flowed down his torso. Bronco snapped another man's neck, broke four men's arms, and killed three right away. It was absolute turmoil.

Everyone was beginning to drop like flies. The sheriff and deputies stood there in utter awe and disbelief. What was happening? No. This wasn't supposed to be happening. The nigger was winning. It was a repeat of Elise's farm, only this time, he was striking back and killing more white men. Men were sprawled across the stone floor of the jail like falling dominoes. They were dead.

Charlie crawled to his feet. His throat was in agony, and blood drained from his mouth. He was fuming. He stared nervously at the sheriff and screamed, "What are you waiting for, Sheriff? Shoot the nigger!"

Deputy Calvin rushed to grab the double-barrel shotgun from the gun closet, and another deputy followed his lead. They hurriedly loaded a few shells into the chamber, cocked the weapon. Before Bronco could turn in their direction, they aimed and fired multiple times his way.

Boom! Boom! Boom! Boom!

The force of the shotguns going off simultaneously compelled Bronco back to some extent and slammed him into a dull stone wall. Still, surprisingly to them, he didn't go down when the smoke cleared. Seeing this, their mouths gaped open, and they became horrified. It was as if they were staring at the devil himself.

"We shot him. We . . . we shot him point-blank with two shotguns," Calvin cried out in a panic. He couldn't believe what he was seeing.

"What the fuck is going on here? What is he?"

"It's . . . it's the devil. That what that nigger is, the devil," a man cried out in fright.

Bronco had had enough. Instead of coming after him, the men were so frightened by what they had witnessed that they began cowardly fleeing toward the exit. Most of their friends were either dead or knocked out unconscious. They ran in fear for their lives, and in doing so, they mistakenly knocked over a kerosene lamp the sheriff had propped on his desk as an alternative light source. It fell over, broke open, and immediately started a fire.

The fire started quickly, creating a solid blaze that rapidly spread through the area, filling the room with thick black smoke. In fear, Deputy Calvin and several other deputies promptly ran from the holding area to the open street. The billowing smoke turned dark as the fire consumed everything in the room. With the out-of-control fire roaring, Bronco calmly exited the jail cell, seemingly unfazed by the blaze. The sheriff was the last man remaining, and as he observed Bronco, he stood there frozen, like an icicle in a blizzard.

There wasn't a relevant explanation of what he saw—some kind of super nigger. The sheriff snapped out of his trance and looked for a weapon to strike him, although nothing seemed to work. But his ego and obsessive hatred wouldn't allow this nigger to win. The niggers would never be his equal. This was his town. He was the reigning authority and justice. Everyone either feared or respected him. But now, this stranger from Harlem was destroying everything he'd built.

"You don't get to win, nigger! This is my town! My fuckin' town!" Sheriff Duke growled through his clenched teeth.

The fire was growing hot, but Sheriff Duke became insane with rage. He, too, seemed undaunted by the intense flames for a moment. Finally, he retrieved an old Colt .45 revolver from the desk drawer and aimed it at Bronco. The man couldn't accept defeat from a nigger.

"I'll kill you, and then I'm gonna kill Elise for bringing you here," he shouted.

The sheriff outstretched his arm with the .45 revolver and emptied the gun at Bronco to no avail.

"Got-damn you, nigger! Why don't you fuckin' die?" he screamed with much animosity as he watched this strong man move toward him in what seemed to be slow motion. "Fuck you!"

Bronco slapped him with an open right and entirely across the face. It rocked the sheriff profoundly. He wobbled, took a step back, and tried to steady himself, almost falling unconscious. It felt like he'd been hit with a hard rock. Sheriff Duke felt vulnerable and scared for the first time in his life.

"I'm going to make sure you never hurt anyone again," Bronco rebuked.

The sheriff was at his mercy suddenly. But there would be no mercy. Bronco grabbed the sheriff by his collar. Sheriff Duke felt his feet fly out from under him, and his entire body became suspended in the air. He couldn't believe how unnatural this nigger's strength was. He felt his demise growing closer.

"This is for Nancy, Sylvester, and the entire Baker family. What you and your men did to them goes unforgiven. And I'm here to correct that tragedy," Bronco spewed.

The sheriff remained utterly helpless. Bronco put the sheriff into a tight bear hug and began to squeeze with all his strength. Suddenly, Sheriff Duke hollered in agony, "Arrgghhh!" as his spine snapped.

Bronco released his tight embrace from around the sheriff, and the man crumpled to the floor, twitching painfully. The intense flames were closing in around them. The heat crackled and became fierce, with the fire licking the walls and sweeping across the ceiling.

Bronco wasn't meant to win, but the sheriff became paralyzed and crippled on the floor. There was nothing else to say to the sheriff. His fate was inevitable. His reign of terror for so many Negros would come to an end tonight. Bronco turned and walked away, leaving the sheriff to scream out, "I'll see you in hell, nigger!"

There was no reason for Bronco to respond. His work was done here. He strolled from the holding area with the ashes and debris falling everywhere. The sheriff could still be heard screaming out in pain and agony, slumped against the floor.

Bronco walked through a wall of flames as he exited the burning sheriff's station. He was immediately met with the surviving men, including Calvin and a few deputies. Everyone was flabbergasted when they saw Bronco walk through a wall of fire unharmed with his clothes scorched. The hatred was still in their eyes, but they were shocked and too scared to move against him.

"Where's the sheriff?" Calvin asked.

"Burning in hell," Bronco responded.

Calvin frowned. His boss was dead, along with many other men, and there wasn't anything he or his men could do about it. They all saw with their own eyes what Bronco was capable of, but they still couldn't believe it. They tried to beat him, stab him, shoot him, and he couldn't be burned. His black skin was magical, and he somehow was unstoppable. What kind of man was he? Where did he come from? And why did this absolute power belong to a nigger? These men were utterly baffled.

Bronco focused on the deputy, who stood in shock in front of the burning building. Several townspeople stood silently behind him. Bronco's demeanor had suddenly shifted, and everyone was now afraid of him. With him having the upper hand, they became submissive and quiet. His muscular dark physique was visible through his singed clothing. Bronco sternly approached the deputy and pulled the badge off his shirt.

"You don't deserve this. None of you do," Bronco said.

Calvin didn't resist or protest. He stood there childlike, pouting but now innocuous. It was apparent that the devil had come to their town to burn it down for their sins against mankind.

"If I ever see you in this town again, I'll kill you and everything associated with you," Bronco threatened the deputy. "Leave, and don't come back here."

Calvin had no choice but to nod in agreement and accept defeat. For the first time in his life, he dropped his eyes to the ground in submission and obedience, similar to how a Black man might have done to a white man. In fact, they all had to bite their tongues and look away from Bronco in fear of his retaliation. It was unthinkable.

As the fire raged and the building began to collapse, Bronco suddenly seemed distracted, lost in thought, and not fully present. He looked to his side and saw three shimmering, smiling figures at the edge of the shadows—Nancy, Sylvester, and her grandmother. They seemed to be at peace. Everyone was at peace. Bronco exhaled and felt liberated. He had fulfilled his purpose and obtained justice for the Baker family.

However, he couldn't relax just yet. He thought about Elise and Kenneth. He had to get to them. They were still in danger. A caravan of armed white men was headed to their community to implement revenge, and Benny Lockheart was intent on keeping his secret. Bronco noticed an old Chevy truck parked nearby and shouted, "Who's truck is that?"

"It's mine," Conway replied.

"I need the damn keys," Bronco demanded.

Conway quickly handed him the keys to his truck, and Bronco got in and raced toward Elise's farm. He was determined not to lose anyone in his life again. He wouldn't allow a repeat of Harlem.

The black community in Morton, Mississippi, came under attack as mobs of white residents started attacking Black residents and destroying homes and businesses.

The violence began at Pastor Brooke's church, leading to a shootout between armed Black and white individuals. The confrontation resulted in casualties on both sides, leaving six white men and three Black men dead and the church on fire.

The situation was tense. Black men refused to be passive in the face of danger. They carried weapons and drove through the streets, including Main Street, seeking retribution. Doc, Washer, JoJo, and Jimmy were among those involved. As news of the violence, including an incident at the sheriff's station, spread throughout the city, chaos ensued. The station was on fire, and lives had been lost, leading to widespread mob violence. White rioters attacked the Black community, resulting in fatalities and the burning and looting of homes and stores. The Mississippi National Guard intervened, attempting to restore order by implementing martial law.

Elise and Kenneth were trying to pick up the pieces after the events that had happened earlier. Elise couldn't help but worry about Bronco. She was convinced that he would be beaten and killed while in jail. However, she could not explain what she had witnessed earlier that night. How did Bronco emerge without severe harm when they were beating him in her home? Was he some kind of invincible angel? Elise wondered if something extraordinary about him made him invincible. In the middle of the night, Elise tried to tidy up her place, but it was hard to shake off what had happened and what she had witnessed.

Kenneth looked like he had lost a big brother. Tears rolled down his cheeks as he sat in his bedroom, completely lost without his idol. He tinkered with the dog tags around his neck, wishing he were strong enough to have helped Bronco when he needed him the most. Bronco had taught him a few moves outside in the yard, including close combat and how to use and handle a knife. Kenneth was eager to learn, and Bronco told him he would become a natural. He wanted to be just like Bronco. He tried to be strong and fearless. He wanted to become a soldier or a warrior to be able to protect his big sister.

Elise glanced at the time on the pendulum clock in the living room. It was after two in the morning. Finally, it was quiet, and she had cleaned up the mess the sheriff and his men had left behind. Elise had yet to learn what was happening in town. She couldn't rest or sleep. She had experienced her own disaster earlier. Unbeknownst to her, things were about to become worse once more.

As Elise was about to turn in for the night and try to get some needed sleep, there was a vital and continued knocking at the front door. It was a desperate knock with a plea to come inside. She heard him scream, "Elise, please open the door. It's me, Pastor Brooke."

She was stunned by the pastor's unexpected visit at such an unusual hour. It was out of character for him. Out of caution, she retrieved a shotgun that she had kept hidden in her bedroom closet, before going to the front door. Elise took a deep breath and approached the door cautiously, hearing the pastor knocking urgently. When she peeked outside, she saw Pastor Brooke pacing frantically on her front porch. He looked frightened.

Elise opened the door with concern, gripping the shotgun in her hands. She asked Pastor Brooke, "Is everything okay?"

He pushed past her and fell to the floor, becoming a heap of mess. His clothes were tattered, and beads of sweat poured from his skin. He was breathless. He had been running, but from what or whom? Elise had never seen him like this. What was happening?

"It's gone. It's all gone. They burned it down," he mumbled.

"What's gone? What's happening?" she asked.

"You haven't heard?"

She hadn't heard anything. She was dealing with her own nightmare, and it felt like this night was never going to end. "No," she replied curiously.

"They're killing everyone," he informed her.

Elise was utterly taken aback. "What?"

"Two carloads of men came to my church, then threw Molotov cocktails through the window. The church caught on fire. When everyone tried to leave, they opened fire on us. Ms. Mary, she's dead."

Elise gasped. "Oh, my God."

"White mobs are setting fires to Black businesses, churches, and people's homes. JoJo, Washer, and others arrived soon after and tried to save the church, but got into a gun battle with them white men. So much death . . ."

The pastor felt a growing sense of uneasiness. He explained to Elise that there had been a fire at the sheriff's station, resulting in the deaths of many white individuals. As a result, white mobs were seeking revenge, prompting some Black men to take up arms to protect their community while others chose to leave the town. Throughout the night, conflict between the two sides persisted.

"You can stay with us for the night, Pastor," Elise said.

Pastor Brooke nodded and thanked her, but he felt like such a coward taking refuge in a young woman's home while people out there were being attacked and dying. He was supposed to be a man of the cloth and of faith. He was supposed to stay and help, but instead, he ran. He felt like he had committed a sin for running. They had burned down his church, and a few of his congregation members had tried to fight back and protect it. Some had lost their lives tonight.

"Where's Bronco?" the pastor asked out of the blue.

Elise sighed heavily and replied, "They came and took him away a few hours ago."

He was shocked by the news. However, Pastor Brooke was not surprised. Deep down, Pastor Brooke harbored a quiet but intense resentment toward the man since he arrived in their community a few weeks ago. He believed that Bronco was trouble. Pastor Brooke thought of Bronco as calm and strong but purposeless, only in town to take advantage of a local farm girl and stir up trouble. However, a few members of his congregation had taken a liking to him and started inviting Bronco into their homes. He was genuinely welcomed and respected. Pastor Brooke deduced that he wanted to dislike Bronco out of jealousy. Pastor Brooke realized that Bronco was not a coward who hid behind words and the podium but instead took action and fought for what he believed in. Now, he understood why Elise had taken him in. Although Bronco had started to gain acceptance from a few people over time, Pastor Brooke couldn't blame tonight's events on Bronco. He knew that these actions were inevitable, regardless of how much the pastor tried to appease the sheriff and white folks. The pastor regretfully acknowledged that they would always be considered unequal and second-class citizens, and their community would always be at risk of being wiped off the map.

"Elise, I was wrong about him," Pastor Brooke began to say.

As the man was about to speak, they suddenly heard a commotion outside her farm. Headlights from two vehicles shone through the window, catching the attention of Elise and the pastor. Elise rushed to the window to see what was happening, and her eyes widened with fear as she realized that their worst nightmare had returned. Two vehicles had pulled up on her land—a sky blue Ford

Hemmings and a brown pickup truck with armed white men in the back.

"Shit!" Elise cursed. "They're back!"

The pastor's heartbeat quickened, hitting him with a tidal wave of fear. Elise ran to Kenneth's bedroom and shouted, "Get underneath the bed, now!"

Kenneth's fear matched the pastor's as he was quickly enveloped by an avalanche of panic. It was happening again. Why? Why couldn't they leave them alone? They had already taken Bronco away. Now, they wanted him and his sister to suffer. Kenneth scowled and thought, *what would Bronco do in this situation?* He wanted to become brave like the man he loved and respected.

Seven armed white men gathered at the front entrance and aimed their guns at the farmhouse. They weren't there to negotiate anyone's surrender. It was termination on sight at the behest of Benny Lockheart. Learning that Bronco was staying there, he figured he had told her his secret. Therefore, everyone needed to go. And when the congressman wanted something done, it was expedited. The men immediately opened fire, raining down a barrage of bullets into the farmhouse.

The gunshots triggered an almost immediate response from Elise. She thrust the shotgun through the front window and returned fire, with both sides quickly firing on each other. Elise was vastly outnumbered. The violence was beginning to take its toll on her. Her eyes were in tears. Her heart was racing and there was the urge to panic. But she knew she had to do whatever to protect her and her little brother. This time she wasn't going to give in to her fear.

Chapter Twenty-seven

The Big Payback

Bronco pressed down on the accelerator of the broken-down pickup truck, trying to give it the speed needed to reach Elise's farm quickly. However, the feeble vehicle shuddered as he accelerated. Bronco, normally invincible, felt more vulnerable than ever. The thought of losing Elise and her little brother terrified him, leaving him feeling desperate and helpless. He had tried to protect them by removing himself from the situation, but fate had somehow placed them back in danger. A few miles away from the farm, Bronco hoped he wasn't too late. He didn't want to lose anyone else in his life.

For the first time, Bronco did something he'd never done before: he prayed. He wasn't religious and didn't believe in God. In the beginning, his mother was a Christian, praying woman, but over time, she'd lost her faith in Christ and God. After the Great Depression and his father's downfall to unemployment and alcoholism, Bronco witnessed his mother's faith go down the drain, and she soon began to suffer and battle her own sins.

Still, there had to be some kind of higher power that was unexplainable because he thought he wasn't human anymore. Some people said he was an angel, but sometimes he felt like a freak show—maybe a demon. He had strength and durability that didn't belong to this realm. Whatever it was, why did it choose him? Was it God?

If there was a God, why would He allow such blood-shed and chaos, especially tonight? Why was there so much hatred and death in this world? Why did whites feel they were superior beings, especially over the Black man? Why the killings? There was no doubt in Bronco's mind that he would kill again. Benny Lockheart and his assailants were going after something he'd fallen in love with. He continued to remind himself that he had a purpose, although he'd brought justice to the Bakers when the sheriff perished in that fire. Was it possible that he could start a new life in Mississippi after all this was over?

Bronco approached the farm and heard gunfire in the distance. He pushed the accelerator to the floor and veered sharply to the right onto the narrow dirt road that led to Elise's farm. His heart and mind were racing. He tightly clenched the steering wheel with both hands, staring angrily ahead through the windshield into the night, where he could barely see anything but the road and passing trees. Ahead, he saw two vehicles with their doors agape, and several men were firing at the farmhouse. Something or someone prevented them from charging any further. It was a standoff. Bronco figured it had to be Elise firing back at them. She needed help, and he would give it to her.

He wasn't going to stop at all but had a plan. His adrenaline rushed the entire time. Bronco turned off the headlights, kept his foot against the accelerator, and the pickup truck roared toward the men and gun-fire. The vehicle came barreling their way, wobbling and weaving at full speed, not stopping. A few lucky ones pivoted cuttingly, noticing the pickup truck speeding to-ward them. They hurriedly moved out of the way before it thunderously crashed into two shooters and a sky blue Ford Hemmings. The crash was deafening, as metal and steel tore into flesh, pinning and crushing one of the shooters between the vehicles and immediately killing another as he was hit and flew nearly a hundred feet into the air and breaking his neck and other bones upon landing. He was dead.

Bronco took a deep breath as he sat in the front seat. Despite being caught amid twisted metal, broken glass, and steel, he was conscious and unharmed, without a scratch on him. With determination, he wriggled and squirmed to free himself. He positioned himself, slightly rotated on his side and managed to kick the driver's door straight off its hinges. Bronco climbed out of the wreckage. The remaining men were stunned by what'd just happened. One of their own was dead, and the other quickly became immobile as he was crushed between the vehicles. He screamed in pain. "Augh! Augh! Someone help me. I can't move. I can't move my legs!"

There was suddenly a loud bang, and the man stopped hollering and screaming. His head had been blown off by a shotgun, his blood sprayed around him, his brains sloshed, and there was this metallic stench of gore. Bronco loomed into their view, carrying the smoking shotgun. His associates were shocked. They recognized Bronco from earlier when he was handcuffed and escorted into the sheriff's station for detainment and possible execution by the lynch mob.

Questioned raced through their minds.

How was he freed?

Why was he still alive?

Why was he in Conway's truck?

What was happening?

Unfortunately, the remaining five men would never find out. They were all living on borrowed time. Going after Elise and Kenneth granted them a death wish. Bronco leveled the shotgun and released another deafening round that ripped through a man's stomach, throwing him off his feet and onto his back—dead. The others returned gunfire as Bronco stood there willingly, far from recoiling or cowering. The burning smell of powder wafted through the air. Bullets that were supposed to slice into him simply flattened against his thick skin and bounced off him like pebbles, leaving the shooters utterly surprised and shocked by what they saw.

"That's not possible," one of the shooters exclaimed.

It left them wide-eyed and bewildered. There was no scientific reason why he was still standing. Bronco stood firm with the heels of his boots planted in the dirt, glaring at them with an emptied shotgun. Those who received the brunt of the shotgun were the lucky ones because now he was going to tear them apart. These men were suddenly hit with a tidal wave of fear, which built with each passing second. They were powerless against him and the oncoming onslaught.

"Whatever you are, nigger, I promise you, you're all—"

The man didn't get to finish his statement. Bronco suddenly charged toward them, head down, arms and legs pumping furiously, and he headed straight for them. Their gunfire remained ineffective as Bronco barreled into them like a steaming locomotive. He put his right fist through the talkative man's chest like it was paper thin. It was a hard enough blow that the man jolted in shock at first, traumatized from the sudden impact and not realizing he was already dead. Bronco intently stared at him, a dead man standing, and uttered, "You was saying?"

His open-mouthed astonishment then wilted when Bronco removed his fist from the gaping hole in his chest, and the man dropped face down into the dirt with his blood pooling thickly underneath him. Silence followed from his peers. They stood frozen in absolute fear by what they'd seen until they remembered to breathe.

Suddenly, one of the men attacked Bronco from behind with a machete swinging wildly. But the machete recoiled against his skin like a bouncing ball against a brick wall. The weapon vibrated in the assailant's grasp, rendering it useless. He stumbled back in awe, not knowing his next move, but it was too late. Bronco grabbed his arm, took the machete from him, and plunged it down into the would-be attacker's skull so deep that it nearly split his face in half.

With two men remaining and seeing their friends brutally ripped apart and killed, their fear continued to take shape. They became paralyzed by panic. To them, Bronco was a monster with some kind of voodoo magic that gave him unnatural durability and strength. In fact, terror gripped them so firmly that one of the men began to pee on himself. They finally realized what they were up against and were now trapped.

"Look, mister, I was just following orders from Mr. Lockheart," one man uttered, his tone trembling. "I just needed the money. We'll leave right now, and I promise we won't be back here."

But it was too late. Bronco was out for blood and revenge, and he figured they would always threaten him and the people he cared about. Bronco quickly stepped toward the coward who had peed on himself and swiftly brought his right hand up, striking the man in the neck over his jugular hard enough to kill him. The man frantically clutched at his throat, gasping and wheezing, finding it difficult to breathe. His screams and voice became mute as his eyes pleadingly became fixed on Bronco for help. He didn't want to die. But tonight, there would be no negotiations with death. Bronco had become the Grim Reaper, and he came to collect. Finally, the man fell to his knees and folded over, still gasping for life until he fell face down into the ground. It was coldhearted and caused the last man standing with a familiar panic grip to tighten around his chest.

He found himself with nowhere to go or to run. Though he wanted to escape, his muscles wouldn't budge. The brown pickup he had arrived in was about thirty feet away. It was close enough to try to reach but far enough to seal his fate. Even if he managed to get to it, he wouldn't be fast enough to climb inside and start the engine. Bronco was too fast. The last man standing quietly surveyed his surroundings, taking in the sight of his deceased acquaintances sprawled across the ground.

"Please. I got a wife and kids," he pleaded.

"Did you think about them before you came here to kill a woman and child?" Bronco countered.

Bronco found it ironic how some violent and racist men could be coldhearted and ruthless toward those they deemed inferior, believing that their white skin color gave them the right to do as they pleased. However, when the tables were turned, and the odds were against them, they would dare to beg for mercy and forgiveness. They came there for a reason, to kill someone he loved. Now, there was no better reason to kill him.

Bronco moved closer to him, backing him into the crashed vehicles. The man manifested his terror through relentless pleas and begging for mercy. He found himself unable to move when Bronco sharply tugged at his shirt and clamped his mighty hand around his thin neck. Bronco lifted him off his feet and began to squeeze with delight. He wanted to watch the light of life slowly fade from his eyes. He started strangling his victim with one hand while having him suspended in the air. Bronco held him in place and squeezed forcefully, feeling his hyoid bone and cervical spine crushing quickly. The man began to choke off his own blood and gasped for breath, and Bronco enjoyed watching his life gradually drain from his eyes as he died in severe pain.

Pastor Brooke witnessed the nightmarish ordeal from the farmhouse. The storm of panic had passed, but he was aghast at what he saw. It was a hellish thing to see. Pastor Brooke was dumbfounded and frightened at the same time. He stared at Bronco as if he were something out of a horror movie. It was as if the man was some demonic creature from the pits of hell. The brutal way he killed those men, why and how? He tried to ignore his fear, but it was a cold-blooded murder. This couldn't be a man. No man could do what Bronco had done.

Elise was both shocked and surprised, yet she remained deceptively calm. Her body felt drained, and her hands were trembling, with a thin veil of anxiety hanging over her like an unwanted shroud. She couldn't handle any more surprises or attacks. Bronco had saved their lives, but at what cost? And what would happen next? She couldn't unsee what she'd just seen him do.

Kenneth witnessed everything unfold from his bedroom and seemed ambivalent about it all. He believed they deserved what happened and was glad they were dead. He felt frightened yet captivated by Bronco's actions, and the sight of several white men sprawled across their farmland was unfathomable. Kenneth viewed Bronco as an ultimate soldier or superhero, similar to the characters he read about in comic books, such as Captain America, Superman, Phantom Stranger, and Batman. However, this superhero was real, and he was Black. Bronco had saved their lives, and Kenneth clutched the dog tags while smiling.

Bronco stood among the deceased, transparent and fully exposed. This was who he was—a killer. Perhaps he was a monster, but now Elise, Kenneth, and the pastor fully saw his capabilities. Suddenly, the realization hit Bronco as he stood before them. Death was going to follow him everywhere he went. Would this change things with him, Elise, and her brother? It continued to daunt him that despite his extraordinary abilities and his desire to protect everyone, he was also cursed. There was no denying it. He was a black hole of death, the Grim Reaper walking the earth in the flesh. And what happened tonight couldn't be undone. The question remained: would they be safer with him not there?

Kenneth was the first to eagerly burst through the front door and run to Bronco. He pushed himself into Bronco's strapping frame and wrapped his arms around his idol to hug him, to thank him, and to say, "Please stay." Elise and Pastor Brooke followed him outside into what appeared to be a war zone. She had never seen so many dead white men in one place. It scared her. And although he had killed them all, there was the fear of more of them coming to take her farm, but this time, coming to finish what they had started—this time, killing her and Kenneth in retribution.

She stared peculiarly at Bronco and uttered, "What just happened?"

"I did what I needed to do to protect you," Bronco said.

"What are you?" she asked him shakingly.

"I don't know. I've been this way for years now, can't explain it," he replied.

"He's a superhero, Elise," Kenneth uttered excitedly. "He is, I's know it. He came here to save us, and he did."

Superhero? Pastor Brooke nearly chuckled at the foolish idea. It was more challenging to accept for him. He didn't believe in superheroes or monsters, but there was no explaining what he saw tonight. His only explanation was that Bronco was a demon in human form or some abomination or curse. Was he human? The pastor couldn't call him an angel. An angel wouldn't have done this.

"I'm no superhero, Kenneth. I'm just a man with some trauma and demons, tryin' to find his way in this world," Bronco replied.

"But you's bulletproof, like Superman. I saw it," Kenneth countered. "We ain't got to be scared no more."

"What happened here, I can't understand it," Pastor Brooke interjected despondently. "This isn't the way. This isn't . . ."

"They all deserved to die, Pastor Brooke. They came here to kill everyone, including you," Bronco chimed.

"But so much death and destruction in one night, my God."

"Do you believe God would allow this? If so, then why?" Bronco said, displeased.

"I don't question His ways, Bronco. I just follow in Him. And I know this isn't the way to a better future. This isn't how we change things," Pastor Brooke replied concretely.

"How do we change it then, Pastor? Please, enlighten me. Forrest Tolson is trying with peaceful marches and protests on City Hall, and they still beat him and killed that boy. We create towns that benefit us, but that they destroy over time. Then they're stealing land from our people, killing families for their greedy cause, and they expect us to just lie down and take it," Bronco rebuked. "What is God's way, Pastor? Please, tell me."

Pastor Brooke stood there, feeling conflicted about Bronco's sudden anger. He understood his anger. He had been a Black man in the South all his life, and he had witnessed the terrors of Jim Crow and the Klan. The oppression by the white man had been a burden for the Black community for generations. He felt he could explain their hatred, but it was a challenge to comprehend Bronco's strength and his willingness to resort to extreme violence. Did these men deserve it? Pastor Brooke believed that only God should judge and have the final word. What he witnessed and experienced tonight would not shake his faith in the Lord. The pastor did not know what had shaped Bronco, but one thing was sure: this was not a creation or the will of the Lord. It couldn't be. Yes, he had felt cowardly earlier, but now he felt awakened, believing he had journeyed through hell tonight.

"Slavery came to an end years ago because it was God's way, and this era of Jim Crow, it will come to an end, too," Pastor Brooke stated. "Second Corinthians 5:7 tells us that it can be difficult to trust God during uncertain times, but as believers we know that His ways are not our ways, and He will ultimately work all things for good. Having faith in difficult times can allow you to find peace in God's presence."

Bronco frowned. "Peace. I've never seen peace, and peace only comes when you have a gun, too, being able to protect yourself."

"An eye for an eye, huh? Unfortunately the problem with that is eventually everyone will end up blind," the pastor said.

"You have your beliefs, and I have mine, Pastor. You is a Black man, but you come from a different world," said Bronco evenly.

"It seems you do too, Bronco. No matter what you believe in, and what you are, I'm going to pray for you. I'm going to pray that someday you'll find your way and find your purpose. We all have a purpose during our time here on earth."

"I believe I already have found my purpose, Pastor," Bronco responded.

Pastor Brooke nodded and exhaled. He gathered his bearings, smiled slightly, and said to Elise and Kenneth, "I need to go. I apologize for coming here during such an untimely and horrific event. I need to go help those in need. A lot is happening, folks are dying, and I can't remain sheltered in your home. I thank you for your kindness, Elise. You're a good Christian woman."

"You don't need to rush off, Pastor. It's still not safe out there. Let the sun rise first before you go out," Elise begged him.

Pastor Brooke displayed a quiet and bright smile, one with knowing and understanding. "I'll be okay, Elise. I shouldn't have lost a fraction of faith from our God. I'm not running cowardly anymore. You and Kenneth take care."

"Pastor, maybe she's right," Bronco concurred. "Maybe you should just wait here and wait it out. It's too dangerous to leave right now."

"Bronco, you have your strength, and I have mines with the Lord," he said wholeheartedly.

The pastor's smile was like a sudden beam of sunlight lighting up the darkest corners of the woods. He exhaled and looked determined to help others, no matter how hellish it was out there. He could no longer remain sheltered. He once again thanked Elise, shook Bronco's hand, and said to him, "I'm going to keep praying for you, Bronco. I believe your purpose isn't just violence and bloodshed. I don't understand, but I know you're not evil."

Bronco smiled. Hey, it was a start.

Pastor Brooke pivoted and slowly walked away from everyone. He soon disappeared into the thick woods that covered Elise's farmland. It would quickly be sunrise and become a new day with more worries. With the pastor gone, Bronco turned to Elise and said, "Go back inside. I'll take care of things out here."

He planned on removing the bodies from her land so it wouldn't bring her any trouble. About two hours of darkness was left before sunrise came, and Bronco needed the cover of night. It would be risky because there was turmoil still happening, and a mob of white men roamed the area looking to kill every Black person they saw.

"No. I'm helping you," she protested.

Elise wasn't taking no for an answer. The following two hours before sunrise, Bronco loaded the bodies into the cab of her pickup truck and drove off to get rid of the bodies. He found a clearing in the woods, and like before, Bronco piled the bodies into an upward heap and set their flesh ablaze. None would be the wiser when they saw the fire. Many fires were happening throughout the community, and one more wouldn't be suspicious. By the time anyone got to the scene with the charred bodies burning, they wouldn't be able to distinguish if they were dead Negros or white men. It took the heat and attention away from Elise's place and left things indistinguishable.

Around noon, everyone was tired. It had been a long night of trying to survive. Kenneth and Elise had fallen asleep in her bedroom while Bronco remained on guard outside on the porch with the shotgun. He sat diligently, feeling the need to accomplish something. There was still no word on whether the massacre or riot had ended. Bronco could see pockets of billowing smoke in the distance and sighed sadly. As he sat there, he felt a sudden, vast emptiness amplifying his feelings of separation and loss. He had found love, but now he couldn't stay to enjoy it. It would be too risky for him to stay there and try to live a decent and purposeful life with Elise. He felt that no matter where he went, there would be no pure happiness for him—no escape from his demons and torment. He couldn't be everywhere at once, and the life of a nomad seemed safer for everyone.

Finally, Elise and Kenneth had awoken from their needed sleep. The sun was bright and hot, the sky was a vast blue stretching endlessly, and there was a calm wind against their skin. Kenneth felt joyful seeing Bronco sitting on their porch, protecting them from what he believed were white devils. He had a smooth calm, and he had a broad smile as if he were looking at a big brother.

"Did you get any sleep?" Elise asked him.

"I'll be fine, Elise."

"You should get some sleep."

"I'm fine, Elise," he protested. "Maybe some coffee."

Elise exhaled and nodded. She turned to go back into the house while Kenneth remained on the porch with Bronco.

"What did you do with their bodies?" he asked Bronco.

"Just be okay knowing they'll never come back around to bother or harm you or your sister again, Kenneth."

Kenneth smiled youthfully. His eyes gleamed with much admiration for Bronco. "I wanna be like you when I get older, Bronco. I wanna fight and protect the people I love. They fear you."

Bronco exhaled sharply and replied, "What I did, I did for you and Elise because it's who I became. But spending these past few weeks with you and your sister, it taught me something. There's more to this life than anger, drinking, and violence. I would do anything to just have a family and be happy, Kenneth. A soldier's life and being a man like me isn't a happy one. You regularly carry the stigma of death with you and can't sleep most nights. I'm vulnerable where I hate it the most, being with you and Elise."

Kenneth heard him, but he was confused. What did he mean? Elise joined them on the porch and handed Bronco his coffee. He took a few careful sips. They stood quietly next to each other for a few minutes, both wondering what would happen next. But Bronco knew what his next move would be. It would be heartbreaking for everyone, especially for him.

"You do know I can't stay here, Elise. They'll come for me," Bronco said dejectedly. "There will be a manhunt. Me being here will only place you and Kenneth in harm's way. I plan to leave by week's end."

"But you's can stop them, Bronco. You can kill them all. You can stay and protect us," Kenneth beseeched, feeling his eyes water.

"No matter what I am or became, I'm still one man. And everywhere I go, death follows me," he proclaimed. "This is the only way for the two of you to remain safe."

"But you promised to teach me how to fight," Kenneth fussed, tears beginning to well in his eyes. "And how we's s'posed to remain safe with you's gone? We ain't safe with you not here."

It was breaking Bronco's heart to see Kenneth cry and worry. But he had to go. His secret was out now, and neither fear, motive, nor curiosity would bring him or anyone he grew close with any peace. Most likely they would try to use them to hurt him.

"You're gonna be okay, Kenneth. You're gonna be strong for your sister, because she needs you to be. You're a man now, the man of this land, and Nancy would be so proud of you. I know it. She misses you as much as you miss her," Bronco proclaimed wholeheartedly.

Kenneth's tears seemed endless. He nodded in conformity and fiddled with Bronco's dog tags around his neck. They'd become a conduit for his courage. "I will."

Bronco smiled. "I know you will,"

Elise stood behind Kenneth and listened. The butterflies swimming around in her stomach made it real. He planned on leaving them, and she didn't want to see him go. She loved him, but she understood his reasoning. If he stayed with them, there would always be a mark on him. Bronco had killed too many men and would forever be haunted by that past staying there. Eventually, they

would come for him and try to figure out a way to hurt
him and then destroy him. It was in their nature. Leaving
Mississippi for good was for the best. They couldn't come
after him if they couldn't find him. Bronco would become
a ghost like those who haunted him.

Bronco had a strong feeling that Elise and Kenneth
would be okay. *Is it faith?* He had no idea, but he felt confident leaving Mississippi, knowing he had fulfilled his
purpose and reason for being there. The sheriff was dead,
and unfortunately, there were many other deaths, too,
both Black and white. Nearly a hundred National Guard
troops arrived in Mississippi to stop the violence and restore law and order in the towns. They declared martial
law, and within twenty-four hours, the troops had managed to suppress most of the remaining violence. The
ordeal was devastating. What they were calling a race
riot was covered by national and African American newspapers. Some were saying that the death toll was eighty.
Twenty-nine whites and fifty-one Black people had perished during the tragedy. The commercial section of
the African American town was looted, burned, and destroyed, including businesses, schools, churches, and
homes. There was a spotlight on Monroe, Mississippi,
and the African American town of Nichol. Members of
the NAACP had arrived via train or bus to give aid, and
preachers and pastors came to help with healing and rebuilding. But the controversy that spread like wildfire
was Benny Lockheart and the investors stealing African
American people's land for pennies on the dollar. And
then it came out that Mr. Lockheart was passing as a
white man. Bronco made sure to reveal the congress-
men's secret before he left Mississippi. He told Elise and
the pastor and went to the newspapers with this information, giving them names and directing them where to
begin looking for the truth. The name Benjamin Boone

was the catalyst of their investigation. It was crushing for Benny's constituents, and the community immediately turned against him.

Benny Lockheart sat in his office, behind his magnificent oak desk, in his high-back leather chair. Pinches of sunlight shined through the barely closed blinds behind him. It was a beautiful day. Yet, Benny sat at his desk quietly and looked despondent and troubled. Everything around him was still and silent. The house was empty. There was no laughter from his daughters filtering in through his office from the hallways, and there were no voices of concern and care from his loving wife. They had left him. Ruth packed her belongings with their daughters, and they stayed with her family. It wasn't sure if she would return. Ruth was angry and devastated that Benny lied to them and her about everything. The rumors of him passing and having a Black father went rampant around town, and overnight, she and her daughters found themselves up against intense criticism and scrutiny. She and her daughters were no longer the socialites and envy of everyone. They began to call her a "nigger lover!"

The phone rang a few times. Benny looked reluctant to answer it. However, he slowly removed the receiver from its cradle and placed the phone to his ear, knowing that the caller wouldn't bring good news. Nothing had been in his favor since word had gotten out about his past, specifically about his mixed-race heritage due to his father.

Instead of saying hello, he listened and heard Mr. Roth say, "Mr. Lockheart, because of unfortunate events that occurred this past week, my investors and I have come to the conclusion that our interest in you and your town will no longer be valuable. We have decided to move on elsewhere. Good day to you, Mr. Lockheart. My regards to your family." The call ended abruptly. Benny Lockheart sat there, deadpan. It was expected.

Everything was falling apart. His career as a congressman was in shambles. Virginia was pregnant with his child, and that news spread like wildfire. Benny felt betrayed by her. But the strange thing was, he still loved her. He wished things could have been different. He wished he could proudly show their child to the world, go on lovely picnics together, kiss each other in public, and become a happy family. But he continued to deceive himself, hiding his true identity because it was easier to live as a prejudiced white man than to face the reality of his mixed heritage being known to everyone.

No more lies. No more hiding. No more pain and no more secrets. Benny Lockheart wanted to be free from it all. So, he opened the drawer to his desk and removed a .38 Special. He continued to sit there, deadpan, and placed the barrel of the gun against his temple. He closed his eyes, exhaled, and squeezed the trigger.

Epilogue

Three Months Later

Bronco patiently waited at the town's bus stop. The lackluster waiting room was a bit cramped, with unkempt bathrooms adorned with plaques and signs reading COLORED WAITING ROOM placed everywhere. These signs were a reminder of the Jim Crow era, and the discrimination Black people faced as second-class citizens. Bronco planned on heading west, perhaps to Arizona, Nevada, or California. He wanted to put as much distance between himself and Mississippi as possible. With his duffel bag in tow, he was leaving town and Elise with mixed feelings.

During his final night with Elise, they had made passionate love most of the night. He was deep inside her and controlling their movements in the bed. Her muscles were clustered beneath her, contracting around his thick erection. As they made love, he would suckle on her breasts and cup them occasionally, not wanting to let them go. Elise had straddled him and would slowly grind on top of him, panting and grunting while feeling Bronco's rough hands grope her breasts and ample buttocks. She felt her desires building and building to a take-off point that caused her skin to tingle. Elise felt Bronco's hand at her throat, breasts, backside, and hips, moving in rhythm with him. Elise continued to throw herself back and forth on top of him, jerking until they both could no longer contain their compulsion, followed by an intense orgasm explosion. That night, Elise fell asleep in his fine arms, her face against his bare, muscular chest, and she didn't want to leave his secure hold.

The day she dropped him off at the bus station was an emotional departure. Kenneth refused to go with them. He didn't want to see him go, so he stayed at the farm. Elise's eyes were damp the entire time she said goodbye to him. She huffed and was saddened. Her breathing became a bit shaky.

"I'm gon' miss you," she'd said.

"I'm gonna miss you too," Bronco admitted.

They shared a final, lingering, passionate kiss, and Bronco had to pull himself away from her. It was excruciating for both of them. Elise looked like she was ready to collapse with grief. She exhaled sharply, wiped away a few tears, and watched Bronco leave her life. She climbed back into her truck and drove back to her farm.

As Bronco waited for his bus, something caught his attention in the distance. A young boy, about 15 years old, was staring at him from across the street. The boy wore a wide-brim hat, a white buttoned shirt, and a black tie. He had big, sad brown eyes, and Bronco realized he was the only one seeing this teenage boy. It was a ghost, and it seemed to be seeking help from him.

It was Emmett Till.

Seven Months Later

Elise sat at the foot of her bed, trying to gather her bearings. Lately, she had had trouble moving. Her breathing became winded, and her feet felt thick and swollen, but the chores on the farm needed doing. It was a hard and harsh winter, but Elise and Kenneth survived it. They were both happy that they still had a farm to look after. After the race riot, it took time to rebuild everything, but with the help of the NAACP and other organizations, their community was coming along fine. Pastor Brooke had rebuilt his church and was determined to be part of the Civil Rights Movement. Beulah and Duncan Goff had returned to Mississippi from Georgia, although they were devastated by their farm burning down. They still owned their land, and with the town's help, they'd begun rebuilding their home. Harland was in Chicago, but he regularly wrote to Elise and Kenneth. He'd gotten employment working in some steel mill and often sent Elise money to help with the farm. Elise missed him. But she missed Bronco every single day.

Elise finally pushed herself off the bed and turned on the radio. She was seven months pregnant with Bronco's baby. The doctors and midwives believed she was having a boy. Elise was happy to hear that. She yearned to reach out to Bronco and inform him that he was having a son. But she had no idea where he was, and it felt daunting to her that she might never see him again.

Elise was starting her day when she immediately heard urgent news about Emmett Till's case. It had happened about a year ago, but the radio announcer said through the airwaves, "It has been confirmed. The bodies of Roy Bryant and J.W. Milam have been found. I repeat, the bodies of Roy Bryant and J.W. Milam have been found twenty miles away from where authorities believed they'd been abducted and killed. The two men, who had been acquitted in the murder of Emmett Till, went missing the same night of their acquittal."

Elise smiled and rubbed her pregnant belly. She knew that Bronco was responsible for their sudden disappearance and subsequent murder. Yes, he was violent, but she knew he wasn't evil. He simply wanted justice for his people. Elise exhaled with her hands against her stomach, closed her eyes, and said, "Please, Bronco. Come back to me."

To Be Continued